THE
ADORED

T.R. Connolly

The Adored

Cover Illustration: "Dream Maker," Klisha Bomopigamago (Roberta Giallo)

This is a work of fiction. The names, places, characters, and incidents either are from the author's imagination or are used factitiously. The brave men and women of the police departments mentioned have my gratitude for the work they do every day to keep our cities and towns safe.

For my wife Kathleen who has made all things possible with her love and her strength and her devotion to our family.

Acknowledgements:

-To Sister Julie Marie who encouraged me when I was 13 and said, "Thomas you should write."

-To my reading group who sent me back to work when I thought I was almost there – thanks Maureen Connolly, Barbara Geraghty, Judy Flagg and Mary Blackwell.

-To the Darien Library Writer's Group who tormented me with endless ways to improve my stories.

CONTENTS

PART

1

1

J ohn Walsh, the police officer who killed Curtis Strong, described it as, "self-defense, a terrible accident."

Curtis Strong had known Willie Stevens for thirty years, ever since they were two years old, living in the same crumbling row house on Henry Street on the Waterside peninsula of Stamford, Connecticut. The neighborhood was not much then, mostly Italian tradesmen, but by 1995 it was worse, owned by slum lords and developers, all waiting for Stamford's redevelopment to continue in this area. It was bleak, devoid of spirit. Willie and Curtis still lived in the neighborhood, which was 80 percent black at the time of Curtis Strong's death, a death that citizens of the neighborhood called legalized murder.

Friday night was Strong's night out with his friend. He would leave work at the Clairol warehouse, walk the seven blocks home through old industrialized Stamford and have dinner with his wife and son, Curtis Jr. Then he would walk the eight blocks to the pool hall on West Main Street where he and Willie would drink beer and play pool until 11:00 p.m.

The pool hall was dark, four tables, lit by four lights, and around the room were chairs where friends of a lifetime of poverty sat in the dark talking and drinking beer. Drugs were prevalent on West Main Street, in the bars and in the pool hall. Drugs first showed up as draftees from the Vietnam War returned with their habits and increased again as soldiers returned from the Gulf War, in less numbers than Vietnam, but with the same drug addictions. The police had always winked at the illegal sale of beer in the pool hall, but a wave of drug related crimes in the area brought greater scrutiny to the establishment. The drugs were something Strong was aware of but oblivious to. He and Stevens were both veterans but had done their time without drugs and had come out of the service with only a thirst for a good night out drinking beer and playing pool.

This night all four tables were in use, and players emerged from the darkened sidelines to place their quarters on the table to play the winners of the current game. Joe Howard ran the pool hall. Howard would just as soon spit on the floor as say hello to his customers, and most times did when they greeted him. He had two tables for singles and two tables for doubles. Willie and Curtis always played doubles and rarely spent fifty cents playing pool for three hours. The challenger paid, and Joe Howard would rack the balls and take the quarter. Most Friday nights they barely spent five dollars between them, usually betting beers for winners, which Joe Howard would get from the cooler and charge the losers $1.50 a bottle.

The headline of the Stamford Advocate read, "One dead, one seriously injured in accidental shooting by police at Westside pool hall." It had started simply. The two young black men who challenged Willie Stevens and Curtis Strong to the next game on the pool table were high on something other than beer. They had been abusive in victory earlier at the other doubles table. Joe Howard told them to pipe down, and they gave him some lip. Willie stepped in and invited the two to put their mouths to work "putting up some bread on the cue." They decided to take on Willie and Curtis, who were considered unbeatable before 10 p.m. but easier after several beers had gone down. It was ten thirty on October 28, 1995, and the challengers were beating the old pros. As the younger of the challengers, Jesse Marks, the one with the scar beneath his left eye, drew his stick back; it hit the arm of a player at the other doubles table, causing him to miss a shot. And causing him to remark, "Hey, asshole, watch what you're doing."

At the moment that Jesse Marks smashed his stick against the temple of the curser, a pair of white police officers entered the pool hall on a "routine drug patrol," as the Advocate stated the next day.

A fist fight erupted between the two players, and the police attempted to break it up. When the larger of the two officers threw the young pool player on top of the table, slamming his head onto the slate surface, his playing partner grabbed the officer's arm. The other police officer, John Walsh, grabbed his gun and said, "Back off nigger or you're dead meat."

Willie Stevens became incensed and stepped forward. "Hey, watch your mouth you white shithead." The officer spun left at a forty-five degree angle and saw Willie advancing towards him. Curtis Strong, sensing the situation had gotten out of hand, rushed to try to grab his friend before he did something stupid. The officer jerked a half step further left on seeing Strong advance and fired a bullet into Strong's heart at a distance of five feet.

2

Reading the Advocate's account of the incident the next day, Jonathan Barnes remarked to his wife, "What the hell is wrong with these people. Look at this, the guy gets killed in a fight at the pool hall and leaves his wife with a twelve-year-old boy, our Parker's age. This place on West Main Street is a cesspool, yet these men leave their families at home and go there to drink and do drugs. I can't understand it. I tell you, Margaret, we will live to see the day when Barnes Construction demolishes that whole blot on the city. That and the hellhole they live in right across the water."

Barnes looked out from the library window of his home on Shippan Point. Across the harbor, beyond the lighthouse, not more than a half mile away, there were beautiful homes, but behind them, by only several hundred yards, was part of the "blight of Stamford," as Barnes called it. Waterside and beyond, Southfield. "A ghetto, we've built ourselves a ghetto, can you believe it. In Stamford, our "gateway to New England," a quote he coined heralding the massive construction project his firm had grabbed to transform the city from blue collar town to corporate headquarters city. "It all has to go," Barnes concluded.

Jonathan Barnes did not have total say as to what would go and what would stay in an ambitious urban renewal plan for Stamford, but as the prime contractor for the city's redevelopment, his advice was sought and heeded. His company's reputation for completing quality work, on time, and under budget gave him more leverage than a contractor might otherwise have. Most contractors, in fact, were not interested in the aesthetics of the work but in the profits. Barnes, a sixth-generation Stamfordite, who could trace his roots to a seventeenth century sea captain trading tea out of Stamford harbor, had what he considered a vested interest in, if not an obligation for, Stamford's future.

In 1920 Parker Barnes Sr. founded the family construction business, two years after he returned from serving as an infantry officer in World War I. He rejected his parents' wishes that he go to Yale, as each male son in the Barnes family had for four generations. Instead he chose to marry Ellen Sullivan, who waited for him for the two years he was in France in the war. He began as an apprentice carpenter and quickly learned the interrelationships that existed among tradesmen. In 1920 he built his first house with the help of five friends—two masons, a carpenter, a plumber and an electrician. By 1925 he had built forty homes and two office buildings in Stamford. Barnes Construction employed twenty people full time including the five original friends.

In the 1920s the trade union movement was gaining momentum, but Barnes never had union problems. His company was still small, but he generously rewarded his employees with a share in the profits and established retirement plans for all employees, a unique innovation at the time.

It was a result of his work on the two office buildings in 1924 that his business tripled in the next five years. Malcolm Leverett, a wealthy developer and financier in New York City, had decided Stamford, his home town, needed more services for a growing class of rich families. The two buildings commissioned by Leverett, both three stories tall, sat across from one another on Summer Street, just up from the Palace Theater. The town was proud of the buildings, and Leverett relished the attention he received in bringing the new office space to Stamford. A generous man, he heaped praise on young Barnes, began using Barnes Construction on all his projects and recommended him to his colleagues in New York.

It was in 1930 that Parker Barnes took the gamble that established him as a most honorable man and employer. After the great stock market crash of 1929, new building projects came to a halt. In the last half of 1930, Barnes paid his employees, then numbering eighty-five, their full salary from his own pocket. Only one new project, a six-family house, had been built by Barnes over that six-month timeframe. It was over Thanksgiving dinner at his father's house that he made the request for $40,000. It was enough money, he rationalized, to subsidize his employees' pay for two years, while enabling him to be the low bidder on a government housing project in the Southfield section of town.

His father, whose fortune was largely intact after the crash, was pleased with his son's benevolence and pleased he felt comfortable asking for the loan. There had been no animosity between the two over Parker's decision to mold his life on his own. His father was quite proud of what he had done in service to the country and starting a business without asking for financial help. Even now he was not asking for himself but for his employees.

The loan was made, and Barnes did become the low bidder on the housing project. The work took two full years, and by its completion in January 1933, new construction projects had started flowing again. Barnes Construction employees never forgot what their owner had done, and as it grew in the thirties and forties, Barnes Construction never had the labor problems that beset the industry. In fact, union organizing campaigns highlighted Barnes as the type of employer all construction companies should be, but until such time as that occurred, they proclaimed, unions would always be needed. This was a fact that never sat well with Barnes' competitors.

Parker Barnes Sr. ran the firm until 1978 and passed the presidency over to his son Jonathan, who at thirty had been in the firm for ten years. While Jonathan had never shown a flair for the people end of running a company, he did have a good head for finance. Parker Sr. felt comfortable turning the business over to his son at this time since three of the original five friends were still with the company as vice presidents. However, when Barnes Sr. died suddenly six months into retirement, the stage was set for Jonathan to become his own man. Quietly, but firmly, from July to November 1980, he forced the retirement of all three of his father's friends. As 1981 began Jonathan Barnes was solely in control of Barnes Construction.

Jonathan and Margaret moved to his father's home in Shippan in 1981 at the request of his mother. Ellen Sullivan Barnes had felt alone in Apple Manor's eighteen rooms with no family and simply her three housekeepers. Before her husband's death, they had planned to move to a smaller home with only one housekeeper. All that had changed and she knew Jonathan had hoped one day to own Apple Manor. This would allow him to have what he wanted and give her regular access to her infant grandson, Parker. She moved to a small suite of three rooms and kept her favorite housekeeper in a two-room apartment across the hall from her.

Ellen Sullivan Barnes observed what her son had done to his father's and her friends, but even as the majority stockholder she would not interfere, for this was her husband's wish. Still she was disappointed in Jonathan, a nice enough husband and father and always a good son, but rather spineless when it came to doing the right thing by people in the business. His main drive seemed for profit and expanding the business, certainly key reasons to be in business, but Mrs. Barnes knew he did not have his father's passion and empathy for his employees. Her husband had driven hard for profit and growth but also proved to be kind, with a loving devotion to his people. Jonathan seemed unable, she reasoned, to make the connection to the company's employees despite the fact that it was the people who made the company strong and prosperous. Even still, in 1995, after fifteen years with Jonathan Barnes as chairman, Barnes Construction's revenue had grown from 50 million dollars in 1980 to 2.5 billion dollars with profits of 300 million dollars.

3

The summer of his twelfth year, the last summer of his father's life, was the happiest for Curtis Strong Jr. His father had signed up to manage his baseball team after being an assistant coach for two years.

They spent endless hours together that spring with son helping father in his new leadership role. One night in March, Curtis Sr. came home with a list of players who would remain on the team from the prior year's roster. "CJ, I need your help," he said to his son. "The draft for the other players for the team is this Saturday afternoon."

"Sure, Dad," replied CJ, the nickname his mother had given him to eliminate the confusion of "Yes. Yes." whenever she called "Curtis."

"We need to rank all these eleven-year-olds who are coming up. With the players we've got coming back from last year's team, we'll have twelve players on a team."

"Let me see the list, Dad," CJ jumped in enthusiastically. "Oh boy, Kenny Smith, pick him first, Spike Johnson second, Leroy third, Alvin fourth," the boy rattled off in rapid succession.

"Whoa, not so fast. These guys are all your friends."

"Yeah, Dad, won't it be great."

"No, it won't be, son. We want to build a winner, and I happen to be aware that Spike has a hole in his glove."

"He doesn't make that many errors, Dad."

"Seventeen, count em, seventeen in fifteen games. That's not many? That's a whole bunch! Now let's get serious. What do we need most?"

"Pitching?" CJ guessed.

"You got it. Besides you, and only when you're on, we've got no pitchers. So our first two choices are going to be pitchers, and after that, two of the other four we draft are going to have to pitch some."

On into the night they plotted, arguing over the merits of this shortstop or that catcher. Finally, when their rating system was finished Strong gave a "1" rating to Eddie Sanders. "Dad, wait a minute. Not him. You've got him mixed up with someone else; he stinks."

"Well, CJ, I'm not too sure how good he is, but his father volunteered to coach. And I happen to know he goes to every game. So, that will give me and Uncle Willie breathing room if we have to work overtime some night. We at least know that Eddie's father will be there to manage the team."

"Oh, that's great, Dad. Mr. Sanders knows even less than Eddie about baseball."

"Don't worry, he'll be in charge. But I'll depend on you to help him put the right lineup together, and you'll be his third base coach if I'm not there."

"Really, you'll let me do a lineup?" CJ glowed with anticipation.

"OK you two," Louise Strong interrupted, "it's ten thirty; let's go, CJ, time for bed."

"Oh, mom, we're almost through, just a little while longer?"

"Come on, son, let's call it a night. I'm all thunk out. We'll work on it some more tomorrow. Head to the bathroom and brush your teeth."

"OK, Dad."

As Strong was leaving his son's room, CJ asked, "Do you think we'll win this year?"

"I know we'll do better than last year."

"Come on, Dad, five wins and ten losses? I know we'll do better than that with you managing, but will we win the championship?"

"Did you think the Red Sox would win last year?"

"Sure, Dad, we always think they're going to win."

"I feel the same way about our team. I think if we get the players we want, we're going to win."

"All right!" CJ yelled in delight.

"But it's going to take a lot of work."

"Don't take the fun out of everything, Dad," CJ smiled at his father.

"Good night, son."

- - - - -

"Dad, Dad," Parker Barnes yelled in a state of excitement running into his father's library. "Mr. Strong, my baseball coach, was killed yesterday," the boy concluded, seeking some explanation from his father.

Jonathan Barnes, alarmed, asked, "What happened, Parker?"

"Right there, Dad, in the newspaper, look, "One dead, one seriously injured in accidental shooting by police at Westside pool hall."

"I saw the story, but I did not notice the name."

"Look, Curtis Strong Sr., see Dad, it's Mr. Strong."

"That's terrible, son. Obviously Mr. Strong should not have been at a place like that," Barnes concluded with his usual judgmental aplomb.

"What do you mean, Dad; it says it was the cop's fault."

"What I mean," the elder Barnes started firmly, "is that in a place like that you can only expect trouble. Look, son, it says right here, 'illegal drinking and drug use regularly occurred,' and there was a fight going on when the police walked in."

"Mr. Curtis was no dope head," young Parker protested, noting his father's distance, as usual. "He wouldn't start a fight with anyone; he wouldn't."

"Perhaps he was just an innocent bystander, son, but that is the wrong place for a married man with children to be."

"Child, Dad," Parker said firmly, "he didn't have children, only CJ," and after a moment he continued, "Can we go to the funeral on Monday?"

"No, son, we'll be out of place there. Now you go off and play with your friends. Don't worry about it."

Parker remembered Curtis Strong in his prayers that night. Mr. Strong. Coach.

He could see his smiling, cajoling face. He also prayed for CJ.

4

The unique, sociological phenomena of multimillionaire contractor's son and poor black laborer's son being on the same baseball team developed from their geographic proximity to each other. The west branch of Stamford harbor was all that divided the rich on the Shippan peninsula from the poor in Waterside. As years passed CJ Strong and Parker Barnes grew to realize that more than water separated their lives. Parker was isolated by his family's wealth, and Curtis was being swallowed by the poverty and crime around him.

In the spring of his seventeenth year, CJ Strong became a man. The event that cloaked itself in manhood occurred as CJ went to a West Main Street corner to meet his best friend, his cousin Billy Stevens. The families became even closer after Curtis Sr.'s death with Willie Stevens acting as a surrogate father to CJ and Mrs. Stevens, Louise Strong's sister, looking out for CJ after school as CJ's mother, Louise, worked to support the two of them.

This night was dark, and as CJ approached the corner of West Main St. and Green Avenue, he saw Billy Stevens up ahead of him. Billy pushed the person beside him into the alley next to the corner store. Curtis called out to Billy and jogged to the alley. Looking into the shadows cast from the street light he heard a desperate yell and saw a figure slump to the ground. The other figure, maybe two people, ran out the back of the alley and hopped over a five-foot fence. CJ ran in and leaned over the body on the ground. It wasn't

Billy. It was a man who appeared to be about twenty-five years old. He looked up at CJ and said, "Please help me; he stabbed me." CJ looked at the man's hands; they were covered in blood flowing from the puncture wound from the knife sticking out of his stomach.

A voice above called out. "What the hell you doing down there. Get away from there." CJ looked up. Then panic overcame him. "She thinks I did this," he thought. For the rest of his life, he would wonder why he did what he did next. He stood up, and as life oozed from the body on the ground, he ran out of the alley, taking the same path that Billy Stevens had a moment before.

CJ ran all the way home, and as he stood in the yard behind his house, he heard sirens in the distance. He tried to stop sweating, to quiet his heart before going in. He knew his mother would see something was wrong. He could not hide problems from her.

He waited a long time in the dark with his back up against the rotting clapboards of his home. He walked to the pear tree at the back of the small yard and sat with his back against it. He could not believe his friend Billy stabbed that man. Maybe it wasn't Billy, he thought, and yet as soon as he thought it, he knew it was Billy. But why? He wouldn't ask, he would never tell, he would never see Billy again. He prayed, "God, please take me out of here, take my mother and me away from this." And as he prayed, it came to him that God would not take him out of this life. He would have to do it himself. He would get back into sports in school, stop wasting his life, start doing homework, and going to church again with his mother. "Only please, God, no more of this," he whispered in the dark.

Louise Strong was in the kitchen drying dishes in the wall-long cast iron sink as CJ walked in the door. "CJ, my, my, ten thirty on a Friday night. You feeling alright, honey?"

"Sure, Mom, just tired; besides, I want to get up early tomorrow and look for a weekend job."

"Oh, my heart," Louise Strong said, feigning an attack, "no, not that, not a job."

"Come on, Mom, knock it off. I'm seventeen; don't you think it's about time I got a job?"

"Yes I do, CJ; I'm just surprised you do too."

"Maybe if I work, you can give up one of your jobs."

"Oh, wouldn't that be nice. Tell me what brought on this rush of responsibility?"

"Nothing," he came back quickly and nervously and continued, "Well, let's just say I'm growing up." With that he turned toward the hallway, kissed his mother on the way by, and said, "Good night, Mom."

Louise Strong put her arms around her son's waist and hugged him. She sensed a shudder as he hugged her; he lowered his head so that his cheek rested upon her head. "Son, are you alright?"

"Yes, Mom, just fine," he answered, feeling the security of his mother's arms tightly around him.

Something happened. Louise Strong knew as her son went off to bed that something happened. She knew she would not find out from him, and she prayed it was not bad. She thought of how big he had become, still feeling him against her.

Later, as she turned out the lights, she thought she must move her son and herself from this area. She feared for him as he was a good boy, but he was drifting. She could probably get an apartment over by the north part of Shippan Avenue. The area had become middle class black in the last few years as families who could, fled the growing bleakness that was Waterside. It was closer to Clairol, where she now worked, having been offered a job by a sympathetic manager after her husband died. An apartment there would also be closer to her second, part-time job, cleaning and washing floors twice weekly at Apple Manor, which she kept from CJ. He would not have appreciated her cleaning floors in his former baseball teammate's home. She had merely told him it was an office building she worked in.

As CJ awoke on Saturday at 9:00 a.m., he smiled, thankful it was Saturday. Then in the kitchen he heard Billy's voice, "Morning, Aunt Louise." The horrible panic from the night before returned instantly to CJ.

Mrs. Strong turned around, pulling her hands out of the wringer washing machine to stick her cheek out to Billy as he walked by.

And kissing the cheek he asked "Is CJ up yet?"

"No, but he should be; he got in real early last night. What were you two doing to get home so early?"

"Well," Billy Stevens started.

"Hey, Billy," CJ emerged from his bedroom and interrupted before any more could be said.

"CJ, what's happening," Billy smiled.

"C'mon, I'm going to look for a job today," CJ replied, taking the newspaper and leading Billy into his room, where he closed the door.

"What's going on?" Billy said.

"Look, I saw you last night," CJ said stretching his tall, broad frame up to his shorter, slighter friend and cousin.

"You saw what last night?" Billy asked, with a smirk.

"I saw you pull that guy in the alley by the corner, and when I got there, he'd been knifed."

"Are you nuts? I don't know what you're talking about. Come on, CJ; me, stab someone, get real."

"Billy, I don't know what you're into, but we're through. I'm never going to say anything, but you and I are finished."

"Hey, whatever you think you saw, you got it wrong. It wasn't me you saw."

At that moment there was a knock at the front door of the four-room apartment. Louise Strong emerged from the kitchen, down the brief hallway past CJ's room to the door. She swung the door open. Two men dressed in jeans, one with a flannel shirt and down vest and the other wearing a heavy, waist-length jacket, stood in the doorway. "Mrs. Strong?" the one with the vest who was unshaven with a Fu Manchu mustache asked.

"Yes," she answered, immediately worried. They felt like police.

"I'm Detective Foley; this is Detective Lodovico. We're with the Stamford Police. Is your son Curtis here?"

She froze; her heart pounded. She felt the same sense of loss as when she was told her husband was dead. She could barely get the words out, "Yes, he is. Is there anything wrong?" she replied in terror. CJ's returning home early Friday night raced to the front of her mind.

"We have a few questions to ask him. Would you please ask him to come and talk with us?" Detective Lodovico asked.

"Yes, just a minute," she said, and she walked the few steps along the narrow hallway to her son's room. She knocked on the door before turning the knob.

"Yes, Mom?" CJ answered, opening the door.

Louise Strong entered. "CJ, there are two police officers here who want to see you."

Instant panic came over CJ. His eyes shot to Billy. Another look of panic. Noticing the look of fear in both boys' faces, Louise Strong said, "CJ, what is this about?"

"I don't know, Mom," he trembled, continuing, "What did they say they wanted?"

"To see you and ask you some questions."

"I don't know what they want," CJ offered, seeming bewildered.

"Well, come and talk with them, and let's get to the bottom of this."

They started up the hallway as Billy headed toward the rear door saying, "CJ, I've got to go; I'll see you later," and he left through the kitchen door, not waiting or looking for a reply.

Louise Strong looked at her son's face. It went empty, and she watched Billy open the door and leave. She started to cry and hugged her son, "CJ, what's happened?"

At that point the two officers appeared, having heard the rear door open and close. Detective Foley spoke, "Curtis Strong?"

"Yes sir," CJ answered.

"I have a warrant for your arrest for the murder of Augusto Santos," Detective Foley said bluntly.

Louise Strong screamed, "Oh, CJ," sobbing.

"Mom, I did not do anything wrong, I promise you."

"Curtis, you'll have to come with us. We will need to search you, and Detective Lodovico will read you your rights."

5

Diversity teemed yet separation continued. Fairfield County had the richness of New York, the poverty of Caracas; the wind of the end of summer, the chill of a winter over the horizon; the bright light of a hopeful morning, the black water of the lightless night; the American Sea that was Long Island Sound, open, reaching from sunrise to sunset and a brackish cove in Norwalk at the End of the World Marina.

Southern Fairfield County—sun and sand, tar and fences. A checkerboard: Greenwich, rich and white; Bridgeport, poor, black and Spanish. Stamford—north and south—well off and white; east and west—laid-off and black. Darien, it's opposite Norwalk, its opposite Westport. Fairfield, worried that Bridgeport's bursting poverty will sweep across it like a giant wave out of Long Island Sound.

High-priced houses, drive-by shootings. New college graduates creating new service sector jobs; drop-outs unable to find low-paying factory jobs lost to the third world. The third world arriving on the door step; the first world throwing open its arms in the name of multi-culturalization and low-cost labor for low-skilled service jobs. America's native black children only able to find minimum wage jobs; America's new minorities competing for those same jobs.

Joy, beauty and happiness. Hate, envy and drugs. The second world confused; the middle class missing.

Curtis Strong Jr. was lost; father killed, son in jail. Nothing made sense. How could a life begun so well be ending like this? Curtis was behind bars, shielding a friend who never had the courage to come forward and save his own friend. Where did friendship begin; when did it end? How could you continue to be true to a friend who was not; why would you?

After CJ had been arrested, his mother spoke with her part-time employer, Jonathan Barnes. Frightened but having no one else to ask for the type of help CJ needed, she relented, swallowing her pride.

"Mr. Barnes, may I ask you a question?"

"Why yes, Mrs. Strong," Barnes said as he relaxed in his library, two days after the murder of Augusto Santos.

"Well, it's about my son, CJ. There was a crime…the other night. A young man was stabbed, and he died."

"Yes, was that over on the West side," Barnes replied barely looking up.

"It was. Well, Mr. Barnes, the police came to my house yesterday. They arrested my son; they think he did it," Louise Strong said, now crying.

"What!" a now startled Barnes replied, standing suddenly and putting his arm around Louise Strong. And rather uncharacteristically, he asked, "How can I help?"

He walked her to a chair in the study, she sat, sobbing uncontrollably. "CJ didn't do it Mr. Barnes; I know that. He told me he didn't, but the police say they have a witness who saw CJ."

"Where is he now, Mrs. Strong?"

"In jail," she said with a plea in her voice.

When he found that CJ did not have a lawyer he said, "I will talk with my attorney, and we will represent CJ. Do not worry about this; I will help you."

After CJ had been in custody for several hours on the night of his arrest, there was agreement by the arresting officers that they had the right man. Here's the usual robbery-murder perp: caught, eyewitness ID'd from the lineup, comes from a broken home—

father shot and killed while attacking a cop in a pool hall. What else could we expect? Maybe a signed confession.

"But why the hell won't he confess?" Detective Lodovico complained to his partner. "All the time we get these kids to confess. Why not this kid?"

"He's locked into this position," Detective John Walsh was saying to the arresting officers, Lodovico and Foley. "He says he came upon the guy and tried to help him. Just like his old man, tried to put a pool cue over my head. Well, that didn't work and neither will this bullshit. We'll break him."

"We will," Lodovico joined in, adding, "especially since the eyewitness didn't see any other figure in the alleyway."

"We need to make the case air-tight, and the confession will do it," continued Walsh. "What we got looks good. We have the knife. We have the eyewitness. And while the eyewitness didn't actually see the stabbing, she did see the Strong kid leaning over the body. Nothing stolen from the dead guy was found at Strong's house. His sneakers have the dead guy's blood on them. Work on the kid some more; I'll work on the eyewitness to help her memory. Get a lie detector for the kid, then call a PD for him; he's got no money for a lawyer."

Two days later, assistant DA Paula Johnson was even less impressed. "Detective Walsh, you have a very marginal case here. This kid has never been in trouble before. Your guys tell me it's unusual not to be able to get a confession when you're offering a kid who did it the kind of plea bargain you went ahead with, without my agreement. And still you want me to put three months of my life into a case this weak. Why?"

"Paula, he did it. What was he doing in the alley? The witness recognized him. He denied being there at first but admits now that he was there. Says he saw someone do it, saw him run, and makes up the story he went to help the poor bastard. He's lying; I'm telling you," Walsh concluded, almost pleading.

"Detective, I need more evidence," Johnson demanded, impatiently.

More evidence appeared. The eye witness's memory became clearer. She now remembered seeing a shiny object being raised back and forth, two or three times, like a knife, into the victim.

Curtis Strong failed a lie detector test, and the bloody knife removed from the victim had Curtis Strong's thumb print on it.

Jonathan Barnes was true to his word and had a member of his lawyer's firm take the case, unfortunately a rather young and inexperienced associate. But as the senior partner later told Barnes, who followed the trial daily, "It was unfortunate. These young bucks need to cut their teeth somewhere, and it was a reasonable case for us to expect to win," and added "Usually, I like to see them win their first one but better luck next time," he told Barnes and they had a laugh. Barnes laughed uncomfortably with Michael Sutton. They had known each other their entire lives, and Barnes had always been intimated by Sutton's bravado. He had wanted to do better for Mrs. Strong. Curtis Strong was tried as an adult for murder, convicted and sentenced to twenty-five years to life in prison.

6

Out of the black water of the lightless night and against the horizon of charcoal clouds, the boat sailed into view. It was a mile offshore, ablaze with energy, as its crew prepared for the annual Stamford to Provincetown race. The yacht "Construction" introduced its owner Jonathan Barnes, Commodore of the Stamford Yacht Club and fierce competitor on the sea. He loved the American Sea, his American Sea. He named it after reading Whitman in college and Whitman's descriptions of life along Long Island Sound. He grew to love the Sound even more as he sailed it competitively all summer while growing up. The Sea's calm surface and strong westerly winds created a paradise for sailors.

Now in the seam, between the clouds of the night and the fog of morning, the boats came, forty in all, rigging rising, speed building, and then the gun—before the sun broke.

This would be Parker Barnes third Provincetown race with his father and his first as Captain. Jonathan Barnes had trained his boy well. He pushed him as a deckhand, no privileges; learn each position, understand wind and sails and lines and men, then bring them all together above the water. "A great race is never won in the water," Jonathan Barnes coached his son, "always above the water, Parker, above the water."

And Parker would reassure his father, "I understand, Dad." While unassuming at seventeen, Parker had grown strong, stayed aware of all going on around him aboard the boat and learned his lessons well. For all of his father's fierce competitiveness at sea, what came through to Parker was not the competitiveness but a love of sailing and of the American Sea.

On this day "Construction" would win the Provincetown race, but clouds of destruction were gathering on the horizon.

The young man had been developing addictions: first smoking and drinking, then marijuana and cocaine. None of his friends from the Brunswick School were aware of anything other than the smoking and drinking. They all did a little of the latter, and one friend, Gideon Bridge, had smoked a few joints with Parker on evenings when they took the "Construction" out for sails. Usually they would take girls from the Greenwich Academy, Brunswick's sister school, on board and they behaved. But when it was just the two of them, they smoked pot.

Even Gideon did not know the seriousness of Parker's drug addiction. Only Lenny "the Liar" Crane knew, along with Barnes' parents, who were to begin a series of shuttles in and out of drug rehabilitation for their son.

The first rehab occurred at Hawk Hill in Chester, Connecticut. The fact that the other Brunswick School families all were off to summer homes helped the Barnes' keep a low profile about Parker's six-week effort at rehabilitation. And in this summer of his seventeenth year, Parker did try. But the following January, his senior year at Brunswick, when Parker's behavior became noticeably more erratic and he went missing for another six weeks, this time to a more intense rehabilitation assignment to the Close Farm in Lakeville, Connecticut, the others knew. They talked about it and how to help young Barnes. They vowed they would not abandon their troubled friend, and true to their word, he was welcomed back with more caring and friendship than he knew he deserved. And he tried; he worked at his program, taking one day at a time of sobriety and abstinence.

There were constant parties in the spring of their senior year and all of the friends made a pledge they would not drink out of respect for Parker. That worked. Barnes continued refraining from drugs and alcohol.

26

Lenny the Liar Crane, another Brunswick friend, wasn't as protective as the other six. He knew Parker's weaknesses, all of them. It wasn't that he wanted to bring Barnes down; he just wanted more of the limelight with the other Brunswick boys, the seven who formed the Brunswick Fund. In the classroom at the time of the Fund's creation, some spark went off inside Crane. It became very important for Lenny to be part of that group. They were generally seen as "the" boys to be with. Some were athletes, some were scholars, but together they were the richest and most popular of the boys at Brunswick. Parker was Lenny's entry, and it was Parker he befriended and even then not so much befriended as served.

Parker Barnes was a tall strapping boy, constantly tanned from sailing in the summer and skiing in Vermont in the winter. His blond hair was long and flowed freely down his neck. He'd had two high school romances. The first ended when the girl moved to Switzerland, and the second ended more disastrously on a double date with Leonard Crane and two sisters.

Graduation had occurred at Brunswick and Parker and Lenny Crane were headed to Columbia in the fall. As happens in a town with the wealth of Greenwich and Stamford, the social scene runs the length of the summer, especially after graduation when there were parties and celebrations night after night for weeks. Every child of privilege had to have their own party. At one of the parties given by a girl who had graduated from Greenwich Academy, Barnes and Lenny met two sisters, Rossie and Judy Leary, who attended Greenwich High School. One girl was a junior and the other a sophomore at the school.

The night began innocently enough; Barnes picked Crane up at his home. At the party, the hosting girl's parents greeted everyone as they arrived. Crane and Barnes believed the two Leary sisters had also graduated. By 9 p.m. the party had swelled to over two hundred. Later in the evening, the police were called, and several young men and women were arrested for alcohol or drug possession, Parker among them. But it wasn't until two months later when Judy Leary's parents showed up with the young lady at the Barnes home that the real problem surfaced.

She was pregnant, Mr. Barnes was told. And Parker had been supplying her with a stream of drugs on their dates over the recent weeks. The parents and the young lady, while from Greenwich, were not well-to-do. The girl was a sophomore at Greenwich High and was fifteen years old at the time Barnes got her pregnant.

Quietly, Jonathan Barnes took care of things once again for Parker. An abortion was performed once it was confirmed that Parker was the father. Legal papers were drawn up, and a sum was paid. And yet another rehab assignment began for young Mr. Barnes.

7

Curtis Strong Jr. was eighteen when his trial ended, and the jury returned a verdict of guilty of second degree murder. The judge sentenced Strong to twenty-five years to life in prison. That night, two years before, sitting in his cell in the Stamford Police jail he tried to envision Auburn, New York, where the maximum security prison he was sentenced to was located. Louise Strong visited her son on the night before he was to be transferred to the upstate New York lockup. She had gone to the library to find out about the prison and the area once the location for Curtis' incarceration was determined. She read stories about the place and its past inmates that terrified her. This was no place for her boy. She felt like she was being slowly strangled as the gears of justice were grinding away at her son. This night she settled on telling Curtis other stories about the area of New York and the town of Auburn and about two of its illustrious citizens, Harriet Tubman and William Seward, both stalwarts in the fight against slavery and for equal rights. She wished they were alive now to stop the injustice her son was undergoing.

On that final night in Stamford with his mother, Curtis put on a brave front, telling her not to worry, flexing his biceps to show his strength and that he would be able to take care of himself. Louise Strong laughed at CJ's bravado but urged him to keep a low profile in that place of monsters.

The initial days at Auburn were wearing: travelling to the prison; processing through so many check points for pictures, finger prints, showers, uniforms, bedding, and arriving at his cell; meeting his cellmate, a sullen southerner who spit on him as the guard turned away. Then there were the work assignments, meeting the doctor and getting a partial physical, digesting the scope of this place that might as well have been on another planet for the different life it presented to him, and most intimidating to him were the twenty-foot-thick walls around the prison that towered over everything in town. What struck him was those walls were keeping him from his freedom for the next twenty-five years and on the other side somewhere, Billy Stevens, the person who did kill Augusto Santos, had his freedom. But Curtis vowed he would not yield—not the name, not the loss, and not to the scum-spitting murderer next to him.

8

Valerie McGuire was in love. It was not something she was looking for, he just happened upon her. Well, not just. Sol Katz, the head lifeguard at Tod's Point for over a quarter of a century, put the two together. At the beach in Old Greenwich, they were training partners as junior lifeguards. When paired up against other guards in training competitions, both being athletes and strong, they won a majority of contests. Whether swimming out to the dummy and bringing it back in, speed dashes up and down the beach or distance swimming, they were the youngest but they were the best. Valerie liked her new friend Eddie Wheelwright. He was well mannered, very good looking and listened to her when she spoke.

Then love arrived, quite unexpectedly. It was another in Sol Katz's endless preparation drills that prompted the thought of love. "Here's how you do it," Katz said hunched awkwardly over the dummy, giving it mouth-to-mouth resuscitation. Valerie wanted to ask when was the last time anyone drowned or even had to be rescued in the calm waters of the Point, but being seventeen she demurred to the wise leader.

"Today we're going to do it live. Each of you will practice it with your partner," Katz intoned. Groans went up among the six pairs of guards; particularly loud from the only male pairing of Parker Barnes and Lenny Crane.

"No way, Mr. Katz," Parker shouted.

"Barnes, I'm not asking you to kiss Crane. If you need to do the job for real, you have to know what it's like. Rubber man here is OK for practice but nothing substitutes for the real thing."

"Nope, not doing it," Barnes replied.

"Stop your whining. Wheelwright, you show Barnes how it's done." The prospect tickled Edward Wheelwright. He found Valerie McGuire quite attractive.

Wheelwright stood up and asked Val to "assume the position."

"Wheelwright, not her. Crane. Perform CPR on Crane."

Edward did as he was told. Crane complied being the dummy he was while the others all cringed. Valerie cringed more than the others. She was looking forward to having Edward place his mouth over hers. She even had it in her mind to put her tongue in his mouth. And now a strange thing happened: She became jealous of Lenny Crane.

There was such a fuss, such noise going up among the young lifeguards after Wheelwright performed CPR on Lenny Crane that Katz called off the broader exercise.

That night lying in her bed, Valerie fell in love with her friend, Edward Wheelwright. Since providence is truly divine, across town in his own bed Edward Wheelwright reached back to the afternoon exercise and envisioned his mouth on Valerie McGuire's. He liked the image as he drifted off to sleep.

His last thought before exploring the depths of teenage sleep was of the girl with the vocabulary of a ghetto punk and the pure heart of a newborn. A smile crossed his lips as he slipped away; she was a girl of clear thought and good nature. She just liked to swear.

9

"This is my world, the kingdom I have been searching for."
Robert Holmes

Upon entering Robert Conetta's Great Questions class at the Brunswick School for the first time, that quote is what his students saw on the chalkboard.

The first question Mr. Conetta posed for his students was, "What did Mr. Holmes mean by that."

The only student who ever got the question right was Sebastian Ball, at least according to Mr. Conetta. Sebastian Ball answered Mr. Conetta's question with the question: "What is 'This' in what context or where is this."

Most students made an assumption of what "This" was and developed their answer accordingly. In Mr. Conetta's logic, one could not possibly answer his question until you understood "This." It was like trying to solve mathematics problems with only one number, he would tell his class.

Robert Conetta had been a teacher at the Brunswick School for twenty-five years. It was in his class that students learned the skill of critical thinking. The subject was a requirement beginning in the third grade, and it continued every year through twelfth grade. Sometimes it was part of a history class, occasionally part of a mathematics class, but generally it was included in a writing and logic class.

Mr. Conetta had this idea: instill in his boys a quest for learning, a desire to find truth. He saw philosophy as a critical subject for students of all ages. He believed in self-discovery and original thought. If the asking of questions was a good method for Socrates as he taught Plato more than two thousand years ago, it would be good for these privileged children of the wealthy. Questions required answers, required thought, and if the questions were posed properly, the boys would search for the answer.

The most fully-developed part of Mr. Conetta's idea was the Great Questions class, itself a twenty-two-week-long search for truth. The formal class was limited to twenty eleventh grade boys, all of whom had to answer twenty questions—one per week with a paper. And one student per week had to present and defend the merits of their answer. The students found out who was presenting each week as they entered the classroom and discovered the defending student's name next to the question of the week.

"Why does the stock market always go up?" had Lenny the Liar's name next to it. That question was one of the few material questions posed by Mr. Conetta, and, as he later explained to Leonard Crane and the class, it was not intended to be a treatise on greed.

It was also in this class that the Brunswick Fund was born.

The Brunswick School began in Greenwich, Connecticut, in 1902 as a school for boys with the intention of keeping them strong and upright as society was seen at the time as getting soft. Along the way it grew to accept five hundred boys from pre-k through high school. The school collectively had the highest per capita income per parent of any school in the world. Along with the aforementioned Sebastian Ball Jr.'s father, there were three billionaires and several others worth hundreds of millions at a time when billionaires were not a dime a dozen. This wealth was the result of both new and old money—the new coming from the finance industry on Wall St. and the old hanging around from the early industrial era of the nineteenth and twentieth centuries.

With a long history of academic and athletic excellence, the school's tuition rivals the leading universities in the world. The results were significant: most students progress to these same leading universities. The school's athletic teams also fared well against much larger rivals and frequently won state titles. Brunswick School also had a strong and proud record of public service, both for the local community and the military. The school affirmed what was possible for young men to achieve. It reaffirmed what was possible for boys four years old at Brunswick as seven toddlers became friends for life. Now, much later, Sebastian Ball, Parker Barnes, Edward March Wheelwright, Gideon Bridge, Kishenlal Moira, Traynor Johnson, and Winston Trout were in personal contact with each other almost every day as they pursued their careers.

Five of the boys grew up in Greenwich, one in Stamford, one town up the coast of Long Island Sound, and one in Darien, two towns up the coast. In the 1990s they came together as the class that would graduate Brunswick and go off to college early in the new millennium. They were inseparable as playmates and classmates. In Mr. Conneta's Great Questions class, it was Edward Wheelwright who answered the question, "How can students of Brunswick School maintain a close lifelong friendship?" with the answer, "Develop the Brunswick Fund." It was the question he was chosen to answer and defend. The other six boys who viewed themselves as brothers immediately bought into Wheelwright's idea. To prove their loyalty to each other the seven persuaded their parents to advance fifty thousand dollars each to open the investment fund. If each student graduated successfully from college, then the parents would advance an additional fifty thousand dollars. The seven had to pay their parents back the full one hundred thousand dollars within five years of graduation. Eddie Wheelwright and Kish Moira were the investment managers of the fund, as seventeen-year-old high school juniors. They took on the duties of monthly reporting to the Brunswick Fund: preparing investment recommendations, providing monthly statements and conducting a monthly business meeting that all seven were required to attend in person or through some form of technology.

Lenny the Liar Crane argued that the fund should be opened to all twenty members of the class. Edward argued that since the seven members of Brunswick Fund had participated in many projects as a team, this was just a natural extension. Edward suggested that Lenny could encourage other members of the class to form a similar fund. After the presentation and as the class dismissed, Lenny sought out other class members to join with him in establishing a similar fund. He had no takers.

Father. Parent, mentor, teacher and friend. Ruler, tyrant, despot and adult. Coach. Disciplinarian. Fathers came in all dimensions. The seven Brunswick brothers had seven fathers, each different and different in their differences. Each of the boys was the only child in their family, and as they grew older, their relationships with their fathers shaped them.

Sebastian Ball Sr. was very similar in style to Arthur Trout. They were exceptionally close to their sons and trusted them the way you trust your best friend—without hesitation. They had each made their sons partners with full authority in their businesses. The Ball, Trout differences? Ball trusted and loved his son Sebastian from the outside. Trout wanted to know what made Winston tick. When Winston was young, Arthur was fascinated that he had helped create such a wonderful, small human being. He knew and loved Winston from the inside. The Balls listened intently to each other and allowed the other full support. But before the listening, they had not a thought of what the other was thinking. Each Trout knew the other intently; they knew what the other wanted to do and would do. They allowed each other that freedom.

Of the seven brothers, it was Parker Barnes who was most troubled in his relationship with his father. Jonathan Barnes insisted that Parker make his own mark in the world through his own efforts, something that the father had not been required to do. Resentment grew in Parker as he found his father distant, dictatorial and condescending. There was an oppression that grew daily in Parker distancing him from fatherly love.

Nothing could have been more opposite than the relationship of Admiral Johnson and his boy Traynor. The support system a frequently absent admiral had in place for Tray was a regimen of self-reliance skills that Tray would carry into adulthood.

Tragedy was the commonality in the lives of the Moiras and Wheelwrights. Captain Kim Moira, hero of the 1971 war with Pakistan, left India for the US after the death of Kishenlal's mother. Kish's mother suffered a painful death due to malaria, and it was a terrible sadness for the boy without the mother who loved him so dearly. However, no less dearly than Cynthia Wheelwright loved her only son as she died young at fifty-eight due to pancreatic cancer. The Wheelwrights' tragedy was compounded by the personal economic collapse of the family fortune, lost by Mark Wheelwright as he kept 90 percent of his fortune in Ocean Bank stock. When the great recession struck, Mark was nearly wiped out. While all seven boys were close at Brunswick, Kish Moira and Edward Wheelwright were among the closest. Later, they both attended Harvard's College and Business School. And from the time they were seventeen, they managed the Brunswick Fund, very successfully, applying lessons learned along the way. It was the best form of education—take what you learn and apply the very day you learn it.

Gideon Bridge was raised mostly by his grandfather, the head of the family law firm. Gideon's father, George, would drift in and out of the boy's life on holidays. Grandfather Roy Bridge and his wife took their daughter-in-law and grandson to live with them after George Bridge divorced his wife for a young woman and became the playboy of Greenwich, spending every waking hour in the company of whichever sports star living in town was not actively playing. In the spring he hung out with a linebacker for the NY Giants, in the summer it was a wing on the Rangers and in the fall and winter it was a pitcher on the Mets. The pitcher and George would always make plans to go to Barbados after October 5th since the Mets were never in the post season. For Gideon it was a life of law. Grandfather Roy Bridge was determined that a Bridge would keep the family law firm alive, and he taught and mentored young Gideon in the ways of the law.

Martha Bridge was somewhat shocked by Gideon's choice of college: Brandeis University. "Isn't that a Jewish school?" his mother asked.

"Sort of mom, but it won't make me Jewish," Gideon replied after they discussed his application.

"Why don't you go to MIT, like Winston?" she pursued. "They win Nobel Prizes all the time there."

"I'm going for the law; their pre-law program is the best. And the sciences, they win more MacArthur Genius Awards than anyone."

She could see his determination, and she did not want to be discouraging, "It sounds like you've done your homework, son. Just don't come back a Jew."

Gideon went to Brandeis, and he did not come back a Jew. He came back a Mormon. Of his six closest friends, his "brothers," three, Gideon, Winston and Edward, were Catholic; Sebastian, Tray and Parker were Protestant; and Kish was Hindu. Religion was in their parents' day who you were; for the brothers, religion had become what you were and that was quickly fading.

On the day Gideon was preparing for his conversion and induction into the Mormon faith, his mother and grandfather accompanied him to the Mormon Temple. Gideon tried reassuring his mother, "Mom, it's still Jesus."

"Gideon, it's not our Jesus," she replied.

During the Baptism Mrs. Bridge cried audibly all through the ceremony. She thought to herself, "If you live long enough, everyone will turn on you."

Not quite, in fact in Gideon's case, he was a Mormon for exactly one and a half years. He felt that religion should help him see things in a new light. When he performed his mission work in Venezuela, he came away unimpressed and uninspired. The happiest day of Mrs. Bridge's life was not when Gideon returned from South America, but when he said, "Mom, you're right, he's not our Jesus," and with that Gideon repatriated himself into the open arms of Catholicism, Harvard Law and the Bridge Law firm.

And now all seven brothers were men, embarking on the work of their lives. Kish and Edward had success in investment banking and kept the Brunswick Fund growing significantly. Traynor Johnson completed his studies at the US Naval Academy and became a Navy Seal. Parker Barnes joined the family construction business after graduating from Columbia with a degree in architecture. Winston Trout did likewise joining this father's solar engineering firm after MIT. And Sebastian Ball Jr., well, the acorn did not fall far from the tree. He went to UPenn's Wharton School, as had his father, and was able to make money as readily as his hedge-fund-owning dad. Together they made a formidable team, and the son had vision and the guts to support his visions. So these seven boys, each an only child of a wealthy family, became "brothers" at the age of four and inseparable as they emerged as adults.

But as they grew life's consequences would affect them; in a most dire way for some.

10

After a year at the Auburn Prison, CJ Strong had settled into a routine of sorts. He found he could handle the day-to-day business of being a prisoner, but what got to him, what weighed on him like a crushing weight was the coercive nature of every second of every day. The physical place was crushing with its thirty-foot-high grey walls and armed guardhouses at the corners of the yard. He remembered his religious teaching that God was omni-present; in Auburn only the guards were omni-present. Whether in his cell, at work in the prison power plant, when reading to illiterate prisoners over lunch two days a week, playing basketball during his hour and half of "freedom" as an honor prisoner, at meals, in showers, or as he went to sleep at night, the omni-present guards hovered, cajoled, prodded, encouraged, threatened, leered, and occasionally looked the other way. And that was when CJ Strong worried the most, when the guards looked the other way. It usually meant a fight with or a beating by other prisoners was about to occur. It also meant older male prisoners were seeking sex from younger male prisoners. He was terrified of that, the threat of that. In his time there, nothing happened. He had been approached by prisoners; guards had suggested that certain prisoners wanted to see him in the back of the library.

Strong felt the only way he could survive at Auburn was to be like his name: Strong. Stronger. Strongest. He needed to have an iron will to move on, to avoid capitulation, which he learned from reading meant to cede, to yield, to give up or in. He would not. He worked out five days a week in the gym. At six-foot-one-inch tall, he was filling out at Auburn. A slim kid turned much more powerful man. Bench presses, curls, squats, push-ups, chin ups, repetitions, hundreds of reps. Till his arms ached, till they cramped. Thousands of sit-ups until he could pop himself up from a lying position without the use of his arms. In the prison yard, he looked forward to the karate taught him by a great black man, a black belt. The black belt took CJ and two Latino prisoners under tutelage and all progressed quickly with the prison yard sensei conferring brown belts, made in the prison shop, on the three after four months.

Near-freedom came to CJ once a month when Louise Strong took the four-hour bus trip to visit her son. It was what CJ treasured the most. Louise Strong always had been a cheerful force in life and in his life. It had been just the two of them for seven years after his father was shot dead in the pool room in Stamford. They knew each other's every feeling. And so it was that during the first two years of imprisonment, there were glorious days in the life of Curtis Strong and in the life of Louise Strong—in the lives and hearts that each adored.

11

I n the early autumn sun on a late September afternoon sitting on a grassy hill, the seven brothers and one girl, one Valerie McGuire, pondered their great questions from Mr. Conetta's Great Questions class. In the girl's case, she pondered the great question: "How much I love Eddie Wheelwright; let me count the ways."

The two young lovers had met as new lifeguards at Tod's Point Beach in Old Greenwich over the summer. And while Parker Barnes and Sebastian Ball also lifeguarded at the Point with Eddie and Valerie and both vied for the freckled faced Miss McGuire's young heart, it was the ramrod straight Wheelwright whom she fell for. Or tripped for, for on the very first day of lifeguard drills, when Valerie stumbled over a rock on a two-mile timed run with nine lifeguards through the woods, only Wheelwright stopped to help her up. In that valiant moment, a small spark ignited between the two, and by the summer's end, the spark grew into an inferno of youthful passion.

When Parker made no progress in his pursuit of Valerie, he simply conceded that Eddie had won the girl. Sebastian Ball was not as gracious. Even then, at seventeen going on eighteen, Sebastian competed with Eddie for girls. Over the prior winter, he had lost the hand of a debutante at Brunswick's sister school, Greenwich Academy, to Wheelwright. Try as he did through the summer to budge Valerie from her loyalty to Wheelwright, she never wavered.

"It's not you, Sebastian. You're fine, you're handsome, you're a leader among your friends, you've got all the right things going for you, including that Mercedes," she told Ball on a walk around the Point. Well, she told him with an outstretched arm and the palm of her right hand pressed against his chest as he tried kissing her. "But I really care about Eddie, so please, let's be friends. I know how much you guys care about each other. Promise me, I won't come between you."

Ball kept the promise. He never made another pass at Eddie's girl-friend, but he did find himself longing. He thought she was the most beautiful girl he had met to that point in his life with her athletically proportioned body, her long brown wavy hair always blowing in the afternoon breeze at the beach, and her tanned freckled skin. He felt he could do so much for a young woman who had no money, no strong economic future. But it was not to be. This time Eddie had won out.

So as the brothers pondered Conetta's great questions the seven had grown to eight. Valerie had been accepted. It turned out to be the only way Eddie Wheelwright would stay focused, if Valerie was included; otherwise, when the boys got together as they did almost daily, if Valerie was not there, neither would Eddie. Or if Eddie was there and Valerie was not, he would be daydreaming about her. She was constant in his thoughts.

Winston Trout, the smartest, offered up his great question as they sat on the grass on the rolling hill of his father's estate overlooking Long Island Sound: "How will I solve the energy crisis?" Given that his father owned Trout Solar, a start-up solar panel inventor and developer; it was a logical problem to set out solving.

The smallest boy in the group, Kish Moira, felt his future and one of the great questions for him lay in, "How to adequately feed the world?"

"Somehow we're not breaking out of our known cosmos," Gideon Bridge said.

"What do you mean, Gid?" an intrigued Valerie asked.

"Kish, your family comes from the most undernourished country on the planet. Winston, your dad is solving the energy crisis. We're doing what we know—where's the challenge?"

"Gid, the challenge is there. If you'll notice, gas for your Audi has almost doubled in the last two years," Winston Trout shot back with a smile.

"Guys," Valerie began, "does your teacher mean what your parents want you to do or what you want to do?" The girl didn't have money but she did have brains.

Sebastian Ball laughed, "Is there a difference?" Not to Ball who was already committed to his father's vast and rich hedge fund. At eighteen Ball worked two afternoons a week at Ball Enterprises.

"Sure, there's a difference," Wheelwright added.

"And?" Ball challenged.

"We need to decide what we need to do to make a difference."

"What the Peace Corps. You and Val?" Ball laughed at the thought Eddie and Valerie had proposed earlier.

"Yes," the female part of the Wheelwright/McGuire brain said. "How can we share democracy with countries where freedom is rare?"

"Come on, Val." Where are you gonna find that? Russia? You and Wheelwright trotting off to Kiev to unleash the Communist downtrodden."

There, he had done it again: Sebastian Ball in all his omniscience, challenging, rejecting and ultimately putting down in irony the ideas of his friends. The brothers and Valerie loved him, for he was superior to them in his world view and in his sense of power. But there were those times when he headed to deep space on a lone ship.

"Nice, real nice, asshole," Gideon Bridge, who took nothing from Ball, enjoined. "For Christ's sake, Sebastian, grow up. For one of us, you're the least of us," the conscience and debater of the group reacted angrily. "You really gotta stop this, 'I'm the lord of the Riff' bullshit, Ball."

A chastened eighteen-year-old Sebastian Ball saw the fire in Bridges eyes. Gideon was the one member of the group whose command of the English language and balls to stand up to him kept Ball in his place. Not above them but one of them.

"How about you, Gid?" Tray Johnson, the Admiral's son asked.

"My great question? I don't know, Tray," a calmed Bridge replied. "I think it's going to be, "How can we help the poor?" I mean we have so much, yet we see so little of what so many cope with. Does that make sense?"

"It does," Parker added. "Mine is similar. How do we not hurt others?" I don't know the answer, but I'm framing my question around that thought. Tray, you?"

"My father always likes to talk about peace. Being the warrior he seems to go to opposites. He always quotes Curtis LeMay, the general who ran the Air Force's Strategic Air Command where they have all the B52 bombers. LeMay was the guy who fire bombed Tokyo in World War II, but when it came time for a motto for his Air Command he chose, 'Peace is our Profession.' So something like that, how do we keep peace in the world?"

"Valerie offered up ours, but I also have a second idea floating around, "How do we remain lifelong friends?"

And in that long day out on the grass at the end of summer, the seven boys and one girl pondered Mr. Conetta's challenge and for some, put in place a framework that would guide their lives.

12

The first thing you notice about the Auburn maximum security prison is the walls. Huge imposing walls. Walls that run for blocks. And as these walls change directions, there are guardhouses sitting atop them, large guardhouses, more like apartments, surrounded by glass.

Robert Chambers, the preppy murderer, served his time there. William Kemmler, the first person executed in the electric chair, got the juice there. Joey Gallo, the mobster who made a mess of Umberto's clam house in Little Italy when they rubbed him out, spent happier days at Auburn. And while the State Asylum for Insane Criminals was part of the Auburn System, Robert Buffum, who was awarded the Medal of Honor by President Abraham Lincoln himself, committed suicide there by slashing his throat in his cell. Some unfortunate things happened to Mr. Buffum after his meeting with the president: he became an uncontrollable alcoholic, suffered psychological damage resulting from his time as a prisoner of war in the hands of Confederates, and he spent three years in a mental hospital. After that hospital stay, he began to drink again, got into an argument with a man who denigrated President Lincoln and shot and killed the man. He was indicted for murder and sent to the Asylum as an insane criminal.

Interestingly, not two miles from the prison is the historic home of William Seward, former US Senator and Abraham Lincoln's Secretary of State, who was brutally stabbed in his Washington home on April 14, 1865, the same night President Lincoln was murdered at the Ford Theater. Seward's attacker, Lewis Powell, was a co-conspirator of John Wilkes Booth. Seward recovered from his injuries and later retired to his home in Auburn where he died on October 10, 1872.

It had started to snow in the morning when he left Stamford on the Greyhound bus to New York. Billy Stevens was to take a bus from New York's Port Authority to visit his cousin, Curtis "CJ" Strong, who had been imprisoned in Auburn for four of his twenty-five years to life sentence. While CJ's and Billy's mothers were sisters and the boys were best friends growing up, Billy had not come to visit CJ in the time he had been at Auburn.

The bus to the prison was free for family members and brought the visitor right to the front gate of the prison. By 11 a.m. the snow had started to accumulate, and some of the people who had been waiting for the bus to Auburn decided to leave after it was delayed one hour. Stevens thought about turning back; after all, he was not looking forward to seeing his friend and telling him what really happened on the night the Guatemalan drug dealer was murdered. It also meant he would not get back to Stamford until after midnight.

Stevens would take the bus. He needed to unburden himself.

The ride was mostly on major highways and took a little over four hours. Stevens and the other passengers visiting the prison went through multiple layers of security including partial body searches.

As they entered the large waiting room, Billy saw Curtis at the far end of the room standing in a gray prison uniform with a smile on his face. His tension melted away. Strong was older and bigger, in fact, stronger looking.

"Billy," Curtis said, smiling as he hugged his cousin. "Thanks for coming to see me."

"I'm sorry, CJ; I should have come sooner," Billy said.

"Damn right, you should have. Sit down." Curtis said as they each took chairs on opposite sides of the metal table.

"How are they treating you here?" Billy asked, forgetting whatever it was he intended to say.

"They're treating me fine." Curtis said, again with a big smile. "And what about you, what have you been up to."

"Trying to stay out of here," he said, then regretted it at once, "I mean…"

Curtis stopped him. "That's OK, it's funny."

"I've had a few jobs, nothing important. Still hang out with some of the same guys on the Westside. You remember Cecil Lane?"

Curtis nodded, "How is Cece; what is he up to? I figured I'd be bunking with him up here sometime."

"He's as crazy as ever, still shooting hoops down at the park in the summer. No one can beat him. He should be pro."

"How's your mother and father?" Curtis asked.

"They're fine. Both said to say hi. Mom said to give you a kiss for her, but we'll let that go." They both laughed.

"Your mom came up with my mom three months ago. I told her to tell you I was going to break out of this place and come and get you if you didn't come and see me." Curtis laughed.

"Man, you must be the happiest guy in here. What the hell are they feeding you?" Billy said, smiling back at the cousin who had been so loyal to him.

"What are you going to do? Complain to city hall? Who'd listen to me?" Curtis said, a statement he'd made to many visitors over the years to help him over the awkwardness of the initial discussion.

"So you forgive me for not coming," Billy Stevens pleaded.

"I do; you don't need to talk about it," Curtis said.

"But I do. It's what kept me away; it's what brought me here now," he said.

"I said we don't need to talk about it," Curtis said more firmly.

"I need to talk about it," Stevens said, his voice rising; he was on the verge of tears. "All this time you have been in here blaming me for it."

"No one is blaming you, Billy, least of all me. I chose to do this." Curtis said.

"Rather than tell on me?" Stevens said, imploringly to his cousin.

"Yes, rather than tell on you." Curtis said, not smugly, but close to it.

"Well, here's the shock: I didn't do it," Billy said to CJ.

"So nothing has changed in four and a half years. What's new?" Curtis said.

"Well, Cuz, how bout if I tell you who did do it?" Billy said smartly, getting a rise now out of CJ.

"How bout if I smack the shit out of you right here. What the fuck are you talking about," Strong said a little more loudly.

A guard was standing with his back against the wall about twenty feet away. He was a bit overweight but big enough to handle visiting day commotions; he leaned forward and quietly said, "Hold it down a bit fellas, will ya?"

CJ raised his hand in acknowledgement.

"Answer me," CJ said with renewed focus.

"That night there was someone else with me. We were buying drugs. My boy was a little high and got agitated when the Guatemalan dealer wanted to see his money," Stevens said to his cousin.

"Why didn't you tell me this before?" CJ demanded, but in a lower, but fiercer tone. "Who the fuck was it?"

Billy Stevens looked to his left and to his right and leaned forward, and in a whisper said, "You may not want to hear it. I came here to make you understand that it wasn't me who did the knifing."

"You're making no sense, Billy. If someone else did it I want to know, I need to know. It'll be my ticket out of this place. Just say it for Christ's sake." CJ demanded.

"You remember those boys who always hang out at the place your Mama works at, the Barnes' house?"

"What about them?"

"You remember the time we played football with them?"

"Yes, I do," Strong said in anticipation.

"Well, it's one of them."

"What are you talking about? Make sense."

"I don't know their names. It was one of them."

"If you don't start making sense, this little visit is over," CJ concluded, confused.

"What I'm telling you it was one of them who did the knife on the dealer."

Worn out from this mental game CJ declared, "It took you four fucking years to dream that up—you, one of the rich white boys, and the Guatemalan hanging out in an alley on the West side of Stamford? Right, that's it?" and he stood up and said derisively, "See you, Cuz."

Curtis Strong started to walk away when Billy Stevens stood up and said, "He needed drugs, I was his dealer, the Guatemalan was my source. That's the God's truth CJ. I am not lying!" he concluded.

Strong stood still for a long minute; he looked at Stevens.

The guard joined in again, "Fellas, if you are going to continue talking, you need to sit down, OK?"

"Got it," Billy said, and he sat back down. Strong paused a moment and then sat down. There was an uncomfortable silence as Strong tried sorting this out.

"What were you doing dealing drugs? You didn't do that," Strong said.

"Well I don't any more. I was just getting started. The white boy was one of four regular customers I had," Stevens told his cousin.

"One of them a druggie? No way," Strong said emphatically.

"I don't know about now, but then he was one screwed-up kid," Billy said, adding, "He had no idea what the fuck he was doing with the drugs. He'd take the crack, and I'd have to babysit him all night. The stuff really screwed him up."

"What happened in that alley," CJ demanded.

"That was the regular place I'd meet the Guatemalan. The kid was so hot for the drugs that night he came with me. I couldn't shake him. The Guatemalan got pissed. Started hassling him. Wanted to see the color of his money. For twenty-dollar hits, he gives the kid a lot of shit. Kid has this knife on him, pulls it out with one hand and says, "Give me the fucking crack." With his other hand, he pulls out a couple of twenties. The Guatemalan lunged for the money. I think the kid thought he was coming for him, and he plugged the thing in his chest. As soon as he did it, he took off," Stevens said.

"What did he tell you when you saw him again," CJ asked.

"I never saw him again. He never came around again."

"I mean you contacted him, right? Told him what happened to me, right?" CJ questioned hard, looking at Billy for an answer that wasn't there.

"No, I never did," he said, dropping his head. "I was so damn afraid; I did nothing for months, for maybe a year after that. I didn't know his name—he'd only come to the corner where I hang. He never came back. Hell, he never even recognized me from the football game at Barnes."

"Why didn't you find out; there had to be some way to find out which one it was. What were you doing after I went away?"

"Not a thing. School, home, the hoops. School, home, the hoops. Moms thought I was just feeling down about what was happening to you," and he looked up and faced Strong, "And I was, CJ; I was hurting for what you were going through. I knew you were doing it for me, and it wasn't me who killed the dealer."

"Shit," CJ said, "Now what am I supposed to do. I'm no better off."

"I know, the Barnes' family looking out for your mother all these years. I know, but I couldn't go there and ask Mrs. Barnes for a list of the boys who visited that day, could I?" Stevens said. And now more resigned he added, "But I can't handle it any longer. I'll do whatever you want. I figured I'd come here and tell you, and we could think it out. Whatever you want. You want me to go to cops and tell them what went down, I will. I'll take my raps. I'm sorry, CJ; I was just so afraid then," as tears welled up in his eyes.

"OK, Billy," Strong said. "I don't know what I'll do, but you don't need to do anything. Don't say a word of this to anyone. Does anyone else know?" he pressed.

"No one."

52

"Then I want your word of honor, on your mother's soul, that you will never say a word of this to anyone unless I tell you to," Strong demanded.

"Yes," Stevens replied.

"Say it for me to hear," Strong pushed.

"On my mother's soul, CJ, I will never tell anyone what I told you unless you tell me to," Stevens said.

Strong looked at his cousin and smiled, "Now I forgive you for letting me rot in this hole for 4 years, 196 days," and looking at his watch, "and 17 hours."

"That bad?" Stevens asked.

"Every goddamn minute," Strong concluded.

When Stevens was gone, when Strong was back in his cell, the memory of the day they joined in a football game at the home of Parker Barnes, now almost eight years ago, returned. He and Billy Stevens had dropped by to get some money for a movie they were taking girls to see that evening. Louise Strong kept a tight leash on CJ since his father was killed. Not that he needed it. He was a good kid, did well in school, loved sports and his friends. So in the morning when CJ asked her for money for a movie that night, she asked him to come by her employers, the Barnes, after school, and it being payday she would have cashed her check and had money for him. He was surprised when she told him it was the Barnes' home she worked at part-time but accepted it as how things were.

When CJ and Billy showed up, they came around the back of the house to the service area, rang the bell, and Louise Strong answered. She greeted the two, gave CJ ten dollars. It was then they heard the eight boys playing football on the rear lawn. The rear lawn at the Barnes' estate was a strip of manicured grass that ran west, down to a private beach, between the tennis courts on the south side to the swimming pool on the north side.

Louise Strong encouraged the boys to join in the game, but they demurred. As they were walking away, Parker Barnes called out.

"CJ, come on. We need two more."

"Go on, you'll have a good time," Mrs. Strong encouraged.

"Let's go kick some ass," Billy said.

They joined the game and played for an hour, two black sons of west side laborers and eight rich kids from Stamford, Darien, and Greenwich.

In his mind he had the image of the perfect day it was. The sun was shining; his mother watched for a while on the side. He could still see her smiling. He remembered Mrs. Barnes coming out to watch, standing beside his mother. He remembered another of the household help bringing out lemonade and water for them afterward. He could see the picture of the ten boys that Mrs. Barnes took.

"That Mrs. Barnes took and gave to Mom," Strong said out loud.

His cellmate, a redneck lifer from Vermont with a constant chip on his shoulder, said, "You talking to me, Bro?"

Barnes learned to ignore him. He snapped back to the picture in his mind. Mom must still have it.

On Sunday when phone calls were allowed, CJ Strong called his mother collect as he always did.

"I talked with my sister, and she said Billy went to see you this week," Louise
Strong said to her son.

"Yes, it was good to see him," CJ replied.

And as they always did, Louise Strong had her son tell her what he was doing each day of the week. She tried to envision the lost moments of her son's life as he recounted his daily experiences, rather his daily drab existence. But this day he seemed more upbeat to her.

"Mom, do you remember the day Billy and I came by your work and ended up playing football with Parker and his friends."

"Like it was yesterday."

"Remember the picture that Mrs. Barnes took and gave you a copy of?"

"Yes, I do."

"Do you think you could find it and bring it next week when you come?"

"I think I know where it is. Feeling a little homesick, Son?"

"Something like that, Mom."

And the next week when Mrs. Strong visited she brought the picture. There they were. The ten of them. And there was his freedom, once Billy could identify which one had stabbed Augusto Santos.

At the end of their visit, CJ said, "I need a big favor. I need you to ask Aunt Jackie to have Billy come back up to see me. I need to talk with him again. It's important."

"Sure I will, what's so important?"

And not wanting to alarm his mother, he downplayed it. "No, it was just so good to see him after so long. I liked the company."

"That's good. I'll be sure to tell her."

That night as he lay back on his bunk, CJ Strong looked at the picture of the ten boys. He looked closely at the eight white faces. Kish Moira was Indian, so it wasn't him. Of the other seven, he wondered who killed Augusto Santos.

13

The meadow at Tod's Point rolled down to Long Island Sound, a great green strip of grass pouring into the sea. Their work as summer lifeguards done, they had one more week before returning to college—he to Harvard, she to Columbia.

"Narragansett, Jersey Shore. Narragansett, Jersey Shore," Valerie intoned as she plucked singular white petals from the wild daisy that grew along the side of the emerald swarth.

"Narragansett," Eddie stated firmly, "We'll get crushed in the traffic over the GW Bridge."

"Narragansett, Jersey Shore," Val continued. "Not so fast, Wheelwright. The law of the petals, rules."

"I'll give you the law of the petals," he said and leaped across the blanket they were picnicking on and landed lengthwise on her. "Let's wrestle."

"I know what wrestling means to you: let's fuck!"

"You are so crude. And so correct," said the Harvard junior as he rolled off her, placing a hand on her hip.

They kissed, touched each other, but when Eddie stared to pull Valerie's bikini bottom down, she punched him in the left side. "Not here!"

"What's wrong?"

"We're out in the open. People passing. Middle of the day."

"It's six. No one comes by here now."

In a case of perfect timing, another young couple appeared at the top of the meadow and began walking toward the would-be lovers.

"Look, it's Kish," Val said.

Wheelwright sat up and smiled as Kishenlal Moira approached with a young woman he did not recognize.

"Great timing, Kish," Wheelwright smiled.

Valerie laughed, "Yeah, Kish, great timing. You saved me."

Moira laughed as he and his friend came to the blanket. Val and Eddie made room as the newcomers sat down.

"Val, Eddie, this is my friend Sophie."

"Hi, Sophie," Val greeted.

The four exchanged pleasantries. Kish then added, by way of saying Sophie is OK, "Sophie goes to MIT."

Impressed, Wheelwright asked, "What year?"

"Junior," the pretty girl said.

"Do you know Winston?" then without giving her a chance to answer, Valerie looked at Moira, "Does Sophie know Winston?" inquiring about their mutual friend Winston Trout who was a third-year student at the Cambridge school.

"Yes, I do," Sophie Sorinku added. "It was Winston who introduced me to Kish a couple of weeks ago."

"Small world," Wheelwright added. "What do you study?"

"Same as Winston, materials science."

"Don't tell me you're going to save the planet too?" Wheelwright laughed, referring to Trout's well-known commitment, among his friends, to alternative forms of energy.

"I'm going to try," Sophie laughed.

"Actually," Kish began, "Sophie is on an internship at Trout Solar."

"Yes," Sophie jumped in, "I didn't know Winston until I started my internship. Then we realized we actually had been in several classes together over the past two years."

"So what brings us by here?" Kish asked with a sly smile.

"You knew we'd be here?"

"I knew you were heading out of town, and I wanted to catch you before you left. You two live here."

"What's up?"

"Ladies, we just need to talk business for a moment," Kish said, rising and beckoning Wheelwright to join him.

Wheelwright rose to about a foot higher than his friend. At six feet two inches to Moira's five foot four inches, Wheelwright was still high school slim, not yet filled out to the man he would become.

"It's the fund," Moira said as the friends walked across the grass, "the last group of stock we bought."

Before Kish could say anything further, Wheelwright interrupted, a deep furrow in his brow, "Damn, I knew there was risk. You tried to talk me out of it."

"No, Eddie, it's not bad. It's good. Today they went up 40 percent. They released earnings early. Revenue and EPS beat by a lot. Guidance for next quarter is up 30 percent on a large new Chinese contract they got. And they announced a stock buyback."

"And we sold?"

"No. I couldn't reach you."

"What? Kish—rule one—25 percent on any investment in a week—we're out."

"Eddie, rule 2. We both decide on investments more than four million dollars."

"What?"

"Yes, with the gain today it pushed those stocks up over four."

Valerie and Sophie chatted and watched as their two young men enjoyed a giddy dance as they walked back to the blanket.

"And we're happy because?" Valerie asked.

The Brunswick Fund was created for the altruistic reason of keeping a group of boys together in a lifelong friendship. The job of managing the fund had always belonged to Wheelwright and Moira. Edward had envisioned it and together they managed it, through high school and now through the first years of college, with extraordinary success. Edward was initially guided by his banker father but more recently relied on the combined research of Kish and himself. They rarely discussed the fund beyond the seven of the boys, Valerie McGuire being the exception.

"Some success with the fund," Eddie replied. Usually the furthest the twenty year would go in discussing the fund in front of anyone else.

"We'll be going," Kish said, "just wanted to share some good news with you." In the early evening in the meadow, the four young people stood. An elderly couple passed by the top of the meadow as the girls hugged. The boys shook hands and hugged the other's girlfriend. "I'll talk with you Kish."

As Kish and Sophie ascended the meadow, Valerie asked Eddie, "Do you think Kish is taking Sophie to the secret garden?"

Eddie turned and looked at Val, his eyes gleaming. "That's our spot. I never talk about that," he said, tugging Valerie back to the blanket.

"Not here, Eddie, didn't you just see that other couple?"

"Then let's go to the garden."

"Let's just stay here for now. It's so pretty this time of day. You can beguile me with your financial exploits."

"Well, last week…"

"I'm kidding. I don't care about that," Valerie said, glancing up and seeing no one else. She rolled over on top of the only boy she had ever loved.

****

Later, as dusk turned to dark, after making love in the open meadow, they lay naked facing the night sky.

"I told you about the problems my father's having, "Eddie said.

"Yes."

"Well, it's getting worse. As much as I know about what he does, it seems I know nothing."

Valerie turned on her side, her breasts spilling onto Eddie's arm. She raised her head up, positioning her elbow to support her head in the palm of her hand. "Is he going to be alright; I mean what else has happened?"

60

"I thought it was just the drinking. But it's not. The problem is what's causing him to drink."

"I don't understand." Val asked, "You want to talk about it."

"Not really," he said, but then he went on, "except my old man worked for Buck Simon at Oceans Bank. Cut him in two, he did. Guy's the nastiest bastard in the world. Even let one of his henchmen can his son before he canned the henchman."

"Over what, I mean I knew your father worked at Oceans, but what did Simon do to him," Val probed, getting more interested.

"Dad was one of Simon's vice presidents. Oversaw risk management. He tried to control Simon from his egomaniacal ambition to put the financial supermarket together. He saw what Simon was doing: buying off the politicians, getting Glass-Stengel repealed, allowing the mega-bank to come into being," Edward said, now sitting back, now leaning forward. Anxious.

"But it was Simon's total disregard for any constraints that got my father. My father played by the rules, he knew what they were, why they existed and he knew what exceptions could be made. Simon was reckless, insulting. Rules, principles, laws. They were a challenge for him. They drove him," Edward said.

"And?" Val chirped in.

Edward sat up, "Dad said that what started to push him over the edge was the abuse of shareholders. Simon rewarded himself and his henchmen fabulously. He spread money around the city buying largess through charity."

"But Simon gives tons to charity. How can you object to that?" Val asked

"He doesn't give two shits for charity. It's the new grease for the system and his ego," Wheelwright added, using his right hand emphatically as if lunging with an epee.

"Huh?" said Val, trying desperately to fathom what Edward meant.

"It's grease. It's ego. It's leverage. It gives him an edge for whatever he wants to do."

"How do you figure?"

"Spitzer when he was Attorney General had his ass. He was going to do time. My father said he never saw the bastard so afraid. Simon met with my father every day, for weeks trying to find a way out. My father was actually enjoying it. All the pain had been worth this to watch the weasel squirm."

Val asked, "But I never heard of an indictment."

"Bingo," Edward said lunging with his epee once again. Smiling sarcastically, he added, "There wasn't. Simon bought Spitzer off."

"Your father told you that?" Val asked.

"The world knew that. Simon paid a 400 million dollar fine."

"Big fine."

"But not with his money. With Oceans' shareholders money."

"And Simon got nothing, right; I mean no personal fine, no indictment, nothing?" Val asked.

"Viola! Except his picture in the *Times* the next week for being a model, generous New Yorker."

"It paid off," Val said, "the charitable giving."

"It became the model for all the other crooks. Spitzer had them all. Let them all buy their way out. The banks were using their investment banks to spin IPOs, give them favorable ratings, and give IPO shares away to favored politicians. Fined ten banks 1.4 billion dollars and not an indictment or day of jail time for any one of the bank heads he caught breaking the law."

"And Spitzer, what does he get out of this?" Val asked, knowing the answer.

"The governor's office."

"But my father didn't leave Oceans because of what ultimately happened there."

"What then?" Val came back.

"When my father tried one last time to get Oceans out of the packaging-of-mortgages business and CDO derivatives before everything turned into the great recession, he said Simon stood in his office and laughed at him.

"He told my father 'mind your own fucking business.'" My father was lost. Simon was up to his ass in creating the financial disaster that took the whole world down for six years. After that the relationship was shot. My father retired early. As if that wasn't enough, Simon got the rolodex out and spread the word through his network in the finance community. My father was done in the industry."

Wheelwright's face reddened in the black night.

"And your father now?" Val asked, sadly.

"It's not a happy ending. He's really troubled. My father thought he'd have freedom after telling me. Now whenever he drinks he comes crying on my shoulder that I shouldn't think badly of him. I don't. I try reassuring him, but it's the financial disaster that destroyed so much. Simon was responsible for it. My father felt he should have done more. He can't get over that his own anger at Simon."

14

Edward Wheelwright was different. He alone was unfazed by all around him, but then he had Valerie McGuire at his side. At sixteen they met at Tod's Point beach in Old Greenwich; the following year they became lifeguards at that beach. Each summer through high school, they spent together; each winter they were mostly apart as their schools were in different towns, their families' social circles in different orbits. Through their separation they grew stronger; through their togetherness they found their life.

Valerie McGuire cared about much and wanted little. Both encompassed Edward Wheelwright, whom she cared for so much and when with him needed so little. When they went to different universities, they were not so far apart. School breaks were often, and with a five-week vacation over the Christmas holiday that brought them home, they saw each other frequently. During the endless summers during their first two years in college, they were together constantly as lifeguards at Tod's Point and as lovers. When not engaged in those activities, they spent time with their mutual friends—Eddie's six "brothers" and their love interests. During the school year once a month, they alternatively took the Acela high speed train—she to Boston and he to Manhattan.

While there was a heart and mental meld between Eddie and Valerie, her focus on Eddie exceeded his for her. He did love her and was not distracted by other young women, but he needed more. Despite the family wealth, and it was considerable as Mark

Wheelwright had been a senior VP at Oceans Bank, Edward strove for something larger. Not for wealth or power, for when Valerie pressed to know what this inner drive was, he could not define it. Not yet.

Valerie thought it was the peer pressure, being tied to his brothers. The Ball's, Barnes' and Bridge's fortunes were great and derived from ownership, even the Trout's fortune was growing significantly with the establishment of Trout Solar and it's coming initial public offering. And yet by establishing the Brunswick Fund as a way to keep their friendship ties tight and grow his investing prowess, Eddie was inextricably linking himself to a subservient role in support of his brothers.

Valerie could see it. She tried nudging Eddie towards self-sufficiency. He was strong, confident, smart, and handsome and did not need the brothers to grow. They, on the other hand, clung to his youthful exuberance and leadership. They relied on him for life outside the stuffiness of the stultifying life they led behind tall hedges and gate houses. Still, it was Edward Wheelwright who needed much and brought everyone along in his quests.

There was a time when they crossed the Charles Bridge, went to the Pantheon and slept in on Sunday mornings in Kensington. They bargained for oil paintings like Bohemians on Nevsky Prospect, ate tomato salads in San Gimigiano, and swam at Majorica. The summers during and after their junior year of college were spent on the modern day version of LeGrande Tour. They took trains from Amsterdam to Bitburg; they took boats on the Rhine and buses up to the other coliseum in Verona or to the Palio in Siena. They fell in and out of love so many times with so many beautiful women the concept of beauty became love. The sight of a stunning Spanish girl in the Prado became the thunderbolt. Walking along Grafton Street beside a redhead with freckles and skin kissed by the air of Eire fulfilled a young man's life.

By the time Eddie and Valerie were seniors in high school, their families became friendlier, realizing there was a very strong bond between their children. The Wheelwrights were monied; the McGuires were middleclass. Through Val and Eddie's college year, they often dined together in each other's homes or at the Wheelwright's Club at Indian Harbor in Greenwich.

So close had the relationship between the two families become, so sure of their future to become one family, that they vacationed together sailing in the Wheelwright yacht to Edgartown during the week after their children's lifeguard duties ended.

At the Wheelwright's summer home on Martha's Vineyard, Mrs. Wheelwright, older than Mrs. McGuire by fifteen years, came to have such affection for Valerie that she seemed more Val's grandmother. In the early morning, Margaret Wheelwright and Valerie McGuire would walk down Katama Road and along South Beach, hand in hand. Mrs. Wheelwright, a kind gentle soul from an earlier time, loved Valerie; she loved the substance of the girl—still a girl, but the future woman was visible. "Bright, kind and loving," was how Mrs. W., as Val called her, described the girl she hoped would one day marry her son.

Valerie was all that and more. During the school year while at Columbia, two nights a week she tutored reading for illegal immigrants on the lower east side of Manhattan. The subway ride from her apartment on One Hundred Tenth Street was a far cry from the circumstances she found in life's nomads from Guatemala, Africa, and China on East Tenth Street.

And from all the joy shared by Valerie and Edward, there came the time when Edward left Valerie McGuire.

15

The late spring snow had stopped falling. He watched the wind through the light snow blowing on the back lawn and out on the Sound. The wind lifted the snow, pushing it up off the ground. It formed into a mass, looked like a ground-bound cloud, and moved over the water. There the wind blew it apart sending the snow shooting upwards, then sideways. Then the wind stopped, and the frozen crystals blew back over and settled in the back yard.

He lifted his glass and drank, immersed in the moment.

Then the ache returned to his head. There were windmills everywhere in his life now. Was what he saw on the ice the wind blowing the snow or was it an unseen windmill kicking up a ruckus?

Don Quixote had nothing on him; Mark Wheelwright laughed out loud, half in, half out of sanity. He was fighting windmills on every front. He had been named in five lawsuits stemming from bank losses in the recent great recession. He filed his own lawsuit against his former employer, Oceans Bank, and he had even filed a lawsuit against the golf course his property abutted, claiming adverse possession of land that he had tended for twenty years that the golf course claimed as its own, and that he knew was theirs, but since they wanted to put a fence up he decided he'd put up a windmill. His anger began with the wrongful death lawsuit against the Riverside Memorial Hospital and two doctors who had misdiagnosed pancreatic cancer that killed his wife of thirty-five years. And he was in the battle of his life with his alcoholism.

It was 7 a.m.; Mark Wheelwright again lifted the glass of bourbon and shook his head. Tears rolled down his cheeks.

****

"You left some stuff out last night," Edward began as he entered the room noticing his father with a drink in his hand.

Mark Wheelwright had a hangover, a bad one. They were all bad lately. His capacity for alcohol had diminished; he was drinking more and remembering less. "Like what?"

"In the office. I was using the computer, and it was there."

"What was?"

"Letters from Valerie's mother."

Edward did not notice his father's reddened face as Edward had looked away, embarrassed to bring this topic up.

"And you read them?"

"Yes."

"Why?'

"Because I saw Valerie's name on the first page I glanced at."

"And?'

"You paid for Valerie's college?"

"Yes."

"Does she know that?"

"Not as far as I know."

"How did this happen?" Edward said, and proceeded with what he thought was the answer; he assailed his father. "You and her mother?"

Mark thought of trying to duck, but he was on the ropes, cornered. "Yes," he blurted out.

"Mrs. McGuire and you?"

"Yes."

"Did Mom know?"

"I don't think so."

"How long did this go on? Is it still going on?"

"No, it's over."

Edward's face was crimson with shame and anger. "How long?'

"Long."

"Long? A year, two years?"

"Almost three."

"Three years. Three goddamn years you had an affair with Valerie's mother! And you knew we were in love, wanting to get married?"

There was a pause, a deafening silence in the room as Mark tried to hang on from the pounding in his head and salvage the relationship with the boy he loved. Edward looked at his father, unmoving, trying to think of the many things this meant.

"Why aren't you two together? Mom's dead. Is this the reason Val's father took off?"

"Probably. She said he suspected something," Mark was breathing heavily, "That he confronted her several times when she was out late. When she seemed a little too close to me or when we would fool around or when the four of us would sail on the boat."

"You were friends with her father. And you would fool around in front of mom?"

"No. It wasn't like that. Look, Val's parents were a great couple. Your mother and I had a lot of fun with them. But they didn't have a pot to piss in. We all knew Val was a top student, that she was going to be part of the family, so when she got accepted to Columbia, Sue confided in me that they had no way to pay for it. We had more money than God, so your mother and I agreed to pay for it. Only Sue knew, Bill McGuire would not have accepted it, so only your mother, Sue, and I knew."

"And the affair, when did it start?"

"Right after Val went off to Columbia. Sue was so proud of Val, so happy and so thankful. It just happened."

"And Val's father never knew?"

"Bill wasn't dumb. He knew they couldn't afford Columbia even on both their salaries. Sue tried telling him it was a combination of student loans and scholarships and their savings. She said he accepted it at first, but then Bill started putting two and two together.

She said he confronted her several times about how they were paying for it all and still had money for travel. Then the questions shifted to her and me. Bill had figured it out. His wife and his friend. He left—just walked out the door."

"And what happened with you and Mrs. McGuire?"

"It took off. Val off in school, Bill gone. I was with her every night."

"And mom?"

"I covered fairly well with work. I always did work long hours. Only then, did I cut back."

"Mom never confronted you?"

"No. I really don't think she knew. She knew Sue was a flirt, but Sue was very sweet to your mother."

"How did it end?"

"Guilt," and Mark Wheelwright paused. Edward could see the tears in his eyes. "I screwed everything up. When your mother was getting sick, I should have reacted sooner. She didn't want to bother with the doctors. Later the doctors said we could have caught it if we had acted sooner."

"What?" Edward fumed.

"I know."

The dreadful pause reappeared. It was a silence between a father and son and all the air was leaking out. A lifetime of love was damaged, maybe beyond repair.

"And once mom dies?"

"When your mother died I knew what I did or rather what I didn't do. I drank more—and more. I went to Sue's every night— drank all night. Could barely get to work. Wasn't effective in work during the financial crisis. Drank more. Sue finally ended it six months ago."

There was no air left in the room. Neither man could breathe.

"I'm sorry, Eddie."

The young Wheelwright got up, looked at his father still seated, and left the room. He did not see Valerie McGuire again. He could not face her, did not return her calls, and when she came to his door, he did not answer.

PART

2

16

Recife, Brazil, is that point in South America that juts furthest east into the Atlantic Ocean. If Pangaea, the original supercontinent of earth, were put back together, Recife would tuck nicely into the African country of Cameroon.

In the sky above the city of Recife, on a day when the sun is not baking the red clay roofs, it is filled with clouds. The clouds come in columns, like they were puffed out of a great chimney. Straight as arrow columns, then rows of them. But not too far inland, mainly along the coast, they float along, like a quiet army.

The boy sits on the sand of BoaViagem beach looking at the clouds, thinking about them. He is the only figure on the beach on this cloudy day. The boy is sitting there in tan shorts with no other clothes. It is not that he is going swimming; these shorts are all the clothes he has. He sits with his arms wrapped around his knees.

A dog has been swimming, and now, emerging from the surf, notices the boy. He shakes the water off of his long, short body. It is sort of like a chain reaction; the water flies off in small beads, beginning at his head and progressing all the way down his body.

Chunk smiles as he sees the dog looking at him. The dog notices the smile and comes slowly to the boy and sits beside him. The two sit on the beach, not communicating, just each with their own thoughts beside each other.

After some time the dog gets up and walks off. He stops once and looks back at the boy. Then the dog turns and goes further down the beach before heading to one of the seaside carne-de-sol stands that specializes in sun-dried beef. Usually the dog can count on the owner for a scrap.

The following day the boy Chunk is walking across the Santo Antonio Bridge, which crosses over the Juquia River as it flows to the sea. The river is a filthy brown cesspool carrying all the elements of city trash: papers, boxes, plastics, rubber, fruit, vegetables, and occasional dead birds. Pieces of clothing float lazily on top, next to tree branches.

At this moment late in the afternoon, four brown mulatto boys, clad only in the same type shorts as the boy, are running on the far side of the bridge, their shoe leather like feet scurrying across the hot cement. They have hold of the same dog that sat beside Chunk yesterday. They lift the dog up and toss him in the river. Then the four boys climb the cement rail and one by one dive into the ooze after the dog. All five swim to shore and climb back up to the street to once again to escape the steaming humidity by launching themselves into the river.

As the boys grab for the dog, he barks, then snaps at them, trying to escape their grasp but longing to be with them. As the four mulattos get their hands on him by grasping one leg each, Chunk approaches them. He is smaller than the other four, but about their age, somewhere in the early teens.

"Hola," he calls. "Put the dog down."

The tallest of the four boys looks over his shoulder and laughs, "OK boys, let's put him down—in the water." And they proceed to toss the mangy cur into the slime.

The new arrival runs to the rail and watches as the dog struggles to get to shore.

The older boy approaches Chunk and tells the others, "Now let's throw this nosy dog in."

As they all laugh and start to move in on Chunk, he promptly flattens the older boy with a punch squarely on the nose. With lightning speed and a face now twisted into a battle glaze, looking more bulldog than human, he rapidly punches and kicks one, then another, till all four boys are down on the cement bridge at once.

He does not say a word; he turns his head and walks away. The four boys, not sure what hit them, all get up and watch as Chunk heads toward the beach. The dog now back up on the bridge, looks at the four boys, and then looks at Chunk. After weighing his options, he follows Chunk.

Chunk walks to and then along the beach that has many bathers in the water this day. He finds a place to sit. Walking along the beach about fifty yards behind him is the dog. And about another fifty yards behind the dog are the four boys.

Chunk DeLuna is fourteen the day he meets his new friends. He has been in Brazil for nine months. His father, who took him with him from Puerto Rico, abandoned him after six months, and for the past three months, Chuck has been living along the beach, sleeping on the beach, or when rousted by the police moving under the piers in the harbor. But now he is no longer alone. He has a dog; he has a group of four new friends.

"Where did you learn to fight like that?" asks the older boy, the first to be punched and the first to go down.

"My father taught me," Chunk tells him.

The littlest one, the boy named Rafael, with a dirty patch over his right eye says, "I never saw that punch coming."

The twins, Pedro and Paco, begin laughing, "That's because you're blind."

"Don't make fun of him," Chunk says. "What happened to your eye?"

"I don't know; it got infected or something. I can't see out of it any more. When I put this patch over, it doesn't hurt as much." Raphael says.

"Can I see it?" Chunk asks.

"Sure," and he lifts the patch up. Chunk winces. It is a mess of infection and oozing puss, red and blue and purplish.

"You need to get to a hospital."

"I've been. They clean it up for me, give me some medicine to wipe on it," Raphael said.

"They've got to do more than that," Chunk says firmly. "I'll go there tomorrow with you." Chunk suddenly feels better than he has in the three months since his father left him.

The older boy Carlos asks Chunk," You talk a little different from us; where are you from?"

"Puerto Rico," he says.

"Where's that?" one of the twins asks.

"It's an island in the Caribbean Sea," Chunk replies.

After a brief geography lesson, Carlos asks him his name.

"Chunk."

"Chunk? That's different. What's it mean."

"Nothing, it doesn't mean anything," Chunk says, realizing he has no idea why his name is Chunk. He knows his given name is Juan DeLuna, but he never thought to ask where Chunk had come from.

The boys tell Chunk their names. They too are homeless, living in the basements of the public housing buildings inland from the beach.

"I used to live down here at the beach, but the police kept hassling me," Carlos tells Chunk.

"Yeah, they do that to me too, but I just move along down by the piers. Mostly it's OK sleeping along here," Chunk replies, adding, "Tonight you boys stay in my house."

The boys smile, knowing they have a new leader. Carlos has been deposed with one punch, but he does not seem to mind.

They talk the rest of the afternoon, and as the sun goes down, they move towards the street to hustle some food from the beachside vendors. The dog tags along.

"Whose dog is this?" Chunk asks.

"No one's, he just comes around," the twin named Pedro says.

"Well, he's part of our gang now," Chunk laughs and reaches back to pat the dog who growls as Chunk approaches too fast. He calms down once he realizes the boy means no harm. Chunk looks at the hair falling out of the dog and notices the mange infestation on his skin.

When they pass by a stand cooking churrasco, Chunk sees a large drum of kerosene off to the side of the stand. He quickly grabs the dog by the scruff of his neck, lifts him up and dunks him just short of his mouth in the drum. The dog howls, a screeching agony, as the open sores are filled with the oil.

"What in hell are you doing," the man cooking in the stand says as he opens a side door to witness the dousing.

"Dog's got the mange," Chunk says.

"Yeah, that will kill the fleas alright and the dog too. What are you kids thinking of. Get the hell out of here," he says dismissively but not angrily.

Chunk puts the dog down, and he runs off, barking at anyone who comes near him. When the boys last see him, he is running towards the water.

"Well, there goes one member of our gang," the twin Paco says.

"Nah," says Chunk, "he'll be back, and he'll thank us for it."

"You're crazy," Carlos tells Chunk admirably.

"Crazy like a garota," Chunk replies.

"Like a girl?" Pedro smiles.

"Yes, they're very clever," Chunk replies.

Later in the evening as the five boys walk along the beach, they talk of their dreams for their gang. As a couple passes by them, suddenly, Carlos and Raphael hit the man to the ground and begin to pummel him.

"Give me your money," Carlos screams at him as the man's girl-friend looks on horrified.

As the man reaches in his pocket from the prone position, Chunk grabs Carlos' arm and pushes him aside. "No, this is not the way."

Chunk leans down to help the man up, "I am sorry. My friend has lost his mind. Please forgive us." He brushes the sand off the back of the man's pants and gently urges him on his way. The terrified couple's pace picks up as they headed up off the beach.

Chunk slaps Carlos hard on the head, and Carlos put up his hands as if to box. Chunk promptly punches him hard in the stomach with his right hand and as he bends forward, hits him in the head with his left hand. Carlos falls to the sand; with a hand outstretched, he pleads with his attacker, "Please, boss, do not hit me again."

Chunk bends down to help Carlos up. The other three gang members hold their ground, not sure what is going on.

"Carlos, my friend, if I am to be your leader, you cannot go attacking people when I am not aware. We do things by planning them. We do not act like retarded people, just jumping on anyone passing by."

"I'm sorry, Chunk," Carlos says remorsefully.

Still later in the evening they discuss holding up a beach concession stand that will be far more profitable. Once the plan is worked out, they decide to try it out on a coco-frio stand. The person working the stand would be up front with the machete and coconuts. The twins Paco and Pedro would approach the stand from the front, appearing to buy a coco-frio. Raphael would keep an eye out, one eye. Carlos and Chunk, the two strongest, would come up from behind the stand and grab the vendor, forcing him to the ground and taking the machete. Then they would take money from his pants and from under the counter. They would take the machete, and all five would flee into the darkness of the beach.

The plan works perfectly, and as they are all running for the beach, with Chunk bringing up the rear, an arm goes around Chunk's neck. It is a police officer who has witnessed the end of the robbery and waited beside a small outbuilding to grab at least one of the robbers. He has Chunk in a choke hold as he calls for help from a partner across the beach boulevard. Just as the other partner is crossing the street and the officer with the choke hold on Chunk is pulling him out towards the street, the officer screams in pain and reaches for his leg. In that second Chunk breaks free and heads toward the dark of the beach, noticing that a small dog has clamped his teeth onto the officer's calf.

"My little dog," Chunk calls out. And with the officer now on the ground, the dog releases him and run off after Chunk.

The five boys and the dog run in the black night toward the piers. There will be no catching them now.

Under the pier they are all patting the hero of the night—the long short dog with the mange, or less of it now.

"We must have a name for a dog like you," Carlos says

"He looks like a hot dog; let's call him hot dog," Raphael says.

"We'll call him Shorty, Cortito," Chunk says naming his dog, "Come here Cortito," now looking at the animal, who moved next to him.

"And we'll call our gang, Rei de Praia, Beach Kings," Chunk raises his hands up and begins a small dance, and the other boys follow, dancing merrily not in their poverty, but in their newfound wealth: the fraternity of the gang. And Cortito wags his tail and barks with his gang.

The following day the five boys, dressed only in their shorts, and one short dog, enter the San Francisco hospital. They go to the emergencia entrance and are told to wait along with the huddled mass of poor seeking help.

After two hours pass and no one calls Raphael's name, Chunk rises to get some attention. "No, Chunk, we must wait our turn," Raphael tells him.

"You sit down, Raphael; I'll be right back," Chunk says as he walks through the doors where other patients have advanced for treatment.

After several minutes Chunk emerges with a doctor standing beside him. He waves Raphael forward and then puts his hand up indicating that the others should wait there.

Chunk accompanies Raphael and the doctor to the triage area as the doctor pulls the curtain behind them. He examines Raphael, calls for a nurse, and tells her several things. She brings a few instruments and places them on a metal table beside the doctor. The doctor takes a magnifying glass and a long, thin metal instrument and has Raphael lay back. He turns on a bright overhead light and proceeds to look in Raphael's injured eye.

After a couple of minutes of probing, he steps back and turns the light off and says to Chunk, "Raphael has a very serious infection under his eye. We need to do a small procedure, get what is in there out, put some antibiotics in, and clean it up. We can do this later this afternoon."

"Good, we'll wait outside." Chunk says.

"No, I need you to leave. Your friend needs to spend the night in the hospital to make sure the infection is reducing. You can come back tomorrow," the doctor concludes.

"I will come back for him tomorrow at noon time." Chunk says. He walks over to the table, puts his arm around Raphael who was now sitting up, and says, "You'll be fine. This is a good doctor. He will make your eye better. Do everything he says and do not be afraid."

"Yes, Chunk. Thank you," a grateful Raphael says.

The doctor says, "Raphael, you stay here, and I'll get you ready in a little while." And the doctor leaves.

As the boys rise to leave, Raphael asks, "What did you say to the doctor, Chunk? They have never taken this much time to find out what was wrong with my eye before."

Chunk reaches into the canvas bag he is carrying and shows Raphael the machete they had stolen from the coco-frio stand the night before. "I told him you were very sick, that you had come here many times and no one had resolved your injury. I said I was here to make sure that this was fixed today. I took the machete out and showed it to him, and I said, "I will cut off the hand of the doctor who refuses to help my friend get better."

That night as the boys prepared to sleep, Carlos asked Chunk to tell them about Puerto Rico, and Chunk began, "It's a beautiful island, but I have no one left there now but my sister, Silvana."

"That's a pretty name, Chunk," Paco said. "Is she beautiful in all the right places?" he finished with a wry smile.

Chunk reached across Pablo and wacked Paco in the head. "She's a nice girl; she's not like the pigs you go after."

17

"I thought I would go mad last night. It was so hot; there was no breeze. I was having trouble sleeping. But it wasn't the heat of the day driving me crazy. It must have been just after midnight—a dog started barking. He was up in the hills somewhere. He kept barking and then another dog joined him in the noise. Then off in the distance other dogs woke up and started barking. Many of them all at once. They made so much noise they woke the roosters, and they started cock–a-doodle, doodling. I thought I would go mad—it was so hot and there was so much noise so late at night. I needed to sleep; I have so much work to do today."

Silvana DeLuna finished the entry in her diary and got out of bed, placing the diary and pen on the small night stand next to her bed.

In the barrio of San Diego, part of the mountain town of San Blas de Illescas de Coamo, Puerto Rico, she has a three-room home. It is made up of a bedroom, a bathroom, and a pantry and two rooms connected that make up work space and kitchen, although more work space than kitchen. The house sits in the Y of two streets becoming one—Avenue Rio de Janeiro and State Road 744, with 744 the surviving road. The doors on either side of the house are always open during the day, so that it gives you a view through the house from either road. The main door opens onto Avenue Rio, and Silvana can be seen ironing from sunrise to sunset. She does the laundry of many citizens of the barrio—their underwear, shirts, blouses, pants, and skirts. It all comes through to her.

On their way to work, the citizens of the barrio stop and drop their clothes off and pick them up on their way home at night. The washer woman of San Blas labors over these garments with two air fans, one at each door. She is a stunning woman, with no fat, only beautiful round curves. Her skin is olive, her shoulder length hair black as coal, and her smile is the smile of your first love. But she smiles little now.

Silvana's three-year-old daughter plays in and out of the house during the day. There is no husband. He is dead. She is lost.

Oh, but there was a time he was here on this earth. She smiles at this, the thought of her dear, her love, the man who gave her the precious girl playing by her feet. She cries as she thinks of the joy her running man gave her.

She moves across the room and takes a paper from a tin box. It is a letter. As she irons, she reads it.

"I am Juan. I run. I left this place of my birth ten years ago, this barrio de San Diego, this Coamo. Now, I am running the hills of my youth once again.

"My father is seventy-six, and he asked me to return. He gave me land by his house, and over the last two years, my cousin Julio has been in charge of building my home. I would return every six months and watch the progress and pay him. It is done, and it is wonderful.

"I know why my father wanted me home. He knows he is dying, and he wants me to care for Lola. She is the same age as him, healthier, but almost blind.

"Life has to have meaning. My life in the states didn't mean much to me. I ran an envelope-making machine for eight years. I made twenty-nine million envelopes. I did that. And I ran. Sometimes I played the guitar in my room. And I played softball on Wednesday nights and drank a few beers. But mostly I made envelopes. That wasn't meaningful. The running kept me alive.

"So now maybe helping my father and mother will be more meaningful. I read books once and awhile. I read that President John

Adams said you only need to do two things—be a good man and lead a useful life.

"I've always been a good man. Now maybe I can lead a more useful life, be more important in others' lives.

"And the other day, as I was running by, I saw you—my beautiful washer woman of San Blas."

Silvana wiped the tears from her eyes. The running man had been too shy; he left the letter under her door. On that morning four years ago, she found the letter. She knew who he was; she would glance up as he ran by. She knew he lived up on the mountain—he always came from that way and returned that way. It kept her mind busy during the day to catch fleeting glimpses of her neighbors and imagine what they were up to. The running man was easy—he was running, he was always running. And he sweat, he sweat more than she did. He had less fat than she did.

Later, on the day she got the letter, he ran by. Silvana put the iron down, walked to the door, and called after him. "Hi, Juan the runner!"

He turned, smiled and kept running.

A little while later he stopped at the door. "Hola, beautiful washer woman of San Blas."

And his life became much more meaningful. And his beautiful, exotic, olive skinned, sweetheart of a girl found joy. And between them they conceived their daughter. And one night before their daughter was one, Silvana became the widow of Coamo.

He was running at dusk, and he was hit by a car. It came around a corner too fast, and he was gone.

She folded the letter, placing it back in the tin.

"Come here, Sweetie, give Mama a hug." Her daughter Mare came over smiling and hugged her mother's leg. Silvana bent down and wrapped the child in her arms.

She straightened up, the girl went back to her play, and Silvana returned to ironing.

This winter we had a lot of rain, she thinks to herself. Everything is so green. The grass by the roadside is tall.

I would like to have time to go up the mountain, to look over the valley, and see the green in the hills. When I was a girl, I remember it being like it is now only a few times. The northern part of the island is always green from lots of rain. But once you come here across the mountains and face the hotter sun from the south, it is more parched and brown. I always remember that. I wish I were a girl again, to run the hills and play again. Ah, but who would iron the clothes of San Blas; who would take care of my baby!

I would trade anything for the sight of my man running by my open door!

At night everything finds its way home. It's like the ocean—the waves come in, crash and yet the tide takes them home. The horses go looking for the grass along these roads—she glances up for a moment looking out the door—but they return to their stalls when the sun sets. The dogs run to their packs in the sun but run home at night. And the roosters, noisy in the morning, herd their hens into the coop when it gets dark. I hope they are quiet tonight.

I wish I had time to be idle. Idleness is part of life here. It is how life is lived, not a mad cluttered world with images and noise. Not television. People stand outside and wave to each other passing by. I used to have more time to talk with my customers, to look up and wave to them.

Conversation in the barrio goes on for hours. Domino games last for days.

Juan liked to plant coconut trees on his land. When we would go to the beach at Isle Verde in San Juan, he would run along the edge of the ocean and return with dozens of small coconut shells that the tide brought in. He loved watching the long fronds poking thru the cracked shells. He would bring them home and nurture them. Last Sunday I walked by the house he built and saw his small trees growing. They love all this rain.

Up where Juan's house is, the road gets very steep. It is like looking down from the top of a roller coaster. I don't know how he ever ran on these roads.

In the winter time, in February, they have a race here in honor of our patron saint, San Blas. The Africans who come for the prize money fly over the hills. They are short people with powerful legs. They remind me of the pigmy people on the other side of the mountain, through the stinking town of Aibonito, with all its chicken processing plants, and down into the valley to Cayey.

Juan was a good strong runner; he had legs so long they looked like stilts. He was tall, and he had a long thin torso. I watched him in the San Blas marathon. He was leading the race at the halfway point; he was even ahead of the Africans coming up the big hill after passing through Coamo. But they caught him on the backside of the race, the downhill part. He was in such pain after the race. He pulled his shoes off, and his feet were calloused and bleeding. I can still see him slamming his shoe down; mad at himself for wearing new socks to run a race. The new socks had caused the bleeding and pain. But he recovered quickly.

At the finish line at the stadium, there was a big celebration with bands and dancing and food. We stayed all night. We danced; even with his feet hurting, he loved to meringue, swung his hips better than the girls. My quiet man would come alive dancing with me, swiveling to the music, throwing his head back as the music flowed through the night air. Coolness. After a hot day in the sun.

Now she looked up as a clap of thunder sounded overhead. She continued ironing, glancing up to look at the rain.

It rains here in slow motion. The water is so light it takes a long time to reach the grass.

After going by Juan's house on Sunday, I left Mare at my Aunt Carmen's house so I could walk into town. The town is always the same but always being repaired. It is old. The plaza around San Blas' church has undergone renovation—new tiles, cement borders, new benches, and they planted new trees. This transformation is magical, still the original plaza but new and green. I like it. Now it is alive with people. Before, the people would not walk over the cracked tiles, and the grey, bleached broken cement sticking up would trip you. There were places to sit, but even the two-foot wall around the plaza was falling down. They have done a wonderful thing fixing it.

The town seems like it has found itself—the people are walking there again, talking, sitting on the benches. And even though it was still hot in the afternoon, the canopy of lotus trees seemed to bring a breeze with it as dappled sunlight squeezes in.

Over by the church, the old, old crape myrtle tree is still there with its fragrant pink flowers hanging down. And they kept the small monuments dedicated to past citizens. I sat by myself on a bench just watching the people and occasionally talking with some of the older women. I didn't know anyone. All of my customers live up on the hill. My friends are all gone, married, and left for other towns or to the States. My best friend, Santa Alba, the beauty queen of Coamo, went to New York to fashion school and never came back. My parents are gone, my mother died, and my father went to Brazil with my little brother, Chunk. My aunt still lives here, over on the first hill, just before my house.

I left the bench I was sitting on and walked down some of the side streets. The music poured from the casitas. At night in town, it is always the music from the casitas; at night in the hills, it is always the dogs waking up the roosters. But over all of this is the fresh island air. Free to breathe, cool on my face.

It started to rain while I was on my walk so I left town to go home. The air here makes its own environment. Rain comes not in waves but in short bursts from a sky so clearly black at night you can see across the Milky Way. In the day the sun is always there, but it can rain seven or eight times during the day. Once, I kept track of it while washing the clothes of my customers; it rained twelve times that day, but not for long and always on the wings of the constant breezes.

As I walked home, I saw life all around me. Everyone in town talking to everyone else, knowing everyone else. In the hills toward home, strolling on the streets were pigs, horses, cats, dogs, and roosters. Billions of roosters. Er-Er-Ering wildly all day; cock-a-doodle, doodling all night.

Here the men are the men. There aren't girly men here. My friend Santa Alba writes to me about all the fun things she is doing in New York. But she does say the men there are more like girls—

she calls them "metro-sexuals." She says there is something in big cities that makes them feminine. Nuh, uh. Not that way here; although, the men do the shopping here. The women? The women stay home, sashay around in too tight jeans and low (really low) cut blouses.

When I reached my aunt's house, we talked for a while; she fixed Mare and me rice and beans and then we walked on home. I told Mare she was never going to wear tight jeans and low cut blouses. She said, "What are you talking about mommy?"

Juan was always very modest, and he liked that I was also. He would shoot his daughter before he ever let her out of the house in clothes like I saw in the plaza today. I will shoot her for him when it comes time. Maybe that is why there are so many children here in San Blas. Almost as many as the roosters.

On our way home we passed a dead tree, arms outstretched, as if saying, "Why me?" It is the only dead tree on the island. Everything is alive here; nothing dies here.

It surprises me that people move from the smaller towns to the bigger cities, not necessarily to San Juan but to cities in the States. They always come back for visits, and many of the older ones who left are moving back here. They have their money and can live here reasonably. One of my customers retired from the phone company in Boston and came back home to live. She can't believe how cheaply she can live here. Maybe I need to raise my prices.

My customer said here she pays no state tax, no town tax, no sales tax, and no real estate tax, except for a twelve dollar annual land tax. Yes, that is true.

Less and less though, I think the children of San Blas are leaving. Many of the things they were previously drawn to are now coming to them. This is good. Jobs and modern conveniences are arriving, and our local culture is being preserved. Some of the things we see on television that happen in the states are thankfully not happening here.

In a lot of ways, we need those jobs and conveniences. I remember reading in my geography books in high school of sixteenth century Spain. I never saw a difference from that book to my hills of San Blas. Local residents ride horses in these hills and on the roads, animals roam freely around the countryside and return home at night and doctors live next to carpenters. Children and parents spend hours in front of their homes talking with passing neighbors and relatives. And relatives, everyone is related here. Up on the mountain, Juan has twenty cousins; ten aunts, his mother is living with one of his cousins; and maybe seven or eight uncles, not always with those same aunts.

The cars are a problem. The roads are too narrow, and every boy from sixteen on has a car. I don't know how their parents can afford these cars for these kids. I can't afford a car, and I work all day. While the parents stay thin, I notice the kids are getting puffy. I think that is from all the television watching. The kids in town didn't look puffy when I walked there Sunday, but I notice my customer's kids—puffy. Not enough exercise. The Spanish diet of chicken and rice and beans is being replaced by fast food. They have now opened a Burger King next to the McDonalds. My customer from the states, the one who retired from the phone company, eats at McDonalds so much they made her customer of the year. I saw her picture on the wall, standing next to the store manager, under the sign that said "Customer of the Year."

And I think we need more doctors here. I took Mare in for her shot on Saturday. By 9 a.m., forty people had shown up, took their tickets and were assigned a "general" time to come back. We did our shopping and came back at our "general" time of 1 p.m., and the doctor was not back from lunch. Mare didn't get her shot until 3 p.m.

A customer walked in, and Silvana popped out of her reflections to help the lady.

Once the customer left, Silvana went back to her thoughts. She thought of Santa Alba, her best friend growing up. She hoped to hear from her again soon.

She put the iron down, walked back across the room, reached in the tin box, and took out the letter. She began to read it again.

18

The Beauty Queen of Coamo left her home town in Puerto Rico to attend the Fashion Institute of Design in Manhattan, Chelsea to be more exact. Even as a young girl she had style and grace, which only added to her beauty, although it was not those assets that helped her become a hometown beauty queen. That distinction belonged to her father, a prosperous land owner and developer of the local golf course. This was the same golf course that tied into the Banos de Coamo, the legendary Fountain of Youth of Ponce DeLeon.

No, Santa Alba owed her beauty title to the three judges who were fellow business men with Edwardo Alba. And it was not that Santa Alba wasn't beautiful, she was, but at seventeen the beauty of San Blas de Coamo and maybe all of Puerto Rico was the school girl Silvana DeLuna. But when the results were announced at the festival of San Francisco, outside the church in Coamo's main plaza, there was much joy. And to think she came in second to her friend Santa Alba filled Silvana with pride. The two hugged each other for more than a few moments. They had been the closest of friends all through school. And it was dear Santa who convinced Silvana to enter the beauty contest. Silvana had demurred. She might be friends with Santa Alba, but she was not in the same class. Santa came from the moneyed part of town, and her father was well respected. The opposite was true for Silvana DeLuna. After her mother died in child birth with Silvana's younger brother Chunk, it was largely Silvana who raised Chunk. Their father was mostly unemployed, due to his constant drinking. And things only got worse when her father took Chunk to live with him in Brazil.

Santa Alba had dreamed of being a fashion designer from her early teens. She read every magazine, her father indulged her with the latest fashions, but mostly she enjoyed drawing up, cutting, and sewing her own clothes. Frequently her own work won more praise from other girls than did the more expensive clothes from San Juan and New York. When she applied to the Fashion Institute, she sent a portfolio of her own drawings along with a dozen pictures of her and Silvana DeLuna modeling her handmade skirts and blouses. The talent was recognized, and she entered the Institute in the fall of her eighteenth year. By twenty-one she had her own apartment on 20th St, next to the Atlantic Theater Company's hall.

In the summers of her second and third year at the Institute, she stayed in Manhattan, or rather Manhattan with all manner of the world's fashion sense stayed in her. Those two summers she interned with Donna Karan and after that second summer was offered the position of associate designer upon graduation.

Life in the big city agreed with the young Latin beauty. Wherever she went men frequently found her irresistible. After graduation she took a designer position with a young up-and-coming Spanish designer, Paulo Cartino, and at twenty-four she was accompanying Paulo and lead designer Simon Lancaster to Paris during Fashion Week.

During that time in Paris, they stayed at a less than elegant hotel in the St. Germain area, the Hotel St Andre de Arts, on Rue St Andre de Arts. The name of the hotel gave it more cache than it deserved. Their rooms were three singles out of seven on the fourth floor of the walkup. Santa's room looked more like a closet off of one of the other rooms. Things were so tight in the small room that when she showered on her first morning in Paris and bent to pick up the soap, she cracked her head on the sink, which protruded into the shower by about five inches.

Paulo asked her about the lump at breakfast and apologized for the less than ideal quarters.

"But, my dear, we are one block from everything elegant in the world. So suck it up for a few more days."

"Oh, it's fine, Paulo," she protested. "I love everything about it, even my bump."

"Sweetie, you should stay on for a few more days after this is over. The more you see of Paris, the better designer you will become."

"Can I," she squealed, again the schoolgirl. "You won't mind if I stay?"

"I'll miss you, but we'll get along. "I'll pay for the hotel; everything else is on you."

"No, Paulo, it will be part of my vacation. But thank you anyway," Santa concluded.

"You bring me the bill when you come home or you're fired. This is a tax deductible investment in the best young designer in New York. The more you observe everything here, the better you'll be at what you do so well."

Simon Lancaster had been quiet during this exchange among the "girls." He worked for Paulo because Paulo needed him, but also Paulo had a hot name and a lot of financial backers. But damn, Lancaster thought, he's such a girl. Even farther gone than Schwarzenegger would say: girly, girl. And this type of adoration between Paulo and Santa only served to tell Lancaster that his days were numbered.

Santa knew it also. Lancaster was a wonderful mentor to her. For the past two years, he had taught her how an idea makes it from a designer's head to a woman's back. He showed her the processes, the upstream and downstream parts of Seventh Ave, from the buyers who bought wonderful fabrics in from Egypt to the wholesalers who helped you break even, even when one of your creations failed.

All the angels and saints are well represented on the streets of Paris, and on their final night together in the City of Light, Paulo Cartino hosted a wonderful dinner for the three at Café Bolivia on Rue St Martin, a right angle between Rues St Germain and St Andre de Arts. At 10 p.m. Paulo paid the check, which was engorged by the two bottles of champagne and three bottles of wine consumed over three hours of gastronomic delights. "You two are on your own," Cartino said. "I've got a 6 a.m. flight back. Simon, you're taking a 10 o'clock flight?"

"Yes, ten, Paulo. So, see you back home," and he rose to hug the boss.

"And Santa, I'm glad you were able to change reservations."

And she also rose, raising her arms with a wide smile, "Paris, three more days in glorious Paris. Thank you, Paulo." And she kissed him on the cheek, as she caught herself, a bit tipsier than she realized.

"OK then, see you. You two behave yourselves," he smiled.

"We'll be along shortly," Lancaster added, "We can't let this good wine go to waste."

"And it is wasting," Santa held her glass out. Lancaster poured, "But not for long."

Paulo left, Lancaster plotted. He had admired this wonderfully bodied beauty for well on the two years they worked together. Her style of dress was always in high fashion but always revealed just a little too much thigh or a little too much breast. It was one element of style he constantly fought over with both Paulo and Santa. The Latins liked the flash of flesh, and while he agreed, there was a line you did not cross. Ladies, especially ladies in the city, trusted their designers to keep them in check. You wanted style, not sex. There was a difference.

But when it came to her personal style of dress, the young beauty did cross the line, and it was sex that persisted. Lancaster had had the thought a hundred times. And while he was older, he knew Santa was intrigued. He was after all, six foot three inches tall, with a perennial tan, perfectly put together both physically and sartorially. He had a Halston formality about him that attracted women.

They left the restaurant arm in arm, strolling the streets of Paris in the evening, eventually back toward the Hotel St Andre de Arts. At a corner, as the street darkened, Simon Lancaster stopped and put his arm around Santa Alba's shoulder. She reached up and kissed him. Their hands began roaming over each other, groping, searching. Lancaster grew frantic, he thought, right here? Alba was hungry, almost growling.

A small, older couple, he with beret, she with a rectangular boxy purse, walked by and seeing the lust before them said something in French.

Pausing, Lancaster looked at the old man and asked the Latin linguist, "What did he say?"

Santa smiled a sweet, slightly drunk smile and said, "He said 'Pigs.' He called us pigs." She started laughing and said something in French to the old man.

"What did you say?" Lancaster laughed.

"Never mind, it wasn't nice," she said.

And now the spell was broken. Lancaster came at Alba, and she put her arms up. "No, Simon. That was fun. But it would be trouble for both of us."

Lancaster, still in heat, said, "Santa," and moved toward her again; this time pinning her against the grey stucco building.

"Simon," a transformed Alba said firmly, "No, I like you, but we're going no further."

Frustrated, hot, in a bad way, he relented.

"Come on," she said taking his hand, "Let's go to bed." Then realizing what she said, added, "Separately!"

"OK, I get it," he smiled, painfully.

The truth was she could not believe she had let herself get to that position. She had maintained absolute professional relationships with everyone along the design process—in and out of Cartino Fashions, no matter who tried coming on. And they did. Designers, buyers, distributors, retailers, presidents, and delivery boys. Men and women. They all tried with zero success. Santa Alba was not easy. Only a man she was willing to marry would she sleep with. And that had happened on two occasions with young men she dated over the past three years. And each time she hoped he was the one, especially the beautiful Irish actor from Atlantic Theater Company. But he was only here for six months with a visiting production from the Irish Repertory Company.

Upon waking to begin her mini-vacation in Paris, she felt a bit of a headache. She would be in this city for three more days all by herself. Never had she thought of such solitude. A city of six million people, and she didn't know a soul but for a few brief introductions at Fashion Week.

She had a list of what to do. It included all the normal sites: Notre Dame, the Pantheon and Victor Hugo's burial place, the Eiffel Tower, the museums, Montmartre and Sacre-Coeur. But first, a run along the Seine would clear her head.

Along this run on a bright, brisk spring day she passed by vendors on the bridges across the Seine. On the side of one artist's stand was a flier for "Carmina Burana" at St. Chappelle. Louis XIV's own chapel, she had read about it on the flight over. Since it was close to Notre Dame, she added it to her list. The flier noted that musicians from the Sorbonne would be performing. She noted the time was 8 p.m. Perfect after a long day, although she did not know the music of "Carmina Burana," she thought it would be exciting nevertheless.

Santa arrived early and was able to purchase a ticket at the door. At seven thirty she was allowed in. This gave her the opportunity to see the stunning stained glass windows. As she walked around the long rectangular chapel, she noted seating was by individual chair. No seats assigned, first come. As other patrons were taking their seats, she walked to the sixth row, as close as she could get to the altar, where apparently they would perform. She sat in the second seat from the aisle.

No sooner had she sat down and the seats began to fill up across the aisle and behind her. Mainly couples. The single seat next to her sat empty, and she placed her coat on the chair.

A man appeared, and said, "Bon nuit," in an American accent.

"Good evening," Santa replied to the tall, well-dressed man.

"Is this seat taken?" he asked.

"No, please," and she pulled her coat off the seat.

"You're from the US?" he asked.

"Yes, Santa Alba," she said smiling, reaching up to shake hands.

"Hi, Edward Wheelwright," he said taking her hand, adding, "Have you heard Carmina Burana before?"

"No, I really came to see the Chapel. Is it good?" she asked.

Confidently, and noting the beauty of the young woman next to him, he straightened and said, "It's music from God."

"That good. I can't wait," Alba said, noting for the first time how handsome Mr. Wheelwright was and how impeccably dressed he was. "I guess that's why everyone is coming in so quickly. "Doesn't look like there are enough seats," she said as people had started to stand along the rear of the Chapel walls.

"I don't know, but I think this is going to be tight. In fact," he said looking across the width of the chapel at about thirty feet and the depth of the altar at about forty feet, "I don't know what to expect."

"I guess we'll find out in a few minutes."

And now leaning toward Santa Alba and smelling the sweetness on the person next to him he said, "No, what I mean is, I was in San Francisco in February. Carmina Burana was at the symphony, and I was alone that night also, so I went to see it. There was a full orchestra of about one hundred and a chorale of about one hundred and seventy. There wasn't an inch of space."

Santa looked at him and said, "I read the flier; it said 'presented by the Sorbonne.' I didn't see much other information. Maybe the price of the ticket should tell us something," she smiled.

"I'm an idiot. I should have thought of that. For twenty-five francs, what can we expect?"

And at that moment they found out just what they could get for twenty-five francs as four individuals walked out of the side sacristy to applause. There were two middle aged men with beards, a young man of about twenty-five, and a young woman about the same age. With them they had two instruments each.

Fear ran through Wheelwright, amazement through Alba.

The beard with the glasses began a dialogue for the two hundred or so gathered.

"Can you understand what he is saying?" Wheelwright asked.

"Yes, he says they're going to play Carmina Burana on baroque instruments."

And then the other beard began with a series of guttural tones. Wheelwright recognized the tune but not much else.

After forty minutes there was an intermission.

Wheelwright and Alba moved together to the back of the chapel. "This is not at all what I expected," he said.

"It is rather terrible," Alba added.

"Thank you," he smiled. "Would you like to get out of here? I mean, are you with anyone or meeting someone?"

"Yes and no. Yes, I would like to get out of here. And no, I'm not with anyone," she answered with a smile.

As they walked out of the Sun King's chapel into the Parisian spring night, Santa Alba thought Edward Wheelwright could be one of those boys a girl takes home to her mother.

They went for a late evening bite to eat at a café filled with young couples on Rue St. Germain. Paris was the ultimate people-watching city; all of the couples were facing the street, making note of who was passing by. A couple of young men poked each other as Santa Alba entered. Alba and Wheelwright soon joined the gawkers, doing less gawking and more sharing of their lives. She lived in New York; he worked in New York but lived in Greenwich. She worked in New York but came from Coamo, Puerto Rico. Many of the young couples seemed to be just passing time together, but apart, as they faced the street, having separate thoughts on who passed by. Santa and Edward faced the street; neither noticing who passed by, who came to the dimly lit café, or who left. Each element of personal history became important, a revelation. Santa awaited every new detail of this young stranger's life; Edward longed to learn more about this beautiful creature beside him. As they faced the street from the café, they sat next to each other. With each intimacy shared, Edward and Santa leaned a little closer to one another until their shoulders, arms, hips, and thighs were touching. She felt fused to Edward; he wanted to kiss her more than he had ever wanted to kiss another woman. He was so close it was searing; she was near enough to inhale. They talked till two in the morning.

After the café owner flashed the lights and several couples rose to leave, Edward asked Santa, "How long are you here."

"Another two days. During the fashion shows, we only got to see models and clingy dresses. So I took another three days."

"Brave girl, staying by yourself. This isn't the safest city," he said, now protectively, "I'm here for four more days. I only have one meeting in the morning, perhaps I could join you on some of your visits tomorrow afternoon?"

"I'd like that very much," Santa said.

Edward Wheelwright walked Santa Alba back to the Hotel St Andre de Arts and as they stood looking, beholding each other, he said, "I really enjoyed meeting you tonight."

"Me too, Edward," Santa replied, hoping he would try to kiss her. She told herself this time she would not protest.

"Should we meet here, right on this spot, at twelve thirty?" he asked.

"We should."

He hesitated, looked at her and smiled, "Good night, Santa." He took her hands in his, raised her right hand and bent his six-foot-two-inch frame to kiss her right hand. Not a long kiss, rather quickly, but she liked it. She liked him.

In the next two days, they lived through the centuries of builders, of writers and of artists. They saw where they were born, they saw their work places, and they saw where they were buried. They visited more churches than must exist. Edward thought, Paris has more churches than New York has bars.

And on the eve of her departure, Santa Alba took Edward Wheelwright to her hotel room, and they made love until it was light. They collapsed in exhaustion.

Wheelwright returned to New York on the fourth day from when they met, and he called Santa Alba. And now over a year later they were inseparable.

She was in love, and her ambition in design had finally taken second place.

He was in love, and his desire to catch up in his financially driven world was in a tie with Santa Alba. She could win, but it was not yet determined. What was determined was his intention to make his fortune. The Brunswick Fund was that vehicle.

And now, after three months together, they decided the best way to handle the time constraints between his living in Greenwich was for them to move in together. They found a larger apartment on Central Park West. He left his home for the first time; she left the rental condo.

Work in the city, live in the city. Anything else fritted away precious moments that could never be recovered.

19

They met with Sebastian Ball and Parker Barnes, after the play, at Dario's, a bar on Christopher Street in New York.

"My father treated us to the show and dinner," Edward March Wheelwright was telling Ball.

"You said that when we talked, where did you eat?" Sebastian asked.

"At AOC, on Bleeker,"added Santa Alba, Wheelwright's lover, "Light French and very reasonable."

"Yes, I've been there. I agree," Sebastian added, "And you saw *Our Town*? How was that Edward, remind you of our days at Brunswick. "Is there much drinking in Grover's Corners, the citizen asked the professor," laughed Ball.

"There was much drinking in Grover's Corners, as I remember our little play. This was actually quite good. Updated, the sentimentality gone. Really nicely contemporized," Edward said.

"Over there at the Barrow Street Theater," Ball pointed out the window to the sign on the corner of Barrow St."

"Yes, but I didn't get it," Santa said.

"The play?" Edward asked.

"No, the rude guy."

"Oh him, what a jerk!"

Here Santa reinforced Edward, "They said we could go to our seats. The crowd was funneling in through the door, and here was this guy standing in the middle of everyone and he's facing us. He wouldn't get out of the way. He was waiting for, looking for someone."

Wheelwright laughed, "Don't tell that!"

"What?" asked Ball.

Santa continued, "Well, Edward said, 'Excuse me,' and the guy never acknowledged it. Edward was right in his face, with people on both sides, sort of crushing in. So Edward got just slightly beside him, looked back to take my hand, and leaned into him, knocking him down. Edward gave him a hand up and the guy was sputtering, but he moved to the side of the crowd."

Edward March Wheelwright stood up next to Santa Alba, excused himself, and went to the men's room. As he smiled at Santa, the smile was higher on one side. He had brown wavy hair, brushed back, not a bed head that a lot of young men are fond of today. He had a long, angular jaw line. His charcoal suit was well tailored and showed a fit man with no bulges in the wrong places. The red pocket handkerchief matched his tie, and as he wove his way through tables, other men and women noticed him. In the men's room, he glanced down. His black shoes had a bright shine to them, a trick his Navy Seal friend, Tray Johnson, taught him.

"You take a cotton ball, dip it in a little cold water, then get some black shoe polish on the cotton ball where it's wet. Then you apply it to your shoe by spreading the polish in circles until it gleams. Then when you put your shoes on you walk tall and think of me out among the hordes protecting you." Wheelwright smiled at the memory of them laughing over Edward's shoeshine lesson. He was glad his friend would soon be home from Afghanistan for their mutual friend Winston's wedding.

Edward rejoined the table with a smile.

"What's amusing?" Sebastian asked.

"The guy I bumped into at the play. He was pretty ugly and arrogant, but his girlfriend was even uglier. And as I looked around I noticed that most of the theater goers were not very pleasant looking."

"That's true," Santa Alba chimed in.

As the waiter took an order of drinks, Edward continued. "I think the best looking guy in the place resembled the Senator, Harry Reid; that's how bad it was.

At that moment, Gideon Bridge, looking rather dapper in his cream colored bow tie with blue shirt and plaid suit arrived. "Hey guys," he greeted the three friends.

"Glad you could make it, Gid," Sebastian smiled, rising to hug his lifelong friend.

"I'll do anything for a ride home," said the former editor of the Harvard Law Review and newest partner in the Bridge Law firm, started fifty-five years earlier by his grandfather.

"What's been going on," Edward asked Bridge as he also hugged him. Now they were partly complete. Four of seven lifelong friends, all still together, all still living in the area, ready to attend the wedding of the first of them to marry and partnering in business investments to build their own wealth, just as their parents had.

"Law's not all it's cracked up to be. The hours are pitiful. Occasionally, there are wonderful, interesting cases, but mostly it's boring," Bridge said, reaching up and signaling for the waiter as he sat down.

"Well you arrived just in time, "Sebastian said, "Edward is giving us a little insight into the ugly people at the theater tonight."

"Sounds like a lawsuit," Bridge said as the waiter arrived. "I'll have a glass of chardonnay, please. Anyone else?"

"I'm OK," Sebastian said, Santa nodded agreement.

"I'll have another," Edward said.

"Yes, sir," the waiter said, glancing at Gideon, who glanced back. Sebastian noticed, as did Edward, and they both burst out laughing. Gideon smiled knowingly, adding, "Edward, please continue with your story."

"Exactly, Gideon, Edward was getting to the interesting part of how he came to see people as less beautiful," Ball added with a dig.

"Don't go there, Sebastian."

"I'm confused, sweetie," Santa said, "Why are we still talking about them?"

"You want to talk ugly, how about Lloyd Blankfein, the CEO over at Goldman Sachs. Did you hear what Blankfein said at a congressional hearing the other day, that he was doing God's work. Now that's ugly."

"Gideon, you're an idiot," Parker said laughing.

"It is true; he did say it," said Edward. "That's part of the arrogance. They get caught with their hands in the cookie jar, and they make statements like that. That's part of what my father shared with me. A few years ago we sat down in the library one night after dinner. He needed to talk, to get it out. We had a few drinks, and it came pouring out. My father played by the rules. He knew what they were, why they existed, and he knew what exceptions could be made. But these guys he worked with at the bank—so arrogant. To make statements like that."

"And?" Gideon chirped in.

Edward leaned forward, "Dad said that what started to push him over the edge was the abuse of shareholders. These guys are taking too much money for themselves. One of the guys at Blackrock made over a billion dollars last year.

Ball, the billionaire's son, roared at that. "You are wacked, Eddie. You're part of that crowd with Obama that wants to play Robin Hood." Gideon was giggling, and Santa even managed a smile.

Edward looked irritated that he was the cause of this unintended merriment.

"I think it's OK to make as much as you can," Santa added.

"I like the way you think," Ball added, as if noticing Santa Alba for the first time.

With understanding sinking in, Edward leaned back, put his arm around Santa and said, "How did we get from some ugly people at the theater to crooks all over New York?" He laughed.

"Well, you are right when they make statements like Blankfein made and then take that much money for pay. They should just shut up and keep a low profile," Sebastian added.

"You're right. Everyone outside of the New York community sees that." Wheelwright paused as the waiter came by. They all passed, with the waiter and Gideon again exchanging glances.

"Gideon, you are hopeless," Santa said, gently slapping him on the arm.

"By the way," Gideon began, "I don't suppose any of you saw Obama's State of the Union tonight?"

"No," Sebastian said, looking at Edward and Santa, who shook their heads.

"What did we miss?" Santa said.

"Well to start with it looked like he was addressing the College of Cardinals with all that white hair and a bunch of black women in yellow dresses," Gideon smiled as the others laughed at the imagery.

And another discussion began about another topic of the day, that of the dysfunction in Washington.

The five friends drank and laughed until midnight when Sebastian saw his driver enter.

"OK boys and girl, let's pack it in. I've got carfare to the west side and back to Greenwich," Ball said, "and by the way, particularly you Gideon, it's all set. Winston's bachelor party is the ninth of next month, Intercontinental, San Juan. We're going down on the seventh and coming back on the eleventh or maybe the twelfth if we haven't found everyone by the eleventh. Tray said he'll be there. And you better be there," he concluded pointing a mocking finger at Gideon.

"I'm ready," Gideon said. "How long is Tray back for. "

Rising and putting an arm around Gideon, Ball said, "the whole month. And everyone can make the wedding in Greenwich on the sixteenth. So let's get this show on the road."

"Umm, I'll be staying in the city tonight," Gideon said, glancing in the direction of the waiter.

Gideon grabbed Edward's arm, "Give us a minute," he said to the others, and guided Wheelwright to a quiet corner. "Eddie, I went along with you there, but you have to stop this stuff with the hate you have and the contempt for the bankers. You're talking about it all the time lately."

"What have you become, the champion of the money lender?" Wheelwright shot back.

"What the hell's wrong with you? They have a pass. They take all the risks in that business and sometimes things don't work out right."

"You mean like the great fucking recession?" Wheelwright snapped.

"Yes, but you more than anyone understand that world. I know what you're saying—but you say it to more and more people. There is a distinction between some banker in Podunk, Idaho, and the financial capital of the world. They take more risks, open up more new markets—for the whole country."

"Damn Gideon, I'm not talking about all bankers, just the crooks."

"Well you just put them all in the same pot. I know what your father went through. You've told us that. I can see it eating at you. Get above it. Got it asshole," he finished with a smile.

"Got it, Gid. I understand. Go see your boyfriend," Wheelwright nodded in the direction of the waiter. And they laughed.

"One last thing, Eddie. Something wrong with Parker?"

"Not that I know of. Why?"

"He didn't say a word while we were here," Gideon, always the observant one, said.

"Probably just a long day."

"Probably."

Sebastian, Parker, Eddie, and Santa tried one last time to get Gideon to come with them, but he resisted. They paid up, said their goodnights, and left. They settled comfortably in the back of the Ball family Bentley. The wealth, the privileged life, the close association with an almost sacred group of friends who had known each other since pre-school made Santa tingle. The outsider, the beauty queen of Coamo, longed to be part of this, longed to be Mrs. Edward March Wheelwright. Mr. Edward March Wheelwright had one thought on his mind—Miss Santa Alba and what was to come when they arrived at their apartment on the upper west side.

20

The Second Baptist Church sits on one of four corners at the intersection of faith and hopelessness. Pacific and Henry Streets in Stamford display the south end in all its glory and horror. The Baptist Church, a playground basketball court, a demolished lock making factory, and a bodega with a large flat roof and a pit bull patrolling atop it complete the four corners. The basketball court is a refuge for scores of young black men, although across the street in front of the bodega on three benches sit an older generation of black men, talking all day, brown paper bags in hand concealing whatever bottle they can afford. These bench men talk with their friends who did not escape the neighborhood. Trapped here now that the path to middle class jobs that once existed in the lock factory have moved, gone to China. And on Sunday all the black women of the neighborhood in their finest dresses, with delicate, beautiful hats, come to the Baptist Church to pray to God, to ask Jesus not to let their sons and grandsons who are playing on the basketball court suffer the same fate as their husbands and brothers who sit in front of the bodega sipping from their brown bags as the pit bull keeps a watchful eye.

It is on these Sundays that Louise Strong comes to church with her sister, Jackie Stevens. The sisters pray and sing. Louise asked for God to welcome her husband, Curtis, into heaven and to protect her son, Curtis Jr., with His grace while he is in Auburn Prison. She asks that Christ place a protective shield over CJ to keep him safe from the fear she knows that exists there. Jackie Stevens asks God to protect her son Billy, to put him on a straighter road that he is on now. Jackie knows that Billy is a criminal; she sees how her boy has changed, almost slithering in and out when he does come home. She sees it in his face, the fear of being caught, of being questioned, of ending up where Curtis is. In all the five years Curtis has been in prison, the two sisters have not talked about anything to do with the crime that CJ is imprisoned for. Louise will tell Jackie about Curtis and how he is doing well. She even took Jackie to see him two times. But they never talk about the crime. Jackie is afraid to ask; Louise is afraid to question.

So the sisters sing and pray. On a particular Sunday, a particularly glorious sunny day, the sisters linger outside talking with other members of their choir. A young woman approached Louise and asked, "Are you Mrs. Strong, Curtis Strong's mother?" Louise and Jackie shot each other glances that said neither recognized the young, well dressed woman.

Louise smiled broadly. No one other than her family had asked about Curtis in more than four years. "Yes, I am." Sensing something personal, Jackie edged away and into a conversation with another member of the choir.

"I'm Kathy Jackson, Mrs. Strong," she began with a beautiful smile that flashed bright white teeth against a complexion of perfect skin like that of the black night sky. "You don't remember me?"

"Should I," Louise hesitated, "Miss Jackson?"

"It's been a long time. Curtis took me to the junior prom at Westhill High."

"Oh, my God," Louise lit up. "Kathy, I'm sorry for not recognizing you. You've gotten even more beautiful than I remember."

And the bright smile of the young woman's face reappeared.

****

Freedom. It was a luxury Curtis Strong had not allowed himself; it was a hope that did not exist. The judge's gavel was final.

Auburn's walls were too high, and the human spirit trapped itself in a Pavlonian jar that it could not jump out of.

Now with this picture, once Billy Stevens returned and identified who killed Augustos Santos and testified that he saw him kill Augustos Santos, CJ would know freedom.

CJ reached for his Bible, the one book he kept close. He opened it and placed the picture in it. He lay back on his mattress, placed his hands behind his head, and closed his eyes. Visions of freedom, of his past freedom flooded forward, rushing to the surface of consciousness as he faded from it: the joy of his father coaching him in baseball, the smile of his mother while cooking dinner, shooting hoops with the boys on court at Henry and Pacific Streets, and a prom date with a quiet young girl.

21

The moneyed class and rich Europeans, namely older French widows, live along Boa Viagem. Their glistening white condominium buildings face east overlooking the beaches of Recife.

The poor live four streets back from the beach in the squalor of windowless public housing. When breezes die down the flies come, attracted to the garbage flung out of the open ports where windows normally fit. A poor woman leans on one of the ports looking toward the ocean for a breeze, looking at where the rich lived, wondering if it is possible for her to move four blocks closer.

Then this woman glances down from her fifth-story port to the houses in the space between the rich and her; that is the next step up the ladder, middle class housing. In the second and third streets from the beach are smaller apartment houses, even a few private homes.

It is five thirty in the morning as she swats a fly away from her face, and she notices a man emerge from one of the private houses below. He is short and powerfully built. He stretches outside of his home and begins an easy jog to the intersection, and he turns left towards the ocean. She loses sight of him and turns to begin her work day.

The man running takes less than a minute to reach the beach on his run. Chunk DeLuna begins every day this way. He knows he must remain strong. He knows his verbal ferocity must be backed up occasionally by physical violence. It is his way of life. What elevated him from homeless loneliness was his brute strength. It enabled him to become leader of his gang, and it enabled him to stay as leader. What came naturally to him was not the brute he had become, but his loyalty to those in his gang and those who helped him. While he was tough on his gang's members, they knew he would defend them at any cost. He took a good share of proceeds from the gang's work for himself, but he was generous to his boys. They would say he was firm but fair.

On this day like so many others just under the equator, the sun will heat the earth's air to one hundred degrees. It is the reason he runs early; already it is eighty degrees. This is also the reason the beach is full of tanned, healthy Recifians walking and swimming before 6 a.m.

There is no wind, only a gentle breeze right on the water at this hour. The water is flat, and as waves move toward shore, they do not so much break as they rise, then just fall. There is no energy in the water, just calm, and perfect for the hundreds of swimmers in early before the work day begins.

Chunk sees the girl playing paddle ball with a young man as she does three or four days every week. The first thing he notices is her bare ass. There is a thong running through it, and her ass is round and firm and glistens on the left cheek as the sun, just coming over the edge of the water, hits it. And as he does every time he passes by he says, "Hola." The boy and the girl call back to him.

This day Chunk does something different—he stops. He finds this girl alluring. Her hair is pulled back tightly. She is several inches taller than Chunk, and the young man with her is several inches taller than her. She is pretty, not beautiful. She has a strong face that shows the mixed race of so many Brazilians. Her body is taut, tight as a drum, abdominal muscles with skin stretched across them, calves with muscles, thighs with a slightly bulging main muscle on the outside of each leg. Her arms are firm but not thin.

She stops playing and looks at the short stranger who always says hello but has never stopped before.

"Do we know you?" she asks with attitude but with a smile.

"I'm Chunk, and I'd like to have a date with you," DeLuna says, now looking at the young man, daring him to speak.

"Why are you looking at him," she says. "Do you want to date him?" and she laughs, a mocking laugh and her brother laughs with her.

Chunk smiles and says, "No," and he looks at her and adds, "I mean no offence to him."

The young man smiles. "There is no offence. Lupe is my sister. But who are you to just ask her for a date? We don't know you."

"Well I say hola to you every morning. I see you out here, and I feel like I know you."

At that Lupe finds herself thinking, I have seen this man in the neighborhood, heard of this man's reputation. She is correct; he is known in the area as the leader of a tough gang of thieves and drug dealers. She thinks he seems friendly enough even though he is hard to look at.

"Just because you say hola does not mean I know you," Lupe says. "The only way you can get to know me better is on a date, so yes, I will go on a date with you. When?"

Lupe Montserrat's brother Jorge is shocked. He also knows of Chunk DeLuna and does not think he is a good choice for Lupe. But he says nothing. He knows more of DeLuna's reputation than Lupe, and DeLuna is the type of man you do not anger.

Chunk smiles broadly, two gold teeth visible where once the canines had been.

Chunk DeLuna does not so much make love as ravishes a girl. This was among his earliest acts of violence. Whatever he wanted he took, usually at night, usually under the piers where girls would come around. That was where the boys of Chunk's gang were; a perfect lure for unsuspecting girls searching for love and finding horror in the form of Chunk DeLuna. If a girl resisted once Chunk began making his form of love, she could easily be punched into submission.

It was a different Chunk who took Lupe to Olinda Churrascaria, a restaurant at the water's edge in the ancient town of Olinda just north of Recife. As waiters carved slices of beef at the table and brought skewers of shrimp, Lupe was aglow. She had never been to a restaurant like this.

Later Chunk took Lupe to his home. She liked what she saw there; DeLuna had so much. Lupe's family was just out of the projects but had not moved into the middle class streets. They began back further, seven streets from the ocean with a small apartment. The Montserrat's had four rooms, with windows, that housed her parents, her older and younger brothers. Chunk had seven rooms all to himself.

"This is nice," she said to DeLuna, looking around at the furniture, large leafed plants and colorful posters on the walls.

"Thanks. Let me show you something else that's nice," as he unzipped his fly and approached her.

"Is this the way you want me to think of you? As a crude pig?" she asked.

DeLuna froze, rage rose up quickly.

"Do you want to make love to me?" Lupe asked the volcano.

"Yes," he said, his hand emerging from inside his fly, relatively disarmed by Lupe's frankness.

"Show me your bedroom," she said with authority. "I am not some tramp for you to screw with. If we are going to make love, we will do it right or not at all."

Chunk nodded. No girl or woman had ever talked to him this way. He walked to the bedroom, and Lupe followed. And Lupe showed Chunk how to make love. She taught him to gently run his hand over her body. She put her arms around his back. It was wide and had no softness to it. She let him hold her round firm ass as he kissed her neck. When he started to suck on her neck she pulled back and slapped him in the face.

DeLuna sat up, enraged, and he raised his arm back to fracture her teeth.

"You touch me," she yelled in his face, "and you'll never touch this body again and you'll never know what heaven is like."

That night she broke him. He became tame, but only for her. And that same week she moved in with him. Chunk DeLuna was twenty-two and had found a soft side to himself. Lupe Montserrat was two months past her sixteenth birthday.

22

It had started to snow in the afternoon. Parker Barnes was having lunch with his former college roommate and friend, Leonard Crane. Barnes was preparing Crane for his "interview" with the BF partners. The fund which had been a private investment vehicle for the seven Brunswick School friends now had become a registered hedge fund and open to wealthy individual investors looking for outsized returns.

Crane had a terrific pedigree, Columbia MBA, five years with Morgan Stanley and two years with Blackthorn Investments, the large hedge fund run by Paul Wolf, based in Greenwich and New York.

"The key thing for you to remember in these discussions, no matter how wealthy and knowledgeable about finance my six partners are," Parker was telling Lenny, "you have more experience than any of them."

"This means a lot to me, Parker; it's a chance to really hit it big. The idea that you and your friends have is surefire. I want to be a part of it," Crane said, almost pleadingly.

"You will be. Just don't give it up. No nervousness or I should say it's OK to be nervous, but you have the answers. There is nothing they can get by you, and I guarantee you that when the night is over, you'll have the job."

"Thanks, dude. I needed to hear that."

"Well, I'm going off. I still need to finish up a couple of things here in the city; I'll see you at McDale's at six thirty. And Lenny, by the way, no "dude" stuff at the meeting. These guys are not dudes."

"Got it," Crane finished as they both rose to leave.

There are real fools in the world. Leonard Crane was one of them. Captain of the water polo team at Columbia, he was aggressive in a way that gives aggression a bad name. In the water he used to pound the ball to land in the face of the competitor; on land he would belittle a client who just wasn't quick enough to understand his investing methodologies. Tenacious, inflexible are also apt descriptors for Crane. In an earlier life he was known as Lenny the Liar, and not because he told the truth.

Maybe it came from his size. He was built like a pit bull, close to the ground with too big a jaw. His head seemed to grow out of the jaw, his shoulders hunching up behind it. Men did cower at the sight of him approaching and women, strangely, found these Quasimodo-features, well, attractive. And that might not be the right word, but it was close. Maybe luring is a better word, not alluring, but luring.

What is surprising though was the loyalty Parker Barnes had for his Columbia roommate. After two years of being rejected by other roommates, Leonard Crane found an accepting roommate in Parker Barnes. They had known each other at Brunswick School where they were in several classes together. They both lived on Stamford's Shippan peninsula; Parker on Ocean Drive West, Leonard on Ocean Drive East, financial worlds apart. Barnes' father developed and built the new Stamford; Crane's father bid for and won all of the cleaning contracts for those office buildings.

As a roommate, at first Barnes found the obnoxious Mr. Crane amusing. Unbred, as wild as he looked, but disciplined when he focused. Leonard Crane would die for a true friend, and he told Barnes he felt that way about him. That statement, that outpouring of need by Crane, allowed Barnes to go beyond Crane's faults and accept him without reservation.

Others did not always see Crane that way. Part of his success at Morgan and Blackthorn Investments came from his large network of people in the financial community. He was surprisingly charming to those who could help him, and he freely shared knowledge with all of his associates. He was not selfish; he was very giving. But when pressed, when he felt trapped, like the time a client called his managing director at Morgan and complained about the promises Crane had made to induce an investment that utterly failed and was far too risky for that client's profile of risk tolerance, he would lie. Crane was working in product sales then. He did sell his products well, and he did tend to inflate possibilities since they were only that, possibilities. Confronted by his manager of the client's claims, he denied promising the outsized returns the client said he had. There was a bit of ping pong as the managing director went back to the client, but when the client produced a tape recording he had made of a phone call with Crane stating what sounded like promises, Crane was trapped in his lie.

He was quietly let go. Many of the brightest MBAs take unusual risks on Wall Street; it is the nature of the financial community. Many are let go, but discretely, without malice, as everyone has secrets and alienation is not an attribute wanted with exiting employees.

But also because of that silence, characters are easily able to slip under the ethical radar and pop up elsewhere. With Crane's experience as a trader, before his promotion to marketing at Morgan, he was eagerly sought at Blackthorn, many of whose younger executives and traders he knew. Trading was profitable at Blackthorn. He was earning in the low three hundred thousands.

However, the character problems persisted. As might be expected with a deeply insecure person, with a history of reacting without thinking when cornered, he would continue his pattern and lie. A series of these incidents had been accumulating at Blackthorn, and the sun was setting on Leonard Crane's financial future.

This particular morning, before his meeting with Parker Barnes, Leonard Crane had been thinking about that future. With time on his hands until their lunchtime meeting, Crane walked up from his apartment on West 112th St, to Olive's at West 116th St and Broadway, directly across from Columbia University's main gate, where he experienced his greatest joys in life.

He sat in the window nursing a cup of coffee. Outside, snow was in the forecast, and it was cold. This was all a game he thought: school, his job, this city. The game, the scam, it was everywhere in the city. Open and galling and people were still falling for it. On the corner of 116th St, he watched as two tall black men played homeless tag. This was their corner. One would work it for four hours, holding the cup and accumulate change from the guilty, and then be relieved by the other. The first man reached in the can, took his earnings from begging and handed the can to the second.

There was no sign on the can, neither man spoke during the hand off. The second began his shift just thrusting the can out to the steady stream of the throng. And the guilty among them, Crane figured about every twentieth person, put something in the can. Occasionally, someone would strike up a conversation. Not to be rude, the can man would quickly end it. This was business, and the can would be thrust out again.

The previous day on 3rd Ave, near 44th St, just up from the UN he passed by a beggar, a Latino, who was holding his can out while talking on a cell phone. As he watched in disbelief, occasionally someone would put money in the can. The Latino would stop talking on the cell phone for a moment and say, "Thank you. God bless you."

Crane wondered now, looking into his coffee, is this where I'm headed, becoming one of the con men of the earth. They were everywhere with their hands out.

Mr. Crane did learn that these men *were* everywhere, not just on the streets but in the offices where he worked. They ran the big banks, they were his managing directors, they were who he was to become. And the lying would help him get there.

In the meantime, he had been on notice at Blackthorn; the next instance of dishonesty or lying and he would be history. That was the way his team leader, Sidney Rogers, put it, "You'll be history,

Crane." The pit bull in Crane reared up in Rogers's office. He went chest to chest with the taller man, who was more than shocked at this behavior.

"Just what the hell do you think you're doing, Crane?" he asked, somewhat fearfully.

And with a further chest bump that moved the man back two feet, Crane replied, "Just letting you know what's in store if my trading desk is suddenly no longer mine."

"What?" Rogers yelled. It was the wrong approach.

"Did you not hear what the fuck I just said?" a Hulk-like character now loomed beneath the incredulous Rogers.

Somewhat trembling, Rogers walked by Crane, opened the door, and did not say another word. Crane smartly took the cue and left.

That was two days before, and he was now grateful that Barnes had been receptive to him interviewing with Brunswick Fund, since his exit paperwork at Blackthorn was probably being prepared at this moment.

McDales's was one of a thousand Irish bars in the city that were located in neighborhoods. In a long narrow room in front, it had two rows of tables looking out on 2nd Ave. Inside a second side street entrance, a large dining room had tables spread about, but back maybe fifteen feet or so from the bar that ran the full length of the dining room. The space was for the four thirty crowd that stood three deep until eight or so in the evening.

At the end of the dining room, there was a short passageway with restrooms on both sides and an entrance into the kitchen on the left. The end of the passageway had a private dining room that seated ten to twelve comfortably at a French country maple table. This evening there were just six at the table; the quarterly meeting of the BF was underway. It was a rite that had been ongoing for nearly ten years. The location floated, many times to accommodate members, but mostly it was held in the city, after work since six of the partners worked or had offices in the city. The other, Traynor Johnson, was a Navy Seal fighting in Afghanistan. This evening only

Traynor was absent. Gideon Bridge came up from Wall St., Sebastian Ball, Edward Wheelwright, Kish Moira, Parker Barnes, and Winston Trout had offices for their businesses in midtown.

"On the agenda that I shot out to you in the e-mail last week is a consideration that we take BF to the next level," Wheelwright was saying as the other five were putting the last touches on dinner, "from private investment vehicle for the seven of us to a formal hedge fund, open to outside investors of independent means: initial investment, half a million."

"Why in hell would you want to leave JP Morgan," Winston Trout said, "to run this little toy? What am I missing, Eddie."

"You want all this grief of dealing with more than us, Edward?" Sebastian Ball laughed.

"You fellas are a piece of cake, compared to what I deal with daily." Wheelwright said, "But really, Winston, we have grown this to a sizeable sum. Twenty-eight million is not a toy. I think we have a strong base to begin, and as we talked the last couple of times and you've seen in the prospectus that Kish and I have put together, we think we can grow it into a sizeable competitor of Sebastian's dad's fund."

"Oh, that's it, is it," mocked Ball.

Kish jumped in, "Yes, we think if the Balls can make that kind of money, imagine what we can do."

The friends laughed; they understood the objectives that were discussed.

Parker Barnes spoke up, "And, Kish, you want to go into this with Eddie?"

"It's time for a change for me and building my own fund is exactly what I need to do right now," Moira said, continuing, "Eddie and I have talked about this for over two years. We see what's out there. Our skills match up with anyone; we have a great client list we can bring with us. We have a strong network. Two of the other guys we want to bring along have outstanding technology backgrounds."

"And," Wheelwright jumped in supportively, "the returns we expect to see will be in the 30 percent per year range, minimum.

Certainly attractive enough for each of you to up your current portfolios."

"We haven't finished dinner, and we're already getting the arm put on us," Gideon Bridge said from his place at the end of the table as he sipped a cup of tea.

Sebastian endorsed the idea first, "I say we go ahead. Hell we can only lose twenty-eight million," and laughing loudly, for he loved to laugh, "and what's twenty-eight million among friends."

"If that's the way Eddie and Kish want to go, I'm also for it," said Gideon

"Parker?" Wheelwright said, since a unanimous vote was required—it was the way they always operated.

"Absolutely."

"And Sebastian, how about Tray?" Kish asked.

"Tray's in; we exchanged e-mails the other day while he was busy killing Taliban," Sebastian laughed again, the easy laugh of the billionaire's son.

"Terrific, thanks guys," Wheelwright said. "And Parker also has a trading and operations manager from Blackthorn's hedge fund he wants us to talk to, Leonard Crane."

Gideon spoke up, "Do we need to speak with him; I mean isn't the management of the fund going to be Eddie and Kish's responsibility. I don't want to be micromanaging you."

"No, it's a fair point," Wheelwright said, "It's just that it's a key position, and I thought you might like to talk with him also."

"Leonard Crane,' Sebastian began, "Don't we know that name," and looking at Barnes said, "Parker, where do we know Crane from."

"He was my roommate at Columbia, terrific financial background." Barnes said.

"No, that's not it. Further back, I just can't get it." Ball concluded.

"He was at Brunswick with us," Barnes offered up.

"Not Lenny the Jew? That's it, isn't it?" Ball said, starting his laugh.

"Parker, is that true, Lenny the Jew?" Gideon enjoined, looking at Sebastian and the both broke up, with the others joining in, including Barnes.

"First off, Lenny's Irish and Catholic," Barnes began.

"And that's better?" Sebastian said, and another round of laughter ensued among the friends.

"If you must remember, at least remember that Lenny always wanted to join the fund," Barnes came back at the other five, "He reminded me only today. He was the one in Mr. Conetta's Great Questions Class who was upset when he couldn't join."

"And now he's waited all these years?" Sebastian kept it up, laughing.

"Damn it, Sebastian, stop it," Gideon laughed, "I can't finish my tea without spilling it.

"Kish and I will talk with him after," Wheelwright said. "He's been having dinner outside with Santa. I'll shoot you guys a note if we take him on. Parker is very high on him."

"OK, sorry for the grief, Parker," Sebastian said sheepishly.

Kish and Wheelwright were impressed with Crane's background, his knowledge and experiences. They were the two most difficult for Crane to get passing marks from since they had the same pedigree. Since they had their own reasons for joining Brunswick Fund full time, they did not press Crane on why he would leave Blackthorn to come with Brunswick Funk at a smaller salary, but with the opportunity for outsized bonuses and eventual partnership. They should have.

23

The screen on Kishenlal Moira's computer popped to life, ablaze in colors, charts and numbers flashing by at the speed of light. The large screen monitor partitioned into four squares showed all he needed to know about the stocks he was buying and selling. The bids and asks constantly dancing, streaming trades flowing like a river, and graphs in red and green showing the trends of the stock. The fourth partition had all the vital data on a particular stock: its selling price, last trade, the daily high and low as well as where it opened today and closed yesterday.

Two additional computers flanked the main one that Kish was concentrating on. He moved back and forth between the computer on the right constantly looking at the main screen as the trades accelerated and now waned. He waited, crouching like a cat. The trajectory of the graph rose higher and higher. The trades were now viral, flowing rapidly as computer trading kicked in, trading hundreds of thousands of shares in seconds. The price rose to eight seventy-five, and knowing it was reaching a crescendo, he pressed the "sell" button on the computer next to him. He looked left and saw his trade of five hundred thousand shares flash by; he pushed a second button, another five hundred thousand shares sold. In the first fifteen minutes of trading, he had made two million dollars as the price leapt from six seventy-five the night before to his selling price of eight seventy-five.

Kish sat back and watched the stock continue as if heading to infinity. It reached $9.10. Then it happened as it does on all viral stocks. The green disappeared from the screen; the peak flattened and abruptly red appeared. The quadrant that showed green as the trades accelerated now showed red as the selloff began as the direction headed south. Bids and asks fluctuated wildly. A brief counter attack began and green flashed again only to be overwhelmed by a sea of red. As the counter attack began, Kish pushed the sell button on a separate screen. He sold three hundred thousand shares short at a price of eight ninety. Two hours later he bought those three hundred thousand shares back at a price of $7.25—another half million dollar profit.

He had sold at the peak one million shares of the original 1.2 million purchase, keeping two hundred thousand as "cover" shares. Over the coming weeks, he would slowly dispose of the other one hundred thousand "cover," which were purchased to deflect attention from SEC computers looking for patterns of trades like his—very large buys before earnings and total sellouts on earnings day. He knew from his friend at the SEC that their computers had a programming flaw that exempted attention for swing trades where there was still a position a week after a sell.

In the two weeks leading up to earnings announcement for Thompson Computers, Kish had bought the shares in trades of ten thousand at a time or less, to stay below the radar. He knew what earnings would be; he knew tech stocks were hot right now and that when announced the earnings would cause a brief sensation. But as happened more and more lately, tech stocks were on a roller coaster, up and down, sometimes 25 percent in either direction, occasionally on the same day.

Once he received news through multiple one-off-from-the-source "sharers" that earnings would beat the street estimates by ten cents and revenues would soar by 50 percent from the prior year and 25 percent from the prior quarter, he put his plan in place. He posted misinformation on as many professional stock blogs as possible, the message: there is real potential for Thompson to miss its numbers. He called the computer to his left, "Lefty;" he would tell his close friends it was like a democrat, always spreading rumors. The computer to his right was his trading machine, and once the misinformation that he spread started to have an effect, he began buying.

In the end, once he had disposed of the remaining two hundred thousand shares for a profit of one dollar apiece, he did the math; 2.7 million dollars, in less than one month. It fit the pattern of profit that was building in the Brunswick Fund.

The fund economics exercise that began with the seven friends from Brunswick School in their junior year of Mr. Conetta's Great Questions class had become a registered hedge fund. While it was generally known only to the seven partners, their banker, the SEC and the IRS until a year ago, it had now started taking on clients with the ability to invest at least five hundred thousand dollars for a three-year lock-up period. And what began as a fifty thousand dollar investment supported by the boys' wealthy parents and supplemented with a second equal investment was now worth 28 million dollars. The total funds under the management of BF would soon grow to ten times that amount.

Kishenlal Moira was the managing director responsible for the trading operations and research. Edward March Wheelwright was the managing partner responsible for everything else, which mainly focused on oversight, administration and marketing.

As two of the original seven Brunswick boys in Brunswick Fund, they had left similar positions; Kish as a director at one of Bear, Stearns hedge funds before it went belly up in the mortgage backed securities crash that brought down the whole market and Edward at JP Morgan where he was a managing director in equity trading. Brunswick Fund would continue growing exponentially for the seven partners.

24

The two Sebastian Balls took a trip to visit Ball-owned companies in Binghamton and Newburgh, New York, and two other non-owned companies with three plants near Pittsburgh. In Pittsburg, one company had two plants along the Monongahela River to the south and the other company had a plant along the Ohio River to the west and north. The younger Sebastian saw a world adrift. An old order had crumbled, the remnants of the industrial age strewn about, rusted hulks in idle by the rivers and streams that spawned an age. The new state had not yet emerged.

In Beaver Falls, Pennsylvania, on the Beaver River before it flows into the Ohio, on first entering the town he saw a home totally burned to the ground, just lying there. The fire was not recent. The house next door had lost its roof and part of its siding in the fire, but repairs were nearly complete. No repairs, no reconstruction was planned for the burned down house. After driving down the main street, a beautiful broad street, but with empty stores, for blocks and blocks, he thought of the old western movies and their false facades. Beaver Falls was now like that—a façade. No, that wasn't it. A façade was false. This was not false. Once this was a thriving, important small town, like hundreds all across the Northeast and Mid-Atlantic. In this area all along the Ohio River sat the remnants of the steel, coke and coal industries. Giant shrouds cover the former plants—these roofs cover the emptiness of the industrial revolution. As America built up and out, the excess was no longer necessary.

When the Japanese flooded the world with cheap steel, this area could not compete.

Carnegie and Frick were gone now, no titans were left. The steel beast lay dying; America had built one new plant in the last fifty years. As the Japanese built twelve new steel plants in that same time, the obituary was being written for a whole way of life—not just businesses, but towns where people made lives and friends, raised children, served their country and died. The grave yards of eastern Ohio and western Pennsylvania are well kept: rows and rows dedicated to servicemen, fresh flowers are still being brought to graves with American flags beside many of the graves. There are no ghosts there. The ghosts are in the towns among the living.

And when those plants closed their doors for good, when the last employees got their buyouts, separation pay, unemployment benefits, and what pensions remained, it was not that generation that was affected. They saw it coming, they heard it daily in work, at union halls—the end was near. For so long they heard it, when the end came it was a relief.

It was their children and their grand-children who wondered what happened. Where would they work, where were their friends moving to, why were the churches nearly empty or worse, closing. How do you close a church? How do you tell children God doesn't live there anymore?

These giant dislocations had been happening for two generations. In the seventies they called the north the rust belt as plants began shutting and snow birds who only flew south in the winter were now migrating to lower cost of living areas in the south and west permanently. Here was an America that helped the world build itself out, and now, with city after city, town after town, was struggling to remain viable or teetering toward forfeiture.

Sebastian had seen these affects before when doing field work for his MBA when he visited shoe factories in Lynn and Brockton, Massachusetts. He saw it in the former All American City of Newburgh, New York, on this trip with his father. Newburg, a cold pitiless place that most Americans would be ashamed of if they saw it. Dickensian in the despair on the faces of the mixed races living

128

there; children, street after street of children, in rags huddling in doorways, their only solace in this life: each other. When the shoe factories emptied out and the work moved to countries south of the equator, it was as if a neutron bomb had gone off in Lynn and Brockton: the structures remained, the people were gone.

These dislocations had always occurred since man first started paying for labor. When a cheaper labor source was found, the work moved there or the people moved to the work accepting the circumstances—Egypt, Greece, Rome, all the same.

England. When the states could produce textiles more cheaply, the manufacturing and design for the equipment moved to the states, bringing vast new wealth to the colonies, just as the world's manufacturing center became China and was now bringing great wealth to that nation.

And these cycles Ball was thinking of no longer took centuries to play out. Now decades would see a nation win an industry and before a generation passed, that same nation would lose out the same way it was won—to a lower cost of labor. Sebastian knew work always moves to the lowest common denominator—the cost of labor. It is how we reward management—hold costs down; it is why we have unions—hold the cost of labor down; it is the way our stockholders decide to invest or not invest in our stock—the cost of revenue—how much did it cost to make, what are the margins for gross profit, operating profit and net profit. It is why our accounting systems would not work properly if we couldn't bean count every hour of labor. Thousands of consultants would be unemployed, for who is it that identifies for management where labor must be cut, where work needs to move off shore.

Ball started to have a vision. He would examine labor intensive industries and their locations. Was it possible to build a virtual environment to continue after the neutron bomb of labor cost took the industry and the work but left the infrastructure. If technology could intervene along with cooperative government, then the cost of labor could be mitigated.

Inside he felt pressed, he needed to do something. If the people with the means who saw these ruins would not act, who would, he asked himself. Something never done before needed doing. Was it possible to establish endowments for towns like Homestead, Pennsylvania, and Steubenville, Ohio, so that when the effects of business downturns and business relocation destabilize a town there would be a permanent backstop that could incent new business and protect citizens from the loss of earning power? He needed to think this out—yes it sounded new and undoable, but colleges and universities sometimes seem to outlive their usefulness in one generation only to bounce back in the next more vital than ever; these institutions were able to survive for hundreds of years because of their endowments; fortunes given by benefactors interested in seeing the school persevere.

In the months following their return from this trip, Sebastian discussed these ideas with his father and, getting quite a bit of encouragement, went to work. He made several additional trips to Ohio and Pennsylvania. When the time was right, he decided he would need to start talking with Winston Trout. He believed Trout was the smartest person on the face of the earth. If Trout Solar were going to build solar panels, they needed to be built here in the states. If the separate elements that went into making a solar panel could all be harnessed in one place, in an entity, in a company, cost could be ameliorated. Scale would matter more than a shrinking labor cost. If power companies would embrace utility scale solar to meet their states laws for upwards of 20 percent of energy generated from clean energy, say within ten years, then a new industry could flourish in America.

25

Some men have a time in the limelight that lasts far beyond them. They don't come often and we remember their names; Einstein, Caesar, Hugo, Gandhi, and Tchaikovsky. But they are rare. Of the billions of people who have inhabited this planet, not many are remembered beyond their own generation. Fame *is* fleeting. Most men shine for no longer than that brief burst of enthusiasm they put behind their great ideas. Human nature conspires against them: the inability of the creators to present their enlightenments, an attention deficit by those who would be their audience, or an inability to persevere and see their ideas to fulfillment.

But the names we remember, the Churchills, Hemingways, Curies, Mandellas, and M.L. Kings, they were more persistent. Their ideas were them, their lives; the ideas burned in them.

Sebastian Ball Jr.'s passion to renew capitalism was the type of vision that could have his name on the minds and lips of future generations. But like all great visions there was possibly remembrance of folly. All together his concepts were utopian; looked at in segments, folly.

****

Sebastian Ball was able to arrange for the monthly Brunswick Fund meeting to take place at Trout Solar's headquarters at 425

Park Ave. This would give him time to meet with Winston Trout to discuss what he felt could be his purpose on the planet. The Fund meeting would take place at 6 p.m. Ball set his meeting with Winston for 4 p.m.

When the secretary showed Sebastian into Winston's office, they hugged as brothers hugged. It was one of the endearing measures of friendship that went to their brotherhood. It was born of seven boys in preschool; seven only-children in a school teeming with the offspring from large rich families. The only child of a rich person is a lonely child; surrounded by maids, nannies, chauffeurs, butlers and gardeners, their parents are engaged in lives of business, social and sporting activities that relegate the life of the child to being reared by others. Out of that loneliness, the seven boys found themselves at four years old the only children in the Brunswick School's preschool program. But then they were not "only," they were seven. As they moved through the Brunswick School, while in different classes or in different sports, they tried as much as possible to arrange togetherness, by requesting specific teachers, specific sports or adding an elective that would guarantee them being in the same class. Other schools may have shied away from allowing this clinging; Brunswick allowed and encouraged the boys to do what they wanted. And when Greenwich Magazine's section on weddings would announce the Winston Trout and Emily Albright marriage, there would be the seven boys, only-children who were never lonely, happily in the wedding party as best men for their lifelong friend.

"Let's sit over here," Winston gestured, and they moved to two chairs by the large picture window that overlooked Park Ave below with its center strip a garden of grass and flowers.

"And what's so urgent?" Winston asked Sebastian.

For twenty minutes Ball went on, non-stop describing the trip he and his father had returned from. He described his horror at the wake of the industrial age. He talked about the cities and the people he saw. The wounds the people had, not the physical, but the emotional: the psychological strain he saw in the eyes of women in Homestead, PA, and "the pitiful condition of the children in the streets of Newburgh, NY." He described the missing people in places like Steubenville, Ohio, and Beaver Falls, PA.

Trout jumped in, "Stop, Sebastian, God, you're depressing me. This can't be what we're going to talk about, is it?"

"Yes," Ball laughed. "How to fix it."

"So now you're a sociologist, out to solve the world's problems," Winston smiled.

"Yup, that's us."

"What do you mean us? Don't go including me in on one of your crusades," Trout said, mindful, that Sebastian Ball really needed more to do. He would spend hours over the course of their years together, regaling his "brothers" with his plans to improve life as they knew it. And to be fair he had made good progress in a number of his philanthropies. Thinking of that good, Winston, checked himself as he noticed Sebastian frowning at his lack of enthusiasm, "OK, what is it. Tell me, what you want to do?"

That brought Ball back, "Winny, here's my idea. I want to solve the energy crisis."

"Doesn't everyone. I was doing it at MIT with the 'vessel,'" Trout added.

"No, I have the full plan. Solve the energy crisis at the same time, put millions of Americans back to work. I'm talking about shining up the rust belt. I'm talking about restabilizing hundreds of cities and towns in middle America," and now warming to his own ideas, "I'm talking about ending America's dependence on foreign oil, on foreign energy sources, and ending our balance of payments deficits with the Middle East and part of those deficits with China."

"You're running for office?" Trout asked, "Congratulations, Sebastian. Which one?"

"No, no!" an excited Ball said, "Not public office you smart ass," Ball chastised his friend. "You're the one always telling us about the importance of solar and the need to solve the energy crisis, right? You have all these panels you need to build, well build them here. In Steubenville, in Newburgh, in Homestead."

"Well, you know my hot buttons, but we can't build the solar industry here. It would be too expensive. It couldn't compete with what the gas and electric utilities offer today. And we couldn't compete against the Chinese who make the panels today; their prices are too low. Right now, price is the only factor that will make solar energy real," Trout said.

"You once told me that the solar industry was too inefficient. What did you mean by that?" Ball said, tossing in a set up.

"It's new. All its elements are scattered around the world. When the steel industry first got going, I told you this before, Carnegie had all those big plants but it was Frick who had the coke processes and plants to produce it that made steel purer and stronger. Carnegie was smart. He bought much of Frick's business then brought Frick himself in to manage it all. And that was a simple industry. Solar—much more complex—and too many special interests in old energy like oil, gas and coal that would fight it and lobby it every step of the way," Trout said with a frustrated gasp.

"But suppose it was in America's interest?" Ball persisted.

"It is in America's interest. It doesn't matter. Old energy's self-interest is first, to them."

"What if I were able to bring the scattered elements of solar together?"

"It would make economic sense."

"What if these elements were all in one company, an American company, creating thousands of jobs in depressed areas?"

"Then you should be running for public office," Trout laughed. "You're such a dreamer, Sebastian."

"But, hypothetically speaking."

"Yes, it would allow everything to scale up and the economics would make sense," Trout said, partly to placate his friend. "But you don't understand all that goes into making a panel."

"I've been enlightening myself."

"Please," Winston smiled, "enlighten me."

"Let's see, you've got sand. You put it in a reactor, add some magic stuff and turn up the heat and presto you've got polysilicon. Then you take that, put it in a furnace, add some more magic stuff, and you've got an ingot. OK so far."

Trout laughed, "So far much easier than steel, huh?"

"Then we take the ingot; slice it up with a "special" saw. Put in an oven, add some more stuff and you've got a wafer," Ball said, adding smugly, "So far it does sound a lot like steel: take an abundant resource from the ground, boil it, bake it, and slice it up."

"Pretty damn funny, Sebastian. It's more complicated," Trout said, sounding a bit defensive, like a person with great knowledge of an industry talking to a neophyte.

"How?" Sebastian said.

"The magic stuff, the technology in the reactors and furnaces, for one. Where it's done, for another," Trout shot back.

"Let's try this, Winny. Suppose you had unlimited resources, here, draw this out," Ball said, reaching and pulling a pad from his brief case. "Draw it. How? Where does it begin and where does it end?"

And taking a pen from his shirt pocket he wrote in process order: "Sand > Reactor > Polisilicon > Furnace/Technology > Ingot > Oven/Technology > Wafer > Technology > Panel > Technology > Module > Sales > Distribution > Customer > Installation," and he said, "That's it at a high level."

"So how's this so different than any other manufacturing and distribution process?" Ball said, rather than asking, as he leaned forward and looked the diagram over.

"It's not particularly difficult that way—the process of a manufacturing business is common. It's the scattered approach and the players. For example, right now at Trout Solar, we do nothing here except invent and design the technology, then we contract with the Chinese to build it according to our specs. They in turn buy the reactors, furnaces and ovens we specify from the US or Germany. We do the selling and contract with installers in different parts of the world. So you can see how fragmented it is. All the elements are scattered."

"Exactly, let's talk about them," Ball said looking Winston in the eyes firmly.

"OK, for starters the Chinese own solar. They are years ahead of the US. By dragging our feet and letting special interests have their way, we gave it to the Chinese. There are maybe ten manufacturing plants in China that have forty acres of solar panel lines in production. We have two that maybe have ten acres. We had a real chance in the 1970s with the original oil shocks, then OPEC. It told us there was a limit. Then the environmental movement in the eighties and nineties. It told us there was a limit. We didn't react, and the Chinese did. Now we're stuck. If we can get out of foreign oil, we'll be stuck with foreign solar. That's it, game over!" Winston told his friend.

"Hah, then why the hell are you in the business, Winny," Ball said, "You're smarter than God; I can't imagine you chasing a lost cause."

"It's almost over, but I think we can make a difference."

"I know you can too," Ball told his friend. "That's why I'm here, Winny. I have been listening to you all these years. Tell me, all those elements under the roof of the Chinese solar companies, who makes them."

"Not the Chinese. You do understand!" Winston said. "I know where you're going. They are assemblers, manufacturers, distributors."

"Exactly. They are not the inventors," Sebastian added and continued, leaning forward once again. "They do innovate, but only in those processes they are engaged in. We can do what they do. They are making solar panels as commodities. But they do have labor costs on their side."

Winston Trout stood up, squinted and faced the window, "The science is coming out of American universities, some in Germany, and from a few companies like ours. Same with the reactors and furnaces; all of them are designed and made in the US and Germany," now he turned and looked down at Sebastian who sat back. "It's the final products that are made in China, and now out of sensitivity to that the Chinese are starting to do panel assembly in the US to get over that hurdle, the same way the Japanese did by building car plants in the South. If we can out-innovate them, if we can produce on a giant scale we can take the labor cost off the table and make all elements here," Trout concluded. He was warming to the conversation. "I'm thirsty, you're whetting my appetite. Want a soda or some water?"

"Sure, Pepsi's fine."

There was a phone on the table between them, and Trout lifted the receiver and asked his assistant for water and a Pepsi. Ball stood to stretch and stood beside Trout at the window.

"This is some beautiful stretch of the city. A minipark right down the middle of the street." Ball said.

"That's why they call it Park Ave," Trout said, as the assistant brought the two drinks in and placed them on the table.

"Hey, I never thought about that before, pretty neat," Ball said, pleased with this tidbit of New York trivia.

"So we've been dancing around on this topic," Trout said. "You know what I know, but I don't know what you know, what you're thinking." It was a question phrased as a statement.

"Winny, I think I've found out what I want to do," Ball said confidently. "I want solar to be America's great new industry. With this economic downturn lagging, I want the country united around it, like the space program. Millions of new jobs, good paying jobs, top technology, and all supported by the government—nationally to drive research towards solar and with significant tax investment credit and with local government to support solar companies with grants of land and buildings and tax breaks. And these local governments work with the companies to build endowments to ensure their futures are secure if new technologies displace their citizens."

"Sebastian, you're way up in the clouds. You're dreaming again."

"No Winny, I want this to be our job. I want to partner with you—for you and me to become the next Carnegie and Frick."

"Ha, ha!" Trout said in a mock laugh. "Sebastian, you are so freaking funny. Where do you get these ideas? And who am I? Carnegie or Frick."

"You're Frick. I just bought Solar Foundries and another smaller company, Solar Installation."

"What? You're mad!" Trout exclaimed, caught off guard. He was aware that Solar Foundries was the leading American manufacturer of all elements needed in the manufacture of solar products from reactors to furnaces, to all the parts required to keep the reactors and furnaces working. He was struck by the boldness of his friend's statement. "You don't know anything about solar."

"No, but you do. I want to buy Trout Solar and put it together with the other two." Sebastian Ball brought his punch line out, and it came out too quickly. Ball could see the shock on his friend's face.

"And what will I do?" Trout asked almost meekly, hurt by his friend's sweeping dreams. He and his billions would just come busting in to take over Winston's father's company, without considering whether there was interest by the Trouts. Winston had trouble with Ball when he went off in his tangents in the past, but they were harmless, but this, this was frightening. A person with no knowledge of an industry would suddenly appoint himself captain of that industry and buy up whatever he chose, including his friend's business. Sebastian Ball: the hammer looking for a nail.

"You would run the combined company, well your father would, with you in a key executive position, and eventually you'd run the company."

"No, Sebastian," an obviously upset Trout said, now standing, facing the window. "The company is not mine to sell."

"You haven't let me finish. I don't want these companies. They'll be yours. I'll have a substantial stake, but the majority will be owned by you and your father. In fact, I won't even be in the company, other than maybe as a board member to help with funding, direction and political stuff. We'll be taking the company private. It will be your company, Winny, only now you'll have all the parts necessary to make it real, to compete with the Chinese," Ball said.

"My God, Sebastian," a now dumbfounded Winston Trout exclaimed. "You are serious."

"I am," a smiling Ball said. "What do you say?"

"I can't say anything. Even though you say you bought two companies, to do all of the other things you said, it is going to take years."

"I've talked with six companies that own the land we could bring everything together on; also to four cities that own buildings and land that they would love to get back on the tax rolls at some point. They will all work with us. I've acquired the rights to two large modern plants in Steubenville, Ohio, and two more up the river in Beaver Falls, PA. I've talked with the governors of both Ohio and Pennsylvania; they are very enthusiastic about the idea and have each set up teams to help us identify what we need," He paused, and looked into Winston Trout's eyes. "Please do this with me, Winny? I need you. We need to do this."

"I can't believe you're that interested, but it sounds like you are. Somehow I'll help you. I'll talk with my father. Then both of us will talk with him."

26

Everything in a father passes emotionally to his son. It was no different for Arthur Trout and his son Winston. And there was no hesitation on the part of the son to accept the love of his father. They were inseparable whenever they were at home, and when away from home, they talked daily.

Winston Trout was a great friend to his Brunswick School mates, and even though he and Traynor Johnson were like brothers, his best friend was his father, Arthur.

Winston chose to attend MIT and not just because his father graduated from MIT. MIT was in his blood from a very young age. Arthur Trout had grown up in Cambridge, and whenever possible the Trout family found a reason to go to that city. Arthur regaled young Winston with his stories of Cambridge, a number of which Kathy Trout did not care for her son to hear. But mostly she allowed Arthur to ramble on with his stories of playing pool in Tom Lynch's pool hall on Hampshire St. "It was dark when you walked in from the sun, and in the back grouchy, angry old Tom Lynch sat, yelling half the time, 'If you're not playing, get the hell out.'" In Tom's you had to get your dime on the table for the next rack.

Attending public schools in Cambridge, Arthur did particularly well. He excelled in math and physics and won one of two scholarships that MIT gave every year to students from the city that housed them. MIT sought the goodwill of the citizens of Cambridge as it constantly battled with the city manager over its fair share contribution for the services the city provided; besides a couple of scholarships annually would not dilute the genius pool that attended the esteemed science school. In the case of Arthur Trout, there was no dilution. He added to the genius pool. His contributions in materials science were significant enough that he stayed to earn his masters and PHD and later became a guest lecturer. He, along with the department of material science, patented several innovations for developing solar panels and modules. With one professor and two other graduate students, he founded Trout Solar Systems. The arrangement worked wonderfully for the school since they received royalties from the patents. The professor, an Indian by the name of Rajit Singh, remained at the school, and the free flow of ideas from theory to practice aided both the school and the company.

Trout Solar was an early player in the war heating up for alternative sources of energy. Arthur Trout sat on several presidential commissions and became a trusted advisor to the Secretary of Energy, Steven Chu, the Nobel laureate who was one of Trout senior's closest friends.

The Cambridge that Arthur Trout grew up in was the Cambridge that Winston Trout grew to love. Father and son would drive by the old pool hall with Arthur imitating old Tom Lynch.

In the winter when they visited, they would take their ice skates, hockey sticks and play one-on-one hockey on the Cambridge common as Arthur did when he grew up. Arthur found it wonderful that the Cambridge Fire Department still hosed down the softball field and made it into the same rink he remembered. The Trouts would always stay at the Sheraton Commander Hotel, just across the street from the common, in back of Harvard Square. It was where Arthur had been staying for twenty years whenever he returned to lecture or work at MIT. The Commander was named for George Washington, Commander of the Continental Army, who took over the army across the street in the common. The hotel was approaching its ninetieth birthday, and it still retained the charm of a boutique European hotel. The Guleserian family had been running the Commander as far back as Arthur could remember and maintained in a quiet luxury that constantly brought former guests back. All of the top law firms still recruited at Harvard Law School out of the hotel's guest rooms, and almost annually Al Gore would come in to help recruit a hot young law student for a favorite firm.

Kathy, Arthur, and Winston enjoyed the intimacy of Harvard Square, its book stores, diversity of restaurants, and on the summer evenings, all those wonderful music groups playing on every corner in the Square. On Sundays the City closes Memorial Drive, the road winding along the Charles River, just east of the square. When the Trouts were coming to Cambridge in the summer, they attached the bike rack to the Mercedes wagon and brought along three bikes to ride for several miles along the Drive.

Kathy Trout, who Arthur met at a mixer for Wellesley girls and MIT boys while both were in their senior year, would tell Arthur that if they ever were to move from Greenwich, CT, where they moved after setting up their company headquarters in New York City, the only acceptable place would be Cambridge. Arthur understood, and he appreciated that Kathy had adopted the city of his youth as well.

One particular Sunday, around the time Winston was graduating from MIT, the family took their bike ride and ended up by the Weeks footbridge, an ancient connection over the Charles River between Harvard College in Cambridge and Harvard Business School in Allston. A sizeable painting of the bridge hung in the Trout home, and it was one of those reminders of Cambridge that was always around. As they parked their bikes by the bridge and sat on the grass nearby, Arthur told his son of a time when, as a seventeen-year-old Cambridge High & Latin School student, he would regularly come to this almost-exact spot on Friday nights with his friends Terry and Junior and drink quarts of Knickerbocker beer.

"But on this particular night we had Ace and the Cosgrove brothers, Jackie and Donnie with us. It was around eleven, and we were all a little high and right behind us on Memorial Drive a police car pulls up. We took off across the bridge like a shot. Going across the bridge we dropped the quart bottles, and they shattered all over the place. We got to the other side, and there were two more police cars waiting for us there," Arthur said smiling.

"Have I heard this story?" Kathy kidded Arthur.

"Go on, Dad," Winston said.

"Well, they were MDC police. They handle all of the parkways around Boston, MDC, Metropolitan District Commission. Anyway, they took us all down to their station, which is right past MIT at Lechmere Square. Turns out they knew most of our fathers. The Cosgrove's father and my father worked for the city. The police said they could call our parents to come and get us. With that Jackie Cosgrove starts begging, "Please, do not call my father, he'll kill me." So one of the officers who took us in says, "I have an idea, Sarge," and he talks to the sergeant. "OK," the sergeant says, "we can call your parents or you can go back to the bridge with the officers and sweep up all the broken glass you left there." It was a good option. The bridge was spotless when we finished, and Friday nights by the river came to a halt."

Winston was laughing, and even though she had heard it before, Kathy Trout still smiled at her husband's youthful adventures.

"Well, go on, finish the story," Kathy offered up.

"There's more? Come on, Dad, out with it." Winston challenged his father.

"Well, this part is tame. After graduating and when I first started coming back to work on developing the company, I would stay at the Commander. They always gave me the same room, really a suite, with a bedroom and a living room. In the living room hung a picture of the Weeks Bridge. So whenever I looked up, there was the reminder of my misspent youth."

"Just like we have a picture of the bridge at home." Winston exclaimed.

"The exact picture we have at home." Arthur said.

"What do you mean?"

"I guess I had been staying here eight or ten nights a month for three years and got to know the owners, the Guleserians, pretty well. They would give me their season tickets to the Red Sox games from time to time. You remember those good seats behind the plate?" he said to Winston.

"The best."

"Compliments of my host. Anyway, when I knew we would not be staying here as much in the future, I went down to see the father and son a few days before returning home. And I told them the Friday night tale of the Weeks Bridge. Two days later as I was checking out, Michael Guleserian meets me at the front desk with the painting that had been in my room for those years and gives it to me as a gift."

"No way. That's how you got that painting?" And when Arthur nodded with Kathy smiling, a now laughing Winston said, "That's cool."

Arthur taught Winston mathematics and physics and materials science right alongside his high school teachers. And the younger Trout wrestled to grasp new ideas and concepts that his father was encouraging him to learn. And he did learn. As he grew there was never a question that the young man would go into his father's business. Winston knew the company as well as anyone in the firm. He spent his summers working there; he did his internships with his father, except for one year, his junior year.

That was the only year, the only summer he wavered. During the course of the school year, he had been working on a project called "the vessel." He talked with his father about it during the spring break, before the end of the school year and the time he was to begin the internship with his father. He wanted to pursue his work a little further but was afraid to disappoint his father. Arthur Trout could tell it was a tough conversation for him.

To listen to Winston talk, his eyes focused, you could see his mind working behind his eyes. He talked rapidly; so fast in fact, it was difficult to understand him. You needed to listen with your mind to what he was saying. The father could see the intelligence on his face, an intelligence that surpassed his own. Winston's face, with many parts, worked as one, his eyes moving, thinking, the lips were saying what the eyes were seeing in the mind. And the hands joined in, punching the air for emphasis, like a conductor. There was tension behind the thinking. You could feel its tightness. He lived in his science.

"So," his father began, "this vessel heats plasma, and as the temperature rises it becomes less stable, right?" Arthur asked his son, wanting to understand. "Well, how hot are you getting it?"

"We're taking it to the temperature of the sun. It gets that hot. But only for one and a half seconds then it starts vibrating and rattling and we need to shut it down."

"What's the purpose of the vessel; what are they ultimately trying to do with it?"

"Solve the energy crisis," Winston said flatly.

Arthur Trout sat back. He thought for a second and said, "Then you should follow your instincts. You'll be trying to do the same thing we're working on at the company with solar, only you are thinking of a much greater scale. It sounds like incrementalism, yes?"

"Certainly, in the next ten years we'll be lucky enough to get it to stay stable for eight or nine seconds. The department has been working on it for fifteen years."

"So make your contribution. We'll wait for you."

"Thanks, Dad," Winston volunteered. And he was genuinely glad that his father gave him the opportunity that summer. Not so much for his incremental contribution, which was significant, but for another opportunity that occurred.

The big boat lumbered across the line. It was the third time in two weeks that it finished third behind Harvard and Boston University in practice runs for the Head of the Charles Regatta that would take place at the beginning of October. It was Winston Trout's final year of eligibility for crew, having begun rowing only in his senior year at MIT. This was a big race, and it drew hundreds along the Charles River, which was nothing compared to the thousands who would line the banks of the river and mob the bridges in the fall.

As the eight men fell back in exhaustion, pushed to their limits by the prodding and pounding of their ninety-six-pound freshman cox, they passed under the Weeks Bridge. Winston smiled. When the boat emerged from the other side, something hit his leg. It was a necklace of some sort. He looked up and saw a smiling, pretty girl looking down. "Sorry," she said. Adding, "Can I have it back?" as the boat continued to move.

"Yes," he hollered, "MIT boat house. Just after the BU Bridge on the Cambridge side."

She had a puzzled look on her face, and then called back, "I'll find it."

"One hour," he yelled back as the boat moved further up the river guided by two rowers as the others recovered. He watched as she walked her bicycle off the bridge. She rode along Memorial Drive beside the boat, looking out at the rowers for a while until the boat turned and started downstream towards Boston.

The girl on the bike stopped, turned around and continued riding along the Drive beside the boat. "Catch Winston guys. He can't take his eyes off his new admirer."

"It's the other way around," Trout laughed. "She can't stop looking at these pipes," and he flexed his muscles in a pose that the girl on the bike noticed. The rest of the crew laughed. She smiled sensing somehow that she was being made fun of.

When the "eight" arrived at the boat house, Winston looked around for the girl on the bike to return her necklace, a plain gold chain with an intricate Murano design in a circular pendant. He thought it expensive, but she was nowhere in sight.

After showering he emerged from the boat house, and the necklace's owner was sitting on the grass with her bike beside her. She popped up, and it was then that her features became clear to Winston. She had medium length brown hair that had a bright shine to it, like it had just been washed. It was pulled back in a ponytail. The hair began where, skin as smooth as he had ever seen, stopped. She smiled at him with almost opaque and yet bright white teeth, perfectly aligned from the brace years. Her eyes smiled along with her mouth; they were hazel.

Winston hung the necklace from his outstretched hand. As she reached for it, he pulled it back. "Not so fast, how do I know this is yours. Do you have any identification that says you are the owner?"

Smiling, she answered, "No, kind, sir. But you will know it is mine, once you see it on me."

Her voice he found was feminine, her words lilting, rolling off her tongue in a way both playful and mature. "Emily Albright," she said, holding out her hand.

"Winston Trout. I'm pleased to meet you," and he was. He could not take his eyes from the picture of loveliness that stood before him in jeans, a white blouse and sandals. Again he held the necklace out, this time in both hands. "May I?" he offered in a gesture she found reassuring, and she turned her back to him so he could put it on her.

As he put the necklace over her head, his hand brushed the top of her head. "Sorry," he said, now taking in her sweet scent, now brushing her shoulder with his arm, and now fearful that this encounter could end, he dropped one end of the chain across the front of her blouse.

"Butterfingers," she said, turning with a smile. She got the loose end of the chain and handed it back to him.

27

One particularly brutal thief, who had broken into a widow's home, beaten her mercilessly while stealing her money, jewels and car was CJ Strong's pride. The man, Jack Doherty, a mean, sinewy brawler from Queens had been on record as among the most difficult of prisoners. It was not unusual for Doherty to spend two months each year in solitary confinement for fighting with other prisoners or guards. At fifty-two years old, Doherty had been in Auburn for thirty-one years and was on track to spend the rest of his life there. Parole had been denied four times, and his sentence had been extended twice. He was viewed as one of the few prisoners who could become eligible for parole, but his behavior was so anti-social he was deemed a continuing and certain danger to society.

As fortune would have it, Jack Doherty was about to undergo involuntary surgery at the hands of the notorious knife fighter Jose Truillo when CJ Strong intervened. The incident that triggered the visit to Truillo's operating room occurred in the prison yard on the basketball court after lunch. Doherty was all elbows as a rebounder, and this time Truillo took a particularly vicious shot to the temple. Jarring enough that the sound travelled across the yard to where Strong was talking with two other men.

Truillo was immediately on Doherty, and as they boxed and wrestled, Truillo became more incensed at his lack of progress in the fight. He pulled a knife from a strap on his calf, a knife fully seven inches long. The knife, a discarded piece of metal in the shop where

Truillo worked, had been hidden away months earlier and daily honed with a sharp edge and thin point. At the moment that the death of Mr. Doherty was poised on the upraised arm of Mr. Truillo, who was now sitting on Doherty with his left hand on Doherty's throat, CJ Strong stepped into the middle of the circle of prisoners around the combatants. He grabbed Truillo's right hand, pulled it back and said, "Jose, you don't want to do that."

The pause was enough of a distraction for Doherty to squirm free as guards pushed through to break up the fight. After some questions Doherty and Truillo were led away; both got thirty days in solitary confinement. On the thirty-first day, Doherty was released from confinement. He saw CJ Strong on the basketball court after lunch.

"Strong," Doherty bellowed.

"Look out, CJ, here comes the madman," said one of the knowing prisoners CJ was talking with.

Strong turned around, expecting trouble but was greeted by Doherty's smile. "I owe you."

Strong knew what he meant but needed no thanks and simply replied, "You're welcome."

"Seriously, Bro, you saved my ass. That punk had me."

"It's OK, Doherty. I'm glad I helped."

"If you ever need anything," Doherty began.

Strong saw an opening, "There is something."

And with that "something," Jack Doherty made a promise to come and read with CJ Strong, twice weekly.

Doherty was not the only one who ended up learning. With two A's in hand from his latest courses, CJ Strong looked forward to sharing them with his mother when she arrived this Saturday. He had finished his work changing oil in three of the power plant motors early in the morning. Now he had freedom to move about the prison that came with his status as an honor inmate. Five years into his prison sentence he had become a popular man. Among the brighter prisoners who met one night a week in a book discussion group, he was viewed as intelligent with insight into classic literature. Among the gym set, he was one of the more powerful inmates, able to bench press 350 pounds, and he frequently coached prisoners on lifting technique. His dedication to his power plant work drew praise from the civilian power plant manager. He made many suggestions for improvement in plant maintenance and on his own initiative drew up an improved maintenance schedule on the forty-year-old boilers. CJ was academically eligible for a degree with the completion of seven more courses, all the time carrying a straight A average.

Where CJ got satisfaction, where he knew he made the best contribution, was in literacy tutoring of other prisoners. He vowed if he ever did get out of prison he would continue to involve himself in teaching reading to the incarcerated. He saw the joy that came into the lives of hopeless men when they read their first book, usually a child's first grade primer. For cruel men, where life had been equally cruel, he saw softening as they read stories; first Jack and Jill, then chapter books like the Lemony Snicket series, then *The Old Man and the Sea*. It never ceased to amaze him how quick the progression was and how many books the men devoured. He saw them as starving men coming to the table.

Then there was Doherty. "I know I promised you I'd come, but this isn't gonna work, Strong," Jack Doherty said to CJ Strong after his first lesson.

Jack Doherty learned to fight before he could read. What little reading he was capable of gradually slipped away as he slipped away from school, first as a truant, then as an unruly student unable to be taught. By the time he was twelve, his formal schooling ended. A single, working mother with three children could barely stay afloat, never mind track down a wayward child who stayed out late seven nights a week.

But here, in Auburn, in the fifty-second year of his life, Jack Doherty learned to read and understand what he was reading. After two months he devoured several first and second grade books a week from a prison library that resembled a children's reading room. In four months CJ found Doherty voracious. A beast of a different sort was awakening in the man. He read everything CJ recommended and would discuss the stories with Strong. In the courtyard they would pace in deep discussion over why Raskolnikov needed to kill the pawnbroker in *Crime and Punishment* or how Santiago persisted in *The Old Man and the Sea*. As they talked about Raskolnikov's justifications, Doherty began crying, thinking back to his own similar crime. When a brutal crime occurred in a book, Doherty looked inside himself. When he read *Les Miserables*, it was he, Doherty, who stole the Bishop's silver. And when the Bishop told the Gendarmes who arrested Jean Val Jean that he had given the stolen silver to Val Jean, Doherty cried. Doherty cried again as he talked with CJ Strong about it and about his own crimes.

28

A man who is learned in his field, one who has spent years in apprenticeship gathering knowledge and applying it to real world tasks is powerful and respected. Chunk DeLuna is that man. Now twenty-nine, he has spent years building his Rei de Praia, his gang of beach kings. And while still a crime problem in the beach areas, the gang had spread north to Olinda and all the way south, from the state of Purnambuco to the state of Bahia and its capital of Salvador. The gang multiplied like fishes and loaves, whereas it began with five and one dog, it now numbered over two hundred. Chunk had changed the gang's name from the youthful beach kings to the more reflective CDL Enterprisa. He liked having his imprimatur on his business: Chunk DeLuna Enterprisa.

CDL had many sources of income for this enterprise. The members began with petty larceny and occasional armed robbery. They moved up to dealing drugs for a Columbian. They expanded into prostitution, gambling, and loan sharking. The crown in the beach kings' empire was a legitimate side of the business: a cement manufacturer. It was bought by Chunk DeLuna for several million dollars, most of which was obtained in fraudulent loans provided by a heavily drug dependent banker. Bribery of public officials became common as the gang gave them kickbacks on construction projects granted to the large cement producer.

DeLuna became increasingly obsessive about his "businesses" as he now called them. The cement producer being the opportunity to give the members of the gang a legitimate face, and while still nowhere near as profitable as drugs, it held promise for the future. However, Chunk found that no matter what business he operated there was always competition. It didn't matter if it was a San Salvadoran drug dealer encroaching on his territories or a Mexican cement producer trying to undercut his prices. The problems were the same; the solutions were the same.

And these problems came up frequently. At one particular meeting concerning the drug operations, Chunk got a report from Paco who ran that portion of the business for the gang. It was an important meeting since the Columbian drug supplier was there with his complaints; in fact, he began the meeting.

"You guys have got to fix this. These blackies from San Salvador are stealing your business, and when they are stealing your business, they are stealing mine also. They don't buy from my cartel but from one of the others. We're losing out here," Roberto Calo told the six men present.

Angel Pagan, a boyhood friend of DeLuna's from San Blas, Puerto Rico, had joined the gang and along with the others, was one of its leaders. Pagan's business was eliminating the competition. Chunk DeLuna was mean; Angel Pagan was frightening. In fact the only reason that the beach kings ever had competition was due to new entries into the marketplace. Experienced dealers left Chunk's business alone; you just did not want to suffer the consequences.

"So Paco," Pagan began, "do you know these guys Roberto is talking about."

"Yes, we have talked about this before. It wasn't a big deal till now," Paco said. "But when they start threatening our street level guys and putting themselves in our buildings to deal, like we're not even there, well, that's enough. Yes, we do need to act."

"You give me the locations, every location where this is happening, and I will take care of it." Pagan said.

Over the next several days, Paco's dealers in and around Recife and Olinda funneled into Paco six main locations where the selling was going on. Some of Paco's men had followed their competitors, and there was also a seventh location where three of the six dealers had gone, most likely a drug factory, processing, cutting and packaging the product as it came in from Columbia.

A second meeting was called after this information was gathered to decide how to approach the competition. Chunk, Paco, Angel, and Roberto the Columbian attended, which was again held at Chunk's home by the water.

"This is what we have so far," Paco proceeded to explain the details of the comings and goings of the encroachers. "Do you need more?"

"You did good, Paco," the Columbian said, "Now, Chunk, go kill them."

This interjection was inappropriate; the Columbian knew it and Chunk got hot. But he decided to let the slight pass. It only mattered that Chunk knew this was his house and his gang and that he, Chunk, not some greasy Colom-ball, as Chunk derisively referred to the Columbian when he wasn't there, would handle his own affairs without any interference.

"Good job, Paco, that's enough for us to go on." DeLuna began, "How do you want to handle it, Angel?"

"I like the idea of the one central place to take out everything at once. From what you have given us, Paco, my guess is your guys did not identify anyone as a leader?" Pagan asked.

"No, except on two of the three times they ended up at the seventh location, in Olinda, my boys said a tall African came outside with the dealers who had gone in.'"

"OK, sounds like it could be from Salvador or from the south side of Recife, where more Africans live," Pagan said, continuing: "Paco, I want one of the guys who went to the seventh house to come with me. Give him all the locations, a description of the dealers, and have him pick me up at my place tomorrow night. We'll drive through the whole thing and see how it looks," and looking at Chunk, Pagan said, "Then I will make a plan Chunk and bring it to you."

"I want to see this plan also," the Columbian said.

""I assure you, you will Roberto," Chunk replied, deciding in that moment that whatever plan was developed, Roberto Calo could go along for the ride and see first-hand what this gang could do when it applied itself.

Throughout history, Olinda was an early rival to Recife, just as the original Portuguese occupiers were rivals of the Dutch invaders who burned down Olinda, the strategic town on the hill. But unlike Recife, not much has changed in Olinda. It was rebuilt in the 1700s and retains much of its colonial heritage.

In Olinda, at 23 Predente de Morais Street, Angel found, by having his men do some close-in snooping, that the occupant was a San Salvadoran, by the name of Eduardo. He had lived in the colorful blue stucco home for about three months. Neighbors noticed men and women coming frequently to the home. The area was residential, the streets still cobblestoned. It was one of the main routes of the carnival procession just before lent—a rite, smaller by far than that of Rio, but no less spirited.

Angel considered the location. Some of Recife's business leaders made their homes there in the large colonial plantation manors by the Santa Lucia Catholic Church. It would be a problem with noise if they were to swarm into the narrow street, three cars filled with his men, busting open the door, and blasting away the competition. There would be too many neighbors at least in the early evening when most of the visitors were there. Angel assumed the dealers came in the evening to drop off the day's proceeds and to pick up a drug supply for the next day. It would be quiet later, but there would be fewer of Eduardo's dealers there. He would have to involve more of his men—stake out all seven locations and strike at the same time to stop alerts.

This was the plan he presented to Chunk, Paco and Roberto Calo, the Columbian.

Chunk would personally do the work at the Olinda house, and Roberto and Paco would accompany him there. The attack would take place in two days using semi-automatic pistols; it would take place at 6 p.m. when many people were still on their way home from work or the beaches. It would be easier for one car with two or three men to leave any one of the seven areas and get into the flow of

156

evening traffic and given that they would only be taking out two or three people in each location, quicker with less chance of a prolonged gun battle.

On the second day, at 5:45 p.m., Chunk, Paco and Roberto parked half a block away from 23 Predente de Morais, on a side street with the car pointed south, down the hill. The sun was still far above the horizon; there was still plenty of sunlight. Chunk sent Paco to the rear of the building.

Chunk and Roberto drew their pistols from under their shirts. A car approached, and they quickly dropped them to their sides until it passed. Chunk stepped up on the one front stair to the door and tried the knob. It was locked. He looked at Roberto, who raised his left hand in a knocking gesture. Chunk shook his head no.

The door was weather beaten, not thin and not strong. Chunk figured he could lean into it, break it open. He made a breaking open motion to Roberto, who shook his head no. In that instant, Roberto knocked loudly. Chunk stepped back, ran at the door and broke it open. A small room to the right had two mattresses and no one in it. He kept running down the hallway, heard voices as he burst into what was the kitchen. One man reached for his gun as Chunk shot him dead. Two others were behind the dead man, and Chunk shot them. A fourth man came in from another room, behind Chunk. He had a knife and as Chunk swung around the taller man slashed at Chunk. Chunk avoided the knife by stepping back. He looked at the man for a second and said, "Never bring a knife to a gun fight," and he shot him dead.

A fifth man, the San Salvadoran, went out the back door. There were three shots, from what sounded like two guns Chunk thought as he ran out the back door. The San Salvadoran was on the ground with a gun in his hand, trying to raise it up. Chunk shot him. Paco was on the ground wounded. Shot in the leg, bleeding.

"Roberto, help me." Chunk said calling to Roberto who came out and was now beside him as he lifted Paco up. "We'll carry him to the car and do a tourniquet there."

Paco said, "You gotta stop the bleeding now. It looks bad Chunk."

"Shut up or it's gonna look a lot worse. You'll live," Chunk said as he and Roberto Calo placed Paco's arms around their necks and carried him back through the house.

There was a large duffel bag on the floor. There were several one kilo bags of cocaine in various stages of being cut and packaged for retail sales. There were piles of money on the counter by the sink.

"Hold him up for a moment," Chunk said, and he grabbed the bag, swept the money off the counter into it, then picked up the bags of cocaine and placed them in the bag. The open ones spilt the white powder over the bag, and the money. Chunk then swung the bag over his shoulder. He replaced Paco's arm around his neck.

They walked out the front door as a car passed by with music blasting and the driver in a trance. They carried Paco around the corner to the car and laid him down in the back seat. Chunk tore off part of his tee shirt and put it into the bullet hole. Paco screamed. "Be quiet. You yell like a girl," Chunk said with a smile, and he laughed. Through his pain, Paco managed a smile.

Then Chunk took off his belt, ripped Paco's pant leg open and wrapped it around the leg, just above the bullet hole. He placed the end of the belt in Paco's hand. "Hold this and keep it tight. It will stop the bleeding till we get you to the doctor."

They drove over the cobblestoned streets with Paco reeling in pain with each bump.

They were down the hill and onto the beach highway back toward Recife in less than a minute. No police.

"You can't take me to a hospital with a gunshot, Chunk," Paco said, adding, "They'll call the cops."

"I have my own doctor. You just relax," and in ten minutes, they crossed the bridge over the Capibaribe River. "Paco, you fool look. And he pointed to three boys diving off the bridge into the river."

"I must be dying," Paco said, half laughing, half crying as he too remembered how he first met Chunk.

"It's a sign from God. You will be fine."

Roberto Calo was silent but impressed with the fearlessness of his business partner and his loyalty to his men.

In another five minutes, they pulled up to a private home in the rich Derby neighborhood. He told Roberto to look after Paco, that he would be right back.

Chunk knocked on the front door of the pink stucco villa with the green tiled roof. A maid answered, and Chunk said something to her. She went away and shortly a man appeared. Paco recognized him; it was the doctor from the hospital many years ago who had saved Raphael's eye.

Chunk spoke with him for a moment. He indicated to Chunk to pull the car into the driveway to the left of the house and to the back, which he did.

The doctor never said a word. He helped Paco out of the car. Chunk and Calo carried him into a small office that the doctor used as a home examining room. They placed Paco on the table. He leaned back and passed out from loss of blood.

The doctor pulled Paco's pants off, leaving him naked from the waist down. He pulled the belt off and pulled the wad of tee shirt out of the bullet hole. It had stopped bleeding. "OK, let me work," indicating to Calo and Chunk they should wait outside. The doctor washed his hands rapidly, and as they started to leave the office, he pulled an instrument bag onto the table.

"Chunk, come back, I can use your help. I need you to hold onto him in case he wakes up. I don't have any anesthesia to give him," the doctor said as he was already prying his way into Paco's thigh with an instrument looking for the bullet.

Paco winced in his semi-coma as the pain increased.

After several minutes of prying, the doctor found the bullet and removed it. He cleaned the wound and put several stitches inside the leg and several more into the outer skin.

"Chunk, I can't do much more for him here. He needs to be in a hospital and may need a transfusion," the doctor said, sweating looking at DeLuna.

"Ain't going to happen, Doc," Chunk said pulling Paco's pants back on him. "You need to tell me what I need to do to help him recover in my house. And I will need you to make a house call tomorrow."

"Sure, Chunk, I'll come by. The best thing right now is to get him into bed resting. He's going to need lots of liquids."

Calo, who stayed also and looked on, found the relationship between respectable doctor and drug dealer fascinating. Fascinating that a doctor would do Chunk's bidding so willingly.

They carried the now partly conscious Paco to Chunk's car and again laid him down in back.

The doctor carried out a small bag and handed it to Chunk. "Here's some more bandages and antiseptic. Change the bandage twice a day and put some of this on the wound. It will help prevent infection. Watch for a fever. If it he gets bad Chunk, you'll have to bring him into a hospital."

"Got it, Doc, thanks," and they drove off.

Over the next week Paco did start to get better. The doctor came by three of the first four days that Paco was at Chunk's home. In this same time frame, Pedro, Paco's twin, took over his brother's drug operation and filled Chunk in on the results of the attack on the rival dealers. Of the six other locations, there was only one person at four of the locations and Paco's men killed all of them. At one location there were two men, and a brief gun battle took place before Paco's men overwhelmed them and killed them. The sixth location was the only failure. One of Paco's men was killed, another wounded. There had been four men in the house. Three were killed, the fourth got away. Paco's men were searching for him. They knew who he was, kidnapped his sister, and told his mother that if he didn't surrender they would cut his sister's head off.

On the fifth day, Chunk ordered it done. "Cut her head off and drop it off on the mother's front door. These people think we're playing with them. Leave a note under the head that if her son ever appears in Purnambuco we will kill her."

Pedro argued that the girl was only fifteen. "She didn't do anything. She doesn't know any of us and can't harm us."

"Pedro," Chunk began angrily, "you know better. No witnesses. Her brother knows what went down, knows who we are. If we let the sister go, he will see it as a sign of our weakness. It will only encourage him."

"But, Chunk?" Pedro pleaded.

"What's the matter with you? Have you gone weak on me? Look what they did to your poor brother. What they did to his men. What they tried to do to our business. No. Do it and don't question me again."

Pedro acknowledged Chunk.

Pedro was troubled; he did not sleep that night, and arose soaking wet with sweat.

She's a kid, he told himself as he drove to the safe house where she was being held. When he got there he entered the house, grabbed the girl, slit her throat and when she was dead he cut off her head. That night he left her head with the note at her mother's front door. After that Chunk's gang never had trouble from the San Salvadorans again.

Chunk, the homeless boy on the beach, had become a murderous menace. The madness that was his behavior grew worse as he got older. It was as if all men, but for those in his enterprise, were competitors and needed to be eliminated. But, he was respectful of customers or those who could help him like the doctor, the good doctor. And as the years passed the respected included the politicians and the builders who were using his cement. He was respectful of them—as long as they did what he wanted.

When Mercosur, the South American free trade treaty, was passed it promised to open a new era of regional growth for all Latin American companies. One export from Argentina and Mexico that quickly found new markets in Brazil was cement. Brazil was going through a great growth spurt and construction was leading that boom. Cement exporters from Argentina and the giant Mexican cement company, Cemex, were posing new problems, more complex than Chunk had ever encountered.

These foreign exporters would offer the cement at a very good price but would also seek to horizontally integrate themselves into the builders by offering a full supply chain: delivering the cement to the site, mixed in their own trucks, they would frame and block the targeted areas, such as foundations or ascending floors. They would do this all for the same price as Chunk's bags of cement, which did not have the added value of the supply chain.

Chunk's cement company, CDL Cement, was significant in size but significantly unprofitable and could not compete. He had professional managers running the company, but his presence was more as a silent partner. As the competition heated up, losses grew, and Chunk became less silent.

His company president, a middle aged man by the name of Ignacio Braun, had been a general manager for one of the divisions of the company. After assuming ownership Chunk met with Ignacio and the chief financial officer. He described what he expected from the company, offered the job of President to Ignacio, who asked Chunk "what about the current president, Juan Lopez."

"Mr. Lopez has a new assignment. Retirement. What other questions do you have for me?"

He had none. He accepted the job, and unfortunately he accepted Chunk's terms: Chunk wanted 20 percent revenue growth and 15 percent net profit. He expected this from a company with 5 percent gross margins that was losing one million dollars on fifty million dollars of sales. The problem for Ignacio would be the way the new company would deal with missed expectations; it would not be a lower performance review, a missed bonus or even a firing. It would be far more personal.

Chunk along with Carlos who was overseeing other businesses would meet with Ignacio and the CFO monthly to review the progress of the cement business.

Sadly for them and their immediate successors progress was not fast enough. Newspapers reported it strange that two presidents of the CDL Cement Company had met violent deaths.

The third time was a charm for DeLuna. He installed Carlos as president along with a new chief financial officer. During the course of the three years that DeLuna and Carlos had been micromanaging, Carlos actually learned quite a bit about the cement business, plumbing its depth with rigorous questioning of everyone in and out of leadership positions. Carlos, in fact, had become quite popular inside the company with midlevel managers. He had risen from the shadows where he had been assigned by Chunk as a special assistant to Ignacio and then succeeded his dead predecessor.

Together with the company's larcenous sales vice president, Carlos put a plan in place to lock out the foreign competition, since local competition had been dealt with already. Each state in Northern Brazil had a director of construction permitting: no permit for a site, no building. Through a series of relationship building experiences with these gentlemen to some of the bordellos in another division of CDL, they treated the state executives like royalty. Plenty of cash changed hands, funded from the drug operations.

Now developers were willing to pay a higher price for CDL cement since dealing with that particular company always made permitting easier, especially when the state directors could see the contract had been signed designating CDL. Each state director was given a significant bonus for every approved permit that carried a CDL contract.

Carlos' sales director for CDL felt like his sales force had been significantly expanded with developers looking to make sure CDL was included in every application, along with state directors only awarding permits to CDL tie ins.

The price rose on cement; CDL learned some of the lessons of horizontal integration and were now selling extended services at much higher prices than those of the Mercosur players who surprisingly just could not compete with CDL.

29

The inner walls of Auburn prison are so high that on a summer's day the sun only hits the full court yard for the one hour from just before noon to just after noon. As he passed through the quadrangle at 1 p.m., no sun shone on three quarters of the grass. CJ Strong was hoping that on this visit by his mother, Billy Stevens would be accompanying her.

"Well, if that no good Billy Stevens isn't here in the next week," his mother told him over the phone two weeks before this visit, "I'll collar him by the ear and drag him here with me."

And when Louise Strong saw the face of her son, she saw the hope sag. She knew what it meant.

"I saw your face, CJ. It dropped when you saw me. Or I should say when you didn't see Billy with me."

"No, I just had a thought about something else."

"No, I know you, CJ. Do you want to tell me what this is about? Something happened when Billy came to visit you, what is it now, six months ago."

"Nothing happened, Mom."

"It has something to do with that picture I brought to you, doesn't it?"

"Mom, let it go. I just enjoyed Billy's visit and would like to see him again."

And on her return to Stamford, Louise Strong wangled an invitation out to dinner with her sister, Jackie, Billy Stevens's mother.

"I went to see CJ the other day," Louise began as they sat in Antonio's, an Italian restaurant they could both walk to on Stamford's West Side and where the food was good and the prices low.

"And how's he doing?" Jackie Stevens asked her older sister.

"Not so good. The time Billy went to see CJ it really perked him up. But Billy hasn't been back and CJ is down."

"Huh," the younger sister replied.

"Why, huh?"

"Well, I didn't say anything at the time, but Billy was totally different after he came back from seeing CJ. I mean he was happy, really happy. He was upbeat for weeks afterward, then it all went away. He became his old gloomy self again."

"I knew it."

"Knew what?"

"After I went to see CJ, after Billy's visit, he had me bring an old photo of the two of them playing football one afternoon at the Barnes, with Parker and a bunch of his friends."

"And?"

"Well, it has something to do with that picture."

"He'll be home in a while. He went with his father to the Y. It's the only time I can expect him home. When we leave here, my dear sister, we're going to have a little talk with Billy. And we'll see that his father is there to help us get to the bottom of what's going on."

"Thanks, Jackie."

"We're all we've got."

"We're all CJ's got."

And like clockwork, at nine fifteen, just after open gym on the courts of the Stamford Y closed, the two men walked in to the presence of the two waiting women.

"Louise, nice surprise," Willy Stevens said to his sister-in-law.

"Hi, Willy. Hi, Billy," Louise laughed, "Sounds like a song."

"Hi, Aunt Louise," Billy said warily. Since the day CJ was arrested, Louise Strong knew Billy Stevens was somehow involved with whatever happened the night Augusto Santos was murdered. She knew the way he slinked into her apartment that morning and the way he slinked out when the detectives showed up to arrest CJ that he was somehow involved. And Billy knew his aunt knew. He was uncomfortable in her presence. He avoided her when he could; he ducked out of family dinners often.

"Boys, we need to have a talk," Jackie Stevens began.

"You don't need me," Billy said.

"You are the one we do need. Daddy, we need you here to help us sort something out," Jackie Stevens said.

"What's up, Louise," Willy Stevens said, looking at Billy with a wondering eye.

And for the next half hour, almost six years after Augusto Santos was killed, Louise Strong went over her concerns from the past few months, going all the way back to the morning after the murder. She ended by saying, "I always knew CJ never killed that man, and you knew it too, didn't you, Billy."

Jackie Stevens gasped at the thought. Willy Stevens looked at his son and said, "If you ever expect to step through that door again, you answer your aunt right now."

"No," Billy began, "I don't. I don't know who did it."

"What does that picture of you and CJ and those boys playing football have to do with it."

"What picture?"

"After you went to see CJ, he became happier. He asked for a picture of all of you playing football at the Barnes house."

"I don't remember any picture."

Willy Stevens backhanded his son in the head, "Tell the damn truth."

"I don't. What picture.

"One day when you and CJ were about sixteen you came by the Barnes."

"I remember that. Some house. I don't remember any picture."

"Mrs. Barnes took a picture of all of you after your game, and she gave me a copy of it. After you went to see CJ, he asked me for the picture, and he asked me to have you come see him again."

"What's in that picture," Billy's father asked him, again raising his hand.

As Billy pulled back from his father, he said, "I don't know."

"You do know, Billy. You knew the morning that you came over to see CJ after that man was killed. I saw your face then. It's the same as now," Louise Strong concluded, staring firmly at Billy Stevens.

Billy sat down. He didn't know how to tell the story. He didn't know how much his parents knew of his outside life. Yes, they knew he was arrested for drug dealing, but he always lied, saying he was only using. He knew what CJ had made him promise on his mother's soul to never tell anyone. But he also knew he wasn't strong.

"I can see you scheming. Don't make something up. Just tell it," his mother said as his father made a move towards him again.

"There's nothing to tell. CJ never did the killing, like he always said."

His father lifted him up by his sweat shirt, "And you, did you do it?"

"Willie," pleaded his wife, Jackie, "Let him tell us what he knows."

Releasing his son, the elder Stevens said, "You let CJ rot in that prison over five years now. Your cousin, your best friend?"

Billy paused, and then spoke. "I do not know who killed that man. That is the truth. I believe CJ when he says he did not do it." The younger Stevens rose, and added, "I'll go see CJ this weekend and find out what this is about," and with that he bolted out the door of the apartment.

30

C hunk DeLuna brought the legitimate arm of his business, cement, to his native Puerto Rico. Building along the Condado and Isle Verde, two resort areas of San Juan close to the international airport, was growing rapidly. Large condominium complexes were springing up at exactly the time DeLuna and Carlos were introducing CDL Enterprisa's cement business to the US territory by bribing a municipal purchasing manager and producing the low bid for a public housing complex. This procurement manager was also influential in bringing DeLuna and CDL to the close knit construction community of San Juan. Quietly and in less than two years, CDL had won major contracts for two condo complexes, the new convention center and an extension of the new runway at the Munoz International Airport.

His experience in meeting all key schedules along with a strong reputation for a quality product and his status as a US citizen allowed DeLuna to expand into New York City as a minority supplier in several small construction bids.

Barnes Construction, over the past several years, had been continuously looking for links into the enormous construction arm of the city of New York. Being able to come to the table with CDL, as a Latino supplier and with CDL's low prices, Barnes was able to win several lucrative contracts with relative ease.

Jonathan Barnes did not have the skill of a general manager able to see the entire scope of his enterprise, nor did he have the relationship building skills required of a master builder that encouraged selection based on personal confidence. What he did possess was the sharpest pencil in town. Quality was a given among the major contractors; the difference maker was the bidding process. With a cement supplier like CDL, Barnes felt he could win even more business.

He asked his son Parker, who was the Vice President of Barnes charged with managing the firm's New York business, to build a relationship with DeLuna. His thinking, that if he could monopolize the Puerto Rican/Brazilian cement manufacturer, other contractors in the city wouldn't be able to get at the large cost difference DeLuna provided, even more so now that CDL was shipping cement in its own massive freighters.

Interestingly, while Parker had only two skills for the construction business, they were critical—architecting with an eye for design and, he had developed, world class relationship building skills. All of the major New York architects appreciated a contractor who was an architect and who could value their designs. The younger Barnes had burnished this reputation on two projects, one on the waterfront expansion project for the aircraft carrier, Intrepid, which had become a major tourist attraction for the City. The second was the TeleLatino building on Broadway at 58th St. The later was the first non-City project Barnes used CDL on. The building's owner was delighted with the price Barnes came up with and even more delighted that Barnes had chosen a Latino contractor for cement and framing of the building.

Outside of work, Parker also brought DeLuna along. He grew to genuinely like the little man. He found DeLuna reminded him of his good friend, Leonard Crane. They had the same animal magnetism—fierce volcanoes bubbling under their surfaces. Besides DeLuna introduced him to the purest form of cocaine he had ever enjoyed.

31

Weeks passed before Billy Stevens made the trip from Stamford to Auburn Prison after promising his parents and Mrs. Strong that he would come.

When they greeted each other in the visitor's area, CJ Strong was more than a bit upset.

"You got the message I wanted to see you. That was almost a year ago. What is wrong with you, why couldn't you come sooner? I need your help to get out of here. This isn't a joke."

Before CJ could continue, in his anxiety Billy broke into CJ's tirade and said, "I'm sorry."

"I don't have time for sorry, Billy. I need your help."

"I'm here now, CJ."

"My Mom had this picture of us all from the football game we played at the Barnes' house and she brought it," and he handed the picture to Billy. "I figured this would let you recognize who you were with that night the guy got knifed."

The guard looked over, and CJ indicated that it was just a picture he was showing to his friend. The guard nodded his head.

Billy looked at the picture; looked at it closely, as it was starting to yellow. "Here, CJ, this is him."

CJ looked over to who Billy was pointing to. "You sure?" he said.

"Yes, of course, I'm sure. That's the kid that killed the drug dealer."

32

On the night Augusto Santos, the Guatemalan drug dealer, was stabbed to death in Stamford, and for which Curtis Strong was sentenced to twenty-five years in prison, something else occurred.

At the Barnes' estate on the Shippan peninsula, a loud crash occurred out back in the garage area. Jonathan Barnes woke at the noise, dressed and went downstairs. The live-in housekeeper was coming in the rear door, helping an injured Parker Barnes into the kitchen area. He was covered in blood.

"Parker, what happened," Barnes senior asked rushing over to help his son sit.

"I hit the garage," an incoherent Parker answered, swaying in the chair.

"What, were you drinking?"

"No, I wasn't drinking."

"Damn it, you're high as a kite," Barnes exclaimed, motioning to the housekeeper, "Get some wet cloths, and let's find out where he's hurt."

They took Parker's jacket off, then his shirt. They began washing the blood off of his hands; there were smudges of blood on his cheeks. There were no cuts.

"What the hell," Jonathan Barnes exclaimed. "Parker, where did all this blood come from?"

"I don't know," a slurring Parker replied, "Oh, yes, I got into a fight."

"A fight, with what," Barnes said, his face reddening, something he did in fits of frustration.

"With my fists. A guy hit me in a bar, and I hit him back."

"Parker, you're making no sense at all. All this blood is from a lot more than a fist fight. Someone lost a lot of blood." Jonathan Barnes began to pace. "I'm going to call the police and see what the hell is going on here."

"No, Dad," Parker stood, "No, do not do that."

"Then start explaining."

"There was a car accident; I was a passenger," Parker began his lie. "We were driving in a VW bug, and he lost control and hit a tree. The glass came in on the two kids in the front seat and cut them up."

"What two kids?" Barnes senior demanded, sensing the lie.

"Friends of mine from the yacht club."

"What friends, what are their names?"

"Why do you care, Dad, I'm OK, they're OK. They went to the hospital and just got a couple of stitches."

"I don't believe you, Parker. Why are you covered in blood?"

"I was helping them out of the car, "

And to the housekeeper, "What does his car look like?"

"It's pretty messed up, Mr. Barnes," June Williams replied.

"Parker, get your lying ass to bed. I'll find out for myself what happened."

"Nothing happened, Dad." Parker pleaded.

"And you're not high on drugs again, and the cars not busted up in the rear yard, and that wasn't blood all over your clothes?" And to Mrs. Williams, Jonathan Barnes said, "June, would you please help him to his room?"

"Yes, sir, Mr. Barnes."

Ellen Barnes entered the kitchen. "Jonathan, what's going on here," and seeing Parker half naked went to her son, "Parker what happened to you."

"Ellen, don't waste your breath on him. He wrecked the car out back, came in here covered in blood and filled with lies," a fuming Jonathan Barnes said. "Something happened with him tonight, and I intend to find out what. Please get him to bed."

"Parker, what is it," And when no response came, "Come on, tell me."

Jonathan Barnes left the room with his son being supported on each arm by the two women. He walked down a small hallway off the kitchen and into his library. He sat at his desk for a moment and made a few notes. "Covered in blood, crashed our car, high on something, doesn't smell of alcohol, says an accident with friends, and went to hospital with them for stitches." He pulled up his electronic rolodex on the screen of the desktop computer. He pressed the screen at a certain entry and listened as a phone rang.

"This is Al Pavia," came the reply after the third ring.

"Captain Pavia, this is Jonathan Barnes, and I have a problem."

One of the privileges that comes from being a leading citizen is that you participate in the civics of the community. Jonathan Barnes was a member of the Police Commission and from time to time found this position very helpful. He had taken a particular liking to Al Pavia, who as a Lieutenant had assisted him on a call out one night when young Parker was about to be arrested for DWI. Pavia, realizing who his patrol officer was about to arrest, mediated, called Mr. Barnes to come and take Parker home, since no accident had occurred in the incident, and that his officer was willing to allow an outcome favorable to Barnes.

Al Pavia arrived at the Barnes home in under an hour. Jonathan Barnes came out to greet him and accompany him inside. "Al, thanks so much for coming right over."

"I'm glad to be of assistance Mr. Barnes," Pavia said as they walked to the library.

Barnes closed the door.

"I did some checking since we talked," Pavia began. "There were a few things that happened tonight. Tell me more about Parker, his condition."

"He came home about an hour ago, and as I said he crashed his car into the garage out back. He was totally disoriented but didn't smell of alcohol. My guess is drugs."

"Right, now tell me again about the blood. Where was it, and you said that Parker had no cuts."

"None," Barnes replied summarily. "But his jacket and shirt were covered in blood. A lot of it. It was on his hands, and he had some on his face. After we took his jacket and shirt off, we couldn't find any cuts."

"OK, and you said something about a car accident with his friends."

"Yes, he said he was in a car with two friends. The car hit a tree and glass came in and cut his friends up. He said in helping them out of the car he got blood on his clothes. He also said they went to the hospital, as I told you, and his friends got stitches. To be honest with you, Al, I don't believe a word he said. Why I called you is I think he's in bigger trouble."

"You might be right. Based on what you told me, I did some quick checking. There was a stabbing on the West side, guy died. Witness says she saw someone leaning over the dead guy, she yelled and the guy took off. A couple of my guys are all over it, but the description of the killer doesn't fit Parker. The woman thought it was black man who did the stabbing. Also, there were a couple of fights downtown around midnight, one of which involved four white guys, well dressed, going at each other. Lot of blood in that one; we have two of the guys in custody. We're looking for the other two who apparently started something in the bar, and these two goons we have were waiting outside for them."

Barnes listened intently trying to find a link, "Anything else, Al."

"There were three separate car accidents. Two involved women and one involved an older man. The one with the old man was the only serious one where there was blood. He's doing well at the hospital now. The hospital told us there was only one case of stitches tonight, a young boy who cut his finger on an open can." Pavia paused as he looked at the small pad he had jotted down the night's adventures. "The only other action we had tonight was a burglary in North Stamford; side window broken in, computer, jewelry and some clothes taken—no suspects. I called the investigating officer, and there was no blood around the smashed-in window.

"Well, Al, it sounds like the fight fits. Imagine, I'm hopeful that he was in a fist fight," Barnes said smiling slightly.

"Mr. Barnes, do you still have Parker's clothes, with the blood on them?" Pavia asked.

"Yes, why Al?"

"I want to handle it properly," Pavia said with a smile.

"Wait here, I'll go get them," Barnes said, as he thought he understood what Pavia meant and went to the kitchen to retrieve them.

Barnes placed the jacket and shirt in a plastic trash bag and brought it to Paiva, who reached in and pulled out the shirt by a non-bloodied corner. He shook his head, "That's a helluva lot of blood, Mr. Barnes. I don't think we have a street fight here," Paiva said as he pulled out the jacket and looked at the blood on it. "Definitely more than a street fight, Mr. Barnes. "See this blot here," Paiva said pointing to an area on the front of the jacket?"

"Yes, what is it?"

"See how it's solid in the middle and then splattered going out from the middle?"

"Yes, yes, what are you getting at?" a flustered Barnes was now pressing.

"It looks like what occurs when an artery is severed and blood flows out—big in the center as it hits and more splattered as it spreads out."

"Jesus, Al what are you saying."

"I think Parker was facing someone who had just been stabbed or shot."

"No, no. There is no way that is what happened."

"Look, Mr. Barnes, I'm here to help. You called me, remember," Paiva said trying to be reassuring. "I think we need to talk with Parker, Mr. Barnes, you and me. Can you get him?"

"Damn, Al, I don't like where this is going."

"Mr. Barnes, we have to know what we're dealing with. If you want me to help you, let me do it."

"He's in no shape to talk with you now. I'll bring him to you in the morning," Barnes said, almost dismissively.

"We need to do this now," and it was not a request from Captain Paiva, and he added, more to comfort Mr. Barnes, "this is the best time to get at the truth, when it is still closest to the occurrence, before the fairy tales get made up."

Barnes relented and went to get his son.

Paiva stood up to get a closer look at the framed pictures on the shelves of the back wall. In one Barnes senior was standing with President Regan, Regan's arm around him, even though they were as tall as one another. In another Barnes was flanked by former Senator Chris Dodd and former Governor John Rowland. "Interesting," Paiva whispered to himself, "a couple of crooks." He saw pictures of Barnes with former Connecticut Governor Ella Grasso, others with Barnes and three people in suits, who he didn't recognize, and finally there was Barnes with the Police Commissioner, Police Chief John Brennan, and newly promoted Captain Paiva. He thought of Barnes strong support with the Commissioner and the Chief, lobbying on his behalf.

Barnes returned with a disheveled Parker. "Parker, this is Captain Paiva," Barnes began, almost gently; "He needs to ask you a few questions. Please answer him truthfully so we can end this night."

Parker Barnes was in a fog. He walked to one of the three large leather chairs on the left side of the room, away from the desk and picture showcase. He collapsed into the chair.

"Parker, this won't take long. Like your father said, I will only ask you a few questions; in fact, you don't need to answer if you don't want to. But, and this is important, if you do answer you must be truthful. Are you OK with this?" Paiva asked to make sure there was comprehension.

"Yes, sir, I understand."

"OK, first off, were you using drugs tonight?"

Barnes senior flinched. Parker looked at his father.

"It's alright, Parker, just answer," Jonathan Barnes told his son. He had never heard him admit to drug use, only agreeing that he would go to treatment since his parents insisted.

"Yes," Parker said quietly.

"Was it crack?" Paiva asked realizing the popularity and easy access to the plague that was overrunning Stamford.

"Yes, sir."

"Good, thanks for being truthful," Paiva said, now pressing forward, "Now where do you usually get your drugs?"

"On the West Side," Parker responded without thinking of the earlier incident.

"Did you go there tonight to buy drugs?" Paiva asked, knowing this answer could change the young man's life forever.

Now thinking about his last answer, Parker hesitated. The elder Barnes quietly told his son, "You're doing fine, Parker, just keep telling the truth."

Now a voice inside Parker urged caution. Was his father about to sell him down the river? He was exhausted.

"I need to go to bed. Can we do this in the morning? I can't think any more."

Paiva now returned to his firmer self. "Parker, we're doing this here in your home as a favor to your father. If we do it in the morning, it will be at the station with a different view point. Do you understand me?"

"Yes, sir," the young Barnes relented. "Yes, I did go there to buy drugs then everything got all screwed up," he concluded, leaning forward with his elbows on his knees and his head in his hands.

"Tell me what happened during the buy. What went wrong?"

"I was in a hurry. I wanted to get it and get out of there. I was with the guy I usually get them from only he didn't have any so he took me to this other guy, a Mexican or something; Billy told me his name was Augusto. Well, he starts playing with me, you know, like, 'Let's see some of your money.' Start's giving me a bunch of shit. I flashed a knife and told him to give me the damn stuff; I was holding the money. Then he lunges towards me, and I stabbed him. I wasn't trying to hurt him, I never hurt anyone before. I was scared shitless; I thought he was going to kill me. He seemed crazy. I don't know why he did that."

While his son was confessing to killing a drug dealer, Jonathan Barnes was weaving in and out of sanity, wondering how this could have happened. He felt like his brain was going to burst. His son, the heir to Barnes Construction. Doing drugs, killing a drug dealer. Christ, carrying a knife.

"What are you doing carrying a knife," it just came out.

Paiva looked at the elder Barnes and said, "Jonathan, why don't you let me continue to ask Parker the questions."

"Yes, of course, Captain Paiva." Barnes said, unwilling to have his son aware of his familiarity with the police captain.

"What happened next," Paiva continued.

"Blood was spurting out all over me. I just ran, took off."

"What time was this?"

"Early, around eight o'clock."

"Then what did you do the rest of the night?" the inquisitor continued.

"I went to Cummings Beach and just sat there all night."

"Did you use drugs there?"

"Yes."

"That's not possible Parker, not at Cummings Beach. I have patrol cars there all night checking the cars in the parking lot," Paiva said in pursuit.

"My car was parked there; you can check. I saw your police writing down the plate number."

"Where were you?"

"On the hill in the woods. It's where we used to go to get away.

"Who saw you there?"

"No one else was there. If there were I would have left," a now more alert Parker Barnes said. "I know what I did; I used what crack I had to get lost for the night." And now looking at his father, "I didn't do it intentionally, Dad. He came at me, and I reacted. I am sorry."

"Alright, I'm done with what I wanted to find out," Paiva said. "Parker, you get back to bed."

Jonathan Barnes, feeling some sympathy now for his son, said, "Captain Paiva, I'm going to walk Parker back to his room. Would you wait for me please?"

"Sure, Mr. Barnes."

And while the elder Barnes took his charge to bed, Paiva began making notes in the small pad he kept in his shirt pocket. Several minutes passed and Jonathan Barnes returned to the library.

"What do you think, Al," a concerned Barnes asked.

"Well we know where the blood came from. I've got a lot of work to do. Leave things to me tonight, hell, I should say this morning. I'll get back to you sometime during the day, most likely after I talk with the investigating officers." Pavia rose, and picked up the white trash bag with the bloody clothes. "I'll take these clothes for safekeeping."

"OK, Al, you know best." Barnes rose to shake Pavia's hand. "Again, thank you very much for coming here. I won't forget it, Al."

"You're welcome, Mr. Barnes."

33

The following afternoon Captain Paiva drove down Shippan Ave, down Rogers Road and in through the gates at the end of the street. He passed through a narrow aisle of tall cypress trees on either side of the car. It reminded him of a trip he took with his mother and father to Italy when he was a small boy. At the end of the aisle sat Apple Manor. Coming in the dark the night before, he missed the beauty and stateliness of the home.

Upon coming out of the aisle of cypress, the view exploded outward. The large Mediterranean stucco home with the terra cotta tile roofs sat in the middle of a rounded two acres. For a 180 degree arc behind the house was water, Long Island Sound. To the left of the house was a tennis court, to the right in the rear were the slightly damaged garages, and behind the house were the swimming pool, a dock for the Barnes yacht and a massive patio.

Paiva drove to the rear of the house, looked at the damage to the garage without exiting his car and returned to the circular drive and parked just beyond the front door.

The housekeeper Mrs. Williams opened the door and greeted Paiva who was in uniform. "Can I help you, officer," she said.

"Yes, I'm here to see Mr. Barnes, he's expecting me."

"Mr. Barnes, Senior, sir?" Mrs. Williams asked, given what she was aware of from the prior evening.

"Yes, Mr. Jonathan Barnes."

"Please come in, I'll let him know you're here."

Paiva entered and stood until Barnes came to meet him.

"Let's go to the library, Al. It will give us privacy." Barnes said leading the way, "How about something to drink?"

"Sure, but just a soda or water."

Barnes left Paiva and went to get two sodas from the kitchen. He passed by their part-time housekeeper who mainly worked weekends, Mrs. Louise Strong.

"Mr. Barnes, I'm sorry to disturb you, but could I speak to you when you have a moment?" Mrs. Strong asked.

"Yes, Louise, I'll be a little while," and knowing she had seen Paiva, added, "I just need to finish up a couple of police commission responsibilities."

"Yes, thank you, Mr. Barnes.

With two Pepsis in hand, Barnes returned to the library.

"Well, did you learn anything new, Al?"

"Quite a lot. Let me begin by saying it looks like everything Parker told us was true. His car was at Cummings Beach, a couple of my guys did get the plate number like he said. Regarding the dead guy, he was a dealer, a Guatemalan with a pretty extensive history of drug dealing, and illegal. Was deported twice and managed to find his way back here. My guys found the knife, some prints on it that they're working on now."

"Jesus, are they Parker's," an alarmed Barnes asked.

"Well, they were. But they aren't now," Paiva said with that slight smile.

"Whew, how did you do that," Barnes said, now relieved.

"One of my best guys is supervising the investigation," Pavia said and added, "You remember John Walsh, we promoted him to Detective Sergeant last year. He came through the commission because he was moving so quickly ahead of a few of his peers. You helped us on it."

"Vaguely, rings a bell, I think," Barnes said, "Hell, Al, I used to have a mind like a steel trap, could remember everything. Now, some stuff slips away. It's why I've got to get Parker through all this crap. He's the one who has to take over in a few years. Some heir apparent I've got here, huh?"

"He's not a bad kid, Mr. Barnes, just having some trouble finding his way," Paiva said, continuing; "Now, I also had another one of my guys do an analysis on the blood on the clothes. It is definitely the Guatemalan's."

"Shit, Al, I'm getting worried, this looks like it's going to catch up to us?" an almost trembling Jonathan Barnes said.

"No, it won't. It won't. These are my guys. What happens in our family stays in our family. I have never had a breach of trust yet, in twenty years of leading men," and for good measure he added, "and I don't intend to start now."

"So what's next," Barnes asked anxiously.

"Nothing on your end. You need to get Parker out of town and into rehab quickly."

"I've already started. I've got a couple of places we're talking to."

"Good, and regarding the murder. There was an eye witness. She believes she knows the kid who she saw leaning over the dealer. A couple of Walsh's guys picked him up this morning. We did a lineup and she picked him out. He's being arraigned on Monday, the poor bastard. So I think we're all set. But this is important: You must get Parker to understand he can never, not once, talk about this to anyone and not to any of those bleeding hearts in rehab."

"I'll make sure it never again enters his mind, under pain of loss of inheritance," Jonathan Barnes concluded, standing now and again offering his hand to Captain Paiva.

"I'll walk out with you, Al," Barnes was saying, and when they exited the front door, "When the weather gets better, maybe you and your wife can come over for an afternoon sail."

"Thanks, Mr. Barnes, I'd really like that," Paiva said, knowing that an invitation would not be forthcoming.

"Al, I do appreciate all you have done. If I can ever help you, you only have to ask."

"You've helped me a lot already. I'll be talking with you, Mr. Barnes."

When Barnes went back inside, he saw Louise Strong dusting in the library. Feeling much better he walked up and said with a smile, "Now, Mrs. Strong, how can I help you."

"Mr. Barnes, may I ask you a question?"

"Why yes, Mrs. Strong," Barnes said as he relaxed in his library.

"Well, it's about my son, CJ. There was a crime…last night. A man was stabbed and he died."

"Yes, was that over on the west side,' Barnes replied barely looking up.

"It was. Well, Mr. Barnes, the police came to my house yesterday. They arrested my son; they think he did it," Louise Strong said, now crying.

Curtis Strong went to prison for the crime Parker Barnes committed. Parker Barnes went on to Columbia and did quite well at the University. His life going forward was occasionally interrupted by bouts of drug abuse and the necessary return to rehab. Overcoming his afflictions was not a Parker Barnes strength. Besides drugs there was an obsession with wealth, and yet he had more money than all the people who had ever existed on earth, except for but two or three thousand. Well, his father had all that wealth, not Parker. Therein lay part of the disarray of his mind. His great dilemma: how to get hold of it now, not when dear old dad chose to give it up.

There was a certain degree of envy for his closest lifelong friends from Brunswick. Their fortunes were similar, but in a number of cases, they had possession of the fortune. Now he didn't want all of it, like Sebastian Ball, whose father loved him so much, confided in him as an alter ego, taught him the business, and for his twenty-first birthday gave him one hundred million dollars, taxes paid. Then again the Balls, as they said, had it all. And they did, with Sebastian senior annually making the Forbes list of the twenty wealthiest men in the world, with an estimated fortune of seven to ten billion dollars.

The esteem for a son and a way of showing it was what gnawed at Parker Barnes, or rather the lack of esteem. And he knew he was responsible for part of it; he did this to himself with his behavior. But not all of it. His father was not like the others. There was a stinginess to him as if he had built Barnes Construction himself and no one else could share in it. Mr. Jonathan Barnes was himself an heir to the fortune and at a very young age and did not need to go begging to daddy every time an opportunity arose.

The other Brunswick boys still locked together for life with friendship and their Brunswick Fund had access. Access was important for esteem. Barnes had to have it. And it is why, as his father did turn elements of the business over to him, such as their New York City holdings, that Parker felt it necessary to take liberties to have that esteem.

And when Brunswick Fund was to go to the next level with each member needing to ante up another two million dollars, it was Parker who early on board was cheerleading the creation of something that would advance his wealth independent of his father. But it was a dangerous move for him, one that he needed to watch carefully, for what he did was write four checks for five hundred thousand dollars each to Brunswick Fund and enter them into the ledger as buying additional properties on the upper west side.

In fact after several months passed and nothing came of the bookkeeping falsification, young Mr. Barnes created several entries on the order of another one million dollars. This he felt would help him live in a style necessary to keep pace with his friends. After all, for someone of his age and station in life, who would someday inherit several hundred million dollars, trying to get by on one 150 thousand dollars per year that his piker father had bestowed on him as salary, just did not do it.

34

So it was on this day that Louise Strong would find her son content, unconcerned with the outside world; his plate, as he would share with her, was full and about to get fuller.

He saw his mother, and he stood up as he always did at the sight of his mother approaching the visiting area table he sat at. Then he noticed, from sixty feet away, as she got closer the other woman, the younger one, was with his mother. She was familiar; somehow, yes, it was Kathy Jackson. He froze; fear or shock, something gripped him. So out of place here.

CJ's smile returned as he hugged his mother. Mrs. Strong said, "I have a surprise for you."

"I can see that," CJ said, and looking at Kathy Jackson, "Hi, aren't you a little out of the neighborhood, Kathy?"

"Hi, CJ," she laughed, "yes, just a bit. And she moved to hug him. CJ put his arms around his high school prom date and girlfriend for too short a time.

For the first time since he had been arrested, he felt a rush, a pleasant rush, almost new. A warmth came over him. He stood back from her. "You are a surprise, a good surprise."

Louise Strong had been hesitant when Kathy Jackson asked her in the previous week to accompany her on her next visit to see CJ. But realized no harm, nothing but goodness would flow from this vibrant bright beauty to her son. She embraced the idea. The surprise worked.

CJ was so taken with the visit he forgot to mention the two A's he had recently received. Louise Strong for the first time in years saw a different flirtatious side of her son. It was a side she was happy to see; it meant he had not lost hope and could adjust quickly, if only there were a way out of this hell.

Louise excused herself, "I'll be back in a minute. That was a long ride, I need to use the restroom." This was too good to interrupt—she would go back out to the waiting room for a while and read a magazine and let CJ and Kathy have time to talk. She saw the connection—it was electric, it was immediate. Louise and Kathy had talked all the way up on the drive, and having Kathy drive saved her from the excruciating boredom of the much longer bus ride . It was such a pleasure to be in a car again and to have time to talk with such a pleasant young woman. Even the scenery seemed to improve along the drive.

As CJ watched his mother pass by the guard at the door, he turned and faced Kathy. "It is so good to see you."

"So how's it really going, CJ?" she asked, assuming he would be able to let his guard down without his mother present.

"Compared to freedom?" he said, but rather than becoming morose, he came right back. "I'm fine; I'm making progress, you know, with school, helping other inmates, sports, my work."

Kathy Jackson knew why she admired CJ Strong. He was a faithful to his name—he was more than that; he could endure, and progress in spite of his circumstances. She remembered how poised he was in the face of the poverty he endured. Kathy Jackson grew up in Stamford's south end, poor, with a family struggling, but when they dated in high school, CJ was downright poor, more poor. Maybe the poorest kid she ever knew. But you didn't know it, not from CJ, not from his appearance which was always fresh, ironed polo shirts and chinos, clean sneakers and he always smelled like a man. It was only when you went to his neighborhood that you saw the poverty. But CJ wasn't poor; he was not poor of spirit. He laughed, he joked, he was a normal, healthy good kid. And now here was that same good kid with that same even disposition making the best of hell.

190

"Tell me about your work. What do you do here? Make license plates?"

CJ laughed, loud enough that it caught the guard's attention. CJ and the guard exchanged looks. CJ nodded.

"License plates? No, I work in the power plant. I've learned plumbing, steam—any type of piping you can think of I can do."

"So when you get out, will you be a plumber?" she asked, nervously, maybe too fast, not knowing what to ask someone who'd been in prison for almost five years.

"I like the sound of that. When I get out," CJ smiled. "Plumbing—maybe, it's a skill. But I also have a straight A average towards my degree."

"Your mother told me you were doing very well with studies here. What are you studying?"

"Economics. Criminal justice."

"That's a strange combination."

"Doh?" he said with his arms outstretched and hands pointing back to himself. As if to say, "Me being here is the strange combination."

He moved the spotlight to her, "So what have you been doing for the past six years? I guess it's been that long." And while they had been standing all this time he moved forward and hugged her again. She could feel the massive strength in her friend. He held her; it was more than a hug. Then he said to her, quietly, "Thank you so much for coming. I have missed you."

And surprising herself, she said, "I miss you, CJ. I'm so glad I'm here."

They separated, a bond formed, and they both sat wondering what came next. This was new for both of them. Kathy knew it was possible when she came to see CJ. She had always cared for the thoughtful boy she dated for so short a time. The memory emerged in her mind—he did not have a lot of money for movies, restaurants, or other places to go. After the prom each date had a longer time between the prior date. Their time together was always meaningful, and now Kathy figured it was just that CJ was shy, broke, and still playing sports with the boys in his free time. CJ's heart was jumping.

Something new was going on, and this would take some figuring out but for now he knew he made a big mistake by not making more of an effort with this sweet girl who was growing into a beautiful woman.

Kathy began, "Well, I got my degree at Fordham." She was glad for the shift, for his interest, so there would be a sharing.

"In what?"

"Criminal justice."

"No way! Why that?"

"I'm a Stamford Police officer."

"What?"

She grinned from ear to ear.

"There is no way someone as beautiful as you is a cop."

She blushed.

"How long?"

"How long what?"

"How long have you been a cop? I mean police officer."

"A year and half. Four years of school."

"Is that what you wanted to do?"

"I wanted law school. I was going to spring you."

"What?" he laughed.

"Yeah. I was going to get my degree and get your stupid conviction tossed."

"You're serious?" CJ said, still questioning was she serious.

"Yes, I am," and Kathy's eyes became watery. CJ saw a tear run down her cheek.

"What's wrong?"

"I'm sorry, CJ. I got distracted."

"It's alright, go on."

"No, I mean I'm sorry I didn't continue on with my law degree. I got distracted." Kathy Jackson wasn't sure how to say what came next and just blurted it out. "I fell in love. Thought I was in love. Got married. The money and grants ran out in my senior year— barely made it out with my degree. Carried some debt out with me. The marriage was over before it got started. I needed a job. Fortunately, color and sex matter in hiring and with my criminal

192

justice degree, Stamford Police hired me. But it was close for a while there; my world came apart."

"I can relate to that," CJ said smiling. They looked at each other, trying to stifle the eruption that was coming. It was no use; they burst out laughing, loudly, and for a long time. CJ looked at the guard who frowned, and CJ held up his hand. But he and Kathy just kept laughing, quietly giggling. CJ pulled his chair next to Kathy's, put his hand on the side of her head and moved forward. They kissed. Kathy was overjoyed—she knew, she knew. CJ was the one all along. CJ felt stronger than he had ever felt. He was part of something, part of someone. For so long it was always he and his mother. But that wasn't the same. This was him, becoming. Becoming part of something else, something mutual. What he felt, she felt. He knew it by the way Kathy's lips welcomed his.

The guard watched the scene of the prisoner and young woman kissing. Kissing was allowed. Guards needed to pay attention to make sure objects were not passing back and forth, but new screening tools were so good the problem was almost non-existent, so a lot was tolerated. As long as it did not get too physical, guards held back.

It did not become too physical. But Kathy Jackson painted a picture in her mind of a ferocious lover coming at her. It was CJ, muscles rippling, handsome to a fault and a warm tender smile only for her. How could such a tender moment in her life play out in such a place as this. She vowed silently that when she was an old lady there would always be a special place in her heart for Auburn Prison.

CJ spoke. "You know what is amazing?"

"What?" she asked.

"The night, the night all this happened, I was going to call you."

"Why didn't you," a now very curious Kathy asked.

"I had dinner early, was about to call you and my cousin Billy came by. He wanted me to go with him that night."

"How can you remember that?" she said wondering how a detail like that would be in CJ's mind so many years later.

"I've had time to reconstruct every minute of that day and the next and the next three months through the trial," he grimaced, grabbing the edge of the table."

"We don't have to talk about that," she said seeing it got to him.

"What bothers me," he added, the grimace continuing "is that this is America. How can something like this happen?"

"I don't know, CJ," she said, realizing for the first time, she was talking to an innocent man who had been in prison for almost five years.

When Kathy was invited by Mrs. Strong to come along, she agreed readily at the time knowing she still had feelings for the boy who let her young heart heat up so many years before. Kathy had followed the story in the news—his arrest, his conviction, and his sentencing. She intended to visit CJ while he was still awaiting trial, but her parents forbade it. At the time she did not know whether CJ was guilty or innocent. The Stamford Advocate had the most unflattering picture she had ever seen of CJ. The reporting presented both sides, CJ's statements about what happened, but the prosecutor's comments, echoed by the police presented a picture of guilt. She was conflicted at the time but decided to obey her parents.

Now, all this time, and here before her, an innocent man sat. Whom she not only still cared about, but now knew she loved. And now Kathy Jackson was a police officer on the force that put him here.

She resolved there must be something she could do. On the way home with Mrs. Strong, Kathy was less talkative. After the weekend, Kathy resolved she would talk with her mentor, an older lieutenant on the police force. Louise Strong was content with the long stretches of silence; pictures of a joyful CJ filled her mind. His last words to her were, "You were always the best mother in the world, but you took it up a notch bringing Kathy. Thank you so much." Louise smiled, closed her eyes as the car moved forward along Route 17, a sign from the Johnson administration proclaiming it "one of America's scenic highways." Louise Johnson found it just beautiful.

35

"Did you ever think of me?"

It was the third time in three months Kathy Jackson had made the trip to Auburn to see CJ. The first with his mother; the next two times by herself on a different Saturday than his mother visited. Kathy did this because she felt CJ would enjoy more companionship and because she realized she loved him.

"No," CJ answered quickly, then on reflection added, "I didn't mean it that way. You were a luxury I could not afford in here."

Kathy didn't know whether to be flattered or hurt. He saw her puzzled look and continued.

"This place requires a lot of focus, a lot of discipline. You can't be soft here; you can't let your guard down. Five years ago being soft would have got me killed. Now, seeing you here, like this, I will take more moments of luxury. If that's OK with you?"

"It will please me very much that you will have me in your thoughts."

36

It was Curtis Strong Jr.'s graduation day. Louise Strong and Kathy Jackson arrived dressed for a big event. Mr. James Ford, an educational administrator and mentor to CJ, sat with Mrs. Strong. On an otherwise perfect summer day, an ideal one for a graduation ceremony, there were others in attendance: the warden, three prison guards, four other prisoners, and their families. The ceremony took place in the prison yard at 3 p.m. There was a dais and several rows of chairs.

It was for James Ford, a retired NYPD detective and administrator of the Cornell Prison Education Program, a day of fulfillment. As a New York City police officer and detective for twenty-eight years, he had arrested and helped send more than two hundred criminals to Auburn Prison. Of the eighteen hundred prisoners there, over nine hundred were from New York City, with most serving terms for murder. Towards the end of his police career, Ford believed there had to be a better way of dealing with crime. He saw the life of a criminal as a revolving door through the justice system.

Ford heard of a program at Auburn attempting education and rehabilitation for prisoners. It was a degree program taught by faculty from Cornell and Cayuga Community College. While the program had the cache of a Cornell degree, no funds came from the State. Both schools along with Sunshine Lady Foundation head

Doris Buffett, the billionaire Warren Buffett's sister, fund the education of the prisoners.

At fifty-two, single and itching for a new challenge, Ford retired, moved to Auburn, New York, and joined the program as its director volunteering to also teach a course on writing.

This day was part of a continuing celebration of life for Ford with special emphasis on "this day." Ford took great interest in the educational development of one particular prisoner: Curtis Strong Jr. Ford found Strong to be the model of a man, not just a prisoner. For his degree Strong matriculated a perfect 4.0 grade point average. He helped Ford research discussion topics, occasionally conducting a class as a teaching assistant might do with a professor. CJ's other activities on "campus" included guiding other student inmates in course selection, leading study teams and coaching on creative writing.

Beyond the education, beyond the good prisoner, Ford saw a good man. When Ford and Strong talked of guilt and innocence, main themes of Ford's writing project course, Ford found an innocent man. There had to be evidence, some trial evidence that could prove what Strong was telling him, that he merely tried to help a fellow human being and was being held in prison for his deed.

PART

3

37

The phone rang on the desk of Vito Boriello, Detective Lieutenant, and Stamford Police Homicide unit. "Boriello," he said picking up the receiver.

"Lieutenant Vito Boriello," the voice emphasized the Vito.

"Yes, speaking."

"Lieutenant, my name is James Ford. I work with inmates at Auburn Correctional Facility," Ford said, getting to the point of the call: "Our tasks deal with the education of the inmates. The Writing Project is one of those tasks, and out of this workshop, I have come across a very interesting story, one I think you'll be interested in," Ford concluded.

Boriello rolled his eyes upward. He had a great growth between his neck and his knees; a huge, hard gut. He rubbed it, trying to calm the ache in it. "Yes, and how may I help you?"

"I'd like to meet with you to share this story; it's from a young inmate who comes from Stamford," Ford said.

"To what end, Mr. Ford?" Boriello asked as he thought about how he would spend his last thirty days on duty before retirement. And, it did not include reading another, "I-didn't-do-it letter."

Before Ford could answer, Boriello added, "Can I ask his name?"

"Curtis Strong. Curtis Strong Jr," Ford replied. "Lieutenant, I think we can both help each other. Being a former homicide detective myself, I can assure you, you will find this story highly interesting. In fact I guarantee it will move you…to act."

"I hate to discourage you, Mr. Ford, but I have a case load…" Boriello was stopped in mid excuse.

"Lieutenant, I'm sure, since you'll be retiring in a month, the case load may permit at least one discussion," Ford said.

Boriello bristled at first, but then was intrigued how he knew his personal circumstance.

"Your place or mine?" Boriello relented, more interested in meeting someone this thorough than in his writing project.

"Thanks, Lieutenant, I'll come there. How's a week from today sound, say 1 p.m.?

The meeting set, Boriello left the calendar open that afternoon. In preparation he ordered up all the files on Curtis Strong.

Curtis Strong, eighteen-year-old black man from Stamford's Waterside section, had stabbed a man to death in an apparent robbery on Stamford's west side. The name rang a bell with Boriello even though the crime occurred more than six years ago. The case was plain vanilla—eye witness identified Strong, thumb print was on the knife, victim's blood was on a sneaker found in his closet, a footprint from that pair of sneakers was found at the scene of the crime. Strong's defense: he was passing by and heard someone moaning and went to his aid. Claimed he saw someone running away. Trial lasted a week, defense attorney from a high-priced firm. District Attorney tried a plea since Strong was a first-time offender, and his victim was a known drug dealer. Arresting officer John Walsh's notes indicate they thought it was a drug buy gone wrong, and Strong got greedy for drugs and money. The plea offer was manslaughter in the second degree, fifteen years to life and allocution to the crime. Strong refused to allocute. Trial portion lasted three days, jury verdict took six days. Sentence: twenty-five years to life.

Boriello was making notes as he read:

-First-time offender

-High-priced attorney. Poor black kid. Why? Who paid?

-No allocution for ten years off. Dead to right on evidence

-Six days for verdict? On a three-day trial?

-The reviewing police lieutenant made a footnote: Strong's father shot and killed by Stamford patrolman.

James Ford was a tall imposing figure, not at all who Boriello envisioned from his calm manner on the phone. They shook hands in the lobby of police headquarters as Boriello escorted Ford to his office.

"I'm thankful you are taking this time, Lieutenant," Ford added once they reached Boriello's office, which was one of five offices along a rear wall. The offices were all enclosed by glass with blinds that could be dropped for privacy.

"Sure, Mr. Ford," Boriello said. "Did you come down this morning?"

"Yes, I drove, just got here. And please, call me Jim."

"OK, Jim, and I'm Vito," Boriello replied in kind. "Then you must be hungry. Let's go get a bite and we can talk. I left plenty of time," then second-guessing himself, "unless you've got a time issue and need to get back on the road."

"Lunch sounds great, Vito. I'm betting the story interests you, so I made reservations to stay over before driving back tomorrow," Ford replied

Boriello did the eye roll, this time noticed by Ford, "I can't wait."

Over a couple of beers and pizza in a large booth at the Colony, a bar/restaurant, with bar being the operative word, they began their discussion. The Colony was close to the police headquarters building and was a favorite lunchtime and after-work hangout for police officers. During lunch Ford and Boriello discussed their careers and some of the major crimes they solved. They laughed over one case they both remembered—that of a bank robber in New York City who handed a note to the teller that was the back side of his business card.

"I'm taking a liking to you, Jim," Boriello said. "I hope you do have something on Curtis Strong. I did a little research so I'm up to speed."

"I knew you would do your homework," Ford smiled.

"By the way, before we talk about Strong, let's discuss this knowledge you have about me," Boriello smiled. "What gives?"

"Oh that, I didn't tell you, but your Chief, John Brennan, he was my mentor when I was a rookie out of the police academy in the city. We've stayed in touch since then."

Boriello smiled, "That son of a bitch. Why didn't he give me a heads-up?"

"He told me you've been looking forward to retirement, but that you were the best he had and may be able to find some time for me," Ford answered.

"Well, only because it's you, Jim, not because of him," Boriello concluded laughing.

Boriello went inside of himself for a split second—the ability to read the tangents was something he prided himself on. Here was a gift right in front of him, and he missed it.

"That's a gotcha for you, Jim; once you mentioned the city and you knew some personal things about me, I should have figured it was Brennan. Well, let's head back to the office and get to talking about Strong, and I'll see if I can get the antenna back up before I fold my tent."

Once back in Boriello's office, Ford plopped down. "Damn, that pizza was good, but two beers at lunch. Now I need a nap."

Boriello laughed with Ford, and added, "But before the nap, let's hear your story."

"First off, Vito, The Writing Project is a course in writing, ethics and confession."

Boriello couldn't resist, "Bet you get a lot of honest answers there?"

"Sometimes. In fact, more often than you would think. This is one of them." Ford continued, "The Project results in a final paper at the end of six weeks of classes. We have the inmates work on their writing skills, no matter the level of them, and you wouldn't believe grown men in their thirties or so writing at a second grade level. We also have them focused on ethical issues: truth, honesty, and trust. The final couple of weeks we want them dealing with what got them incarcerated, so we talk about the importance of guilt and confession. Accepting what has been done; acknowledging responsibility for it is very important.

"A lot of DAs would be interested in that," Boriello interjected.

"We don't entirely expect that they will confess what they did; what we see mostly are short works of fiction where the antagonist takes the blame, you know, admits guilt for what he has done. The story becomes a metaphor for their lives, for self-confession," Ford looked at Boriello, his eyes seeking.

"I get it. And this stuff works?" Boriello asked.

"We hope. We're trying to see if there's a correlation between hostility in the inmates who don't participate in the program and those who do. Most of our boys aren't going anywhere for a long time, if at all. We need them to play nice while there at Auburn."

"So here's Mr. Strong's story. While you're reading it, I'll go say hi to Chief Brennan if you point me in the right direction," Ford said rising, handing Boriello the stapled paper.

"OK, go across and out the door, take a right and he's down the hallway on the left. You want me to call and see if he's got some time."

"No thanks, Vito, I told him I was meeting with you today and said I'd stop by to say hello. I'll be right back."

With that Ford left and Boriello began reading. The story had about eight typewritten pages. Strong used it as a summary of his life, who he was and how he came to be at Auburn. Family unit consisted of father, mother, and CJ Jr. Father was killed by Stamford patrolman John Walsh. Strong pointed out, the same John Walsh who supervised the arresting officers and presented evidence against him on the stand during his trial for the murder of Augusto Santos, a Guatemalan drug dealer. He stressed he did not do it, that he heard someone moaning in the alley and saw a person run off as he approached. He tried helping the man, who had a knife sticking out of the middle of his chest. He didn't touch the knife because he did not know whether that would hurt the man worse than he was already hurt. He heard evidence that there was a thumbprint on the knife; whosever it was, it was not his. Maybe if there was a thumbprint it belonged to the real killer. Strong said he heard all of the evidence against him; if he was guilty and knowing that, why wouldn't he take a plea and save himself ten years. Simply because he did not do it. Since he had been at Auburn, Strong stated he earned a college degree. He has never been punished at Auburn as he leads a disciplined life, doing his work at the prison, sports, and working out and educating himself for when he is ultimately vindicated. He knows this will happen he says; he just doesn't know when. He stated he had never been in trouble before or since. As further proof, he said the jury was somehow pushed to this verdict when they did not seem inclined. He said the jury foreman, twice, had sent a note to the judge that they were deadlocked and could not reach a verdict, but both times the judge ordered them to work some more. He felt there was something else behind the scenes he could not see—he wrote that he thought it had to do with this Police Officer John Walsh. Boriello paused here thinking about Walsh for a minute—good cop, rose quickly, lots of arrests, made sergeant, on the strength of his investigations and convictions. And it was this last thing that obviously Jim Ford wanted Boriello's help on: he had recently learned who the dark figure in the night was that killed the Guatemalan. He could not say, would not say, as he had his reasons, but the police should relook at all the evidence. He said they may or may not find the killer, but they would certainly find that he did not kill anyone.

Boriello said this outloud to himself, "What the hell kind of bullshit is this," and at that moment Jim Ford reentered the office.

"Chief said to say hello," said Ford.

"He could get off his fat ass and come and say it in person," Boriello said ruffled, "Say, Jim, what gives here. I see nothing other than creative writing 101."

"Except…" said Ford.

"What, except now he knows who did it and won't say. Is this a riddle? I know and I'm not telling," Boriello went on mockingly, "You cops figure it out, and if you do I get out." Well, Curtis my boy, if we don't figure it out you stay in the slammer for the next twenty years or so."

"The "except" thing is what I want to talk with you about," Ford said. "I got to know Curtis over the period of the program, took an interest in him, you might say. Not too many guys have I ever questioned why they are there. Him I do. I went through his background over the last five and a half years. He's an honorable man, done lots of good things at Auburn. He's helped a lot of inmates much older than him come to grips with some pretty awful things in their lives. He's a peacemaker—any time there is trouble, he's never in it but always will step forward to help calm things down. Saved a guard's ass when one inmate put a knife to his throat, talked the guy down. Participates in everything offered to him that will help him grow. He's also strong as an ox. He's put on sixty pounds since he came to Auburn and not an ounce of it is fat. Even got a degree while there."

"And?" Boriello, wasn't convinced of anything.

"And I talked to him about his story several times. Not a fact, not a word, nothing has changed from what he wrote. In fact I now believe every single thing he has said. My request is twofold. Believe along with me—and investigate this story as if it is fact, find the discrepancies and where the fault lines are," Ford said.

"That's asking a lot, Jimbo," Boriello said seriously, "My retirement will not be put off."

"Fair enough. But, most of the facts he writes about should be fairly easy to prove or disprove. Although I would like to hear from one of the jurors just what went on in that jury room."

"I'll help you, but this is almost six years old. We need to talk with a few people who may or may not be around anymore. I do have a number of my own questions already," Boriello said.

"Mind sharing them with me," Ford asked.

"No. I'll share," and they talked about Strong's first offender status, the high priced lawyer and a poor black kid and who pays, not allocuting for a ten-year reduction, "Hell," he stopped, "with that evidence you and I would have taken the plea." He continued with his own concerns about the length of time the verdict took, if the evidence was so clear. He confirmed to Ford that yes, it was Detective Walsh who had shot and killed Strong's father. "I've also now got the files and facts on the father's shooting. Sketchy, shouldn't have happened."

"Just that last item alone has got to make you a little skeptical," Ford said with a deep tone in his voice as his head shook from side to side.

Boriello, head down, confessed trouble with that also, "I'm not saying it was wrong, just needs more looking into. We have a number of multi-generational criminals around town."

"Well, then," Ford began, "should I leave you for now to do some sleuthing and come back in the morning?"

"Nice try, Detective," Boriello said as he picked up the phone and dialed as Ford looked on. "Honey, I'm bringing a guest home for dinner, work, and a sleepover. Can you arrange everything there?" he said with a wink to Ford, "Good, thanks. We'll be home around six."

"I don't want to impose," Ford begged.

"Man doesn't want to impose, does he. And me with thirty days to retirement. Well Mr. Ford you just got yourself a partner, but only for a month. We're on the clock now."

Boriello's home was less than half a mile from police headquarters. Ford had the feeling that Boriello's whole life didn't stray more than a half mile from headquarters. He had found himself a good cop to help investigate the truth in Curtis Strong's story.

Rosa Boriello still had the accent her parents brought with them from Verona, Italy. And Ford found out she had the incredible Italian skill of preparing food as if from heaven. That night at Boriello's home the two used the den that Boriello had turned into a home office, desks with two computers, chalkboard, printer/copier, and phones.

At the end of the night, both having reviewed the Stamford Police Department's reports on Strong senior's shooting and Strong junior's arrest and prosecution, along with Strong junior's file from Auburn, the two detectives came up with a checklist of to dos, split them up, and agreed to talk in one week:

-Vito's to dos:

Thumb print—analysis not in file; go to forensics and confirm

Juror—get names and addresses, contact at least two, ask about the process and the judge's push back

Judge Mortensen?

Defense Lawyer—talk with: who hired, who paid, why?

First time offender—school counselor, teacher, mother: what kind of kid was he

Who was Augusto Santos, dealer, up the line, priors?

John Walsh—father and son? Talk with Walsh's supervisors.

Jim's to dos:

Talk with Strong; he must tell who committed murder, otherwise he'll never be free—police need more than "I know but can't or won't tell"

If he was helping Santos, why did he run off, not in his story or police evidence

Talk with Strong cellmates—has he ever said he knew who did it

Find out who visited or wrote to Strong in two months prior to his writing the story down

38

They were all there, all except the current Democratic senator from Connecticut, Richard Blumenthal. He had not been invited.

On this night with the sun setting over Barnes' private beach in back of the house they call "Apple Manor," Barnes would surprise his guests, and shock some, by announcing that he would run for the US senate in the Democratic primaries. His good friend Senator Joe Lieberman had given every indication that he would run for the seat he had held for over thirty years, but then decided to drop out.

Barnes was very good at politics; after all it was through his other good friend former Senator Chris Dodd, who chose Hollywood over Washington, sensing he would have been defeated, that Barnes began courting powerful politicians that could help his firm. Dodd received substantial contributions for his reelection campaigns from Barnes, and he won new building projects for the banks that were building trading floors and new operations in Stamford, CT. In fact, Barnes Construction had won every major bank building project since banks began exiting New York City in the late nineties.

Bankers knew of the relationship between the Democratic senator, who happened to be Chairman of the Senate Banking Committee and Barnes, something that Barnes was not shy about sharing as he discussed new projects. Barnes had an uncanny knack for getting involved early and often with all parties to the process of attracting and outfitting new businesses coming to Connecticut.

But now Joe Lieberman was hanging it up, and Barnes felt the country had had enough of politicians like Dodd. After all it was on Dodd's watch the great recession began while he moved his family to Iowa to run in the Iowa caucuses for President of the US against Barrack Obama and Hillary Clinton. If that wasn't enough to turn the tide against him, he was also receiving subprime loans on his property thru the VIP program being operated by Angelo Mozzillo, CEO of Countrywide Mortgages and one of the instigators of the country's financial meltdown.

On this night Jonathan Barnes would propose a bold new future for America; one that would right the wrongs of excessive greed and put the crooks in jail. His main opponent for the Democratic nomination would be the state's Attorney General, Michael Samuels. Samuels had been deputy AG under Richard Blumenthal. It was Richard Blumenthal, who the prior year had run for and won Dodd's seat. And it was Blumenthal who had endorsed Samuels for the Lieberman seat. Between Blumenthal and Samuels, it looked to Barnes like they were trying to keep the two seats in the Temple.

However, Barnes had a silver bullet for him. It wasn't two months before that an ex-US Congressman from Connecticut, at a party right here in Barnes home had shared that the announced candidacy of Samuels was doomed for failure.

"Why?" Barnes asked, while standing in a circle of six men, enjoying after-dinner conversation.

"Well, Jonathan, it's like this. Louis Samuels is a decent guy, but he fancies himself a war hero," Harold Andrews offered up.

"Wait a minute, you're getting him confused with Blumenthal," Barnes said.

One of the other guests, a hedge fund manager named Barry Cohen, jumped in, "Congressman, what are you talking about? He is a Marine and served in Vietnam. I heard him say it myself."

"Well, he is and he isn't," the ex-Congressman, coyly offered. "You see, he is in the Marine reserves but never served on active duty."

Another guest, Mike Slade, the editor of the local paper, joined in, "I think you have it wrong Congressman. This is Richard Blumenthal you're thinking about."

"Listen to me boys," Harold Andrews said. "He is a clone of Blumenthal. A clone so closely developed he even has the same weaknesses as Richard."

"I've also heard him say in speeches that when he returned from Vietnam he was spit on. He is a very strong backer of Veterans, Congressman. I'd be careful about spreading this stuff around about him," Barry Cohen said.

"Are we all going crazy? The things we're attributing to Samuels are the issues everyone had with Blumenthal. Right?" asked Barnes.

The ex-Congressman at this point was a little embarrassed by the hostility towards him. "I bring this up in our conversation because lately, since he announced he was running for Lieberman's seat, I am hearing more and more of the war hero stuff. And frankly, Louis is a friend of mine. I like the guy even though we're from different political worlds. I would never say anything against him unless I knew it to be true. What you gentlemen have just confirmed are the exact lies that are going to come out. He never served in Vietnam and, therefore, was never spit upon when he returned. Maybe the tobacco industry might have spit on him." The six men shared a laugh since as the Assistant AG he had pushed Blumenthal's agenda and brought a successful suit against the tobacco industry.

"Let me just finish this," the ex-Congressman continued, "and it's going to vetted, that Louis only joined the Marines after all other options ran out before he was drafted, exactly the same as Richard. He had at least five deferments at the height of the Vietnam War. When his selective service number, after his last deferment, showed he was likely to be drafted into the Army, Richard joined the Marine Reserves in DC, and so did Louis, in a unit that was almost assured of never seeing active duty in Nam. They spent their active duty weekends running toys for tots programs. All I'm trying to do is put the truth out there early before anyone goes too far supporting him. When this comes out, he's unelectable."

"That's what they said about Richard Blumenthal when all this Marine stuff came out about him. Congressman, I find the whole subject rather unnerving. Could we end the discussion with the agreement it will not be any of us who will spill these beans and keep these stories going? That strategy did not work for the Republicans against Richard, and it won't work for us against Louis Samuels in the primaries." Jonathan Barnes uprightly concluded.

The ex-Congressman smiled and said, "Agreed."

The others all said "agreed."

Later that particular night Jonathan Barnes pulled the local newspaper editor Mike Slade aside. "Mike, what do you know about this stuff on Samuels?"

"First I've heard of it, Jonathan," he said to his longtime patron. It was Jonathan Barnes who saw to it that Mike Slade got the post of editor when it opened up. Barnes had been overwhelmingly delighted by an in-depth story that Slade did on the construction industry in Connecticut, particularly the building of the new Stamford and specifically on the design and quality of the buildings being built by Barnes Construction."

"Mike, I need you to get to the bottom of this. Give it everything you've got," and Barnes added, "You know that conversation you keep having with me, telling me to run for the Senate? Well this may be the exact opportunity to run. There is no Republican candidate that can beat us, certainly not the wrestling babe. If this is true about Samuels, then the field is wide open on our side. I might be wrong, but I don't think the voters will stand for two fake war heroes in a row. It's our chance."

"I agree. This is great news," Slade said enthusiastically.

"Not a word, Mike. Not a single word. If all of what the Congressman said is true, I just might do it. But first I need confirmation. I need you to research this personally, no one else. Understood?" Barnes ordered.

"Understood," Slade accepted.

Two weeks later Barnes began planning his campaign as Mike Slade confirmed everything the Congressman had said.

In the six weeks prior to this night's party, Barnes billed the evening as a "discussion about the future of Connecticut."

"Who else to lead the discussion," Slade encouraged Barnes in the days leading up to this evening as he camped out at Barnes residence planning the announcement.

And they were all there. Everyone who could help Barnes win the party nomination and the general election in the fall, and some who could help him lose it.

Before the evening began, Jonathan went to Parker's suite in the gate house, where Parker stayed when not in his apartment in the city. Barnes Sr. didn't knock on entering and went up to his son, who rose and not more than one foot, nose to nose, told Parker, "From this point on in our lives, your behavior is going to be different. I'm taking a considerable risk running for senate, which will be announced tonight. I do not need any more issues from your life interfering with my life. Is that understood?"

As happened in most conversations between the two Barnes males, it was one way, directed from father to son. Yes, there were good reasons for Jonathan Barnes' concern for his son's behavior. Word getting out that the younger Barnes had a significant substance abuse problem would not help a run for the senate. However, Parker Barnes was blind to his father's concern. His whole life had been lived in the intimidating shadow of the man that Parker had increasingly grown to hate.

"Is that understood?" Barnes senior repeated.

"Yes, sir," the cowered Parker replied.

Those that could help him win were the local politicians and state representatives: two US Congressmen, and the mayors of the six largest cities in Connecticut. Also present were the moneyed class: the hedge fund owners who would centralize their hundreds of thousands of dollars behind the campaign of those who would help them avoid financial regulation; the bankers were there still as cheap as ever, contributing their meager thousands, but expecting exceptions from the Congress for their trading operations that had become huge profit centers. There were the investment fund leaders who contributed heavily, selfishly, to the one or two individuals in the state government who directed state workers and teachers' retirement funds their way.

Then there were other scammers, less respectable, but no less sinister: the jewelry dealer seeking big ticket buyers, the Broadway star from Greenwich with the fading light looking for support through theater owners friendly with Barnes. Paulo Cartino, president of his own line of women's wear, came with his top designer, Santa Alba. Cartino, a Connecticut resident, was a reasonably large contributor to political causes. Santa Alba was designing a new branded line of ladies casual wear. While all the men would talk politics, the retailer and his designer would share with the women guests their new ideas and seek financial backers.

Also looming at the far end of the semicircular balcony, richly dressed but looking awkward was the squat figure of Juan "Chunk" DeLuna, businessman by day, a villain in a tux by night.

How was it possible that the molester of Cuomo from so long ago could possibly end up on this night in the same house as the molestee, one beauty queen of Coamo?

DeLuna, the businessman, was here doing relationship building as he continued to stretch his drug-funded cement business empire further north. DeLuna now with a decent grasp of business had been importing Brazilian cement to the US for the past few years. But it was not until he got two large contracts with Barnes Construction that he established himself as a player.

DeLuna was one of thirty Barnes subcontracting companies, whose leaders were invited to Jonathan Barnes home for the evening. Hors d'oeuvres were served outside on the balcony over-looking Long Island Sound; at dinner guests were seated in the cavernous dining hall with a fireplace at one end that ten men standing tall could fit in. After dinner the invitation tucked in Chunk's ill-fitting uniform informed the guests there would be a discussion on the future of Connecticut in the south salon.

216

And there was Senor DeLuna's arm candy, a beauty queen in her own right, but not from Coamo. Many miles, many years and many bodies later, DeLuna had himself a tall slender, exotic beauty from Recife, Brazil. Lupe Montserrat had grown into an attractive woman who knew how to wear a backless, clingy evening gown.

In a room of one hundred people, beautiful women always spot beautiful women. DeLuna's woman and the beauty queen of San Blas spotted each other after dinner in the south salon. Their eyes then went to see who the other had snagged. The Brazilian beauty saw the tall thin designer and thought well of her opponent. Santa Alba could not see a man beside this other lady, then the crowd moved and she spied the short squat Chunk DeLuna. "She has a penguin," Alba thought of the man in the tight tux. Alba thought she saw something else, something familiar, but she shook it off. There was nothing familiar in that little man.

Jonathan Barnes now rose to a lectern as everyone gathered round: the glitterati of the state, the corporate titans, and the financial buzzards with their wives, who to a woman were largely unaware they were married to scoundrels. He began:

"Ladies and gentlemen, thank you so much for coming tonight. And what a beautiful night." And the gathered applauded.

He continued, "I have reached that age when I understand if we could only be born at seventy and gradually approach eighteen, life would be much more informed and happier." And the gathered laughed, heartily with Barnes who led the laughter. "Since that is not to be and still concerned about my immortal soul, I made a deal with God some years ago. I am not a politician and shall always try to do right if God will not make me one." And the laughter erupted again, bringing some to an awareness of a side of Jonathan they had not seen before. Really, a side of Mark Twain they hadn't seen before.

"Tonight, my friends, I want to share with you a vision I have for our country and for our great state of Connecticut. We are living through one of the great periods in the history of the world, and we live in the greatest country in the history of the world. It is because of America and Americans whose compassion for their fellow man knows no bounds that the world did not slip back into the dark ages. We have been through much in less than 250 years as a nation. We have overcome much. We have helped the world overcome much. And yet here we are, just a decade and a half into the twenty-first century and everything seems to be unraveling.

I want to talk about some of these things that are causing this unraveling, and I do not use the word lightly:

"First, the nation is just emerging from the deepest depression since 1929. Yes, depression. The academy called it a recession, the politicians fearing they may be tainted since it happened on their watch called it a recession, and the housing and financial cabal that help orchestrate it called it a recession."

At this point a number of bankers in the audience glanced at one another wondering where Barnes was going with this.

"But I've talked with Americans, and what I hear them saying is that it was a depression—they've lost their jobs that have been outsourced to India and China or their companies have been taken over by private equity firms who stripped their companies bare and put them into bankruptcy and put the profits in their pockets."

Now Barnes had succeeded in making the hedge fund guys a little queasy, dredging up one of their profitable tactics.

"These Americans, citizens of Connecticut, aren't asking for the handouts that Wall Street wants; they don't want to be bailed out, all they want is to work."

There was some applause at this point from a number of the local politicians who had been watching tax revenues dry up with the drop in private sector jobs. The Mayor of Bridgeport, a stocky Latino, whispered to the Mayor of Hartford standing next to him, "Does this sound like a political speech." The tall thin, slightly balding but youthful mayor of the state capital replied, "I think his deal with God is coming undone." And they shared a quiet snicker.

"The engine of enterprise is being led by a greedy group of people who really think they are *earning* all this money they are taking from their firms. They're not; they're stealing from the stockholders, the employees and the citizens of our country. How do

I know this, because Steven Schwartzman is not worth his pay of one billion dollars in one year; because the financial industry is raping and pillaging the life savings and stock holding of most Americans. The average investor is just trying to do good research in quality companies, make an investment and hope the company invested in does well so that when they retire they'll have a nice nest egg." Here Barnes paused, looked out over the audience and roared: "Well, I've got news for them. You're dreaming. Everything is stacked against you. The banks, hedge funds and trading houses are betting against you; they're shorting your stocks, they're naked shorting them, they buy for their own accounts before they execute your orders and stocks they recommend to you. Why, these same people are selling them behind your backs. They're betting against you. So our citizens think it's them and the company they invested in. It's not. There's this giant middle man taking his cut of every penny he can get his hand on."

The bankers and hedge funds leaders in the room were quite uncomfortable at this point. They were visibly moving in place.

"And the politicians are no better." And they began squirming wondering what was coming next from Barnes.

"These politicians fill their coffers with special interest money and call focus groups together from the financial industry whenever they're proposing new legislation to get their input. Not to write good laws and regulations but to ensure they do not make their donors unhappy." There was an audible sigh arising. "Now," and he looked into the faces of his banker friends, "I'm just using the financial industry as an example of one of the things wrong with the country. There's too much money in the system corrupting it. From the owners to the politicians, it is infecting everything we're doing. It has to stop. Just look at the financial meltdown. The whole food chain—from the individual expecting they could buy a house with no money down, no credit and no way to pay for it, to the mortgage broker or lending banker with little due diligence on the borrower's ability to repay, to Fanny and Freddie who backed those loans, to the bankers who packaged them and sliced and diced them into derivatives that are worthless, and to the insurance companies that insured the worthless derivatives. And did I hear the head of Goldman Sachs, Lloyd Blankfein, say that he is doing God's work? I did. It's corrupt. He's corrupt if he thinks for one minute we're buying that. We need to overhaul pay practices, lending and financial regulations, and need better ethical standards.

"This cannot be done by those who created it. We need new leadership in all the too-big-to-fail institutions, whether they're banks, insurance companies, home builders, or auto companies. If you are part of the problem today, you cannot stay at the top and fix it, you're too invested in the old ways of doing things. This goes for Washington too. The people in place today, the ones responsible for oversight need to leave. "And this is tough for me to say, but my good friend, Chris Dodd, should have retired a lot sooner than a few years ago."

Shock, set in. Among politicians there they all knew of the friendship of the two men. The bankers who had been so cozy with Dodd disagreed, their heads shaking "No."

"Thirty-seven years of public service was pretty good. Chris had done a lot for our state and our country, but it is going to take a new breed of men and women in Congress to bring about the changes needed. Richard Blumenthal may think being a hero is about hosting a children's toy party; it's not. And now we have Louis Samuels, some call him 'son of Blumenthal,' who closely resembles the same ethical lapses that Richard stands for.

"And speaking of doing a lot for our country, it is the men and women of our Armed Services who are doing a lot for our country. But we now have two wars going at once. President Obama will tell you the wars in Iraq and Afghanistan are over. They are not. We began the war in Afghanistan to avenge nine eleven and the murder of thirty-five hundred Americans in those four savage attacks. But we are now at the point between Iraq and Afghanistan that we have lost more American soldiers than we lost citizens on nine eleven, and now ISIS or ISIL. George Bush was wrong when he started the Iraq war. Barrack Obama was wrong when he expanded the Afghanistan war. What will Obama be asking us to ante up to fight ISIS?"

Applause broke out. "What is this all about?" "Where did this large canvas that Jonathan Barnes was painting on come from?" "How will this night end?" These were the thoughts of the guests listening to this stem-winding speech by Barnes.

"Another area as citizens we need to be concerned about are our rights. Our rights," he bellowed. "Not the rights of terrorists. The current administration, God love them, wants to Mirandize terrorists. Why, so they can't help us catch their buddies. They want to give them fair trials under American laws and institutions that they only want to destroy. And now this administration, that many of us were so fervent about only a few years ago, now this administration wants to sue Arizona for trying to protect its borders. This administration that was pledged to resolving, fairly, the immigration issue has lost its way. There are millions of mostly Latino families living peacefully in the United States doing meaningful work, and now there is a call in Congress to ship them all back to Mexico, Guatemala or Venezuela. That is definitely not the answer. America is large enough for all of them and more. We have always been a nation of immigrants, it is our life blood, and it is who we are."

More loud applause. The Mayor of Bridgeport said to the Mayor of Hartford, "I like where this going. I think I have someone to vote for." The Hartford Mayor, his son serving in Afghanistan, smiled politely, "Maybe."

"Finally,"

"Thank God," said Chunk DeLuna, his tux now starting to choke his bulky little body, "what a windbag."

"Finally, our country, our state, and our cities need to exercise fiscal restraint. We are a nation of debtors. If we do not want to become a nation of paupers, we need to act now. American supremacy is not a given. Greece, Rome, England, Holland, Spain, and France once all led the world. There are many nations with controllable labor costs and balanced budgets that want to supplant the US as world leaders. Most economists say they will. Brazil, India, Russia, and China, the so called BRICs, are all lining up for world leadership. It's inevitable, they say. Not me. American supremacy is a given, and it's a given based on the goodness of our nation, its guarantees of freedom, and its love of liberty. But some work needs to be done. And this is why I called us all together tonight.

We need to work together, all of us. I see seven key things that need to be done to keep America and our state great. I put them on this small card being handed out to you now."

On cue, the waiters and waitresses walked among the gathered and handed the cards out. From one group, a loud burst of applause came. This area was mostly family and friends. As the others turned the cards over, they saw emblazoned the slogan "Barnes or Bust" and beneath it "Vote for Jonathan Y. Barnes for United States Senate."

And the applause grew wider as the rest of the audience looked up and saw their friend and associate declaring his candidacy for United States Senator from Connecticut.

"Thank you, I thought I would be subtle in declaring my candidacy since the issue is not about me, it's about getting America going now. And if you help me get elected I promise you two things: One, I won't stay long; I think it will take just one term to implement the imperatives I mentioned. I am just not willing to stand on the sidelines any longer. We must act now. Two, if we are fortunate to be elected to the United States Senate, I promise you will not have a missing voice in Washington. I will lead."

Barnes paused here as applause erupted. "Thank you for coming tonight."

There was more applause, louder now. Even some the bankers in the audience who had been criticized could feel the sincerity in Barnes.

Jonathan Barnes looked out on his audience. In all the talks he had given in his life, none was ever personal, none was never about him. He felt different; he felt his adrenaline pumping. He felt quite young at this moment.

"I need all of you with me; can I count on you?" he asked and they responded. To a person they clapped and hooted loudly for the declaration Jonathan Barnes was making. Barnes made his way down from the slightly raised podium and waded into his friends and associates.

It was a serious speech, narrow in scope, but important in the minds of almost everyone there. Everyone except Senor DeLuna who cynically ran out of the ability to pay attention halfway through and started playing around with the olive skin on the back of Lupe Montserrat.

Later that evening as couples discussed Barnes' talk and had drinks, a small combo played a mix of jazz and popular Broadway tunes at the rear of the room. Santa Alba and her boss/date, Paulo Cartino, passed by the Brazilian beauty and her friend.

Santa froze as she heard the words, "Hello, Santa Alba, from Coamo." She kept walking arm in arm with Cartino. To herself she screamed, "Please let it be my imagination."

The designer stopped, "Santa, he spoke to you. Do you know him?" he asked.

Santa's heart stopped. She tugged at Cartino's arm, "I do not, come on."

But the nightmare was real. She now knew who it was.

He called after her, "Santa, do you not recognize me?"

This time she turned. She looked at him. Oh, how is this possible—Chunk DeLuna.

"It's me, Chunk," he said in clear English.

The horror returned in an instant: Chunk crawling on top of her in the night; he put one strong little hand over her mouth as she slept next to his sister, Silvana. His other hand he put under her night gown, moving it up her leg. He was twelve then; she was thirteen. She bit his fingers and screamed. Silvana awoke, and Mr. DeLuna came running into the room.

Santa was young then. She should have kept the incident to herself. But she told people—her parents, her teachers, her friends. Chunk DeLuna became a pariah at twelve. Shortly after, his father took him to Brazil to live. Silvana was left in San Blas to be raised by her aunt. Santa, even at thirteen, by retelling the incident sullied her own reputation. At eighteen she was glad to be moving to New York to attend the Fashion Institute.

Santa and Silvana formed a pact after that night. Nothing would ever come between their friendship.

Santa's mind returned to reality: How in this entire world can this small beast be here, here at this beautiful party? She pulled Paulo's arm and walked away.

The young woman from Recife looked puzzled. "Do you know that girl?" she asked Chunk. "She seemed to recognize you, but she just walked away."

"She recognized me alright," he said.

"Why didn't she speak to you?" Lupe asked, followed by another question, "Who is she?"

"Let's just say an old friend from Puerto Rico," DeLuna replied. He then spotted one of Barnes' bankers, and DeLuna walked in his direction. Lupe looked over her shoulder towards Santa Alba as Chunk nudged her forward.

The other men here this night at Jonathan Barnes invitation were not as grotesque as DeLuna, but some were just as evil. Not the businessmen who created jobs, enabled meaningful lives, made products, and paid taxes. Not them, they weren't all good but most were. The evil lied in the non-productive set, the leeches, the skimmers, and the hangers on. Dressed in fine clothes, ladies in silk gowns, men in tuxedos, all sporting rich tans at the beginning of summer, they lived a life none of them knew in their families growing up. It was a life they would not relinquish under any circumstances. What they had was theirs; others would have to fend for themselves just as they had. Even now, survival was important, more important.

39

After Harvard Law, Gideon Bridge joined Bridge Law, run by his grandfather Roy Bridge. He spent his first two years litigating. By twenty-four he was supervising junior lawyers; at twenty-six he was managing a section and its P&L statement. When he turned twenty-seven, he was the firm's youngest partner. At least daily he and his grandfather discussed cases, what assignments should be made and what Gideon should be thinking of next. As the recession had ended, they talked of beefing up the mergers and acquisitions area.

Gideon Bridge knew corporate law but absorbed more of it daily. He spent prodigious amounts of time every month learning and staying current with new law that was constantly being made in the court rooms of the world. Corporate law was becoming boundaryless. Giant global companies were in every country in the world; precedents established in one country were quickly being adopted in other countries. He used his firm's electronic data bases and internet subscription services to research in depth the thinking behind landmark cases. He loved the law and his grandfather for mentoring him into it. It was not unusual for the older man and his grandson to fly to London to hear lectures on "the origins of English property law," which created the foundation for much of America's law on property rights. And when a prominent English executive got caught with his hand in the cookie jar, the two would occasionally drop in on a trial at the Old Bailey courthouse.

His spare time in his mid-twenties was devoted almost entirely to catching up with his Brunswick brothers after the lost year and half in Venezuela with his Mormon fling. More recently where he spent his time was shifting; a new interest had formed.

It began one winter night after a business dinner in lower Manhattan. As he walked into the bitter cold, a cold blown in by a west wind whipping off the Hudson River, a young homeless girl was begging outside the restaurant on Chambers Street. The temperature that day did not rise above twenty degrees, setting the stage for a ten-degree night.

Gideon reached in his pocket and pulled out some change, probably a dollar fifty in quarters. He placed them in the girl's outstretched hands. Hands he noticed that wore no gloves; hands that were, were...blue. He stopped and watched as the half-frozen girl tried to get her right hand to pick the quarters out of her left hand. After fumbling for a moment, she dropped three of them. Gideon stepped forward towards the girl, and she looked up. She could not have been more than seventeen. He bent down, picked the quarters up, and handed them to her again.

"Thanks," she said weakly.

Gideon took his wool lined leather gloves off and offered them to the girl. She eagerly grabbed them and tried pulling one on. She could not separate her fingers to push them into the finger holes. Gideon tried helping, and as he touched her small hands, they felt hard and cold, like they were dead.

"What's your name," he said to her.

"Anne," she replied with a half-smile.

"Do you live around here?"

"Over in Meatpacking, when I can find boxes."

Gideon cringed. "Anne, I think you have very bad frost bite on your hands. You need to get to a hospital."

"I'll be alright," and she rose from the steps she was sitting on. "Thanks for the gloves." And she walked off into the night.

Three nights later Gideon went to the Bowery Mission with ten pairs of gloves. The first time he came to the Bowery Mission he was more interested in knowing their needs at that point. The mission director, a small, thin Irish lady named Karen Kiernan, was profusely grateful. She explained the goals of the Bowery Mission, and while conceived in the great depression in the 1930s to care for souls who found themselves lost, homeless and near starvation as a result of the market crashes, one common denominator over the years was found among these souls: the tendency to turn to alcohol and, in the last twenty years, to drugs of any kind. Kiernan explained some of the drivers of these tendencies were now reversing the process; it was the drugs that were causing loss of jobs, resulting in homelessness.

Beginning every October Gideon regularly brought a bag of fur lined gloves, men's and women's, maybe fifty pair in all to the Mission. He does this throughout the winter every month up through March. He could not get the image of the frozen dead hand of Anne out of his mind.

Mrs. Kiernan was grateful for Bridge's donation, since gloves, something as simple as gloves, were one of the most important items the mission needed during winter months, and despite all the clothing donated to the mission, the one item donors did not seem to think about was gloves.

Having a benefactor like Bridge met some of the Mission's critical needs and helped to keep the operating budget whole. Some months he brought more gloves depending on needs expressed by Mrs. Kiernan.

By his second year of helping the Mission, Bridge was contributing in other ways. His personal donation had uplifted the budget by 25 percent, enough to allow the mission to bring back the part-time psychiatric counselor let go during the recession when donations nearly dried up. Bridge's donations were so significant that the budget prior to 2007 was almost completely restored.

Mrs. Kiernan convinced Bridge to come onto the board of the Mission with her. He was heartily welcomed by the other six members: two from Wall Street, one from the Media, one Congressman from the Mission's district, one retired police commissioner, and one Catholic auxiliary bishop.

In a very short time, Bridge took on other projects for the Mission: providing pro-bono legal representation to many formerly respectable men who had lost everything and gone astray into crimes like burglary, spousal abuse, if there was still a spouse to strike out at, and creating public disturbances.

A strong link existed between the Catholic Church and the Mission. Since its founding there had always been a priest, monsignor, or now, a bishop on the board. And for good reason, more than half of all needy men and women, since the mission started tracking demographic data, were of the Catholic religion.

In Gideon Bridge's third year helping the Mission and his first year on the board, in a quiet ceremony Mrs. Kiernan, Bishop John Foley and retired police commissioner William Flaherty presented to Gideon Bridge the "Heart of New York" award. No press covered this event; in fact, the other board members did not know it took place. Of the now eight board members, including Bridge, only the four of them knew of the award, except for the eight others who had received the same award over the past seventy years. And while there were no written criteria, the three permanent members currently charged with administering it, Kiernan, Foley and Flaherty, held individual giving from the heart as most important. Additionally, a personal revelation needed to take place to bring the individual to the Mission. In Bridge's case he related to Kiernan, when he first showed up at the door to help, the story of the homeless waif he gave his gloves to. And it was the searing reminder of the poor girl's condition that continued to drive Bridge's spirit, initiating his gloves program, his substantial personal giving to aid the Mission's needs, his coming onto the board on his own time, and representing the legal needs of the poor on his own and with his firm's resources. They saw Bridge as having a deep personal commitment to help his fellow man. Gideon Bridge did all that and asked nothing. In fact, his Brunswick brothers knew nothing of it.

Bishop Foley arranged for a private dinner in the rectory of St Patrick's Cathedral. Just the four individuals were to be at the dinner. The one requirement for this award was that the recipient be Catholic, which Bridge was, by birth, by sacraments, by way of the circuitous route from the Catholic faith to Mormonism and back again, even if not by consistent practice.

While Bridge was aware the board wanted to thank him, he was surprised by the location, that only three members of the board would be there, and that he was asked to say nothing of the event to anyone, board members or otherwise.

When he arrived at the rectory, he was ushered in by Bishop Foley to a private dining room that was set for five places. In short order he found out the fifth place was for Cardinal Patrick Quinn. Bridge was shocked, pleased to meet him, but wondered what was going on. This was more than the simple recognition Mrs. Kiernan had discussed.

To begin the dinner, it was not any of the board members who spoke but Cardinal Quinn.

"My new friend in Jesus, Gideon Bridge. Welcome. I'm afraid you have stumbled onto a most grateful organization charged by the Catholic Church to silently help the neediest among us, those who are in danger of losing their immortal souls," he paused. "Let us eat, thank Jesus for his sacrifice and yours, and after dinner we will talk more of your good work."

And they ate in the large room with candle sconces on the walls. In front of each guest at the round table was one round fat candle.

When dinner was over, the Cardinal stood, walked around the table, hugged each of the other three, and thanked them for their service to Christ and their fellow man.

Bridge was on edge now. This had the ring of ceremony about it. It was eerie for him, like something out of a medieval novel he had read. It was taking on a formality he was not comfortable with. He was not a practicing Catholic, and yet, he felt he was at the center of his religion this night. He no longer went to mass or received sacraments. Not that he was ever largely aware of all of the mysteries of the Catholic Church, he wasn't that interested. He believed in God, at least he had gotten that far. He wasn't sure if Christ was the Son of God, really, although he believed what Jesus Christ did, believed in the good way Christ lived his life as a model. And while Gideon Bridge led an alternative life style, complete with loving his fellow MAN, he believed fervently that Jesus Christ, man

Prophet or Son of God, changed the world forever by his teaching that every life was precious.

"Gideon," the Cardinal began, "we have asked you here tonight to thank you for the gift of love you so obviously have for your fellow man. And we want to thank you for all those needy men and women you have helped, that you will never meet, until you get to heaven."

The Cardinal's words echoed in the dim chamber and now he approached Gideon, hugged him. The Cardinal walked back to his place seating and picked up a small black box. He opened it and walked to Gideon.

Bridge looked at the box. It contained a gold ring. In the center of the ring as it widened was a cross. To the sides of the cross were four quadrants: two smaller and two larger. They had glass in them and beneath the glass was something beige.

The Cardinal lifted the ring out, and said, "Take this Gideon as a symbol of our love for you and our thanks to you. Wear it as a symbol of Christ's love for his fellow man."

Bridge stuck out his left hand; he put his ring finger forward. The Cardinal gestured to Bridges right hand which Gideon put forward as the Cardinal placed it on his finger. It slid on easily, a little snug at the knuckle, but an almost perfect fit. Mrs. Kiernan smiled at her good estimate at the Bridge ring size.

"Thank you, your Eminence," Gideon said, and turning to his fellow board members he said, "This is a little much."

"It is an early appreciation," Commissioner Flaherty said, "of all the good work you will do in your life. And he reached his right hand to shake Bridge's hand when Gideon noticed that the Commissioner had the same ring. As Mrs. Kiernan and Bishop Foley shook his hand, he noticed the same ring on their hands.

Gideon's suspicion of ceremony rang true. "Something else is going on here," he smiled seriously, "This ring, our ring, your presence Cardinal Quinn."

"Bishop Foley told me in addition to a good heart, you had a good brain. Capable of sniffing out a scheme, yes?"

Bridge smiled, he relaxed a bit, "Yes," he said.

"What we have done tonight," Cardinal Quinn said, "is welcome you into the Sacred Society of the Heart of Jesus Christ."

"But this is not," Bridge began protesting. Had he been allowed to finish he would have said, "Right. I'm Catholic in name only."

He was stopped at "Not."

"I'm aware you're not what we call a Sunday Catholic," the Cardinal went on. "That's good. Gideon, you practice Christ's teachings every day by the love you have shown for your most vulnerable fellow men and women."

"No, this is not right. I'll be a terrible representative of the Church. You'll be ridiculed for giving something like this to me," Bridge again protested, and he confessed, "I'm a sinner."

"Yes you are," Archbishop Foley said, "as is Mrs. Kiernan, Commissioner Flaherty, me, and even Cardinal Quinn, although maybe less so, Cardinal?"

"Not at all, John," Quinn laughed. "We all sin, each in our own way. These matters we can take up with God. He forgives us; He knows we sin. He loves us anyway. And while you sin, Gideon, the contradiction in your life, in all our lives, is that we act as Jesus instructed us. You reach out your hand to your fellow man knowing that he is sinning: taking drugs, drinking, stealing, and whatever else. It is why, in that ring, under that glass at the center is a relic of our church. A relic from the time Jesus walked on this earth. It is a fragment from the burial robe of Jesus."

Bridges eyes moistened; he no longer rejected this gift. His heart began to race at the same time his knees got weak. Cardinal Quinn walked over to him as he sobbed and put his arms around him.

40

Leonard Crane's office with the Brunswick Fund was at 515 Madison Ave. When he got the call from Alice Kraft, he suggested they meet in the coffee shop at the Roosevelt Hotel, about halfway between where she worked at Blackthorn Investments, a boutique investment bank, with offices in New York on Sixth Ave at 44th St. It was the "baby call" they had often joked about when they worked together at Blackthorn. If you ever get the "baby call," you drop everything and come as fast as you can since the baby's coming. In their language it meant there is something so hot it would be life changing.

When he put the receiver down, he was reaching for his suit coat. An administrative aid asked him a question as he passed her desk, and he put his hand out, palm facing up, accompanied by, "Hold it; I'll be back in one hour." The elevator cooperated by waiting on the 37th floor; he pushed the button and the door opened. He was out the front door less than one minute after he hung up. His pace down Madison shifted from a fast walk to running-for-the-train quick. He was there in less than ten minutes. Alice arrived at the first floor coffee shop during the eleventh minute.

He had seated himself at a small, round patio table, and when he saw her smiling face, he rose to greet her.

"Hi, I'm glad you called; I was beginning to miss you," he said

"Nice try, Lenny, but you will be glad I called," Alice said, managing a smile.

"What does nice try mean?" a puzzled Crane asked.

"There was nothing to miss. We worked together. We conspired together. We just never got to consummate the conspiracy…until now."

"The first baby call."

"And if things go right, the only one we will ever need," she finished.

Their stories were similar; they were cut from the same cloth. They had worked on trading desks in the same group for Blackthorn. The managing directors at Blackthorn protected their planned actions much more so than other firms with trading operations. Traders had little latitude but to execute as quickly as possible the tactics that their floor directors gave them.

Over drinks one night, many drinks, they drew up the baby call plan. If there was ever a piece of exceptional information that came across their desks before it went public and they could find a way to share it, execute on it independently and profit greatly, secretly then they would make the call. As long as they worked for Blackthorn that would not have been possible without bringing in yet another party on the outside. With Crane out on his own at Brunswick Fund, it could work. At his going away party, again over drinks, they toasted to the day the baby call would be made.

"So, what is it, Alice. What's so hot," Crane began.

"It's the biggest heads-up I have ever heard of and naturally can't act on it without someone else. One of our clients just got three spectacular orders from their customers. It will be out in three days, four at the most. Blackthorn has asked them to sit on it while they buy up every share they can," Kraft finished, taking a deep breath.

A waitress came over, and they held up their discussion to order coffees.

Once the waitress stepped away, Crane began again. "Who is it; what's the deal?"

"I need your help," she said

"I know that." Crane said thinking to himself, well yeah, baby call; of course you need my help. "How do you want me to help?"

"I want a significant consideration," Alice said

"Alice, it depends."

"Lenny, this is bigger than anything either of us has ever seen."

"What then."

"A considerable amount."

"What's considerable?" he continued parrying.

"Twenty-five percent of the profits."

"Ridiculous, we could never do that much," Lenny the Liar said truthfully.

"I have others I can go to. I came to you because you know how to do these things," Alice said in a way that let him feel in control.

"I can set up accounts for the transfer, Alice, but not that much."

"What will you offer me?" she said, a bit exasperated.

"Depends,' he added equally exasperated over the unknown.

"Damn it, Lenny, we don't have time for this. It is a scorcher and because of the industry trading, it will most likely not attract a lot of attention."

It got Crane thinking…could he put this together himself. Maybe. He knew Blackthorn's investment banking clients, he knew their industry expertise, and he knew most of the clients Alice worked with. It was obviously in the solar industry, her strength, but who.

"I'll talk to my partners. But you have to give me more than this."

"I thought you had control?" she asked somewhat surprised.

"I do."

"Then let's make the deal right here, right now!" she said raising her voice.

The waitress, paused, as she was about to put the coffees down, not wanting to interrupt. Alice pulled her hands, which had been flailing, back so she could place the cups down. She thanked her and the waitress left.

"Ten percent of the net," he said, overriding his deal-doing capabilities.

"It's worth more than that," Kraft insisted.

"How much do you figure I can buy?"

"Three to four million shares at ten."

"Ten." He had it; a solar stock that Blackthorn was heavy into had to be Rocket Solar. He had to stay focused.

"And what do you think it will go to?" he asked matter of factly.

"Twenty in two days, that's what your buddy Sid Rogers says."

"Sid's driving this?" Crane said. It was almost too good to be true. He could take the whole thing right out from underneath the bastard Rogers, the bastard that drove him out of Blackthorn.

"He and the client exec on the investment banking side, they're buying shares, lots."

So much for separation of church and state, Crane thought. It was one of the biggest lies on the street; that there was even the slightest separation of investment banking and research from the trading side of the house.

Alice decided to press the issue. "When you hear what's going down, you'll agree."

"I need the afternoon. By five I'll get back to you." Lenny lied. He needed every moment to drive this. While Alice saw this as her opportunity, it definitely was Lenny's chance to score very big.

Alice misread the stall, "OK, but here's what I want. At least 10 percent, plus one million. The one million must be deposited within four days in this Swiss account under the name Nora Hodge," and she handed him a piece of paper with the notation, "UBS account 19-24601."

"Who's Nora Hodge?" Lenny said, now humoring her.

"It was my mother's maiden name; I set the account up last year, preparing for a day like today. And, the 10 percent within a month after you sell," she said confidently.

"And you must begin buying tonight; otherwise, you'll lose some of the high profit. Lenny, this is so good. It can be worth forty million to you guys. For four days work, maybe two weeks selling it out. Asking for three to four million isn't too much, is it?" she said confidently, but tailed off with "is it?"

"Alright then, let me get working on it," he said conclusively

"Lenny, here's my cell phone number, let me have yours. These are the only phones we should use since they are looking at everything after Galleon."

"You're right, here's mine. I'll call you by five." He handed her his card.

From the time he left the Roosevelt till he showed up in Edward Wheelwright's office, nine minutes had passed, and Leonard Crane was out of breath as he closed Wheelwright's door.

41

There's a point in your life when you openly talk about your dreams and what you hope to accomplish.

There is a time somewhere after that you realize you're only here for so long and there are only so many prime years. Then you do one of two things—you pick up the pace or you give up.

Edward Wheelwright was picking up the pace. He was behind in the race. His father's career got cut short at Oceans Bank when he might have risen to the top. All of Wheelwright's friends were "there" where Edward wanted to be. He could feel the tug of failure, and every time he did he slapped it away. But it was there—the fear of failure, the failure to achieve, but most clearly, the failure to keep up with his friends whose wealth now far outshone the Wheelwright's.

Once the revised charter for Brunswick Fund had been approved for hedge fund status, Wheelwright set out on the search for investors beyond the funding of forty million put up by the seven original partners. Sebastian Ball controlled roughly 30 percent of the fund as he put up his and Tray's additional assessment of two million each—which he did tell Tray about and which Tray objected to but Sebastian halted further discussion, telling Tray they could settle up later after profits. "For the time being," he told Tray, "it's important that you concentrate on killing Taliban."

Each of the other partners came up with the two million assessment, mostly from their own personal funds as their parents had been transferring large sums of wealth to them each year as the very rich do. Only Parker Barnes had difficulty gathering the funds. His father was one of the few not bought into the transfer of great wealth to the young, and his father believed that young Barnes had to earn it from his own merit. Jonathan Barnes did not go along with much of what the Brunswick School group did with their wealth. He viewed it as taking initiative away from the young.

Since young Barnes was now deeply invested in Barnes Construction as a corporate vice president and managing their New York City properties, he did have considerable access to funds and made four payments into Brunswick Fund of five hundred thousand dollars each, the signature approval level he possessed. The journal entries showed up as property purchases, but the funds were not retrievable in the event Barnes needed to repatriate them back to the company since there was a three-year tie up required with the Brunswick Fund terms. Since Barnes Construction found itself flush with new projects and revenues hitting record levels, Parker saw there would be no issues.

Wheelwright also had tasked the seven to identify potential investors in family, friends and businesses to gather an additional ten million in investments for Brunswick Fund to bring it to a respectable fifty million dollars, which Edward figured would be substantial enough to attract very large funds to off-load a portion of their risks with Brunswick Fund, particularly since they had a track record of successful growth. Sebastian Ball was so committed to Brunswick Fund he added the ten million from his personal funds.

In Wheelwright's initial discussion with Kish Moira and Lenny Crane, they took inventory of which clients they would be bringing with them and in what amounts would they be investing. This discussion yielded more than they expected: Wheelwright had five clients, including a university endowment, which together brought forty million. Kishenlal was bringing three of his former team members with him and between the four brought eight clients and fifty-five million in investments. Lenny Crane had two former team members from Blackthorn join him and twelve million between the three.

Over the course of the next several months, the more moneyed members of Brunswick Fund, namely Sebastian Ball, Winston Trout, and Gideon Bridge, also scouted up clients for the fund to the tune of 240 million. Four hundred fifteen million dollars in total was very good for a new hedge fund, but nowhere near the likes of Blackthorn or Steven Cohen's former SAC whose assets under management were in the twenty billion dollar range and in the new form (after cheating) still amounted to fifteen billion.

Other topics that Edward Wheelwright focused constantly on besides sources of funds were sources of leads and where to put the money in the fund. There were four parts of the firm—marketing and bringing money in, investing and analysis of where to put the money, technology and the tools for investing and reporting, and general administration of the firm like compliance, finance and personnel. In those first months, Edward and Kish hired eight additional staff bringing Brunswick Fund up to twenty-two members in total with the core focused on investing and trading.

Wheelwright spent the majority of his time with his traders and their managers, Kish and Lenny. Monday mornings were the worst. Wheelwright would bring all traders into the conference room and begin quizzing them on investment strategies, which industries, which companies, what countries, "where are you putting our money and why," he would begin, and then call someone out, "You, Jim Keough, you blew it last week on the trade for Johnson Controls. You stayed too late. Damn it, you made your profit target, why weren't you out. You're costing me money." Jim Keough needn't answer; the question was rhetorical, until he heard, "Well Keough, what do you have to say, where the fuck is your head?" Then Mr. Keough needed to answer.

This went on from 7 a.m. to about eight-thirty, getting all the traders in a killing mood. Then he would set them free on the public. It was never a pretty sight—in this short period of time, Brunswick Fund had become one of the most aggressive traders on the street and were developing a reputation for fantastic timing and ruthless execution. They usually followed the old FIFO accounting rule, first in and first out. You did excellent analysis of where to put your money, and you got in and out quickly, driving the price relentlessly until the general public caught on and the price went viral. And as the investment would gather steam, you were the first one out. You don't violate that rule, as Mr. Keough did and try to stretch to get a larger bonus. "Next time you'll find your ass out on the street, Mr. Keough, you got that?" "Yes, sir, Mr. Wheelwright!"

Yes, sir, Mr. Wheelwright. You bet your ass, Mr. Wheelwright thought.

It was also necessary to discuss the quality of investment development theory. Benjamin Graham, the economist and father of value investing, taught that you needed to make a decent return on any investment but that you also needed to protect the underlying asset from loss. So Wheelwright drilled them all on hedging strategies to protect the capital of the firm. But he also went into deep lead development with the managers of the firm; defined weekly sessions occurred with Edward, Kish and Lenny and of the unsaid but common use of insider leads, how they would be identified, couched and what the sources would be. For the sharks of Wall Street, all investments were made on insider information; it was just a matter of how cleverly you could cover it and keep any paper and technology trails at arm's length. The information was everywhere; everyone had it. They would brag about it over tennis, slobber it out late over drinks, and be screwed out of it by some hustling trader with big tits. Wheelwright's favorite saying was, "No one on the Street can keep a secret, no one. We just have to keep listening, eventually we'll be told."

For teaching examples of how not to trade on inside information, Wheelwright would use the weekly scandal as evidence. Galleon Group was a favorite late example.

"What we're not going to do is pay for any inside information," Wheelwright said. "If it falls in our laps, we don't need to know the inside source. Then it's not inside information. It's like air; it's just there, known. Information always has to be a one-off, which Galleon refined. But they were dumb in execution with paper, phone, and text trails everywhere leading back to who their suppliers were."

Kish added, "Roomy Khan, what was Raj thinking. He knew the Feds had her from her helping him before. He had to know she was being watched."

Leonard the liar joined in, "We can't use anyone that careless. The approach I have used pretty well is a rolodex that includes about fifty sources. These are in our core industries, tech, solar, finance, and pharma. I classify the sources as a, b or c.

"A sources spread inside information to drive the price of the stock they already bought. As it keeps going up, they're selling all the time. They'll be invisible in an SEC action.

"B sources are those that share but want some information in return. This is easy, because you just give them all your A source stocks, driving those stocks higher. But the trade is a mutual exchange.

"C sources are 'the' insider, and what they want is something tangible in return. They want the cash. What Galleon did with the secret payments to Swiss accounts worked brilliantly. Some traders also want the cash done this way."

Kish nodded.

"The C stuff is the most dangerous," Edward said, "We don't do C. Ever. Everything one off. Is that clear?" he said firmly, staring at Crane, red faced.

That was the way Edward operated. And now here stood Leonard Crane with his tip from Alice Kraft.

"I don't like the sound of it," Edward Wheelwright was telling Crane. "It's inside information. You're not sure who the company is and it's happening in a few days. What am I missing, Crane?" he said in a rather irritated tone looking up from his desk.

"Wait. How can it be inside information when we don't even know what company it is or even the industry?" Crane said defensively yet confidently.

"You said it yourself," Wheelwright came back, "you can figure it out."

"But that's not the same as insider information. We do not have a name."

"Maybe," Wheelwright paused between the may and the be.

"We have to try. It's a gift."

"Your friend won't see it that way."

"I can end that right now." Crane said.

"How?"

"I call her back and say we're not interested. She said she had others to take it to. Done deal."

"And then what?" Wheelwright wondered what Crane was planning next.

"I go after it with everything I have. I'll get Fallon who was with me at Blackthorn on it."

"No. If you're going to start looking, you do it all by yourself," Wheelwright said, no longer indifferent to the idea.

"And what you need to be doing is freeing up some capital so we can go after it, once I convince you its right," Crane said, more peer to peer than subordinate to owner.

"Don't worry about anything but your end. You need to do two things: one, get on the phone right now with your friend and close it out. Slam the door, but politely.

Second, come back in here by six with three possible names and why it could be any of the three, but why we need to buy just one." Wheelwright said seeking comprehension.

"But it will only be one, "Crane said.

"Do your homework, damn it. If you want to buy this, it's got to be air tight," Wheelwright finished.

"Got it," Crane said, rising, and as he exited, "See you at six."

"Catch the door," Wheelwright said.

As Crane closed the door, Edward Wheelwright sat thinking about what Crane was proposing. Then he picked up his phone and pressed one of the six programmed numbers.

"Trout Solar, Mr. Trout's office," the female assistant answered.

"Is Winston there, please," Wheelwright asked.

In the meantime Leonard Crane made his call, "Alice?"

"Lenny?" Alice Kraft answered.

"Yes. Alice, I talked with my guys, and there is no interest here. Sorry."

"What do you mean no interest?" Alice Kraft said irately.

"They don't want to get involved."

"Lenny, what are you talking about? It's a no brainer," she came back at him.

"Alice, they don't want to pay the money; it would be too difficult."

"Then you can pay me separately from your share," she persisted.

"I couldn't make it worth your while, Alice. You did say you had other sources," Crane said curtly.

"I do but I trusted you. We talked about this, about doing one of these. It is a way to kill it."

"Alice, if it were my money I would," Crane said hoping this exchange would soon end.

"Lenny, you fuck. I know you. You're going ahead with it, aren't you?" she said, now steaming.

"Alice, I don't even know the company."

"So no one can tag you with insider info, right Lenny." She waited, and there was no reply. "Well it's Rocket Solar. So now you have insider info. Better not use it, you bastard," and she was gone.

"Alice," Crane said into the emptiness of the network. "Goddamnit," and he slammed phone down on his desk. "Fuck."

Crane went to work doing research on Blackthorn clients from an old database listing he lifted before he left the company. He found five solar firms in the eight to twelve dollar price range. He quickly eliminated two based on price. The other three he began pulling the numbers: number of shares, float, revenues, earnings per share, profit. He zeroed in on margins, particularly gross and operating. He dug down through Bloomberg, Gartner, and Reuters databases tracking ratings and expectations.

He went to the analyst reports on those following the solar stocks. Two of the companies were followed by four analysts each, the third, had three that reported on it. He pulled up the analyst reports on his desktop and quickly skimmed each.

Of the three companies, two made solar wafers and panels. The third, Rocket Solar, made the reactors that converted sand to silicon and furnaces that turned the silicon into solar ingots that were then sliced into wafers. One of the analysts writing about Rocket Solar stated what Crane felt were two very promising comments. The first mentioned that "in viewing the landscape of solar, the producers of solar wafers and panels have recently seen large increases in orders from Germany and Spain, thanks to the generous subsidies for their solar industry." It was dated one week earlier. The second comment stated, "If the demand continues for solar modules, pricing will dramatically increase since all major Chinese manufacturers are reportedly operating at capacity." That confirms it, Crane thought.

Crane also noted the share volume on Rocket Solar had risen 35 percent; for the other two solar companies, one had share volume remaining the same and the other increased slightly, about 3 percent.

At 5:45 p.m. Crane was standing in Wheelwright's doorway.

"I've got it," Crane said.

"Show me," Wheelwright said, and he moved to the round conference table by the window overlooking Madison Ave. He gestured to Crane to have a seat.

Crane proceeded to show the eight solar companies that Blackthorn followed, reported on and invested in. He narrowed it to the three in the general price range of ten per share. He then went through comparisons of each company's business and all key statistics. "But here's the clincher on Rocket Solar," Crane said enthusiastically. "In addition to heavy demand and full capacity,

Rocket Solar is the only one of the three making the solar reactors and furnaces." He then proceeded to share the analyst comments.

"So, you can see, Edward, it is Rocket Solar that will be getting these large contracts," Crane concluded.

Wheelwright stared at Crane, "And how did you handle it with your friend at Blackthorn?"

"She's fine."

"How did you handle it," Wheelwright said, frustrated in not getting a full answer. In fact, "frustrated" had become a common reaction for Wheelwright when dealing with Crane. Kish had also voiced similar concern about not being able to get straight answers when it came to trading operations. They had discussed this feeling the very night before, "You always get an almost answer, no details, not the full truth," was how Kish Moira described it.

This type dealing left Wheelwright so uncomfortable that not only were they not going to invest in Rocket Solar, they were not going to invest any further in Leonard Crane.

"Lenny," Wheelwright began, "we're not going to do this, and as you and I have talked about, things are not going as I would like, so we're going to part here. We'll give you six months' severance, I'm sorry things haven't worked out for you and Brunswick."

Crane was stunned. Not only did he not have an investor for this opportunity of a lifetime, he no longer had a job.

So fixed was Crane on getting into Rocket Solar, he barely acknowledged Wheelwright, and that he was unemployed once again. Crane was met at Wheelwright's office door by a security guard who, after Crane removed his personal belongings, escorted him out of the offices.

What Wheelwright did not tell Crane were the results of three phone calls that afternoon. The first was a returned phone call from Winston Trout. "Yes, it was true," he confirmed to Wheelwright, "all the solars are flat out right now. The European subsidies are creating huge demand. It might be gone when they change governments, but right now they want solar energy. You might try your old flame Val Samson; you know she's at Blackthorn now."

"I did not know," Wheelwright came back.

"She calls me every week looking for an edge. Give her a buzz, she'll do anything for Eddie Wheelwright," Trout taunted, laughing.

"Funny guy. Thanks, Win, I will give her a buzz," Wheelwright said, adding, "And since you are so flat out, how about you and your bride picking up the tab for dinner Saturday."

"Great with me, name the place," Trout said.

"Santa likes La Bretagne, over on the Post Road."

"Eight o'clock?"

"Great, you're a prince, Win," and Wheelwright meant it. Winston Trout was the most decent human being he had ever met. Besides Valerie McGuire Samson.

The second phone call was one he made to the former, future Mrs. Edward Wheelwright, Valerie Samson. He pulled up his rolodex and found Val Samson's cell phone.

"Val, I need a favor," Wheelwright said as she answered. And after five minutes of awkward small talk about friends and health and work, he got to the point. "I've heard some things about one of your solar companies, about large contracts about to be announced."

Distraught, after the spark of hearing his voice lit her up, she said, "I'm working on research now, Eddie, let me snoop around. I'll give you a call back."

And she did call back, the same afternoon, "I think I've got an oops here, Eddie."

"What do you mean, Val?" he asked.

"Well, the first person I talked with knew exactly what I was looking for," Samson said, and added. "One of the traders here I know pretty well, Alice Kraft, trades a number of the solar stocks, so I went to her. Turns out she was shoveling this story about Rocket Solar over to one of your guys, Lenny Crane, also one of our former guys," Samson stopped. "How'm I doin so far?"

"Pretty good, Val," he said and asked, "but what the hell is this Kraft girl up to?"

"Trying to make a buck," Samson said. "Look, you need to absolutely kill this thing dead. She's a good girl, smart, and has got a future, but somehow she got plotting with this guy Crane and came up with a get rich quick scheme."

"I can fix it on my end, but what about her. Are you going to get her out of Blackthorn? This isn't good, Val."

"I know. Look let me handle this here. Nothing has happened on this end, and I presume by your call you haven't done anything either. Right?"

"Yes, that's right."

"Well, I'm going to swear her to a blood oath to never, ever try some shit like this again. Not only will it cost her her career, she'll end up in jail. She's just the kind of perp the SEC likes. Put the little people in jail, get the partners to pay big fines and everything goes forward."

"Got it, thanks, Val, I'll handle things here."

"How you and you girlfriend doing?" she had to ask.

"We're doing pretty well. And how about your marriage?"

"It's good, Eddie. David is wonderful, but he's no Edward Wheelwright," Valerie Simpson said sadly.

Wheelwright was shocked. Shocked that the girl he was going to marry, the girl he deserted after nine years of dating and engagement, felt that way. He was mortified that she was carrying that pain. "I'm sorry, Val."

"I know, Eddie." And then almost offhandedly, "Before I forget the two brothers who own Rocket, they're not buying, they're selling. After talking with Alice, I dug a little deeper. Seems Alice's boss is working with Rockets owners. They may be kicking back to him. I understand the industry a bit, and Rocket's technology is out of date. They won't be able to catch up with the new thin film and higher efficiency reactors and furnaces that are now being made. They got a few Chinese solar wafer manufacturers to place big orders. These Chinese companies couldn't get financing in China, and when Rocket said they would carry them for up to a year for new equipment, they signed up. Looks like Blackthorn's plan is goose it up while the brothers sell, announce the orders, buy some more, put out a buy recommendation, and then sell everything. Apparently they think there is enough that the transactions won't appear out of line. Then sometime, six months down the road the orders fall through."

"What," exclaimed Wheelwright? "How is that possible, Val?"

"Volume, Eddie, everything is volume. There is enough for everyone if you have volume, and with these orders it'll explode. At least for a while."

"Madness. Thanks, Val. I love you."

"I'll always love you, Eddie."

Not one half hour after Wheelwright hung up the phone, his secretary came in. "I have an Alice Kraft on the line; she says it's urgent she talk with you."

"Thanks, I'll take it. Please close the door," and he picked up the phone, "Wheelwright."

"Mr. Wheelwright, my name is Alice Kraft," she began meekly. After apologizing profusely for trying to give the information to Crane, she swore it would never happen again. She said she had talked with a senior person at Blackthorn and now realizes the consequences of her actions. She made sure he knew the name of the firm was Rocket Solar, just in case Crane was able to talk him into investing. At least this would dissuade them, knowing that she knew it was insider information.

Wheelwright thought, Valerie was right. This girl was smart. Killed two birds at once. Prevented Brunswick from going forward and laid down on her sword at the same time. Clever.

"Thanks for calling, Miss Kraft. I can assure you Brunswick would not have acted on the information that you mentioned. As for what you attempted to do, I'll leave that to your conscience for the future. There's plenty of money to be made here. You sound like a smart person. Just work hard and it'll happen," and he hung up before any further words were exchanged.

So the short happy life of Leonard Crane at Brunswick Fund came to an abrupt end and Wheelwright let out a deep sigh, "Man that guy was trouble. Thank you, Val."

After the phone calls, after the conversation and exit of Crane, Wheelwright found himself thinking about Rocket Solar. Would he have done it? What if the calls to Trout and Samson came back positive? What if Alice Kraft did not call? Would he have gone after Rocket Solar? He was worried that he might have; he was thankful that he didn't.

The thought nagged at him. But what about the next time? What about picking up the pace, the temptation to catch up quickly? He did not have the answer.

42

It came to her in a flash when Sidney Rogers, the managing director of trading, said he needed a buy recommendation on Rocket Solar. Rogers said it would help their firm, Blackthorn Investments, get Rocket Solar's investment banking business, namely an expanded stock offering that Rocket was tossing feelers out about. Samson, earlier in the week, had talked with Alice Kraft and knew Rogers was buying hundreds of thousands of shares of Rocket Solar for himself and Blackthorn.

"You want me to give you a buy recommendation on Rocket?" Valerie Samson asked, incredulously.

"Yes," he said. "They're going to issue a new offering for expansion. That business is important to us."

"Why now? You know their technology is second rate."

"Look, we did their IPO. We'll look foolish if we don't get the follow-on," Rogers said, just a bit annoyed at the pushback.

Samson was thinking, this was important to Blackthorn, important for Rogers. This might be the chance. While Rogers was the managing director for Blackthorn's trading operations, Valerie Samson reported up the line through the investment banking side of Blackthorn; it was not unusual for trading to push research for recommendations.

"I'll begin working on it. I'll try to have it tonight."

"Great, Val, we need this business," and Rogers turned to leave her office.

"I could use some help with something, Sid," she said.

"Sure, what is it?" the managing director asked.

"You have a big say at the 92nd St. Y. I mean your kids go there, Carol's on the board."

"Yes"

"I would like to have my son Edward go there to the day care and then pre-school."

"It's quite a trek from Greenwich to the Y, Val."

"I'm moving back to the city. I need a great place for him to be cared for."

Rogers approached her desk, "What's wrong with Greenwich. Everyone in the city is trying to get there to buy a house, get a good education for their kids."

"Everyone has it wrong then or maybe it's just not working for me," Val Samson said, frustrated with having to defend her request.

"What about David. He hasn't said anything about moving back into the city," Rogers said, referring to Samson's husband, David, who also worked at Backthorn but in the bond department.

"That's not working for me either."

"I'm sorry to hear that. I'll talk with Carol tonight."

"Thanks, Sid, and please keep this conversation between you and me. David is not really in on it yet," Samson said, not sure she could rely on Rogers to keep it to himself.

"My lips are sealed. But please don't get your hopes up. You know it is quite difficult to get in those programs."

"I know. I just appreciate you trying."

"And the recommendation for Rocket?" he said with a smile on his face.

"I'm on it," she said as Rogers winked at her and left her office.

Through the afternoon Val Samson worked on a review of all Rocket Solar data. She put her quantitative hat on; using all her analytical skills to write a favorable report on a company that would be out of business in two years.

Rogers stopped in her office at 6 p.m. on his way out the door. "How's the write-up coming?"

"About another two hours."

"OK, send it to me at home tonight. I'll read it, and we'll do some iterative work to get it complete by Monday."

"Sure thing," she replied and he left.

And as the offices around her emptied on this Friday evening, dark fell on Manhattan. New York at night was life for Valerie Samson. The restaurants, the shows, the clubs, the conversation, the friends; every week someplace new, every week she and Eddie would turn the city inside out. And now there was no Eddie, he left her.

In the daylight when she had her apartment here, she would run in the Park and on the east side along the river. When she had time, and she always had time when she lived in the city, she would sit in Bryant Park—just sit at one of the wrought iron tables and pull the heavy iron chairs out across the slate. She could hear that sound, feel it on her teeth; she could see the dappled sunlight coming through the tall London Plane trees. On Thursday nights she would sit on Bryant's big rectangular lawn and watch movies with her girl-friends. They would bring a blanket, popcorn, and bottles of wine or soda.

Valerie Samson shook her head bringing her back from this vision. Damn Eddie, she thought.

When the report on Rocket Solar was complete, the last thing she needed to do was rate it. Blackthorn had three ratings: Buy, Hold and Sell. She read the report one more time; she liked the effort she put into analyzing Rocket's share of the Chinese market for their solar reactors that make the polysilicon and the furnaces that convert the polysilicon into ingots, which the Chinese solar manufacturers then slice into wafers, put wafers together to form panels, adding wires that make the module complete. Rocket was clearly the world's market leader with almost 70 percent market share. Add to this that the Chinese were the leading solar panel manufacturers in the world and you had Rocket as the foundry of the entire industry. Rocket Solar was easily the most visible name in the small but technologically influential American solar industry. Samson said all that and put her rating at the top of the page and pressed the "send" button. She packed up and headed for Grand Central and the 8:10 train to Greenwich.

"Sell," the voice of Sidney Rogers screamed as he opened Samson's report on his home Dell. He read the report again and dialed Samson's cell phone.

On the train she heard her Apple iPhone. It was Rogers. She connected him.

"Sell," he screamed again, this time into Val's ear. It was so loud the man next to her on the train looked at her. "Are you fucking crazy? Is this some fucking joke, Val?"

Valerie wondered what question he wanted her to answer first. Samson was aware that Rogers had been buying Rocket Solar heavily for weeks, so it sounded to her like he was taking this personal.

"Sid, it is what it is," she said, playing back one of his favorite copouts.

"No, Val, it isn't what it is."

Trying to talk quietly, Val turned away from the man next to her and faced the window as the train passed through Harlem.

"Sid, they won't be around in two years. They haven't kept up. They've been milking old technology too long," she told him, quoting from the critical part of her report that earned Rocket the "Sell" rating.

"That's exactly why they want to put a new stock offering into the market. I told them this a year ago. I have them at the point where they know they need to do it," Rogers said in a pleading tone.

"Sid, they might have had enough time had they done something a year ago. Now Trout Solar has all the key technology for the next generation. Rocket took too much money out of the company. Those two brothers are rascals," and as she said it she looked around nervously, had she been overheard. She did not notice any cocked ears, and the passenger next to her was now napping.

"Sid, I'm on the train, can we talk about this Monday?"

"We can, but you need to change the last part of the write-up about them "keeping up." Just take it out and it reads OK. You know what the overall recommendation needs to be. Don't be going soft on me, Val."

"Sid, have you talked to Carol yet?"

There was a pause. "So that's what this is about. Fuck you, Val. Fix the goddamn report."

Oops, she smiled; bad timing on that question. "Absolutely not, you know it isn't," she replied and continued, "But I do need that spot at the Y. Please talk with her. Thanks, Sid," and she shut her phone off, not wanting to hear the next rant. It was Friday night, and Val Samson was taking the weekend off.

****

Saturday morning came and the multi-tasking young mother was jogging on the road that loops around Tod's Point in Old Greenwich, CT. The point juts out into Long Island Sound; it is a peninsula and along its south side Long Island sits, seven miles out. On a clear day like this, the towers of the Throgs Neck and Whitestone bridges are visible, and to the right of them Manhattan.

She was pushing her young son in the three-wheeled carriage with her right hand. She had a dog leash wrapped around the hand. The dumb-as-a-rock Irish setter on the end of the leash was loping along in stride with her. The woman held a cell phone to her left ear; she was straining to hear the end of her friend's recorded cell phone message. She needed to tell him some important news, news that will help her escape this suburban sinking.

Val Samson was vibrant, but flagging. Still strong and fit, she had been a scholarship soccer player at Columbia. She graduated with honors from Wharton. At twenty-five she ran a highly profitable trading desk at Citi Bank. At night and on the weekends, she was pursued by several wealthy young men. Before she married her condo in Chelsea was paid for.

And here she was entangled with all these non-city chains around her neck: a home in Greenwich, CT, a baby, a stroller, an oversized dog, and a good but dull husband.

And there was Edward Wheelwright. Still free, still unencumbered, with everything, still striving. And Valerie Samson, with nothing, needing everything.

The work was still there, her equities analysis operation at Blackthorn thriving and challenging. But only that. So much was missing—if only Edward and not David.

David was one of those brainy little dudes that powerful young women somehow become attracted to or somehow get trapped in one of their brainy little plots to snare beautiful women. Edward represented risk, to her sense of self, to her organized life, that sense of control she had over every element of her life. With David she could keep her freedom. He worshiped her; whatever she wanted she could have. Not so with Edward. He was the man. It was about him. It could not possibly work; she loved him too much. But he left her. And she still did not know why.

Because Valerie knew the game, she was valuable. Most equities firms and their managing directors did not get it. She did. The markets had become casinos. The concept that an individual investor by carefully researching stocks, with enough foresight and discipline, could over time, through dollar cost averaging their investments in stocks, build substantial savings that would carry through to the end of life; that concept was gone. There was no new model so the investment banks and trading houses began concocting new ones: ring it up!

How could the investing public on one side, with capital hungry corporations on the other side, not see the giant and ever growing leech between them? You couldn't miss it. At every turn it was there sucking the blood of earned money from the process and the people. Short selling, naked shorting, front running, insider trading, publishing worthless equities analysis and recommendations, creating questionable derivatives, courting and corrupting not-so-ignorant politicians who thrived on the Street's largess; and this giant leech was equipped with tools that let them front run, sell clients stock at the same time they shorted it, collaborate across firms with electronic hand signals, orchestrate flash sell-offs that would confound even their peers, yet be celebrated nightly for the simple deviousness of their workings. Insider trading had become so common that whenever the SEC started an investigation, it would immediately grow exponentially; there was no end to the links, cells, pods, pools, firms, and individuals involved in it.

The giant financial leech had become so big it was the industry. Right there, in plain sight with full support of the governing legislative and regulatory bodies, who themselves were made up of smaller leeches shuttling back and forth between the mother ship.

Valerie did get it. She thrived on it. On the very edge of criminality and yet without penalties for doing what she did. It was all legal, all written down in laws, exceptions, loop holes, and company policies for all to see. Transparency. How could it be wrong? In the post-god, post-values world of the street, it was so wrong, it was right.

David didn't get any of this. He would never believe his bride was involved in a criminal enterprise. It wasn't that she wanted him to believe she was a criminal. She wanted him to know it; she wanted someone else who got it to know how clever she was at the game. There she said it. That wasn't David; it was Edward. Edward could help her wash the slime off with rationality. David could not.

Valerie thought about her recent telephone conversation with Edward Wheelwright. There was an opening; it was not too late. She needed to share an idea that would fulfill his striving and end her emptiness.

"Edward, when you get this message, please call me. It's urgent. Good urgent. Eddie, it's great urgent."

Jim Conroy, the New York City police detective monitoring Valerie Samson's phone, was part of a continuing investigation into insider trading. The cybercrime unit of the department had linked up with the Securities Exchange Commission to crack down on all forms of pillage occurring in the investment community.

Detective Conroy captured the message digitally that Valerie Samson had left Edward Wheelwright and the phone numbers of the sender and receiver. As the data was entered into the data base file on Rocket Solar, Detective Conroy noted that the Wheelwright number was new and may not mean anything. He traced the Wheelwright number; it was for a cell phone registered to Edward Wheelwright, III, address 671 Central Park West.

Monday came quickly. Val took the early train and was at her desk by 7 a.m. At seven fifteen Sid Rogers was in her office.

"I don't appreciate being blanked out for the weekend," Rogers said in an aggravated tone.

"Well, good morning to you, Sid," Samson said, almost jauntily.

"Sorry about the shouting on Friday, Val. But I need the report done right."

"How'd your discussion with Carol go?" Val said.

"It is that!" he almost shouted. "Damn, Val!"

"Damn, Sid. This is important to me too," she said, rising in her chair. "I need to be back in the city."

"And David?"

"I told you; this does not concern him. Let it go at that."

Sid Rogers knew David Samson. They both ran trading desks at Blackthorn before David moved to the other side of the world at Blackthorn: bonds.

"Is he coming with you to the city?"

"Sid, Carol. What did she say?"

"She said 'yes.' She can get your son into the day care and that will give him a leg up in a couple of years as well as get him on the list for pre-school."

Val Samson sat back in her chair, an immense burden lifting.

"Thanks, Sid, that's awesome."

"The report?"

"By noontime."

"Good," Rogers said.

Val Samson was home by eleven fifteen. Her nanny was just bringing little Edward home in the carriage when the phone rang.

"Hello," she answered, not noticing it was her husband's office number.

"Val, what's going on? Sid Rogers just came to see me. He wanted to know where you were. He said you left work, and he couldn't reach you or your cell."

"David, I needed to come home," Valerie told her husband in a pained tone.

"What's wrong? Is Edward OK?"

"He's fine."

"Then what is it?" David asked again in his nasally city accent.

"Nothing. I'll tell you when you're home."

"I'm not home tonight, remember? I leave for Chicago from the office today. I did mention I'm gone till next Thursday. Can we talk tonight?"

"No, it's nothing, I'll tell you next week when were together. Have a good trip," and she hung up. The "what" she planned to tell him was that their marriage was over.

43

"Parker, I need to meet with you," Leonard Crane said urgently as Parker Barnes answered his office phone. "Are you still in the city?" Crane was sitting at his outdoor office in Central Park calling from his cellphone, once again unemployed.

"Lenny, what's up?" And he listened… "Yes, I'm just finishing up. I'm about to get the car," Barnes responded.

"I need to see you right now. And it's going to be awhile,' Crane continued in an excited manner.

"Why don't we grab dinner at Cite, say in half an hour?"

"Yes, that's terrific. I'll see you then." Crane concluded.

"Lenny, are you OK?" Barnes asked, sensing the heightened state Crane was obviously in.

"Yes, fine, Parker. I have an opportunity I think you'll want to hear about."

"Looking forward to it. See you it a bit," Barnes finished, smiling to himself. Life was never dull with Leonard Crane around.

Barnes arrived at Cite Grille, the fashionable eatery, on West 51st. It was a favorite of the TV crowd from Sixth Ave. He spotted Crane right away seated at a table across the foyer to the right.

Barnes couldn't help noticing Mike Francesca, the sports talk show host, already having dinner two tables away with Jim Nance, the sports announcer. Francesca better stop drinking those giant Cokes on his show, Barnes thought to himself, noticing his girth.

"Hey, Lenny," Barnes announced when Crane's eyes, which had been trained on Parker since he entered through the revolving door, met his.

"Did you see who's over there?" Crane asked nodding toward the talking heads.

As Barnes reached out to shake Crane's hand, he said, "Yeah, I did. Mikey boy better back off from the table," Barnes concluded as he sat down. The comment was just loud enough where Francesca thought he heard something about himself and looked around at the two friends with a scowl.

"So, how are things going with you, Eddie and Kish?" Barnes asked, now focused on his friend.

Crane tucked his chin in and pulled his head slightly down, "Not well."

"Not well? How?" Barnes said.

"I'm out. Eddie fired me," Crane said looking up.

"What the hell happened," a now impatient Barnes asked.

"I got a tip from a girl I worked with over at Blackthorn. They're doing a lot of investments in solar. We had a pact when we last worked together. If either of us ever got something that was game or life changing, the other could execute it and we'd share the profits. I talked to Eddie about it. It seemed like he was interested at first, then later on he comes back and cans me."

"That's a little weird," Barnes said, adding, "Must be something more, Lenny, Eddie's a pretty fair guy."

"Well, I had a couple of minor screwups, nothing major, in the last couple of months, but this was the reason. This tip."

"What was the tip?"

"Eddie said it was insider information. He said if we acted on it they could trace it directly back to my friend Alice, and therefore to Blackthorn, who has the solar company as a client."

"Well, if he saw it that way, you can't argue with him. Look, I get it. I'll talk with him. See if we can get you reinstated," Barnes said empathetically.

"Thanks, Parker, but that won't do any good. He was pretty emphatic, and I see his point, "Crane said.

"Then, that's not why you wanted to talk with me, getting hired back?" Barnes asked.

"It's the tip, Parker. It's good as gold. Just sitting there. It's worth millions. This is the once in a life time shot you get to do it all at once," Crane said, suddenly alive.

A waiter appeared and asked about drinks. Barnes ordered a bottle of San Pellegrino. "Do you want to share a bottle of the water, Lenny," Barnes asked.

"Sure, sounds great," Crane said fully aware of his friend's past addictions and willing to forego an alcoholic drink.

The waiter left menus and hustled off.

Barnes said, without any more than casual interest, "Tell me about the tip."

One never knows why an obnoxious person will not give up when they've lost or why an impulsive person won't use sources available to them to confirm facts. Whatever the reasons, Crane and Barnes were toxic together and set off on a ruinous cause that night. Perhaps desire overcame judgment or longing for independence outdid reliance on knowledgeable sources. Crane ignored the danger he knew to be present, especially after Alice's warning. Barnes could have counseled with Wheelwright or Trout but didn't. Crane's case for riches put Barnes in the thrall of becoming his own man. Barnes and Crane met with Kish Moira later that night, told him what they wanted to do, and Barnes gave Kish eight checks in denominations of five hundred thousand dollars to buy Rocket Solar on margin.

A life of risk can be compounded in so many ways. Taking risks in his past to buy drugs or drive while drinking or "borrowing" from Barnes Construction to invest in Brunswick Fund were all measured, and while individually destructive, not compounding, in the way Parker Barnes now exposed himself.

His impulsiveness pushed him into a risk category he had not been in before. Risk spread across multiple fronts. He dared take insider information and use it to buy stock; he was taking information from a source who, while a friend, had a reputation for lying; he compounded the risk by taking four million dollars from his father's company without authorization after discovering he had the ability to write checks above his authorized level; he was buying a stock he knew nothing about without any personal due diligence; and he was buying the stock on margin, which allowed him to buy twice as much as he had the money for by borrowing from his account at Brunswick Fund.

There was no thought to the potential for loss; it would take a miracle for this process, with all its potential pitfalls, to turn out right. Crane, the same person who maliciously smacked the ball into the face of his water polo opponents in college, now recklessly ignored the legal danger and played to Barnes' weakness of desire for quick wealth. Barnes, the builder's son who repeatedly gave into impulses that drove his addictions, moved forward toward self-destruction.

44

Billy Stevens hid in the back of the parking lot of the Stamford Mall. He had walked to this spot earlier. The parking lot was particularly full this Friday night. It was still early, and Billy figured he could ID a rich woman, snatch her handbag, and beat it out the side stairway into the foot traffic by the Bank Street Brewery across the street.

He was right; there were hundreds of walkers this dark night— many working late in the office tower adjoining the mall, others going to the restaurants and clubs just up the street at Park Place, and still others going to the condo complexes that had sprung up in downtown Stamford to accommodate the giant new trading floors of some of the world's largest investment banks. Even Donald Trump had just completed a luxury forty-story condo. Stamford was fast morphing into a segment of New York City—build big financial services and their trading floors, build lots of tony condos, add in a hot nightlife scene, and they will come: lots of expensively educated twenty and thirty somethings did.

Stevens had come up the stairway fifteen minutes earlier. It was a rarely used stairwell. Most shoppers drove into the mall; walkers generally avoided the few isolated traps like this stairwell.

Stevens was unemployed once again; nothing seemed to work. The drug dealer he worked for wanted all of his guys to have regular jobs in addition to dealing. Stevens would keep jobs for a month or two, somebody would give him a hard time, Stevens would give him some lip back, next thing you know Billy's gone. Always worked the same way. This time it wasn't his fault. He was driving policies around for an insurance company. Stopped for a red light, light turns green, he goes. Then wham, guy runs a red light and the company car is wrecked. Cops cited the other guy for running the red light; when they asked for Stevens' license, he didn't have one. Insurance company fired him on the spot. He asked for another chance since it wasn't his fault and said he'd get the license. Office manager was so upset he walked Stevens to the front door of the office, opened it, and just pointed the way out. Stevens, never one to shy from a confrontation, grabbed the door knob, pulled the door closed behind him, not quietly but loudly, strongly, pulling-it-through-the-other-side-closed, closed so strongly that the glass in the seven-foot-high door came chasing after Stevens with a shattering screech and crash.

That was two hours ago. Now he needed money for a buy. Imagine that, Billy Stevens needing money for a buy. He'd told his friend Curtis Strong that he was no longer into that game; he was so far into it. He was using up the profits anyway he could to get the products into him: smoking, needles, inhaling.

His supplier cut him loose. Said he was bad for business. Said he couldn't have a runner, a dealer using like Stevens was. Casual use was OK with the supplier but you had to control it. Not Billy, it had him, it wouldn't let him go. He was in love with the stuff. He'd wake up in the morning, if he ever got to sleep, thinking about his first hit of the day.

The supplier was a son-of-a-bitch; he was very strict. But that wasn't the problem that he was a tough business man. He was tough. And the tougher he had to get, the meaner he became. There were a lot of things said about him, about where he came from and how he got started. Stevens believed most of it because he had seen the supplier, had seen him beat guys up for welching on a debt. He made Stevens go to a customer's house one time with him when the customer wouldn't pay. He knocked on the guy's door, and when his wife answered and said he wasn't there, he punched her in the mouth, hard, knocking out the front teeth. She was bleeding like

268

crazy. Billy's supplier tells her, "Get your old man to pay my boy Billy by tomorrow night or I'll come back and knock the rest of your teeth out."

When he woke up the next morning, Billy Stevens found an envelope that had been slipped under his door. All the money due was paid.

Now he was on furlough from the supplier. He told Billy to get right or don't come back. He needed to get back, and the supplier needed him back—he had grown into one of his better dealers. He had a steady group of customers and had brought along two tiers of subdealers. The money that flowed to him overwhelmed Stevens. As much as he made, he was always broke. Using, gambling, or spending way too much, especially on the girls. The girls were the worst. They'd party with him for days, days, and then they'd be gone and so would his money.

So here he was, biding his time, waiting for a mark that he could take easily and disappear with a few hundred—enough to have a good time.

This night he was all alone. The Brazilian supplier had given his territory to one of his amigos. He promised if Stevens got himself straight he'd give it back to him—but only after he was straight for a month. A month, he'd die in a month without a steady source of funds to get right, but not straight. It was a balancing act; you could still use and manage it and be right. To get straight, like Pedro wanted, well, that was asking too much.

There she is he told himself. Excited at the prospect of the money.

A middle aged woman, neatly dressed, probably a business woman by the look of her clothes, had exited the mall door and was walking directly to where Stevens had located himself behind a large reinforcing column. The stairway was off to his right. To his left, along the rear most wall in the parking lot, was a row of four cars with one space in between the third and fourth car.

Don't go to the fourth car, Stevens said to himself. It won't work with the open space next to it.

She continued walking, glancing over her shoulder, as if thinking she were being followed. I'm in front of you bitch, Stevens laughed in his mind.

She was, yes, she was going to the second car—cover and close to the stairwell.

Stevens pulled back further into the recess. He couldn't see her now, but could hear her reaching in for the keys; she was close. He looked, she had her hand bag up, and she was beside the car, only she was facing him. He crouched down and began to move.

The woman got the keys out of her handbag and turned to put the key in the door of the Chrysler 300. As her right hand went out to insert the key, Stevens struck. He hit her in the head with his left arm in a swiping motion to knock her down. She fell backwards but stayed on her feet. Stevens reached across her arm to get the bag. He had it and started to pull. She wouldn't let go.

"Let go of it, bitch," he yelled at her.

She screamed. She screamed loud; she was going to tell the whole world. He had to act fast—he took a quick glance as he tousled with her. No one else was nearby. He let go of the handbag, put his left arm against her neck and pushed her against the first car. It set off the car alarm. She screeched even louder now. His head was pounding. With his right hand he reached in his rear pocked and pulled out a knife. It came alive as he flicked it open. In one motion he plunged it into her stomach. She kept screaming. He brought the knife back up to his shoulder, removed his left arm from her neck, and stuck the point in her throat, pushing as it entered. He left it there.

Stevens grabbed the handbag from the falling woman, and ran. As he got to the stairwell he heard someone yelling over by the mall entrance. Two men, they were coming towards him, yelling at him. He was now in the stairwell, rifling the purse blindly as he leapt two, three stairs at a time in his downward flight. He found it, her wallet. He dropped the bag and secured the wallet inside his jacket.

He could hear the two men behind him, yelling something. What was it they were saying? He heard a static sound from a two-way radio.

"Stop, police," they were shouting. Holy shit, cops. Where did they come from? He was now steps from the door that would take him to the street when he heard the first shot, or was it that he felt it first. He couldn't be sure, now he was hit, bleeding somewhere around his left leg. He couldn't stop. He got to the door and exited.

He saw the throngs of people just down the walk in front of him. Not more than thirty yards, then he would be able to mix and disappear.

As he looked ahead right in front of him, a Stamford Police car had screeched to a halt. Two policemen exited, one drawing his gun. A second car, unmarked, pulled up, another man jumped out with a gun drawn.

Stevens reeled. There was an area to the right; it was narrow, was fronted by some bushes and seemed to be an alley in back of the street front stores. He dashed for it, the pain in his leg unbearable. Once behind the bushes and hidden in the alley, he bent down and took a nine millimeter hand gun from an ankle holster. The first of the two cops trailing him stumbled out of the door, and he fired wildly at them hoping to hold them off as he made a getaway. The two pulled themselves back into the cover of the stairwell.

Stevens turned to run, then looked back again to see if he was being pursued. A second shot rang out; it hit Stevens in the left side, knocking him to the ground.

The man in plain clothes quickly was upon Stevens.

Now Stevens knew; this was how it was going to end. He could feel the pain, the blood gushing out of him, his life slipping away, quickly. The man was saying something to him. The man kicked the gun out of his hand. He could feel he was going to pass out. CJ, what about CJ. He was in there; he was going to be in there forever and he didn't do it. His last thoughts? He felt himself coming back; it was clearing up. Now he could hear the man. "Don't move, don't make a move or I'll blow your fucking brains out." Too late, I'm done. But CJ.

"Listen, you gotta help me. CJ didn't do it."

"What's that asshole; you didn't just knife that woman upstairs," the detective said as he reached inside Stevens's jacket and retrieved her wallet.

"No, I did that. But seven years ago, another knifing." Stevens struggled to talk. He struggled to break the confidence he had promised Strong, tell him, tell him, Parker Barnes did it. But I made a promise to CJ that I wouldn't.

"Go ahead get it out," the detective said sarcastically. "I love deathbed confessions."

"Curtis Strong was convicted of killing Augusto Santos seven years ago," Stevens gasped, not much time left, he could feel himself slipping. "I was dealing drugs from Santos and knifed him. Strong was just walking by and tried to help the guy when he heard him moaning. I swear on my mother's soul. Strong is in Auburn; he was convicted. You gotta tell someone they got the wrong guy. I did that," Stevens said. And he died.

The detective looked at Stevens then hollered over his shoulder to the others, "All clear, he's down," and as the uniformed police started forward, Detective Sergeant John Walsh leaned down and said to the dead man, "Probably the only decent thing you've ever done in your life you sorry son of a bitch. Too bad your little secret is going to die with you."

Officer Larry Bell came up beside Walsh. "We've got an ambulance on the way for the woman upstairs. She's in real bad shape, lost a lot of blood. Is he dead?" and seeing Walsh nod, added, "Good shooting. Bastard almost got us coming out the door. You know this guy, Sarge? I heard him talking to you. What did he say?" Bell asked.

"Seen him around a lot. Know he's got a record, Strong or something like that." Walsh said absentmindedly thinking about the mountain of paperwork coming when there was a fatal shooting by police. Walsh added, "Here's the woman's wallet. Let's find out who she is and contact some family."

Other officers arrived; sirens could be heard in the distance as more police along with an ambulance sped to this site.

45

Vito Boriello thought about what he and Jim Ford had agreed on, essentially, to try to prove that an innocent man had been sitting in prison in upstate New York for ten years. Across the country there were more and more project innocence task forces emerging, particularly as forensic science, technology and law school researchers came into being.

In the case of Curtis Strong Jr. no new science or technology would come into play, and the only researchers seeking to help Mr. Strong were Ford and Boriello.

In devising a list of to-dos, Boriello and Ford took those that would be easiest for them to handle from their respective locations. Boriello had begun his list and was coming up empty. Thumb print: yes, evidence and fingerprints confirmed that the thumb print on the knife that killed Augusto Santos was Strong's. Strong said he had not touched the knife in trying to help save Santos' life upon finding him hurt. Boriello ruled it a push—trying to save the guy's life he may have inadvertently touched it.

First time offender—talk with community adults, what kind of kid was Strong. Here Boriello got good feedback, the guidance counselor at Westhill High School remembered Strong, even after seven years.

"He was a good kid; his mother always showed interest. His grades were good, not great, but he had a future. Killing someone, being involved in drugs—absolutely not!" Jim Frisoli told Boreillo over the phone.

"Jim, let me ask you, did the Strong's defense counsel ask you to testify in his behalf?" Boriello pursued.

"No, never got a call. And I'd have spoken up for him," Frisoli went on. "I've been in this job twenty years, taught ten years before that, and you get to know kids. It doesn't matter what part of town they're from. You know these kids. I can guarantee you that Curtis Strong would never hurt anyone. He was not into drugs or alcohol—he was very clear eyed. Bright kid, you know what I mean, Vito?"

"I do, Jim," the detective said to the guidance counselor he had known for half his life, both having grown up on Stamford's West Side with neither ever moving anywhere else. "Thanks for your help. I may need to call on you again?'

"Sure, Vito, anytime," Frisoli said.

What Frisoli was telling Boriello was exactly what he was hearing from Ford and from a completely different environment. Frisoli also gave Boriello the name of one of Strong's teachers, and he contacted her. Another confirmation. Good person, you knew he didn't have it in him to do evil. Good student. Peacemaker. Well, how in the bloody hell, Boreillo thought could this happen. Couldn't anyone believe that a good kid would rush to help someone in trouble? Something very wrong here. Either Strong was very good at pulling the wool over adults' eyes or a grave injustice had been committed. He was leaning towards the later.

And Augusto Santos, the man Curtis Strong had been convicted of killing, Boriello found out through a search of police data bases was an illegal immigrant with three prior arrests. One arrest was for domestic abuse; the other two were arrests for dealing drugs. In the first case he served one year in jail and was deported to Guatemala. Two years after deportation he was arrested again in Stamford for dealing drugs but cooperated with police and helped bring down part of a larger drug gang operating to supply the downtown business crowd. Charges were quietly dropped, his name never surfaced, and he was released. That was six months before his murder. A note in the file also indicated that he had crack cocaine in his possession at the time of his death. The theory of the killing was that it was a dispute over drugs. In Boriello's mind, more evidence of innocence since Strong had a good reputation as a drug- and alcohol-free kid.

Boriello still had the judge and defense lawyer to talk with, but first he wanted to hear from a juror just what they saw. That is if he could find one willing to talk about the trial. He picked the names of two of jurors. One, Ann Lofrano, lived on the West Side. These connections to the old Italian neighborhood Boriello grew up in helped him throughout his career. He didn't know the family but knew the Lofrano name.

The small cape on Burwood Ave was like one hundred others in the six-block by four-block area. At the head of the neighborhood was St. Clement of Rome Catholic Church, where all guidance originated growing up.

Ann Lofrano, a small, wide woman of about sixty, in a floral print house dress, slapped her leg and howled. "He was the funniest priest we ever had."

"And he gave penances of whole rosaries," Vito said, laughing also.

"I wouldn't know about that," she said with a twinkle in her eye and laughed again.

"So, Ann," Boriello began, "I don't want to take up too much of your time, let me go over why I'm here."

"Yes, Lieutenant, you mentioned it was a jury I served on?"

"Yes, and call me Vito. It was the Curtis Strong trial."

"Yes, I remember. It's the only jury I ever served on," and Lofrano tensed and her face suddenly got older, more wrinkles showed up. "I'll never do it again."

"Why, what happened?" Boriello asked, now very interested.

"Why? The kid was innocent!" she blurted out.

Boriello was startled by statement. "What? How do you know he was innocent? How did the jury convict him?"

"Everyone knew he was innocent. Maybe more now, as time passes, but it was so clear he didn't kill that man. But at the time I think the police confused us. No offense intended, Vito."

"None taken, Ann. Tell me, how did the police confuse you?"

"The prosecutor badgered everyone. The judge made us continue to deliberate, when we were hung up ten to two for acquittal," she said, looking at the worn carpet beneath their feet.

"Whoa, just a minute, Ann. Slow down just a bit," Boriello encouraged her.

And over the next half hour, Ann Lofrano reconstructed how she, and the jury in its own innocence, let itself be led by the police, the prosecutor and the judge to a decision, now seen by her as one of horror—convicting an innocent man.

"There was reasonable doubt on everything they showed us. That boy was a good kid. No record, doing well in school, but no one stuck up for him. But the one who really did him in was that police sergeant, Walsh. The prosecutor led Walsh and us along with him through every detail of that night in a way that made it look like he did it, if you believed them. Walsh told us they had his fingerprints on the knife, they had a sneaker print in the blood beside the dead man, and that same sneaker was found in Curtis Strong's closet. So that was all the evidence we had; it was so one sided. As I said no one stuck up for the kid. His lawyer was a lump. He only brought one person as a character witness for him, a teacher. He never challenged the police version at all, except in his summary to us that gave Strong's version of Strong trying to help Santos."

"But if you were voting ten to two to acquit, how is it that he was convicted? " Boriello asked, clearly not understanding.

"When we were deliberating, we asked for the transcript of Sergeant Walsh's testimony. The foreman of the jury, who was one of the two originally voting to convict, used that testimony like a hammer on us. I still remember the way he pounded the table, and he was a big man, worked in construction, I think."

Boriello did not like what he was hearing. Dominant men acting as foremen had swayed more than one jury in Boriello's career. It went against all logic that honest citizens, confronted with reasonable doubt of a person's guilt, would nonetheless vote to convict that person if there were strong enough or coercive enough energy in the jury room.

Lofrano continued, Boriello could see, needing to get this burden out. "He would slam his fist down on the table. He says to us, "Look, they have Strong's fingerprints on the knife. His sneaker left a bloody footprint at the murder scene. This same sneaker was found in his home with Augusto Santos' blood on it." Then he would slam his fist down again. "What are we waiting for, he did it, damn it." Then he said, "Let's vote again." The next vote was seven to five to acquit. But that was all he needed, to see that we could be moved. I felt like I was in a lynch mob."

She stopped, got up, and went to the kitchen, which adjoined the living room they had been sitting in. Boriello saw her grab a dish towel and wipe her eyes. With her back to him, she said, "I need a glass of water, would you like one, Vito?"

"Yes, Ann, please."

As she sat back down, Boriello could see the redness in her eyes, and as she looked up, he looked at his glass.

"Anyway, pardon me," she said, "This was going on for days. Every day another one of us would weaken. I know we're not supposed to, but a couple of us, three, talked one night and said we were not going to change our vote from not guilty to guilty. About the fourth day, the judge came in the jury room and said something like, "This is a very important case. An innocent man has been killed, and the police have worked very hard to bring him justice. I am not going to allow a hung jury. Please work harder to come to a unanimous decision."

"That's not possible," said Boriello, his Italian temper rising.

"It's true," Mrs. Lofrano continued. "Our original position, the ten of us voting not guilty, was that we understood what the police were saying, but there was just as much likelihood that what the defense attorney said was true—that the boy heard a cry for help, went to his aid, and in the process got fingerprints on the knife and blood on his sneaker. But that damn foreman just kept pounding the table, going over what Sergeant Walsh said when the prosecutor asked him, "Now, Sergeant, in your experience, have you ever seen an innocent man run off when he was trying to help a victim?"

"No, not once," Walsh said. And the foreman slammed the table in the jury room again, saying, "No, not once." Walsh continued, I remember him saying, "If you went into that alley to help a dying man, you don't run off like you're guilty. Mr. Strong committed that murder; those are his fingerprints on the knife and Mr. Santos blood on his shoes." And that awful defense attorney never objected, never challenged any of the police witnesses. It was like he had no idea what he was doing. I feel really bad for that kid. Is he still in prison?"

"Yes, more six and a half years now," Boriello said looking at a woman who aged since he had come into her home.

"I went to his sentencing," Lofrano said, "almost no one there. Only his mother and another black lady she sat with at the trial. Defense attorney never came back, was out of town on some 'deal.' They had to have a public defender sit with Mr. Strong."

Boriello shook his head.

"And, don't let me forget this, they sent a seventeen-year-old boy to that awful prison. I went to the library. I read about that place, Auburn. A murderous hell hole. God forgive me for what I've been a part of," and tears rolled down her face, yet she did not cry.

"Ann, I believe like you that Mr. Strong is innocent. We are going to appeal his conviction and try to get it thrown out. Will you be willing to submit a statement if we are able to get a hearing for Curtis?"

"I'll come there myself. Maybe I can undo some of the awfulness of what we did. And you need to talk to other jurors too. I'm not the only one who felt this way. Please talk with Mary Clark; she lives over in Springdale and with Francine Brown. I'm not sure where she lives anymore, but she used to live in Glenbrook."

Boriello had been taking notes as Lofrano spoke and finished them with a note of the two ladies and the Stamford neighborhoods they were from.

At the door as she was seeing him out, Boriello gave Lofrano a hug. He could see she needed one.

46

"C J, I've met with a detective in Stamford who agreed to help. We've come up with a number of things we need to track down the answers to. But one of those things is you," James Ford was saying to Curtis Strong in Ford's office, where it was customary for him to counsel one on one with convicts.

"How's that, Mr. Ford," Strong said.

"Detective Boriello, the man I'm working with, and I agree; you need to tell us how you now know who is responsible for the crime you have been convicted of."

"I appreciate what you are doing for me, but if you look at the other end, where this began, you'll find out," Strong replied.

"CJ," Ford said, tensing up, "This isn't some riddle. If you ever hope to come out of here, you've got to help us. It's been more than six years. Evidence is thin, memories fade."

"Mr. Ford, are you talking with my lawyer, the prosecutor, and the jurors? And the cops? Talk to that cop who testified against us, the one who killed my father. Talk to Walsh, he knows what's going on."

"Why Walsh?"

"Don't you think it's odd, he killed my father and he's the one the prosecutor calls to present evidence against me? It's more than just too coincident," Strong said, his voice firm but rising a bit.

"Yes it is and Detective Boriello is looking in to that."

"Then, what? You don't need any more from me."

"I'm afraid we do. Do you think Walsh is going to open up to Detective Boriello and tell him he was wrong, they got the wrong guy? It doesn't work like that. We expect Walsh will stick to his story. If you can't give us something powerful, no judge will rehear your case even if we find tangential stuff."

"What stuff?" Strong asked wondering what they had found so far.

"Tangential. You know. Related stuff that ties the pieces together. Without a strong center of proof, anything else we find is out on the wing. I agree that when we look at the evidence and we choose to believe you, it makes sense. We need something stronger. A jury already made a determination that could have gone either way."

"No, it couldn't. Not the way the prosecutor pushed. Not the way my attorney blew it for me by challenging nothing. Not the way they pushed the jurors. I know what was going on in that jury room. I knew it took way too long for the verdict."

"And that was then, this is now. Don't you see that?"

"I do; I get it."

"Then help me; help yourself."

"Let me think what I can share. Can you let me think about this and can we talk tomorrow?"

"Don't think CJ, just spit it out. I'll come back tomorrow. But I don't want any more mystery. If you are innocent and I believe you, you have to help me get you out. You! Not the people in Stamford. You apparently have the key pieces that are missing here, and we need them. So, put your thoughts together and tell me tomorrow. Yes?" Ford concluded with a question intended to be responded to.

"Let me work on it," Strong said. "Thank you, Mr. Ford.

Ford rose, shook CJ's hand and showed him out.

Immanuel Kant once wrote that, "out of the crooked timber of humanity no straight thing was ever made." Kant may have been thinking of Parker Barnes or his father. But he was not thinking of the Strong men. CJ was the seed of the Strong soldier, Curtis Strong who pushed his friend Willie Stevens down and ended up taking shrapnel from a grenade thrown by a renegade Arab American solider during Desert Storm in 1991. And here was his son, Curtis Jr., being loyal for almost seven years, first to a friend and cousin he believed committed the crime and willing to stay loyal now knowing who did commit the crime, but unwilling to turn on the son of his mother's employer.

Mr. Kant's crooked timber metaphor worked in thinking about the Barnes: Jonathan and Parker, the former a selfish bully to his son; the son, a drug-addled, ungrounded child of twenty-seven. The crooked timber of this father and son covered up a murder by the son and allowed an innocent boy to go to jail.

PART

4

47

The tide turned. And as the moon tugged at the sea, the waves clawed at the shore, like a stubborn child refusing to leave the beach at the end of the day.

The real child, who was three, walked along the shore carrying a yellow bucket in her left hand. She picked up small shells and found a few pieces of sea glass. Every few minutes she wound her way back to her mother, Silvana DeLuna, who was sitting on a red blanket about ten feet back from water's edge. They were alone at this end of the beach although a group of children could be heard further back towards the high rise condos. A mile away, at the opposite end of this mile long crescent, stood the luxury hotels of Isla Verde beach, San Juan, Puerto Rico.

Santa Alba had called her lifelong friend, Silvana DeLuna, and invited her to stay at the Intercontinental Hotel for four days.

"There's a bachelor party for one of Edward's friends. They're staying for four days, and I'm coming along to protect my interests from all you Latina lovers. Ha!" Santa Alba laughed.

"I can't, Santa, but thank you so much for asking," Silvana said of the request, made one month earlier.

"Why not? It will be wonderful for us to catch up on the world," the beauty queen of Coamo pressed on.

"First of all, who would mind Mare? Second of all, I have a business, customers. They pay for my work. I cannot just close the door on them."

"Do you mean you never take a vacation?" Santa asked.

"Not in the three years I have been doing this by myself," Silvana replied.

"Does this mean you will never take a vacation?" Santa said, almost cynically.

"I don't know; I haven't thought much about it."

"Suppose you had to close, what would you do?"

And that was the right question. Silvana answered, "Well, my aunt could cover for me for a few days, and I would take Mare with me."

"So?" Santa waited.

"I'll ask." Silvana replied. "But what about Mare, where would she stay?"

"Out on the beach somewhere," Santa laughed, almost hysterically.

And the two young women giggled at the thought of spending four days together at Isla Verde.

The child was a copy of her mother—the same gold olive skin, the long black hair and black piercing eyes. Both mother and daughter were sinewy but strong. Now Silvana, wearing a Sienna orange bikini filled with curves that could barely be contained, touched the little girl's head as she came to show her mother her shell and seaweed treasures. Silvana exhibited delight in her child's discoveries. They laughed. They sat next to one another looking out at the sea.

After a while they shared a sandwich; both sat cross legged and talked softly to one another. The sun was hot. They rose, ran to the water and let the ocean cool their bodies. They returned to the blanket and lay down. Mare used Silvana's outstretched arm for a pillow while the mother rejoiced in the salt water wet body of the young child she gave birth to. The steady cool breeze coming off the water kept them comfortable. And Silvana thought of Juan; how he would have loved a day like this.

Silvana turned to Mare and kissed her head, and as she did the little girl raised her right arm up and around her mother's neck. She softly touched her mother's cheek and slowly drifted off to sleep to the quiet roar of the waves.

Tray Johnson, running along the beach, observed this mother-daughter tenderness occurring before him. He saw the resemblance of mother in the daughter. He thought about a beautiful woman like that, only occasionally though, as thoughts of battles and strategies and his men always occupied his mind. This respite to celebrate Winston Trout's imminent demise as a bachelor was good. Granted it would only be for four days, but just to be able to see the scene he had witnessed refreshed a part of him that was in mothballs. Now thirty yards past the mother and daughter, he recalled details of the two of them; he even noticed that the young mother did not have a ring, thinking that may not be unusual today as many young couples do not bother marrying or sharing traditions. He saw the mother placing a tender kiss on the child's head and felt the love pass to the child. Something stirred in him, something missing. As he neared the end of the beach, it rose up in an eroded slant making it more difficult to run on; he turned and headed back, hoping to see the mother once again.

When the girl awoke, her mother packed their things in a beach bag; they began the walk back to the hotel.

Up ahead Tray saw the mother and daughter holding hands and walking in the same direction he was headed. The girl dropped her bucket, and she pulled her mother's hand to stop. Johnson, now right behind them, bent down, picked up the bucket, and handed it to the girl. She smiled at him. As Johnson, still kneeling, looked up he saw the full measure of this woman before him. She looked down at Tray, and he rose up, now above her five-foot-seven-inch frame. At six feet two inches, he smiled at the mother; she smiled back and said to Mare, "What do you say, Mare?""

"Gracias," the three-year-old, who was multilingual like her mother, replied.

Wanting to continue some form of conversation, Tray said, "A beautiful day."

"Yes, it is," Silvana said now taking Mare's hand once more.

Stymied, Johnson began his run again, turning and waving to the child.

Silvana watched Johnson run ahead. From the back he looked like Juan only stronger. She thought of her running man, and then she thought of what a beautiful day this was. And she looked ahead at Johnson.

Silvana now knew this was a good idea that Santa Alba had for her and Mare to join her at Isla Verde. Only arriving this particular morning, she felt as if she had been away for days. She felt renewed. This was the beginning of a wonderfully brief vacation.

Back at the hotel, as Silvana and Mare came up the sand by the cabanas and beach umbrellas, Santa was waving furiously, calling to her. She was surrounded by six pale white bodies.

"Silvana, come, meet Edward," she called as she ran to her friend and linked arms. Santa Alba had arrived the night before, alone, wanting to make sure everything was as she had arranged. She wanted this first trip to her homeland by Edward and his friends to be memorable. That night she drove a rental car to her parents' home in Coamo and spent the night. In the morning she drove to the San Blas barrio and retrieved Silvana and Mare.

"Sweetie," she said to Silvana, "if it's the last thing I do I'm going to get you out of this place.

Silvana laughed, "What, the barrio is no good for the beauty queen any longer."

"We can do better. There is a bigger life out there waiting for us," Santa said

Silvana laughed, "Well, we better get going before it changes its mind."

At the Intercontinental, Santa booked a two-bedroom suite on the top floor for them. It had an enormous living area facing the beach with a bedroom on each side, each with its own sumptuous bath.

Silvana flushed at the luxury. "These things exist? These things exist right on our own island?'

They laughed; crazy laughs thinking that this part of island life had been kept from them as children. And now here they were enjoying the sea.

"You go off with Mare for the day. Later on the boys will be here, and you can meet them," Santa had said.

"But, "Silvana began and paused.

"What," Santa said

"Um, is Edward staying here with you?" Silvana asked and immediately regretted it.

"No way," Santa laughed the throaty laugh she had learned in New York. "The boys are in the other rooms going down the hall. Two to a suite, like us. They can look out for each other. I'm just here to keep my man tame. We will see them at the beach during the day, but the rest of the time they have put together their own plans."

"Don't you want to spend time with him here?" Silvana said looking out towards the sea through the wall of glass.

"Just a little bit," Santa said, continuing, "I have my best friend in the whole world here, and I want to catch up on Coamo. Besides, those friends can be big bad wolves. You can protect me."

"And…who's going to protect me?" Silvana said striking a pose with hands on hips.

"I will, Mama," Mare said somewhat seriously.

The two friends laughed loudly, and Mare joined in, pleased that she made her mother happy.

"And Edward, this is the only friend I have ever needed besides you," Santa said, gently nudging Silvana into the semicircle of beach chairs and umbrellas that faced the sea.

Edward stood up to shake hands, with his right hand covering his eyes from the afternoon sun directly behind Silvana's head.

"I have heard so much about you from Santa," Edward said with a sweetness that made Santa proud of him. "I am happy to finally meet you."

The other partners in the Brunswick Fund all stood as if called out for revile by a morning bugle. One by one Santa did the introductions adding something unique about each man. Each of them invariably noticed the stunning beauty of Silvana and gave each other knowing glances or discreet smiles. Silvana and Santa both noticed it as if the wolves were eyeing a prey. They just smiled at each other broadly, almost proudly. Santa thought that Edward's second glance at Silvana lasted a little too long.

"This is the poor dear who is leaving us," Santa said flirting with Winston Trout,

"He is the guest of honor here."

"And last but best; I've saved our protector and a US Navy Seal. This is Tray Johnson," Santa said, and noticing a more fixed look from Silvana towards Johnson, added, "He flew in from Afghanistan just to meet you," Santa concluded and moved to sit by Edward.

The over-the-top introduction snapped the diminutive Silvana DeLuna out of whatever it was that intrigued her for the moment, an earlier thought.

Tray Johnson never heard a word Santa said. He could not believe who stood before him. It was over. This was never going to work. Not in four days, not in four lifetimes. How, he wrestled with himself, was he ever going to leave this island and this woman.

He put his hand out to shake hers, and as he did he smiled and he trembled. He had killed Taliban and taken fire to divert attention from one of his wounded men. He never flinched, until now. He felt weak in his stomach.

Johnson looked down at the mini-me of the vision before him. He knelt down in the sand and put his hand out to the small child. "Hola," he said with a smile that Mare returned along with her hand.

"Mama, it's the nice man who picked up my bucket."

"Yes, honey, I know," Silvana said as she knelt down in the sand, the three of them almost in a huddle. She looked at him. "Oh, my God," she thought. Her eyes welled up with tears, she looked away.

"What's wrong," Tray said quietly.

Over the next four days, the boys showed up at various times at the beach and with different combinations of new friends. Parker

Barnes and Sebastian Ball came on the second day with twin sisters, gathered the previous evening from the dance floor of the El San Juan Resort and Casino next on the beach to the Intercontinental. On the third day, Eddie came to the beach with the former NLF star Dijon Sanders and a Sanders fan following that doubled the size of the Brunswick beach huddle. On the fourth day, Gideon Bridge came arm and arm with the most handsome Latin man any of the friends had ever seen.

Later Gideon remarked to Santa, "My goodness, in Puerto Rico, even the men are beautiful."

"Gideon, you truly are awful!" Santa said as the two of them laughed.

The evenings always began sanely with dinner at a different restaurant arranged by, but not attended by, Santa Alba. Limos picked the seven up at the hotel and returned them at night. The one precaution that Santa gave the friends: "This is not the upper east side. There are serious criminals looking for you. You go out at night together, and you come back together. And you don't leave paradise. Isla Verde beach and these resorts and casinos have everything you need."

They agreed.

The only incident, if it could be called an incident, was the third evening when Parker Barnes went missing. In the morning of the fourth day, his suite mate, Sebastian Ball, called the others. There was no Parker to be found.

Late in the afternoon Barnes arrived at the beach looking worn. His account of a night with a wild woman of San Juan got the others laughing. Sebastian Ball knew otherwise. Parker had gone back to Mr. Fantasy. He knew the look on his friend of a lifetime; he knew the toll that the cocaine took on Barnes every time he slipped. Rehabilitation had been an ongoing event in Barnes life, now up to number six. Different incidents called for different lengths of stay. Some required lengthier stays to avoid incarceration for possession; others were shorter based on the insistence of his parents that he get help. They all worked for a short time, but then the relapse always occurred.

And Tray, well, there were no incidents, no staying out late with his friends; in fact, they barely saw him, mainly at dinner. Each night he went to bed at an early hour and rose with the sun.

Santa Alba and Silvana's daughter, Mare, became best friends. Santa never had an opportunity to keep much of an eye on Edward as she was busy half of the day playing with Mare. Where was Silvana?

In the morning Silvana would walk out to the beach at seven before many of the locals went for their morning beach activity. There she and Tray would walk along the beach. This pattern went on for the next three days and for hours each morning. In the afternoon at lunch, they would return to the hotel and have lunch with Mare on the beach at the Hungry Sailor. Then the three of them would walk off hand in hand for another three hours to the deserted end of the beach.

On the morning of the fifth day as they were all returning home, great dread overcame Tray Johnson. When he woke he was in a panic. Going into battle against a mortal enemy had been easier by far. There was no fear, no longing and no impending sense of great loss.

Silvana and he had said their goodbyes the previous night at 1 a.m. while the remainder of the pre-wedding party made a night of it at the El San Juan. Santa was to drive Silvana and Mare back to the barrio early in the morning. Tray had a 6 a.m. flight back to Kennedy. And except for the next two days in which he would be participating in brief patriotic celebration and Navy Seal demonstration of effectiveness, he would be home on leave for two more weeks. Winston Trout's wedding was in a week.

And from the panic he felt when he woke came the answer. He showered, shaved, packed, and went to Silvana's door at 4:30 a.m., knocking quietly.

She answered it after a time, wiping sleep from her eyes and smiling broadly at Tray.

"I'm coming back for you in three days." Johnson said confidently.

"What are you talking about, Tray," Silvana said, puzzled, since in their confusion on how to conclude this wonderful time in both their lives, they agreed on writing and when Tray returned from Afghanistan the following year he would come to see her.

"I am not leaving you. I want you to come with me in three days." Johnson said.

"That's impossible," Silvana said, knowing this would not work. "We've only known each other three days. I can't just take Mare, leave my business, and go to the States for two or three weeks while you're on leave."

"I don't want you to; I want you to marry me. I never want to be anywhere you are not." Johnson said.

"Tray, I care for you so much. But this is so fast." Silvana pleaded. "Please don't do this to me. Don't do this to us."

The Seal straightened up, "I'm doing this for us. You know you are all I want, and I know you feel the same way. There is nothing we cannot do together. In three days I'll come back. I want you and Mare to come with me. While I'm away you can have the guesthouse at my parent's place. In one year I will come back for good. I will try to cut it in half and complete my service in the New York area."

"You're serious. You must be mad. Tray, please think," Silvana begged, tears streaming down her face.

"I am thinking more clearly," and he placed both his hands on her shoulders, "more clearly than any time in my life. Please believe me, Silvana. I love you more than life."

"No, Tray, I can't," she cried.

"Do you love me?" he asked.

"You said it right; I do know we love each other."

"Then trust me."

"Tray, I'm hardly over the loss of Juan."

"I will give you time on that, you need that, but let me help you." He looked at her; he was not winning this battle. "In three days I will come back, and will you at least think about it and talk with me about it."

"Yes, I will talk." She said firmly but lovingly, "But…"

"Don't," he put his finger to her lips, then removed it and kissed her lips. "In three days," he kissed her again. "Now get back to bed. I love you, Silvana."

"Oh, Tray, I do love you. Please, please, please be real. Don't let me hurt?" she said crying, now stamping her foot down in a moment of insistence.

"You will never hurt. I promise."

And he was gone.

Santa was just coming down the hallway from her night out with the bachelor party and passed Tray Johnson who hugged her without saying a word.

"What was that about?" Santa asked as she met Silvana at the door to their room

"Don't ask," Silvana smiled as they entered the suite.

"What did he want?" Santa asked

"You do not need to ask," Silvana laughed, the tears still on her cheeks

"What do you mean," Santa smiled, but didn't quite get it.

"Tray wants me to come with him in three days. He asked me to marry him. He wants me to wait for him in the States."

"WHAT," Santa said so loudly, that Silvana had to put her finger to her lips.

"Aren't you happy for me?"

"Of course," Santa now laughed out loud, "But it's not fair. I've been working on Edward for over two years and not a peep. Here you come along and in four days have a proposal. What's fair about that," she smiled, hurt and happy. And now, "So you're going right?"

"No, I'm not. How can I. I just met him." Silvana said, unable to find a way out of her dilemma.

"Listen to me. Do you love him?" Santa asked

"Like I never thought I would again. Like the world is mine. Yes I love him, madly."

And this exploding romance was not the only surprise that would occur with the group of seven friends. The visit ending bachelor party, earlier the night before, was full of surprises.

48

The final night of Winston Trout's bachelor party took place amid the pulsating rhythms at the El San Juan Hotel.

It was Saturday night in San Juan and the great mahogany lobby and bar of the hotel overflowed as hundreds crowded in to hear the Latin gods of music. And there on the dance floor was this girl, this vision in red, swaying, throwing her head back with long hair flowing, laughing. Even as the Gipsy Kings sang and strummed guitars and beat their drums, they could not take their eyes off the beauty before them. By herself on the dance floor, something had set her free. She flowed with their music, the music moved her across the floor as she swung her hips toward the band and then out towards the crowd emphasizing the beat. The lead singer, a raspy baritone, stretched his neck upward to reach the higher notes of "Bomboleo," but his roving eyes never left the girl as she danced, stomped, and clapped her hands before his band.

She might have been a belly dancer with the contortions she took her hips through. Her floor-length red skirt stopped at her bare tight waist. A red and black blouse was tied just below breasts that flowed out from the open buttons. When she spun around clapping, her hands over her head, a black thong was revealed through the thin fabric of the flaming skirt.

If you only gauged this young woman by her dress and appearance, you would think differently of her. This beauty with black eyes had a long angular face with rouge on her cheeks. Her smile showed bright white teeth framed by flaming red lipstick that matched the color of her skirt. But what throbbed under those clothes, the perfectly proportioned body of an athlete and the spirit of this wild girl was infectiously charming to all watching her, and they swayed with her and the music of the Kings.

She danced, first by herself, then with another woman. The space around them got smaller as the crowd leaned in to get a closer look. Next she reached out to an older man, then other men, as the song pulsated on and on for six or seven minutes. The floor grew smaller still as more men sought immortality in a dance with this divine creature.

And she was gracious, dancing with each man as if they were on a date. Latin men are good dancers at any age and most gave the girl a good partner, if only for a half minute before they faded.

The old men puffed—maybe one last chance. The young men puffed up—maybe a first chance with a daring and attractive girl.

And Sebastian Ball, who along with Winston Trout, Gideon Bridge, and Tray Johnson and Silvana DeLuna had been watching from ten feet away, was on fire. The roulette tables still were the main attraction for two others in the party: Parker Barnes and the dancing girl's date, Edward Wheelwright.

When the music of "Bomboleo" stopped, the dripping wet Santa Alba left the floor to uproarious applause and rushed to the large round lounge area the group had reserved. Silvana and Tray roared with laughter at Santa's outrageous performance. Winston, the groom-to-be, was trying to be true in thought, and Gideon, well, he was not indifferent, smiling broadly and clapping enthusiastically along with the throng.

The lead singer of the Kings took out a handkerchief to wipe away the sweat as the audience continued their roar. He smiled and pointed to Santa. A spotlight went on her as she made her way to the table, and the roar got louder. Like a rock star she turned, smiling, laughing and waved to the band.

Sebastian was the first up from the table to welcome Santa back from her dance-a-thon. She rushed into his arms, and he hugged the sopping wet body of this object of a new desire.

Sebastian Ball had known Edward Wheelwright all his life, and he had known Santa Alba for two years. He did not know what to do. Santa had ignited something in him, in a space he was unaware of. He was afraid and saw risk, but there was this desire he had never known.

"My God, Santa, what in the hell was that?" he gasped and the others laughed.

Silvana and Tray came to Santa and hugged her as did Winston and Gideon.

Much of the crowd that was standing in every part of the lobby watched the reunion of Santa with her friends and knew there was a special party; some longed to join in.

Sebastian, his linen shirt wet from Santa's embrace, alone remained standing as his friends sat back down in the large semi-circular booth. This was the young man who facilitated other's needs. He had no needs—until this moment. Now, Sebastian felt a tugging at his life's values. Before this moment he was happy for Edward and Santa. Now, he saw that Santa was crying out for attention, attention that Edward more and more was denying her.

His question to himself that he must have answered this night was, would Santa be interested in him as she had been with Edward. Edward had much to offer a girl, Sebastian thought: he was handsome, fit, and remote and focused on money. It's a good thing to be a striver but not for its own sake. There had to be something all that focus was for; it couldn't of itself be fulfilling. Sebastian understood this and would not lose his focus. And while Wheelwright had looks and charm, looks did not totally escape the Ball gene pool, nor was he out of shape. If Sebastian Ball was remote, he thought, it may be his money that was off putting; it certainly was not him. Finally, he was not focused on money; it was just there, in enormous quantities, billions, for him and whomever he chose for a bride, to do with as they must.

Sebastian came back to reality and rejoined the group but determined to move forward this night. He sat at the end of the booth, next to Santa Alba and could feel the heat still flowing out. The air near her body was hot.

Santa took Sebastian's arm, still laughing, blushing as she looked up at him. It was a look he had not known before. "Did you like my dance, Sweetie?"

Ball's heart stopped. Had he heard wrong? Absolutely not. Then what? How was this possible? The moment he desires this stunning creature she is his. It was not possible; she must be toying with him. She is just being her charming self; although in all the time he'd known her, he had never seen this. What was all this for—this dance, this attire; rather who was this for? Him? Edward? To make him jealous, to make him take notice. If it was to get taken notice of, mission accomplished. Four hundred men AND women all wanted a night in bed with this wild girl.

"I loved your dance, every moment of it, my dear." Ball replied, to Santa, not loud enough for all to hear but not a whisper.

"Thank you, Sebastian," and she nuzzled up to him.

I will go mad, he thought.

"Santa, where is Edward? I can't believe he missed this." Ball said.

"I didn't do this for Edward."

"Then who, you certainly went to a lot of effort. By the way, the thong is a nice touch." He kidded, pushing hard.

"Who do you think?" she questioned.

He decided to go for it, "Me, you did this for me. For us?"

Santa looked at him and began to laugh. And she laughed and laughed, and the others were silenced by her throaty laugh and her broad smile that revealed two rows of perfect white teeth. Sebastian's face got red, he froze.

And now they listened as she spoke. "Sebastian, you are so silly; you are so funny. This is for Winston. In one week he will be married; this is to help him get prepared." And now looking at a pale Winston she asked, "So, Winston, are you prepared?"

"Santa, I am more ready than I ever thought I'd be. Thank you. The next gift you can give me is to teach my bride how to do that."

"Winston, sweetie, you need to be born here. It's in the DNA." Santa laughed and her friends, including Sebastian, joined in laughing with her. And they drank.

The Gipsy Kings continued playing. Couples took to the dance floor. Several men came over to ask Santa to dance, and she politely declined. After a while Santa noticed that Sebastian had gotten unusually quiet. As a slow song started, Santa grabbed Sebastian's hand.

"Come, dance with me," she said in an excited tone.

"Thanks, Santa, but I'd like to just sit here and watch," a strangely subdued Ball replied.

"There wasn't a question mark at the end of my sentence. Come on," she persisted, rising with his hand in hers.

The big man reluctantly rose and followed Santa to the dance floor. As they neared the circle, the crowd parted and began cheering, hoping for an encore. Santa gently raised her arm, and they quieted, respecting her space.

"What's the matter, Sebastian? You got so quiet."

Bravely he said, "Santa, I'm having the time of my life. This is wonderful. The music of this island is wonderful."

"But there was something else I missed. What was it?" She tilted her head. "You went cold when I said my little surprise was for the groom-to-be. I thought it was so funny when you said you thought I danced and dressed like this for you. Only you weren't trying to be funny, were you?" Santa asked.

"Farthest thing from my mind," Sebastian replied.

"What happened, what did I do to let you think that?"

"Honestly?" he asked

"Honestly," she said as they waltzed slowly across the dimly lit floor.

"You awoke something in me," he said, short and sweet.

"Or something in you awoke?" she replied.

"You," he retorted.

"How," she asked.

"I have no idea. Something was never there and now something is there." He said, not understanding himself but fully understanding what he was missing.

"Good," she said.

"What?" Sebastian said looking at her, realizing she did not understand what pain she was inflicting on him.

"I said good. It is good isn't it, Sebastian?"

"It's only good if it was intended. It's only good if it works. Otherwise it's like waking up in a dark room and bumping into something and wondering what the hell was that," he replied.

"Come with me," and they left the dance floor. She led him out past the reception desk, outside and into the night. The evening air was pierced by the song of the coqui, the tiny frog of the island that sits in the palm trees. Santa led Sebastian past the pool area and out onto the darkened beach.

She sat on the sand and pulled Sebastian down beside her.

When he was seated beside her, she pushed him back, leaned into him and across his chest and kissed him.

He lay immobile, his lips reaching hers, longing for hers, hungry for hers. He rolled her over, placing himself half on her, reaching for her hip. He thought: Oh, that hip. And he felt the thin line of the black thong. The fire was lit. He kissed her passionately; she responded fiercely.

They went at each other, unbuttoning, sliding what would slide, pulling what would pull until they lay on the beach naked.

Not a word was spoken from the time Santa said "come with me," on the dance floor. Two hours later they lay beside each other, cool from the 2 a.m. breeze, spent.

Spent is the right word. He took his large frame and placed it on top of her strong body and kissed her passionately and inserted himself into her and then pumped for all he was worth. She enveloped him. She wrapped herself around him every possible way—around his large, long probe; around his strong, wide back; around his head; around his legs with her powerfully strong legs. It was if an octopus was on him, a pulsating octopus. For whenever he pumped, she met him. And when he pulled back, she pulled back. And this went on for over an hour, pumping at and into each other. When they came, covered in sand and sweat, a second period of love making began. Then they took each other's clothes and wiped the sand and moisture away from their bodies and they stood. They began foreplay as afterplay, exploring every crevice and curve and organ that had not been fully explored before the rush to fulfillment. They touched each other with their toes, their hands, and their mouths. And when they were licked clean, they lay back down in the sand, spent.

"Do you still think my surprise wasn't for you?" she teased.

"I don't care about the surprise; I have the real thing," and Sebastian reached over and gently ran a hand over one of the breasts that had been bulging through the blouse during her dance.

Lying naked in the pitch black of the night, Sebastian and Santa looked out to the stars. With nothing but a bright night sky above them, it was as if they were there, out in the universe, floating through time.

Sebastian thought of the stars and their energy. He knew all things were possible. He believed what Winston always told him, that man's discoveries are just evidence that God left behind.

He knew that energy from the sun was the answer, that it could provide most of the energy the earth required to run things. God had left many clues on how to harness the sun's energy. He concluded he and Winston Trout would find those clues and fulfill God's plan.

He rose up on an elbow and looked at the beauty queen of Coamo in her naked glory. For the first time in the young titan's life, he wanted something. And he wanted more and more of her.

And out among the stars, with palm trees rustling in the early morning breeze, they made love again. And again.

Later, as Sebastian looked at Santa, she asked him, "What will we tell Edward?"

And now that the lust had been fulfilled, he wondered, what would he tell Edward. He hadn't had time to think. He must think, and an injured conscience was beginning to weigh in: his friend, Edward.

49

—————

T raynor Johnson was the athlete of the boys from Brunswick. He played baseball with abandon and football without fear. He was salutorian of Brunswick, behind his best friend and valedictorian Winston Trout.

Traynor was not of the wealth that existed at Brunswick. His father was a rear admiral, who when he retired from the Navy, he settled in Greenwich, CT. When the admiral applied to Brunswick for Traynor, tuition was waived and every year for the fourteen years Traynor spent there with the friends of his life. A grateful and loyal Brunswick School valued service to America, and for the Board of Overseers at Brunswick, there could be no greater loyalty than to spend one's working life in military service. Those same board members also were aware their sons could benefit from association with a child reared by an admiral. And they were correct in that regard. The friends of Traynor Johnson were stronger because of his fire for life, and they were smarter because of the depth of knowledge he pursued. In their activities he was direct. He would not veer off course. If a friend was moved to misdirection, it was always Traynor who could be depended upon to guide them back on course. He was straight and respectful. He never lied.

But Traynor Johnson also benefited from his friendship with the six members of the Brunswick School Investment Fund, never more so than from Winston Trout. If Parker Barnes was off with his father learning the construction business in a summer, it was Trout who was readily available to be with Johnson. When Sebastian Ball spent part of his winter vacation skiing in Utah, Johnson and Trout made it their business to be together. They were there for each other, not that Sebastian, Kish, Parker, Edward, or Gideon would not give up anything for each other, but of the seven, the two closest friends were Winston and Traynor.

And while they were not planning to sit with one another on the trip home from Puerto Rico, Winston convinced Sebastian to swap first class seats and sit with Parker so he could sit with Traynor. "I've got business to talk over with Tray, really important business."

When Winston plopped into the heavy leather seat, which sat two abreast in the front of the Boeing 767, Johnson saw a worried look on his friends face.

"Getting nervous now, huh, Winny?" Johnson asked.

"Not about the wedding, if that's what you mean, Tray," Winston Trout replied.

"Then what, you don't seem yourself?" Johnson persisted.

"Then what? I've been watching you for the past four days, Tray. You're in some kind of fog. What's wrong?" Winston, ever the concerned friend, asked.

"Ha, Winny, I think I'm in love," a jubilant Johnson blurted out, surprising himself with the words.

"That would be with Silvana, Santa's friend, I'd presume."

"You would presume correctly."

"Sebastian told me that it may be more serious than love," Trout continued probing. "I can't imagine what could be more serious than love. What do you think he meant by that?"

"Sebastian should not worry too much about my affairs; after all, I think he may have gone further than he should have last night," Johnson confided.

"Why do you say that, Tray?" Trout asked.

"After Santa and Sebastian left, Eddie came looking for Santa when he finished with the casino. We told him that we thought she had gone up to her room. Eddie came back a half hour later and said she wasn't in her room," Johnson finished.

"Oh, oh," Trout said, a look of surprise coming over his face.

"And," Johnson began.

"There's an 'and,'" Trout smiled.

"Isn't there always," Johnson smiled also, "but this is not funny. AND, this morning when I went to say goodbye to Silvana, Santa was just coming in at 4:30."

"What's that mean," a now confused Trout asked his friend.

"Well, you probably went up to your room around 1 a.m., and Santa left before you. When Eddie finished up, it was around two thirty; when he came back down after looking for Santa, it was around four. So where was Santa from say twelve thirty till after four?"

"OK, I get it. I have a better question. Where was Sebastian till after three," Trout posited.

"You should have asked him before you gave up your seat to come inquiring about my love life," Tray said to his friend.

Winston rose as if to go ask Sebastian.

Johnson grabbed his arm laughing, "Sit your ass down, Winny."

And they both got silly for a moment thinking of the complications about to set in among their friends.

"Alright, enough of that," Trout finished with a smile, "Back to you. So tell me about Silvana. We haven't seen enough of you these few days to know what's going on there. But Sebastian says it's more than just puppy love."

Tray almost laughed now, "How in the heck does Sebastian Ball know so much about Silvana and me?" and Johnson paused for a moment, "Unless," and he stopped.

"Unless," Trout continued Johnson's train of thought, "he heard it from Santa who got it from Silvana."

"When did he let on how much he knew about Silvana and me?" Tray asked.

"This morning before you came down for the ride over to the airport," Trout reported.

"Then that confirms a lot more than you were looking for. Yes, I'm in love, but yes, Sebastian was spending time with Santa," Johnson analyzed.

"Tray, my boy, I am not interested one bit in what Sebastian and Santa were up to last night. If Eddie loses her, it will be his own fault. He doesn't pay enough attention to the girl and last night she was crying out for it. So let's get back to you. How bad is it?"

Trout persisted.

"As bad as it can get. I love her, and I'm going to marry her," Tray confessed.

"Ah, Tray, four days. Just a bit in a hurry are we."

"As much in a hurry as I've ever been. I knew it the second I saw her, Winny. I don't know how that's possible but that's what happened."

"Are you sure it's not being on leave, being here in this country with all these beautiful women. You know what Gideon says."

"Yes, I know. "In Puerto Rico, even the men are beautiful," and the two friends laughed loudly, enough so that it annoyed a passenger in the row ahead who was trying to nap.

From behind them they heard the loud voice of Sebastian Ball call out, "Can you people up front hold it down," a rather large laugh followed.

"Well, the one thing I notice," Trout said, "is that you're looking a little weak in the knees. So what's next?"

"I'm coming back in three days." Johnson said assuredly.

"What? There's a thing called my wedding on Saturday," Trout said incredulously.

"I know. I'll be there, you know that. I've got a lot to take care of in a short period of time."

"Tray, like what? What can't wait?"

"Well, I've got to talk with my father. I want Silvana and her daughter to move into the guesthouse while I'm gone," as Johnson said this Trout just shook his head. "Then I've got to plan the next year to get assigned back here as quick as possible."

"You start thinking like that and you'll get your head blown off when you go back to Kabul. You keep focused. If she's still here when you come home, then go see her. But after four days Tray, to upset your whole life, it's not good."

"Look, Winny, don't say anything to the other guys."

"Don't say anything? That's all they're talking about. 'Who's cast a spell on Tray? Who's this mysterious spirit who knocked Tray senseless?' Seriously, none of us have ever seen you like this."

"Me neither," Johnson concluded.

50

On his return from San Juan, Tray Johnson was met at Kennedy Airport by his father, the Admiral. Tray had taken a speaking engagement for the Greenwich Veterans of Foreign Wars, and his father drove him to the Burning Tree Country Club to give the talk.

He was introduced warmly to the audience of roughly two hundred men as one of Greenwich's own. Tray Johnson was Brunswick School alum, the son of a Rear Admiral, a US Naval Academy graduate, and currently a Lieutenant and Navy Seal serving in Afghanistan. The applause for each life stage Johnson passed through was long and well meant. His speech had been prepared more than two months before as he agreed to speak at the request of his father, who was a member of both the Veterans group and the Country Club.

"Finally," Lt. Traynor Johnson spoke to the rapt attention of those who had served before him, and while listening to him, realized they were being well represented now, "territorialism is one of life's most primitive manifestations. Trees battle adjacent trees for light in a silent overhead war. Ant colonies destroy one another over the invasion of a tunnel system. The Native American Indian fought to the death for what was part of his existence: land, more than that, the earth. And the Arabs will never let Israel live in peace as they view that land as theirs.

"The British, who invented the rule of law, tried to clarify things legally in the Middle East. At the end of World War I, they accepted an outsized leadership role in carving up and codifying the remnants of the Ottoman Empire. Where those states exist today is much the same as Winston Churchill, as Britain's Colonial Secretary, and his colleagues defined them from 1917 to about 1922 in a series of declarations, agreements, correspondences, and papers. The problem is that they conflict and shift commitments regarding the division and governance of the Middle East. And as Britain exited the empire business totally, some of these same problems occurred as they partitioned India and Pakistan.

"Since that time nothing has worked well. All of the wars in Europe and the Middle East after the Peace of 1919 resulted from the mistakes and arrogance of the victors. World War II, Iraq, Iran, the six-day war, Afghanistan, India versus Pakistan I, II and III, and the War on Terror all spring from that period in time.

"What America is working for now is to bring the peace process along. General Curtis Lemay, former Air Force Chief of Staff, stamped the slogan; Peace is Our Profession, on the Strategic Air Command, the wing of the Air Force at the time that had all of America's nuclear bombers under its mandate. Teddy Roosevelt said 'America should walk softly and carry a big stick.' Both of those concepts are embodied in our efforts in Iraq, Afghanistan and Pakistan. We must be strong but humble among the people we are trying to help. The past hatred must end; war must end.

"We must realize that territorialism is instinctive and one of nature's first inclinations. We must help the world find solutions peacefully and fairly. That is not what has happened to date.

"Thank you for having me here today. It is great to be back in Greenwich, to be with you once again."

There was sustained applause, but none more than from Admiral Johnson.

Later after the hand shaking and one-on-one chats, while walking out to the car, Admiral Johnson said: "Tray, that was an excellent talk, well-thought-out and well received. Now this other news you shared with me on the ride from the airport we need to spend more time on." And the discussion began in the car on the way to their home, not ten minutes from the Club, and continued at home.

"I want you knowing what you are doing. I want it so well-thought-out that you are asking me in advance for what help you'll need from me," the Admiral Johnson told his son.

"Thanks, Dad," Tray Johnson told his father.

"What does your friend Silvana think of coming here so quickly? Has she told her family?"

"No, sir. And she doesn't think much of it herself."

"Tray," the Admiral said, somewhat frustrated, "what are you thinking? And when would you expect her to come here?"

"Soon."

"Tray. This is, and I don't want to be judgmental, but it is rash."

"I agree. I know. It goes against all my development. I know it's not like me. But I don't think I've ever been in love before," the younger Johnson said to his father.

"It doesn't sound like it to me," his father said.

The circular nature of this discussion lasted almost thirty minutes: question, answer, question, answer. And with each question posed, Tray Johnson was more convinced how right his feelings for Silvana DeLuna were. And with each question answered, Admiral Johnson grew more worried about his son's decision making in this process.

"Son," the exasperated Admiral said, "you and I both know this is not like you. It is not well-thought-out. So you still have some more thinking to do. I am here, however you need me, for whatever counsel you want. In the end, Tray, it is your life. Whatever you decide, whether you think I'm on board or not, I will support you and do what you ask me to."

"Thank you, sir," the grateful son said.

"One more important thing, Tray. In the Navy men are addicted to two things—their ship and her crew. That's somewhat true in life."

"How do you mean, sir?"

"The men I've known in and out of the Navy all seem to have two addictions—to a thing and a person. Usually they're aligned; when they're not, problems can occur."

"You're trying to tell me something, and I'm missing it," Tray stated.

"I see you so committed to your mission with the Seals it is an addiction. That's good. Navy men thrive on their mission; it is addictive."

"And my other addiction?"

"It was your men, is your men. But this new romance, all you are trying to do here in such a short time span, it will be in conflict with your devotion to your men."

"I'm sorry, sir; I don't see it that way at all."

"No, you wouldn't, Tray. That early step of romance, when infatuation occurs, is blinding."

"But you were in love once."

"Yes, I still am, but when I went off to sea, it was done. I knew your mother was here, waiting for me. It was not a distraction."

"Exactly, and Silvana will be here for me."

"It is not done. Your heart is not settled."

"Can we talk about something else?" Tray pleaded.

The Admiral rattled off in quick succession: "Parker Barnes—drugs and Lenny Crane; Winston Trout—solar energy and Emily Albright."

"No Dad, not even close, something else."

"Those two examples are in harmony."

"Alright, I give. How are they in harmony?"

"Take Parker, unfortunately his addiction is to drugs, almost unbreakable. His friendship with Crane supersedes his relationship with the other six of you because of his addiction and which I'm sure Crane assists him in."

"Well we've talked about that before, Lenny probably is a person who supports Parker's drug habit."

"And therefore, Parker has his two addictions in harmony."

The Navy Seal shook his head. There was logic to his father's thinking, but he felt it was forced.

"And Winston," the Admiral began.

"Forget Winston, that's an easy one. I get that."

"OK, let's talk about Sebastian or Eddie Wheelwright."

"Why all my friends?"

"These are examples we can both relate to. I've known them as long as you have, if not as well."

"What's your theory with Sebastian?"

"The thing is power. The person is you seven brothers. He uses power all the time. He does a good deal of exercising it through the seven of you."

"He's being helpful."

"That's a way to look at it. But he would be in conflict if you boys rejected his power."

Tray laughed, "Have you always had these ideas."

"Frames."

"Frames?"

"They're frames to help you see things about people. You can break them down further to view courage or fear. I gave you an approach a while back to think about, that would help you see those characteristics in your men."

"Yes. But have you always thought of my friends in those terms too?"

"This is how I've taught myself in life. It's a helpful way to see people and what they're up to, what they're capable of."

"And Eddie?"

"Ah. Conflicted."

"How so?"

"He's driven. Committed to playing the game and succeeding. He lives it and breathes it. Consistently. And while he was with Valerie McGuire, she fed that. She had the same desires he had."

Tray looked at his father. "Where are you getting this stuff? You're scaring me."

"Now I hear from you and your friends he's got this new hot number."

"Santa?"

"That's what I hear. And I imagine his focus had been quite divided."

"Why? Santa can't be his addiction; can't she get him in harmony?"

"Not that. But Valerie is undone."

"What. You don't know that."

"Yes, I do know that. You don't spend half your life loving someone and just end it over a wild fling."

"So all these talks we had and all this time."

"And the time you bring the boys by and you would all catch me up on your adventures, I paid attention. It's what I do. A sailor is always alert."

"I see some application."

"You need to think about it. Being unsettled, unresolved in your two addictions in life is not good. Get in harmony with yourself."

"I will think about it."

"The last thing I'll say on the subject is that this seems more one-sided than it should be."

"I'll make it up to you, Dad."

"I don't mean me, dummy."

"You mean Silvana," Tray replied.

"Yes, it seems your impetuousness will override her judgment of what is best for her and her daughter. It almost sounds as if you are the solution to her problems."

"Dad, what do you mean?"

"Tray, think about it. She's a single mother. You say she runs a small laundry by herself. She lives in a small town. Obviously she is not well-to-do."

"It's not like that," a now younger son said to his father.

"Tray, when you're in love, nothing seems as it is. But trust me. A young woman alone in the world with a child needs the security a man can provide."

"And I want to. I love her."

"But you need to find out if she loves you."

"I know she does. We are of one mind," a now confident Tray Johnson told his father.

"Infatuation is a beautiful feeling. It will lift you up to heights you could not imagine. But when infatuation ends, there is no safety net to catch you. And it does end. And what was built during the period of infatuation needs to have a strong enough foundation to survive. Many people wake up six months into their lives together, about the time infatuation ends and wonder who it is they are sitting across the table from in the morning."

"Dad," the younger Johnson smiled.

"Don't "Dad" me on this one. I've been there a few times more than you. And I got very lucky that the woman I sit across the table from every morning still loves me. Why, I don't know since I was on a boat away from her in most of our younger years."

"And this may happen to me also."

"But, son, we did have more than three days together before we decided to move in together," a wearying father said to his son. "Alright, you're tiring an old man out. You've gotten my advice. Now it's up to you to think this through."

Traynor Johnson rose and saluted his father, as he always did when leaving the Admiral. The Admiral rose, smiled, returned the salute, and hugged the young man he loved.

51

The power plant that is El Yunque, the Puerto Rican rain forest, begins early at the first light. The yuccas awake, long fronded palms take in the morning moisture and the areca plants begin pumping out oxygen. The fresh, damp, aromatic air rises out of the rain forest.

Left to their devices the clouds would drift gently to the east. But it is from the east that the winds from Africa come. As the winds reach the green island, they split up—going north and south. On this day it is southern African winds that push the clouds of air from El Yunque to the south. And when the winds push the clouds over the dry mountains that divide Puerto Rico, they encounter the parched, hot air of the south.

Silvana awoke to the crack of thunder. She sat up with a start. Was that the door, was he there? Then she heard another crack of thunder. It was 6 a.m.; it was the third day. Would he come? No, he would not. She was deluding herself for even thinking something so foolish could occur. But what if he did come? What would she tell him?

"What would I tell him?" Silvana DeLuna asked herself out loud, disturbing the sleep of her young daughter, Mare. She had thought of nothing since she saw Tray at her hotel room door three days earlier. Yet, she had not brought herself to a conclusion. She could not let herself reach a conclusion. If the crazy, crazy dream of a life that Tray had proposed were not to happen, the loss would be too great. She would have deluded herself like a young school girl. If he came, he came. Then they would talk. If he didn't come, he didn't come. She would have to be crazy to think that this could happen.

She pushed the thought from her mind and rose to begin her day.

In Coamo you are known by your name and what you do or did. Santa Alba was the Beauty Queen of Coamo; Juan, the runner of San Diego; Silvana, the washer woman of San Blas; and Silvana's aunt, Carmen, the seamstress of Coamo.

On the morning Santa Alba drove Silvana and Mare home from their brief vacation in San Juan, Silvana kept the laundry closed. Once they said their goodbyes, Silvana and Mare went to Tia Carmen's home. It was Carmen who had half-raised Silvana when her mother died, and it was Carmen who finished raising Silvana when her father left for Brazil with her brother, Chunk; Carmen was sort of a mid-wife of life. She was the family member who provided the nurturing and care. When Silvana lost Juan and almost her will to live afterwards, it was Carmen who brought Silvana back helping her realize the beauty of the child she and Juan created. She helped her appreciate every day she was alive to help Mare develop.

And it was to Carmen that Silvana now turned for advice on the matter at hand.

"Have you lost what little sense I gave you," Carmen screamed at Silvana upon hearing Tray's proposal.

"But, Auntie," Silvana began.

Before another word came out, Carmen was berating Silvana for acting, well, like a little school girl.

This discussion went on for most of the afternoon. Finally mentally drained, Carmen sent Silvana out. "Don't let me hear any more of this crazy talk," Carmen said as she kissed Silvana and Mare as they were leaving. "And if that sailor boy shows up on your doorstep, get rid of him. And if you don't have the courage to do it, send him over to me, and I'll take care of it."

"Bye, Carmen," Silvana said using the older woman's first name, which she did when Carmen got over the top on advice.

318

At midnight as the eve of the third day would become early morning hours, Silvana sat in an old chair outside her house. Mare was long asleep. The air was heavy and damp, not after a rain but before it. The calm shut out all the noise of the island.

Silvana was in a mild panic. She would be a fright without any sleep. And what was I thinking, bringing him here, to see me in this element with my washing all about.

But with time to herself, she resigned her fate to God. She blessed herself. I am who I am, and I know who Tray is. He will come. We will have a life together. Mare will have a whole family.

52

Later in the afternoon, resigned that Tray Johnson would not come, Silvana opened the doors of her home and business. The morning rain gave way to the dry heat of a mountain facing south towards the equator. Mare played with a favorite doll in the bedroom. Silvana hung a load of whites on the clothes lines in the small rear yard.

Silvana came back in and began pressing shirts that were hung on hangers but not yet ironed. She found that shirts with a label that said they were made in Egypt were the easiest to iron of all cotton. She wondered why. Why would cotton grown in one part of the world be so different from every other county; why would the iron smoothly glide through Egyptian cotton yet get snarled up in cotton from Jordan or Vietnam? Was this because of the soil and the way cotton was grown or was it more in the making of the shirt, the types of looms they used to process the cotton? Silvana remembered seeing in her school books the large factories in Massachusetts that produced textiles in the past. There were giant floors of machines and hundreds of women working at the machines. She remembered the story of one factory, with five floors and more than three hundred machines on each floor, that had collapsed killing more than one thousand women working there. The book said there was so much shaking from all those machines that it shook the building apart.

Silvana finished the ironing, put a thin wire around the group of six shirts, attached the right number to the bottom of the first shirt with a pin, and hung them beside other shirts waiting for pick up.

Next, she grabbed the broom, swept the floor that passed between the two doors, and emptied the dust pan into a waste basket by the front door where the afternoon sun continued blazing in.

Silvana started the next load of wash. Underwear! Of all the work she did, the one job she felt worse about was washing other people's underwear. It wasn't that the job was beneath her; it was the condition of the clothing when it was brought in. The stains, the yellow and brown stains sickened her. Some were from the owners soiling themselves; some were from wearing the same underwear multiple times. And stink! Awful. The worst part of this job would be the customers who wanted to argue that Silvana did not get their underwear clean enough. "Maybe if you didn't pee all over yourself they wouldn't be so yellow," well, that was what she wanted to tell them. Or "Maybe if you didn't wear the same panties six days in a row they wouldn't smell like a dead skunk." But she never did. She held her tongue, usually adding. "They might be getting older from washing so much," or "the cotton from Brazil yellows more than others," or when all else failed, "I'll add more bleach next time and leave them in the sun longer." Eventually, customers accepted her explanation. Eventually, Silvana came to realize that customers, no matter who they were, just liked feeling there was someone beneath them and whom they could berate. It wasn't personal; it was just life.

Here this magnificent beauty accepted life as it was given to her. Not complaining about what was not, but thankful for what was. For Mare. And, when he was here on earth, for Juan. And in moments like this, when what almost was, she would shed a tear. Not many but a few to help her in her sentiments.

Once the underwear was done and as she was hanging it out back, she wondered why, in those pictures of the textile plants, it was women who ran all those machines. And when the rumbling of five floors of machines got so strong they shook the building apart, it was women who lay dead and buried under the machines and bricks. Where were the men? What did they do?

Silvana went back inside; she was beginning to sweat. She wiped her brow and sat on a wooden chair by the kitchen table. From there she could see Mare playing in the bedroom. The child was happy and talking with her doll.

A shadow came over the front door, and as she looked up, the blazing sun outlined, like an eclipse, the figure of a man. The man was not moving, just standing there looking in at her. She could see his frame; it was black against a white surrounding light so bright she could not distinguish any features.

Silvana did not move. She sat paralyzed by hope.

And then the man spoke, "Well, do you have your bags packed?"

53

"Tray, like you, I have responsibilities. I cannot just walk away from them. I have customers. My aunt, when my mother died, loaned me the money to buy this laundry to support myself. It is how Mare and I live. I cannot just walk out on this," Silvana said.

Tray was downcast. He assumed she loved him as much. Silvana in her wisdom could see the hurt boy in the man.

"Tray, I know what you want. I want the same thing. But you are going in a week back to Afghanistan, and you'll be gone almost a year. What am I to do? Who will I know? How will I get food? Where will I work?"

"I will take care of all those things," he said.

"You cannot. You will not be there," Silvana spoke more firmly, not angrily, but her voice rose, so that the child came in from the other room and looked at her mother. And Silvana continued, "I must do things for myself."

"My father will help. You will have my money and money to live on. My car will be there for you."

"But you won't be. And Tray, this is how basic the argument is: do you even know I don't drive? Don't know how to and don't have a car here. I know I can learn but I want you there teaching me new things. I am different than you are knowing me. I look like other girls you may have known, but I am not."

Tray looked puzzled, "Yes, different. More beautiful, more loving, more honest.

"Tray, you have travelled the world. You are rich; your friends are all rich. You live in modern cities. Have you noticed what you are standing on? It is a dirt floor."

"Silvana, that doesn't matter," he said.

"It matters to me. It matters that you know who I am and where I am from. And it does matter if you are not there. You need to know me, about me, how I live. I once loved a man, Mare's father, Juan. He was from here. He knew how I lived and his life was different once, but he knew how I lived. And he improved my life in many ways because he knew these things about me."

"I will learn," Tray said, now embracing Silvana.

"Start learning now. Stay here, stay with us until you have to go to war."

Tray called Winston. Winston was not happy, but he understood. Two days before his wedding his best man would not be able to come. He was staying in Puerto Rico with Silvana until he needed to return to duty.

Later, Winston called Sebastian and told him. "But what did Tray say?" Sebastian asked.

"He said he found the woman he was going to marry, and he needed every second with her before going back. Sebastian, he's in love. I know the feeling, and I'm OK with it."

"I'm not. I'm OK with the love part, but these are things the seven of us have talked about our whole lives, that if we were alive we would not miss being part of each other lives. I'll call him."

"No, leave him alone. He's only home for two more weeks."

When they hung up, Sebastian called Tray.

"Tray, you can't miss Winny's wedding."

"Sebastian, don't make this harder than it is," Tray said from the front stoop of Silvana's house. "I leave four days after the wedding. So I've got nine days all together. I need every moment right here."

"You're going to be best man," Sebastian said.

"You're going to be best man," Tray shot back.

"But he wants you. It's one of your life responsibilities. You know how your dad always says you only have two responsibilities in life: 'visit the sick and bury the dead.' Well add a third to the Admiral's list: 'attend your best friend's wedding.'"

"Aahhhhh," Tray screamed.

Silvana called, "What's wrong," as she finished ironing a pair of slacks.

"Nothing, Silvana," he called back.

"What did you say?" Sebastian said.

"Silvana. I was talking to Silvana," Tray said, now frustrated at this game of ping pong.

"Sebastian, I need you to square this with the guys. This is going to be the most important two weeks of my life."

"Can you spare one of them for us?"

"I can't possibly do all that and still have Silvana."

"That's not what I asked. Can you spare one day?"

"I could if I was there and only have to pull out for a day, but I can't."

"I'm sending my plane. It will pick you up that Saturday at 7 a.m., have you here at noon. Service is at 5 p.m., reception at seven, dancing till eleven, back on the plane at midnight, back in Puerto Rico by 4 a.m. One day. For us."

54

Thirty-four egrets, seven of them great egrets, foraged in the brackish inlet. Soon the U-shaped eddy would be flushed by the incoming tide, as the waters of Long Island Sound flowed under the two walking bridges, one at each end of the inlet.

On the other side of the peninsula of Tod's Point was the beach. Directly east, the beach looks out on a universe divided: the darker waters of the sound, the lighter air of the sky. This view was framed on the left by the Shippan peninsula of Stamford, at its furthest point, Stamford Lighthouse. To the right the intersection of the sky and the sea are interrupted by Long Island.

A tall ship plies these waters pressing the environmental movement through short seaborne classes. The ship sat now exactly on the sharp line of the horizon; were it not known to be round, the earth seemed to be calling this four-master over the edge.

There were no flat spots on the American sea this day; a steady breeze from the northeast rippled the water. As the gentle waves made their break on the shore, not twenty feet from where Edward Wheelwright sat, he suddenly turned, startled by the now pounding waves. For thirty seconds, no more, wave after wave rolled over loudly as the sea began to retreat. The tide was turning.

This second weekend in June found the temperature unusually warm, in the high eighties. The breeze cut the heat that loomed inland.

The "Mayor of Tod's Point," Sol Katz, wandered along the beach greeting his fellow beachgoers as if running for political office. He was shrouded in a white safari hat. On the front of the hat, cut into the center, was a small battery powered fan.

Older couples all knew Sol; the newcomers, young men who worked in the banks in the city found him odd, school girls shied away from him, and toddlers like his fan. Katz had been head lifeguard here for thirty years and still trained and qualified all lifeguards. His season started on Memorial Day and didn't end till Labor Day.

As he neared the farther, quiet end of the beach, he spotted Edward Wheelwright.

Wheelwright came to the beach at Tod's Point this day for two reasons: to think through what happened with Santa Alba and to meet with Valerie Samson.

Santa had not come back from Puerto Rico with Edward, and he had not called her. He assumed she was at their apartment in the City. He assumed she was packing to move out.

On the flight back from San Juan, Gideon Bridge told him what happened at the El San Juan. The outfit, the dancing, and Santa leaving with Sebastian Ball. Wheelwright began replaying the conversation with Bridge.

"Rat bastard," Wheelwright said.

"Edward, don't be too hard on him. It took every ounce of strength for me not to break training and pursue her," Gideon said. "Training" was how he referred to his queer self. He was in training when he was on the prowl for handsome young men.

"Rat bastard," Wheelwright repeated.

"You know, Eddie, you've got no one to blame but yourself," Bridge went on, "You have a gorgeous girl who adores you, and you ignore her all the time."

"Gideon, that's bullshit!" Wheelwright shot back.

"Not hardly, my man," the dapper lawyer, dressed, even on the plane, in a tan gabardine suit, blue shirt, and a bronze and aqua bow tie, said to his friend. "You live at work. You're never satisfied.

That's not to say the rest of us are anything but overjoyed with your performance on the Fund. But you don't let down. If it's not the market, its things like the gaming tables in San Juan. You have to have a life, Edward."

There was silence between them and then Gideon spoke. "If Santa didn't know you were straight, she might think you and Kish were going at it. You're inseparable. And Kish, you've made him a slave. He couldn't come to Puerto Rico for Winny's party?"

"That wasn't me," Wheelwright protested, "That was Kish. He's as driven as me." "That was you," Bridge insisted, "Kish had a life once. No one has seen him socially for months."

"And you mentioned you like the returns of the fund," Wheelwright offered, tensing. "What is it, Gideon, returns or social life?"

"Eddie, this is not about us. It's about you. You forget the reason for the creation of the Brunswick Fund. What was your great question in Mr. Conetta's class—'How can we stay friends for life?'"

"I remember."

"And the answer?"

"Create the fund."

"And working backward," Bridge persisted, "why, once again?"

"How can we stay friends for life?"

"Exactly! Not money. Friendship."

"What are you saying, Gideon?" Wheelwright pawed at Bridge seeking what he did not want to hear.

"Eddie, it's not about the money. I appreciate all I can get, but frankly, there isn't a prayer in the world I'll ever be able to figure out what the hell to do with what I already have."

Wheelwright paused. For him, it had become about money; it was his way up. While there was wealth in all of the Brunswick Fund families, there was wealth and there was wealth. Admiral Johnson's million or two was not Sebastian Ball Sr's billions. The Moira's few small businesses worth several million were not the Barnes Construction's billion. The Wheelwrights dwindled, few million coming on the back of the Edward's father's financial career were not the Bridge Law Firm's hundreds of millions or the Trout's newly minted IPO hundred million. In the back of his mind, way back deep, Gideon's argument was creating a stir. What was it? Wheelwright had a hold of it. Don't let it go. And it was slipping away.

And now, again, here on the beach.

Damn it, almost had it, he said to himself. Money, friendship. Something about glue. He couldn't hold the thought. It was too far recessed, an echo.

Then his mind flipped back to the plane, and he heard Gideon's counsel, "Step back, Eddie, hire a couple of professional managers to run this thing, but give yourself some room, and pay attention to your girl."

"Yeah, I hired a professional manager based on Parker's recommendation. Had to can him. Crane was a liar and a crook. Santa. Screw her. Tart. And Sebastian. The rat bastard.

And that was about the way the conversation went on their flight back from Winston Trout's bachelor party in San Juan. Wheelwright was so upset he convinced Gideon Bridge to take a separate flight back with him, different from the one Ball and the others were on.

Now, Wheelwright stretched out on the beach blanket, let out a sigh and waited for Valerie Samson on the beach of their youth.

On his return he had been surprised by her phone call. It seemed almost fateful. He was intrigued by her anxiety over this opportunity she wanted to share with him. He was more intrigued by the tone he detected when he asked, "How's your family." She sounded as flat and uninspired as he had ever heard this spirited young woman whom he had known forever.

Wheelwright sat up and applied sun screen to further the early summer tan he had started in San Juan. He was at that end of the beach that was more Cape Cod like, with small dunes, sea grass and a big sand apron stretching into the Sound.

This beach, a refuge, a 147 acre peninsula, the former estate of a nineteenth century Scottish tycoon, was where the seven friends had grown up. This was their space, their time away from parents, unsupervised by teachers and coaches, out from under the wings of nannies, chauffeurs and housekeepers—no adults allowed. The Point's woods was their laboratory. This is where they experimented with smoking, first sexual contacts, alcohol, and, for a few, drugs.

When they were seventeen, Edward, Parker, Valerie, and Tray worked as lifeguards for the man now approaching Edward.

"Wheelwright," Sol Katz, "the mayor of Tod's Point" boomed out. "Where the hell's the rest of your bunch?"

Wheelwright looked up and saw his old mentor and, not ten feet behind him, Valerie Samson.

Edward got up and gave the older man, who now seemed so much smaller, a hug. "One of them is right behind you," Wheelwright said to Katz.

Katz turned, his white Safari hat, sitting back on his head. "Umm, Vvv, Valerie!"

"Can I get one of those hugs?" she asked as she neared the old head lifeguard, arms outstretched.

"You sure can, sweetheart," and he embraced another of his younger charges.

"You two look fit enough to get up on those chairs right now," Katz said pointing down the beach to the lifeguard chairs.

"And you remember me?" Valerie asked. "How? It's been so long."

"I never forgot the name of one of you kids. Know the year you were guards, know your names, and how old you were then, which means I can easily figure out how old you are now if you're not careful," Katz said, before a second thought. "In fact you two were guards the same summers. And you were a thing for a while."

Valerie and Edward glanced at each other quickly.

"Great memory, Sol," Edward said. "You're looking great."

"There are three stages of life, Wheelwright," Katz said with a smile, "youth, maturity, and you're looking great." The three of them looked at each other and broke up in laughter.

After more memory exchanges and catching, up the "Mayor" went on his way.

Val called after him, "Does that fan in the helmet still work?"

Sol raised his hand and made an OK sign with his fingers.

"Eddie, that's so amazing running into Sol at the exact moment we see each other. For a second, it's like time stood still."

"I agree. And look at you. It is like time stood still. You're more beautiful than ever," Wheelwright said looking at the taut, tanned body in shorts and a knit top. Valerie not only looked fit, she was strong. At five-foot-nine-inches tall, an hour glass figure with the square shoulders of a swimmer and the legs of a college soccer player, she was an impressive woman.

"And you've taken good care of the Wheelwright legacy," she said admiring the obvious strength in his shoulders and arms. "Still a gym rat?"

"Only reason I'm alive," he replied.

And they hugged. And they stood there awkwardly in each other's arms. They moved apart and smiled. Valerie turned and picked up the beach chair she had dropped. She opened it and placed it next to Edward's. She placed a Gucci beach bag next to his sneakers at the foot of the blanket. She pulled her top over her head and slipped off the shorts, revealing a neon green bikini. Wheelwright flinched when he saw and remembered the stunning body beneath the bikini. He reached down, opened the cooler and offered Val a beer. "Yes, yes," she said thirstily.

They both sat.

"A lot to talk about, Val. It's been a long time."

"Two years goes by pretty quick. A lot has happened," she said twisting the top off of the ice cold Anchor Steam beer.

"You first," he said

"This idea I called you about. It's an opportunity we cannot pass up."

"No, not that. We'll get to that," Wheelwright said. "Tell me about you. On the phone you didn't sound like Val McGuire.

"No, I'm not that girl anymore, Eddie. I'm Val Samson: mother, housewife, suburbanite extraordinaire."

"And you're not happy?" What's going on here, he thought to himself. What am I doing asking that question, pressing her like that. Are you taking glee in whatever burden she's carrying?

Simultaneously, she thought: what's going on here. Is he trying to put me in my place? Am I so obvious a mental mess that he can come on like that? Careful.

She looked away. "I'm OK. It's just a new life. It'll take a while to keep it all in perspective. Isn't that what you always told me Eddie? Keep it all in perspective. I wish the hell I kept it in perspective," and on an impulse she decided to get it out. "But I was so upset you dumped me I dashed into this and it sucks." She was looking into Wheelwright's eyes now. Fire in her eyes. Tears. She was smiling. That horrid smile of a beautiful woman, hurt by a man, and nothing could be done about it. It was done.

"Your husband?"

"David's a good guy. He's a nerd. I let him rush me," she stopped. Two minutes. Two minutes talking and I've humiliated myself. She thought when he agreed to meet with her that nothing would matter, that they would stay on a higher plane, only talk about the deal. The deal was nowhere in the discussion, and she was on the floor. Pick yourself up, get it all out. "And now I'm stuck. The only thing I have is my work," she stopped again. "The gym keeps you alive. My work keeps me alive."

"What about your baby?"

"He's wonderful. If I could, I'd snatch him up, move back into the city, get a nanny and live happily ever after. You have to see him, Eddie, he's beautiful. I do love him; it's everything that surrounds us that I hate."

"That's what you get for marrying a Jew."

"Edward Wheelwright, that's bullshit."

"Bullshit it is. A McGuire marrying a Jew. I didn't believe it when I heard it."

"You're the fucking reason," a fiery Samson said with a bittersweet smile.

"That's it. It's my fault you're miserable?" he questioned.

"If you married me like you fucking promised, I wouldn't be in this shit," she laughed hilariously. It was a real laugh. A roar. Old tears streamed down her cheeks, the sad sentiment having passed.

Wheelwright laughed with her, "That's the McGuire I know. Indomitable. Able to spit in the eye of the devil."

"You are the fucking devil, you know," and the laughter continued. The anger out, unbottled after these two years. "You fuck, you promised to marry me."

"If you hadn't been so damn pushy, I would have," he said.

"Pushy! Pushy? I gave you half my fucking life. How long am I supposed to wait?"

"Till I'm ready," Wheelwright said.

"Are you ready now?" she asked impetuously. In fact, stunned by her own question, but she decided to wait for an answer. And it wasn't long in coming.

"Why, are you going to run away with me if I say yes?"

"I'll drive." And they both laughed the way they had their whole lives. "Now answer my fucking question. Are you fucking ready now?"

"Jesus. That mouth, Val. You kiss your baby with those lips."

She punched him hard on the arm, "Answer the fucking question," she screamed.

"Maybe," he said, looking at her seriously.

Valerie Samson looked at Edward Wheelwright. Humph. How to proceed? Push it. No. Rub it in, same old procrastination. Yes, but no. Probe? Yes. "What happened?" she said caringly at first. Then she asked it again with a little more vinegar, "What happened with you and little Miss San Juan?"

"It wasn't Miss San Juan," Edward said a little defensively, then in keeping with their openness, "just little Miss Mountain Town."

"What happened, Edward?" her voice now raised in a sing-song way.

"I think she slept with Sebastian."

"She would cheat on you? With Sebastian? Ugh!" she said disgustedly.

"That's my Val," he said, smiling at her way of phrasing it.

"Well, I agree he's got more money than God, but he's so full of himself and his do-goodness that he couldn't piss if he didn't have a valet or chauffer to help him.

"Val, it's Sebastian," he protested.

"I know."

"When did you feel that way about him?" Wheelwright said, genuinely surprised.

"How about forever," she offered.

"Always?

"Always!" she repeated. "He was too good for anyone. Even his "magnificent seven."

"Magnificent seven?" he wondered where Val got that from.

"You guys were always so funny with your Brunswick thing. There were other people on the earth, and some of us thought you were pretty great without the group thing."

"But the group is about loyalty and friendship."

"Tell me I didn't just hear that. Sebastian. Santa. Same bed. Loyalty. Wrong word, Eddie. If Sebastian didn't have you boys for play things he'd still be home sucking Mrs. Ball's tit."

"When we leave here, you're going straight to confession," he said.

"When we leave here, we're going straight to bed," she said.

55

A nd they did. Metaphorically. The desire returned—it remained, untouched with time, reawakened.

"Let's go," Edward said, standing now, starting to pant.

Smiling, Valerie said, "Where?"

"In back of the secret garden, the old mansion tower."

She knew the spot, she laughed and got up. She kissed him. "You're so creative," and touched his cheek.

"There are times when expediency means something. I figure you'd understand."

They left their beach gear on the sand, took the blanket, and got into Edward's BMW and drove to the southern end of the peninsula and up a narrow path by the cow barn. They walked through the secret garden, a walled rectangle that looked out from a bluff over the sound and the sailing club below. They followed a path into the woods stopping to kiss and grope, gaining heat as they progressed down the path and then back up to the plateau that was all that remained of the Tod mansion, except for a round twenty-five-foot stone turret at the rear of the plateau. It had an open entrance that curled in a half circle enclosing visitors from view. The stone masons that Tod had brought in from Italy to build his estate had even included a cantilevered bench, that was a slab of stone imbedded in the turret's walls and that now found itself supporting a prone Valerie Samson, who was beneath Edward Wheelwright, on the beach blanket.

The bathing suits had come off quicker this time than they did the first time the couple explored this space nine years ago.

Nothing had changed. The passion, the love making, the meeting of pounding bodies all remained intense, only more so now by the desperation of the woman and the timely rediscovery by the man. And when they reached the climax to the reignition of what had always been torrid love making, they could hear the voices of children approaching the plateau.

They laughed and dressed quickly and retraced the path back toward the car, passing two pre-teen boys along the way. The boys turned to look at Valerie's body and giggled to themselves. Valerie and Edward smiled at each other.

"They would have got quite an education if they came along two minutes earlier," she said, her arm around Edward's waist.

"Naw, I'd have scared the shit out of them if they got too close."

"With a growl or that big thing in your pants?"

Edward laughed as he continued to be reminded how fast Valerie was in any situation and how she always kept him happy. She was right, he told himself. It wasn't that he was procrastinating on their future. It was a damn accident, a confluence of incidents: finding his father's papers that he had paid for Val's college, learning about his father's affair with Val's mother, and being in Paris, couple of days of partial downtime, meets an exciting and beautiful girl. He owed Valerie for the way he ended their relationship—their engagement, their planned life, their friendship—and that was why there had been no contact for the two years even though they were in the same business, in the same city.

When they reached the BMW, Valerie pressed up against Edward. "Eddie, I want you again," she said looking up at him, the passion not yet subsided.

"Me too, Val," he said. And then putting his arms around her he said he was sorry. "You should hate me, but you don't. I shouldn't have returned your call. I don't deserve to be in your life." He kissed her, and he remembered what it felt like to care deeply, sympathetically, lovingly for someone. The girl he had loved his

340

whole life, who had promised to be his wife, and who he dismissed so easily was now standing before him. He thought, this moment should remain. They kissed again.

The moment was interrupted as a group of boys and girls came up the path from the cow barn that was now used for sailing lessons and boat and sail storage.

"That's twice with the kids," he said.

"I can stay over," Valerie said. He looked startled, and then smiled, always a surprise—this girl.

"What about your husband?"

"He's fine. He's out of town, our nanny is with my baby, and I'm in the city with a girlfriend."

"And what if I didn't say, 'Maybe?'" he said with a laugh.

"But you did," and she punched him in the stomach.

"Let's go take a swim."

They swam in the chilly, late spring water of the Sound. They raced; they played in the water as they had as teenagers. Val's bikini top came off, and she quickly pulled it back up. "It's a tanning suit, not a swim suit," she told the admiring Edward.

As they toweled off by the beach chairs, from a distance a person would have thought Edward and Valerie were a happily married couple. They held hands as they emerged from the water, smiling, drying each other, hugging, spreading out beside each other on the blanket on their stomachs, looking at each other as they talked, constantly smiling and laughing.

The girl was back in the woman. In an afternoon she had been given her spirit back.

They rolled over and were on their backs on the blanket now, her head resting on his arm. "Where will we spend the night?" she asked, following it with a suggestion, "How about that sleazy hotel in Stamford by Exit 9."

"How about my house?" he offered, "I've kept my space in the guesthouse."

She smiled. "That would be very nice, Eddie."

They lay in the sun silently after that decision; each with their own perceptions of what was occurring. Each with their own hopes of what this meant. At this moment if they laid out all they felt and all they were thinking, they would not have been apart by more than the breeze of a flapping butterfly wing.

After some time Valerie spoke, "Now, can I talk with you about this opportunity?"

"Isn't that why we're here?" Edward laughed.

"You fuck," she said laughing. They both giggled themselves silly at what they were finding in each other once again.

56

The white Colonial home sits at the end of a private road in Old Greenwich, just up the road from Tod's Point. Its smaller counterpart, the former carriage house on the estate, serves as the living quarters for Edward Wheelwright when he is not staying at his apartment in the city. It is to the right and front of the main house. The two acres overlook Long Island Sound. There is a tennis court in back of the carriage house and a swimming pool to the right of the main house in back of the tennis court. The main driveway was moved to the left of the property some years before, and when driving through the tall hedges and winding diagonally to the right, the Wheelwright estate appears before you: main house, pool, tennis court, and carriage house, all framed by the same high hedge that fronts the property.

Val Samson always pictured herself as the mistress of the property, and as she and Edward pulled in through the hedges, she felt her pulse quicken.

"This was to be my home," she said to Edward.

"It is to be your home," Wheelwright responded. "Let's see Dad first. Seeing you will cheer him up."

"When he heard we had split up, he was pissed," he said as they pulled in front of the large home.

"At me?" Val asked, puzzled.

"No, of course not. At me. For ending our engagement. This will be a shock to him."

Inside his home, Mark Wheelwright, the former Senior Vice President for Risk Management at Oceans Bank, was playing it over in his mind. It was all there, all for the taking—the merger, bringing together the three main financial elements: banking, investment banking, and insurance. Then it was gone.

Oceans Bank was a target from the beginning. Everyone wanted something from it. That was why it made perfect sense. But the target was too big. It couldn't feed all the fish in the ocean. The capital demand in New York City was astounding. Everyone came calling; everyone saw the advantages of one-stop financial shopping. The borrowers, empire builders who wanted to create the next skyscraper to fit their egos pushed the bank for higher and higher leverage—less capital put in, more of the total cost borrowed, spread over longer and longer time frames. But it was all in a market that was overbuilt, with depressed rental prices.

He lifted his glass, took a drink and said out loud, "What were we thinking?"

And then he remembered, we were thinking we were big enough, we had the three-legged stool. The retail bank for the world, the investment bank for profit and tough times, and the backing of the insurance giant would outweigh the risks of recessionary times. Our ego started to match our customers. We were morphing, no longer bankers, our roots, and not yet the new moneymen for all seasons.

There we were snug in the middle of Wall Street, admired for our inventiveness, for our boldness. But it was inevitable. The target was too big. After the borrowers came the beggars. Congressmen, senators, prospective presidents, all with their hands out. All offering us a seat at the table. Access. And we bellied up to the bar with them.

The more we dealt with the borrowers and the beggars, the more we felt part of them. We saw the target also; it was enormous. We raised our salaries, our bonuses skyrocketed. We felt like ball players. Our parachutes were no longer golden; they were platinum. Payoffs for silence about the plunder were taking place.

And the wealth spread across the world. Our offices reached everywhere. Civilization demanded prosperity, and we were capable of financing it all. Even the little guy wanted in. Sure, a home with nothing down, no payments for a year and low interest for five years. You don't have a job; that's hilarious. Get one. You'll need it when the loan resets in five years or when the Fed raises rates. But for now, don't worry about it. That's what we told them. We didn't learn from the dot com bubble. Same thing happened: big target, lots of money available. Start-up. Sure we can finance you. The banks became angel investors. The mentality of the investment bank permeated the lending bank. No revenue, no problem. You have a business plan; it's on the back of a napkin? Your plant is in your garage? How much do you want? Then the crash of the technology bubble.

Where was I, the risk guy? I was there. I was part of it. I saw it happening. I helped it happen. Sure I raised my hand, "But…"

But I wasn't effective. I raised my hand like the good traffic cop I was. Trying to slow the speeders down. I gave them warnings, and they said thank you and sped off.

So now, I would be smarter, this time with the housing situation, we would all be smarter after the dot com ending.

Still, though, the target was too big. After nine eleven we realized we had become a different kind of target. Terrorists saw us as evil. Saw capitalism as evil. Us. Bankers. Evil? And there it was. We had changed. We had become evil. Even the beggars were after us now. They saw us as a quick way from congressman to senator. We became a stepping stone from Attorney General to Governor. They were shoo-ins. Spitzer used us. Cuomo used us. The same guys that wanted to shackle us also made sure we paid a thousand dollars a plate for a table of ten at every rubber chicken dinner they popped in on. Damn. They were worse than us. They'd have us under indictment for conspiring to fix rates and at the same time have their underlings looking for us to send a bundle of contributions to the campaign. They expected a grand from every vice president in the bank. They even knew how many vice presidents we had—and it was too many.

When they would find Oceans Bank in the cookie jar, they'd find fault using some law or other to find us conspiring. But never us as individuals, not by name. Always Oceans Bank. Always an exorbitant fine of three or four hundred million. Paid for by the bank, not by the guilty conspirators. By the bank, meaning the stockholders. But no one ever went to jail, not once. With Spitzer, he got ten banks all at once. Got them to pay one billion in fines. But not a single person went to jail, especially not Buck Simon.

John Paul Simon knew his way around the beggars. He knew how to feed them. Our Chairman, my boss, was the cleverest. He had fought to have laws changed and barriers removed that would give him more elbow room in the crowded world financial marketplace. He had always felt after nine eleven that it was the Arabs against the Jews. He knew what the real target was. Or so he told me and everyone else.

But John Paul Simon was the master of reputation building. First the financial supermarket, then the philanthropy, and the negotiated settlements, all to protect the reputation, all to protect him. He knew what leverage was, he knew how to grease palms, and he knew how to slip from the clutches of the beggars. With the competition he had the sharpest elbows in town. But even he, even Buck Simon, couldn't hold back the tsunami that was the housing crisis, that became the financial crisis, that became the great recession. He could not stop our downfall. And it's all gone. It was a tsunami; it wiped everything off the map. Oceans Bank is gone, in bankruptcy, a shell of its former self, trying to reorganize. They sold our building on John Street to London Equity Holdings. Most of the people are gone, laid off, and then eventually fired when there was nothing left. Everyone wiped out. Here I was risk executive for the biggest bank in the world and I had most of my life savings all tied up in Oceans stock—from fifty dollars a share to five hundredths of a cent—three hundred thousand shares worthless.

Mark Wheelwright had played this story over and over in his mind every day for the past two years. And the story never changed. He picked up his glass. Took one more drink. From the window in the library of his home, he looked out on the beauty of Long Island. He placed the glass of whiskey back on the desk and opened the desk draw. He looked at the gun and reached and touched it.

"Dad," Edward called out as he entered the rear door. "Dad, I have a surprise for you."

Quickly, Mark closed the drawer and turned the key to lock it. "In here Eddie," and he rose to greet his son.

And Edward and Valerie walked in.

When Mark Wheelwright turned, there was his son and Valerie McGuire.

A smile broke out on Wheelwright senior's face. "I had a flashback. For a second I thought that was Val McGuire standing beside you."

And Valerie went to his arms and hugged him.

"My God, it is you," he said laughing.

Valerie blushed. "It is so good to see you Mr. W.," she said. "It's been too long."

"It has been too long," Eddie joined in.

"So," Mark paused, drawing out the "oh", that meant, "what's up here?"

And on cue Eddie said, "Val and I are back together."

Valerie beamed at the confirmation. And they talked for a good hour. Val was married, had a son, but going to get a divorce. No, David does not know yet. He's out of town.

Eddie explained more fully to his father why he and Santa were no more and that Santa had moved on to Sebastian.

And when Mark said to Valerie, "You must be more than a bit upset with her for what she did to you, breaking the two of you up." Eddie was speechless.

But not Valerie. She said quickly, "No, I don't hate her for taking Eddie from me. She's the reason he'll do a better job loving me this time."

A tear came out of Eddie's right eye. Valerie saw it, and she kissed his cheek. "I'm sorry," she whispered. "It's OK; it's true," he said back softly. "I know it is," she said and the three of them laughed like they had on so many occasions over years. Like the four of them used to.

And they all realized that Mrs. Wheelwright was always a part of that laughter.

"I'm so sorry, still, about Mrs. Wheelwright," Valerie said.

"Thank you, Val," Mark said as he hugged Valerie again.

"I didn't love him. I loved you and Mrs. W.," she said smiling.

"Now about your son?" Mark Wheelwright asked.

"Yes, he's wonderful. Almost two now. I'll bring him by tomorrow, if that's alright?"

"That would be wonderful," the senior Wheelwright said.

"Dad, we're going to stay in the guesthouse tonight."

Mark Wheelwright said "OK, we'll see you in the morning. Can we have breakfast together?"

"Sure," Edward said.

"I don't suppose you'll be wanting to go to Mass with me in the morning?" Mark asked.

Valerie spoke up, "Can we take a rain check till next Sunday."

"Yes, you can have a rain check anytime with me, Val," the senior Wheelwright said, gave Val a hug and concluded, "Off you go. I can see the two of you have a lot in front of you. See you in the morning." And he left the room.

Valerie and Edward went to the guesthouse, wrapped in excitement and fear.

57

As they came back together, as the fog of betrayal opened the heart of the girl he had always loved, he saw her depth. Rather, he saw the depths to which he had subjected her. He had been wrong; walking out so easily on the girl he had forever promised to marry, he had driven her to a place of humiliation.

In fact that first night when they reunited in love, he was about to learn just how deep the humiliation was.

As they were about to enter the two-story colonial guesthouse, Edward stopped, picked Valerie up in his arms, and carried her across the threshold.

"This is late coming, but we will do this the right way, soon," Edward told a tearful Valerie.

"Are you serious?" Val asked, shocked.

"Never more in my life, if you'll have me," Eddie said, realizing the second chance that was playing out on this day.

"There are a few things I need your help with, so after you show me around, I want to sit down and talk."

The guesthouse was quaint, just enough to accommodate a family. It had three bedrooms, three baths, and a great room overlooking the pool. The house had been updated several years earlier and had a comfortable feel to it, like it had been lived in. Edward had kept it up and frequently stayed there whenever he was in Greenwich. A few days earlier, upon return from Puerto Rico, he slipped easily into a new life that he could not have imagined would change again a week later. They chose the larger bedroom to put Valerie's overnight bag in; it had a king sized bed. Valerie jumped on it and Edward followed and they made love again, more slowly than before, but more passionately.

Later, Edward poured both Val and himself a glass of white wine, and they sat on the back patio, beside the pool in the quiet, warm night.

"I need to tell you something right now before we do anything else," Val said. "I'm very afraid of what you will think of me, but I need you to know something right now."

"What great secret must I know; is this the big idea you've wanted to tell me all day?"

"No, Eddie, it's…" and Valerie started to cry.

"Val, what is it, are you ok?"

"I hope so, Eddie, I'm scared, for the first time in my life. I just have you back, and I don't want to lose you," Valerie said, looking at Edward with pleading in her eyes.

Edward laughed, "You're going to lose me if you don't tell me this great secret. There is nothing you can say that will change how I feel about you."

"I hope so. Well, you know I need to tell David about us."

"Yes. But that's not it, right?"

"No, you know I told you I married David on the rebound from you. That I was so hurt and he chased me."

"Yes, I know that."

"Well, there was a reason I got married. I was pregnant, Eddie."

"You mean there was someone else between the time you left me and when you married David."

"No, Eddie, there was no one else," she paused here, unsure of how he would take what she was about to say. "After you left me, I found out I was pregnant. My baby boy is our son."

Edward Wheelwright sat straight up; he put his glass down on the table. He rose and stood beside Valerie's chair. He stood for a moment thinking about what he had just heard. He looked down at Valerie. She had fear in her eyes.

He knelt down beside her. "Val, it's true?"

"Yes, Eddie, it is. His name is Edward."

"I don't know what to say," Wheelwright said as he put an arm around Valerie, and there was a silence, then he asked, "Why didn't you tell me?"

"What would I have said? I tried thinking of words a thousand times. I actually came to believe that you would never know. Not that I didn't want you to know, I never knew how I would tell you. I never knew what would happen if I did. "

"Didn't you think I would care for my son?" Wheelwright asked quietly.

"Of course I knew you would, but you made a decision to leave. I didn't think you would want to be bothered by me or the baby. I didn't want to tie you down if that wasn't what you wanted."

"Oh, Val, It's alright. I'm so sorry. And I'm so glad."

"You are?" Valerie said, in a way, both relieved and startled.

"Yes, I love you. I made terrible mistakes that hurt our lives. Having a son, our son, as we come back together is wonderful. When can I see him?"

Valerie was overjoyed. She put her hands on either side of Eddie's face, caressed it and cried.

58

The bottle was opened early. The first drink poured by 9 a.m. Mark Wheelwright was looking out his study window, looking towards the sea, when he caught a glimpse of people coming through his rear yard from the right. There was a man, a woman, and a small boy in the middle, walking, holding his parents hands. It was a dream, an illusion: Mark, his departed wife, and his son Edward. He looked at the glass of whiskey, shivered from his late night of drinking the prior evening.

As he stared at his glass, he thought about the idea of his son and Valerie moving into the guesthouse. He wasn't sure he liked the idea with her still married.

Wheelwright looked up from the glass, and there was the young family again, only this time they were outside of his window, not ten feet away looking in at him. He looked closer. It was his son, Edward, but not as the child, as the man, and Valerie and what must be her little boy. They smiled in at him, waved, and walked to the back door. Wheelwright moved to the kitchen, drink in hand, and dumped it out in the sink just as they opened the kitchen door.

"Hi, Dad," Edward said.

"Hi, Mr. W," Valerie added.

They all looked down at the little boy, all of two-years-old, walking steadily, and the boy looked up at Mark Wheelwright and said, "Papa."

Valerie and Edward laughed as Valerie bent down to him.

Mark Wheelwright was hung over. He didn't like the joke.

"Dad, he's your grandson," the younger Wheelwright said.

"That's nice of you two, but he's not my grandson," said the older man in a sharp tone with the emphasis on "my."

"Can we go in the family room and talk?" Edward said to his father.

"Sure," Mark said, a little upset with the way this day was starting out. He didn't like the idea of a married woman living in his guesthouse. He liked it even less if they were going to try to pass the baby off in some charade as Edward's and that he was the grandfather. Has the persecution of an old man no end, he thought, the image of a bottle looming on the horizon of his mind.

When they were seated in the family room, the little boy sat on the floor holding a fluffy toy rabbit.

"We need to tell you something, Mr. W," Valerie began.

"Something quite wonderful, Dad," Edward said.

"You're going to get married, finally," Mark said with a smile and with a touch of sarcasm.

"Yes," Edward said, "but something better."

"Well let's have it," Mark was tiring of the game. He needed them gone and a refill of what he had just poured down the drain.

"This little boy is your grandson, Mr. W. When Eddie left me, I was pregnant. I never told him because he no longer wanted me, and I assumed he wouldn't want the baby. I decided to have the baby, and wanting to have a normal family life and a father for the baby, I rushed into marriage."

The older Wheelwright became very alert. He sat forward and looked at the boy. He could see a resemblance to his son. The same eyes, blue. The same jaw line, the dark brown hair. He got up and walked to the boy, bent down and picked him up. He took the boy with him and sat down in his favorite chair with the boy on his lap.

"Papa," Edward Wheelwright Jr. said looking at his grandfather.

Mark Wheelwright laughed a long natural laugh. A laugh Edward had not heard for a long time.

Later when Valerie and Edward and his grandson left, Mark Wheelwright went to the den, got his bottle of whiskey. He went to the kitchen, poured himself a glass, touched it against the bottle, and said, "Here's to you old friend; we will be saying goodbye here." He drank the glass down in one gulp and poured the rest of the bottle down the drain.

59

———✦✦✦✦———

They hadn't spoken in the four days since they returned from San Juan and now Sebastian Ball had his secretary arrange a luncheon meeting with Edward Wheelwright at Ben Benson's Steak House on W. 52nd St.

Sebastian arrived early, anxious over how to begin this discussion. After all, he figured, he had never been in this position before, having to apologize.

Edward Wheelwright came in the door at exactly 1 p.m. He looked at his lifelong friend and could see the dread in Sebastian's face. Wheelwright thought to himself, he should be worried. Sleeping with my girl. Well, my former girl.

In the intervening time, Santa Alba had moved out of the apartment that Wheelwright and she shared without a word being exchanged between the two. She knew she had to leave; Wheelwright knew she would leave.

When Santa Alba told Silvana DeLuna that she had been sleeping with Sebastian, Silvana berated her friend.

"How could you do that to Edward? You are the one who told me how much you loved him."

"I know, I did. But, Eddie stopped caring," an exhausted Alba stated in that first phone call back to her friend, on the day after she returned from Puerto Rico. Alba was in a panic. She was in the apartment knowing she would not be here in a week, yet not knowing where she would be living after that week. Edward's world had become her world. And now she had chosen Sebastian. Would Sebastian want her to move in with him, would they find a place together, and why hadn't Sebastian called since they returned. Why hadn't Edward called, even if to tell her to get out. Well, she thought to herself, at least Sebastian did text her that he needed to fix things with Eddie. But now, four days, no calls. "Will someone please call?"

Who called was Sebastian's secretary to ask if Edward would be willing to have lunch at Ben Benson's. Edward thought, why not at his club. "Oh, I get it," he said to himself, "He thinks I'll make a scene."

"Yes, Gail, Benson's is fine," he told the secretary and began to think, "how should I deal with Sebastian?"

Ben Benson's had always been a favorite of Sebastian, a lusty meat eater, and now he and Edward were face-to-face, sitting at a table toward the rear of the restaurant.

The owner came to the table, recognizing Sebastian, "Nice to see you again, Mr. Ball."

"Hello, Ben. This is my good friend Edward Wheelwright."

"A pleasure to meet you, sir. Can I get you gentlemen a beverage?"

"A bottle of San Pellegrino, yes, Eddie?"

"That would be fine."

When Benson stepped away, Wheelwright spoke first.

"I thought it was you who told me," Wheelwright said, "Character is what happens when no one is looking."

"I'm sorry, Edward," Ball said hurriedly, "I could not help myself."

"Bullshit," Wheelwright said, a bit too loud, as Ball cringed that others would overhear.

"Eddie, she threw herself at me. I've never seen anything like it. I don't know how you kept your hands off of her."

"Sebastian, are you out of your mind? She wasn't yours to take."

"Edward, she had this outfit on, this red skirt, and a matching blouse tied around her waist and she was bulging out..."

"Stop. Listen to yourself," Wheelwright said, now more pissed off, listening to his friend's feeble excuse. "Like it was Santa's fault you took her."

"Eddie, you ask anyone there. It was absurd what she did. The entire dance floor was after her," a still enthralled Ball was reporting. "She heated that place up to a fever pitch with her dancing. I had never seen anything like it. I know why she did what she did. She obviously wanted to taunt you for leaving her alone so much in San Juan."

"That was the plan, Sebastian. She was to set things up and get out of the way. She wanted to see her friend Silvana and spend time with her. That was the way the whole thing was arranged."

"Well, that certainly is not how she played it."

And then the owner came by with their bottle of sparkling water, "I'll leave you gentlemen to look over the menu, and my nephew, Jimmy, will be serving you today."

"Thank you, Ben," Sebastian spoke up.

Once the owner was out of earshot, Wheelwright spoke again. "I don't care how she played it, I expected more from you Sebastian. Loyalty. Friendship. Remember those words you always repeat?"

"I do," a humbled Ball said.

"Well, don't they apply to you? Just the rest of us?"

"No they apply to me," Ball said. And now pleadingly, "Eddie, honest to God, I was helpless. She could have had anything I had."

"Could have had?"

"Well, I don't know how you feel going forward. I mean where we are. The three of us."

"What do you mean the three of us?"

"Edward, you're not making this easy for me," Ball sort of whined.

"Oh, Sebastian, I'm sorry. Is this difficult for you?" Wheelwright kept the pressure on.

"It's damn difficult, and you know it. You don't have to be enjoying this so much."

"Stick with where you are. What do you mean by the three of us?" Wheelwright said.

"I mean, do you still want her?"

"Do I still want who? " Edward Wheelwright said

"Damn it, Eddie, stop it."

"Sebastian, you haven't said her name once since we've been talking."

"Santa, Santa Alba. Do you still want her?"

Relentless, Wheelwright said, "Why do you ask?"

"Because I want to know if you are in love with her."

"What do you think?"

"I think not. But do you want her back?" Ball asked his friend.

"Why do you need to know this? Let me say it a different way, make it easier for you. Do you want her?"

"Yes, Edward. I do," a chastened but grateful Ball said. Grateful to his friend for allowing him to get his feelings out.

"Then she's yours," Wheelwright said looking his friend in the eye.

"Yes, it's alright with you?" an excited Ball asked.

"Sebastian, it's not alright. It will never be alright. But, it is what it is, as they say these days." Wheelwright said. "You took advantage of a flirting girl. Worse, you took advantage of our friendship."

"How can I make it up to you," Ball implored, unaware how stupid this sounded to Wheelwright.

"Sebastian, we are friends. We will always be friends, no matter what. There are times we will test that friendship, and this is one of them. Somehow we will get through this. I'm pissed off now, but I'll get over it," Wheelwright went on, "But don't think you can ever make this up to me. You can't. But it's done, and I accept it."

"I'm sorry, Eddie," Ball said.

"I believe you, Sebastian. Now what are we having to eat?"

"Thank you, Eddie."

"You're welcome, Sebastian, now let's eat."

"One more thing," Ball asked, "How do we go on with our group?"

"Just fine. Santa's your girl now."

"But what about the others, how do we explain it to Kish and Winston and the others?

"How do you explain it to them, Sebastian?"

"Eddie, you've got to help me out here."

"Sebastian, it's not that hard."

"It is for me, Eddie. You've had these beautiful girls your whole life. I..."

"Stop, Sebastian. We broke up. That's what you tell them. That's what I'll tell them. So it's done."

"But they know about San Juan, about me and her."

"Sebastian, she is yours. You don't need to explain to anyone."

"We're going to move into my apartment here."

"That's good; that will be a relief to her knowing where she's going to live."

"When we're all together, how will you be with her?" Sebastian asked.

"You really want to get everything lined up."

"Yes, I do. I don't want awkward moments for you or her"

"Or yourself."

"Or myself. Yes," Ball relented. "I don't want any of us to be uncomfortable."

"Well, I have an idea that will help all of us. Why don't we all have dinner in a couple of days before the wedding."

"That's a great idea," Ball exclaimed, jumping on the words as they escaped Wheelwrights mouth.

"I'll arrange it, you, Santa, Val, and me."

"Val?"

"Valerie Samson, formerly Valerie McGuire."

"You dog," Sebastian smiled, for the first time.

"Things have a way of working out."

"You two are back together?"

"Just about. A few things to work out, like her marriage and her son. But yes, we're back together."

"That's great, Eddie. Santa will be happy for you."

Wheelwright thought to himself, not too happy. He knew the passion he and Santa had for each other. He knew that Sebastian would not be able to satisfy the depths of Santa's passions, but he did believe Sebastian could help her in other ways. A billionaire has ways to compensate for shortcomings. And they weren't many, but Edward was aware of Sebastian's almost goofiness around beautiful women. Sebastian, he could see, was just lustful enough to put everything at Santa's disposal, and Santa was just, not too much, but just worldly enough to enjoy, and make work, what her billionaire had to offer.

"When I was at Penn," Sebastian began, "I read Pablo Neruda, the Chilean poet. I found it amazing the fire he had in his soul for women. When he fell in love, the world changed for him. His passions overwhelmed him. He described women as goddesses who consumed him, who became him. They fused in heat. Their minds..."

"Sebastian, stop. Christ, you're not with Santa, you're with me. So you've discovered lust."

"No, Eddie, it's more than..."

"Stop. I know. But Sebastian, you don't talk about this stuff. You do it; you feel it. That's it."

"I haven't been there before," a half-smiling Ball said to his friend.

"Enjoy it," Wheelwright said, and he wanted to add, "while it lasts," but he did not want to be cynical with Sebastian. He did know the feeling himself, and he was enjoying it once again with one Valerie McGuire.

60

One of the first things your eyes notice when you enter the Colony Grille, after you notice the people in noisy conversation, is the pictures on the wall. It's like stepping back in time, to the 1940s. Picture after picture of boys from Stamford who went off to war and came home. Solo pictures of privates smiling in their dress uniform after completing basic training, group pictures of sailors home on leave in uniform with their civilian friends, and in the end pictures of big parties, held right here, of dozens of soldiers after the war. There are hundreds of pictures on the wall behind the bar, which has twenty stools along its length and scores more above the booths across from the bar. In the next room, the dining room, with booths on both sides of the aisle, there are more pictures of these World War II soldiers and sailors.

It is a place where time stands still. There were no other wars here, only WWII. No pictures of men who served in Korea or Vietnam. No pictures of Stamford men who went off in America's business in Grenada, Lebanon, Somalia, or Desert Storm. No pictures of those who fought in the war on terror in Iraq or Afghanistan. Just WWII.

The Colony is that kind of place. Hard-nosed, regular guys. Workers. Middle class men. Ball players—hundreds of ball players from the fields down the street at Cummings Park.

And the policemen of Stamford. The Colony was theirs. They served in the wars just as their fathers had. All of these men had uncles or older family friends in those WWII pictures. The police played on those softball teams. And they sought refuge here in each other's company from the horrors they witnessed every day being cops.

Some sought more refuge than others; some needed more refuge than others. And when they stayed, night after night closing the place up, with nowhere to go, having lost their families in the personal war, it was their fellow officers who got them home.

John Walsh didn't always need refuge. He was a large man, and when he came here as a young cop, a power hitter on the police Waterside team, he ate the pizza, enjoyed the beer and companionship, and went home.

But in his third year on the force something happened to change him. Everyone in his unit thought he did well to recover from the depression after accidentally shooting Curtis Strong Sr. in a West Side pool hall. A month after the shooting he was back in uniform. The following summer he had his best year on the police softball team, and when the team won the city championship, no man was happier, or so it seemed.

In some of the pictures on the walls of the Colony, the ones taken at the parties after the war ended, the soldiers are smiling as much as others. On closer inspection some of those smiles seem to be masking sadness or even fear that had insinuated itself into their lives after the danger passed.

And to look at the smile on the face of big John Walsh, the same sadness could be seen. And underneath, it was there—fear.

Walsh was here, this night, with fellow officers to have a couple of beers after their shift. Only this night he was drinking more rapidly, words starting to slur, laughter a little louder, and stories a bit more exaggerated. One after another the stories about this felon or that perp. There were six other officers with Walsh, and they were holding court in the Colony "dining room." Their own area was to the far end, away from the booths, which gave them a little more leeway with their bravado. Most of the regular customers knew the cops liked that area and let them be; they needed the release after dealing with some of the prizes of Stamford.

"And he says, 'but I wasn't even there officer,'" Walsh was laughing, "and we have three witnesses including his mother who nailed his ass." They laughed the laughs of comrades in arms who knew the idiocy of the people they dealt with.

The night went on, each of the officers anteing up their contribution to the stories. The pictures of beer kept coming.

Around 11 p.m. two officers left, five others remained. It was then that the fear that was suppressed in Walsh raised itself to the surface.

Willie Stevens had confessed to Walsh as he lay dying. Stevens had to release Curtis Strong from the prison he had kept him in by not coming forward. And just as Stevens suffered, now Walsh carried the burden. Not only had he accidentally killed Strong's father, he was the supervising sergeant on Curtis Strong Jr's murder conviction. To help his Captain Pavia at the time, he falsified evidence that implicated Strong. At that time, now six years past, he believed Strong was part of it, so it was no sweat if he put the knife in the drug dealer or not. He was there; he was part of it.

Now, with Strong innocent, it was eating at him. What was he to do?

"The kid I nailed last month, Stevens, complete fool. Went from having a nice little business dealing on the West Side to falling in love with his product. Got pushed out and left to fend for himself, he became a robber, snatch and grab. But this fool doesn't just take the poor woman's bag; he's got to kill her. Stabs her in the neck and leaves the knife in. Like this," demonstrating he picks up a table knife raises it over his head and plunges down on Larry Bell, stopping just above his head and then laughing. They all laugh at the dramatics. "So anyway," he pauses to refill his mug and gulp down half of it, "we get into a shootout, and I nail the little shit. So then he goes into this confession, 'CJ Strong's innocent,' and tells me a drug dealer that got knifed ten years ago, says he did it, not the kid Strong who got sent up to Auburn for twenty-five to life." He stopped before the punch line to take a drink, looked at the officers there with him to make sure he had their attention with this story.

"So what happened," another officer asked eagerly, "did Strong go free?"

"Fuck, no," and he paused, a thought, a judgement needed to be made. Continue or stop. What the hell, these are my people. "I told the fucker as he died that it was the only decent thing he'd ever done. Too bad his stupid little secret had to die with him. And poof," with that Walsh made a twisted face and cocked his head to the side to feign death. And they laughed some more. Well, the others did. Larry Bell didn't. He wasn't quite as high as the others, and it didn't strike him as all that funny.

61

A nd this story from the prior week was what Officer Larry Bell was recounting for Detective Lieutenant Vito Boriello.

"Lieutenant, I hate to say it, but I think Detective John Walsh is involved in a cover-up of a murder or more," Officer Larry Bell began. He had called Boriello the day before and asked to see him about a departmental matter that was quite serious. He needed complete confidentiality in their discussion, as he could be wrong on what he was about to tell Boriello. The Lieutenant reassured Bell.

"Let's take a walk," Boriello said to Bell. Boriello was never big on sitting across from anyone expecting to hear the whole truth. He found that difficult conversations always seemed easier while walking and talking. This was difficult, to be sure; a fellow officer, coming to him with some evidence of malfeasance by another officer.

They left Stamford Police Headquarters, walked up Hoyt Street to the corner of North Street and made a left, proceeding west into the afternoon sun.

"So you, Walsh and three other officers were at the Colony having a few? When was this," Boriello asked.

"A week ago, last Friday night."

"And here we are, a week gone by. What took you so long to come see me?"

"Isn't it obvious? Cops talk trash all the time, bullshit about their cases. But this had a ring of truth to it; it sounds real. And I remember the meanness that came over Walsh's face when he said what he said."

"Which was?"

Bell pulled out a small three-by-five note pad. "Here, I wrote it down afterwards, it bothered me so much. He said: "I told the fucker as he died that it was the only decent thing he'd ever done. Too bad his stupid little secret had to die with him."

"Wait," Boriello said, "You're ahead of me. Who's doing the dying and what's the secret."

"Sorry, Lieutenant. The murder/robbery that took place at the mall, where Walsh shot the killer. The killer's name was Billy Stevens."

"I remember the case very well. So what's the secret he tells Walsh?"

"He says a friend of his, CJ Strong, is innocent of a murder charge that he's doing twenty-five to life for it. I also went back and checked this out. CJ Strong was convicted of murdering a drug dealer on the West side about seven years ago. According to Walsh that night, Stevens confesses to Walsh that Strong didn't commit the murder, that it was he, Stevens, who did it." Bell paused to look at his notes. Boriello rolled what he was hearing over in his mind; what an interesting turn providence was taking. Jim Ford up at Auburn would be pleased to hear this, he thought.

Bell continued, "The part about Stevens confessing that he killed the guy Strong is serving time for is not part of the official record of Walsh's shooting of Stevens. I checked."

"Let's begin from the beginning. You and the other officers are shooting the shit." Boriello stops to give Bell room to fill in the blanks.

"Each one of us are talking about crazy collars, and Walsh comes out with this story. Says after he shot Stevens he ran up, kicked the gun out of his hand and the kid says, "You gotta help me. C.J Strong is innocent. He's in jail. He didn't kill anyone." Walsh says the kid knows he's dying and is trying to use him to relieve his sins."

"So Stevens tells Walsh, Strong did not kill anyone?" Boriello asks.

"Yes."

"Does he say who did?"

"Yes, like I wrote down. Stevens tells Walsh he did it."

"Who was the other guy killed?"

"Augusto Santos. That's who Strong is doing time for killing."

"OK, I'm aware of that."

"You've got some memory, Lieutenant, more than six years ago," Bell said.

"Something came up recently on the same crime," Boriello confided. Actually, Boriello found it a strange coincidence; what strange fate could possibly be bringing these two separate streams of information about Augusto Santos' death and Curtis Strong's innocence to the confluence of Boriello's mind.

"Tell me, what else happened?" Boriello asked.

"At the bar or with Stevens' confession?"

"Either one," Boriello decided to leave it open-ended to see where this officer took it.

"Well, Walsh went on with the story, tells the kid, 'too bad your lousy little secret's going to die with you.' We actually laughed; no, as I recall, I didn't. That was when I saw the reality in it. I saw the way Walsh was telling the story. But at that point we figured that was the punch line so the laughter just came. But that wasn't the punch line."

Boriello grabbed his arm as they came to the corner of Summer Street. Bell started to walk out just as a car came speeding by.

"Didn't they teach you anything at the police academy? You only cross on green. Come on, let's cross this way, and we can get a DQ," Boriello said and they crossed North Street to the Dairy Queen on the corner.

"What'll you have?" the lieutenant asked the younger officer.

"Whatever you're having," Bell said, wondering if Boriello was believing what he was hearing. After all he was being quite casual about the whole thing, going for a walk and an ice cream. He wondered now if he had made a mistake coming forward.

"Two medium vanilla cones, dipped," Boriello requested.

"You got it, Bud," the enthusiastic teenaged boy behind the steel counter said. Then he added, "Whoops, sorry, Lieutenant Boriello."

"That's OK, Richie; just make them right," Boriello said to Richie Pisano, who lived two blocks from Boriello and whom he was able to help out in traffic court several months earlier at the request of his mother, a high school classmate of the lieutenant.

Boriello paid, took the two cones and walked to a nearby table. "Can you grab a couple of napkins," he said, over his shoulder, to Officer Bell.

As traffic whizzed down Summer Street, the two police officers ate their ice cream. Boriello picked up where they left off. "So what was the punch line?"

Bell looked at Boriello and was reassured by the disarming manner of the short fat cop. "Walsh said, 'Strong did it. That's how I got my detective shield.'"

"That's what he said?"

"Those exact words, and he added, 'The little shit thinks he's gonna save his buddy's ass now that he's history.' Then one of the other cops, Pete Ozowelski, asks Walsh, 'But what if it's true?' Walsh starts laughing hysterically, says to Ozo, 'After he takes the blame himself, he changes his mind. Says it was Parker Barnes.' Ozo says, 'Who's that?' Walsh laughs at Ozo and says, 'The son of the guy who built Stamford. The son of the next senator.' Ozo then says and he starts laughing, 'Did he blame me?' The guys cracked up. Walsh says, 'Exactly. Lying through his teeth, looking to do a good deed for his friend.' We all laughed then as Walsh makes like a judge with a gavel, slams his fist down on the table and says, 'Case closed,' and after a minute he adds, 'still.'"

Boriello rose, took one last lick of his cone. He tossed his cone in the trash can; Bell who was now beside him did the same. Boriello led as they began walking back up North Street opposite of the side they walked down.

"What do you think about what you heard?" Boriello knew he was redundant, but he wanted Bell to sum it up.

"Walsh had had a few, but what he was telling us, the way he told it, I'd say it was true. There is one other thing I almost forgot. I was with Walsh the day he shot Stevens. He did save us. The kid had us pinned down, and Walsh came up from his blind side. When I went up to Walsh right after he shot him, I hear him talking to Stevens who's dying. I asked him if he knew the kid. He said he'd 'seen him around, he had a record, name's Strong or something like that.' Holy shit," Bell said realizing for the first time why he believed what Walsh said at the Colony was true.

"That last part again. Where did that come from?"

"It was in the back of my mind. I completely forgot about it. Maybe it was why I came forward."

"It sounds that way to me; that's a pretty important piece of information, a Freudian slip on the part of Walsh," the seasoned officer said. "Let's just keep this between you and me right now. But I'd like you to write down the whole conversation just like you told it to me."

"Sure, Lieutenant. What's next?"

"I'm not sure, but at some point we'll have to go before a judge. You'll have to testify against Walsh. Are you willing?"

"I don't have anything against Walsh, but if it's true then, there's an innocent man in prison for someone else's crime. Yes, I will testify to what I heard."

That Friday evening Boriello phoned James Ford at his home in Auburn, New York. He relayed the whole story as Bell had told it.

"That's it," Ford exclaimed. "That's the missing evidence that will free him."

"I know. Point is, now I need to prove it."

"You're going to confront Walsh?" Ford asked.

"Have to. Got to get his side of it. We need to think through how we get him to confirm what he said to Bell, how we get him to confirm what the Stevens kid said to him."

"You want some help in putting the line of questioning together."

"No, I'll kick it around over the weekend, and when I have it finished, I'll go over it with you. Say Monday morning."

"Good enough. Thanks, Vito, great work."

"Thanks nothing. It just walked in the door. A bluebird."

"Funny."

"What's funny?"

"That's what I used to call a key piece of evidence that just appeared, just like a bluebird."

"Maybe that's where I got it. Your buddy Chief Brennan used to say the same thing."

62

"Walsh!" Boriello said to the detective as he approached his cubicle.

"What's up, Lieutenant," John Walsh said as he lifted his head and spied Vito Boriello.

"I need a little time to talk. What's good for you?"

"I'm OK now. Where?"

"My office."

"I'll be there in a minute," Walsh said somewhat puzzled since, while he knew Boriello, they were not working together on any case. Maybe, Walsh thought, since the Lieutenant was retiring, it was about his position. Something that Walsh saw himself ready for.

Walsh walked into Boriello's office, and Boriello motioned with his head in a way that said, "Shut the door."

"I'm working on an aspect of an old case of yours, and I have a few questions."

"Sure, which case?"

"Curtis Strong."

"OK, which one?"

"Which one?" Boriello repeated back to Walsh.

"Yeah, I had two. The father or the son."

"The son," Boriello said, getting it. But then he added, "Maybe you could tell me about both. Kind of strange to have had major cases with both a father and a son."

"Strange as hell, Lieutenant," Walsh said, now a little suspicious that Boriello knew they were both major cases. "Can you tell me what this is about?"

"No, not right now," Boriello decided he would not put Walsh at ease, not yet. "Just tell me about the cases, beginning with the oldest one."

"The father, Curtis Strong Sr.," Walsh began, and finding himself ill at ease, proceeded cautiously. "There was an argument in a pool hall on the West Side. A bunch of guys had been drinking. We were on drug patrol. Came into a situation that escalated quickly. Strong had a friend who got belligerent, made a move on me and my partner. I pulled my gun, Strong stepped in closer. I fired. He went down. Dead at the scene," he paused. Then began, "The son, he..."

"Hold up. Before we get to the son, "Boriello said

"Yes"

"Well, I know this is a long time ago, but why'd you pull your gun in that situation?"

"Self-defense."

"Had Strong or his friend touched you?"

"No, Lieutenant," Walsh said through teeth clenched in a tightened jaw. "Hey, what's this about? I was cleared of that."

"I'm curious. Why'd you fire?"

"I saw Strong's friend as a threat. Strong came even closer. It was dark; there were a lot of guys in the shadows. It got out of hand pretty fast. It was an accident," Walsh said, now sweating profusely from his forehead.

"OK, thanks. Now tell me about the son's case."

"Completely different. No link at all. Just weird fate to have caught both cases."

"Tell me about it," Boriello said, pushing away from the desk, hands behind his head.

"Two of my guys picked it up when a drug dealer got knifed."

"Your guys?"

"We didn't have a sergeant in homicide then; I was acting."

"Didn't you make it right around that time, detective sergeant?"

"Yes," Walsh felt fear. There was a man leaning back in his chair with a fat belly sticking out who knew something and wasn't saying what it was. He had to be careful. Something wasn't right. He was being asked all these questions, and he didn't like the course of discussion. He would play along but only for a little while longer.

"OK, so your two guys," and Boriello emphasized "your," "they draw the case and what about it."

"Well, as you said, I made detective sergeant shortly after this case and Strong's conviction. I knew I was up for it. So I watched cases like this very closely, evidence chain of custody, forensics, crime scene thoroughness, witnesses interviews, meetings with DA, witness preparation, you name it, I was bird dogging this case. It was one of the first murder cases I was acting sergeant on."

"So you would have worked on witness preparation with the DA before going to the stand?"

"I already said that. Yes, I wanted to make sure we crossed every t and dotted every i."

"And you had to make sure they got the facts right, I mean, what they witnessed?"

"Yes. In this case, there was just one witness who saw Strong clearly, saw him stab the guy."

"Now, as part of my research, I talked with the witness and she said she recognized Strong from the neighborhood, but she never really did see him stab anyone. She said he was in the alleyway, and she could see the two men, one lying on the ground, which was why she called out."

"That's not what she said to me, and that's not what she said on the stand to the jury."

"Well, that's another problem. You see, it seems like the jury got worked over too."

"Stop right there, Lieutenant. No one got worked over, and if anyone is telling you this, they're full of shit. We went by the book. This was a simple case of robbery/murder. Cut and dry."

"Tell me, detective," Boriello said, "did you or your guys think that Strong could be innocent? That he was telling the truth? "

"Why? Why would I think that? He did it. All the evidence pointed to him. His thumb print, the bloody sneaker in his room, an eye witness who testified under oath it was Strong she saw stab Santos. Why would I think Strong was telling the truth? That's his attorney's job."

"And how about his attorney, do you think he gave him good representation?"

"He didn't say much. Hell, what could he say, we had his client dead to right," Walsh said, gaining confidence, enough now to go on the offensive. "All right, Lieutenant, now it's time for you to answer a few questions."

"I'm not through."

"I'm through talking until you tell me what the hell this is about," Walsh said, sitting forward and about to rise from the chair.

"Tell me about the Stevens shooting."

"No, you tell me what the hell this is about."

"It's about too many coincidences. I need you to help me sort these out. First the two Strongs and then Stevens. All three major cases, all three involving deaths, all three related to the Strongs."

"Billy Stevens was a murderer, and I took him down—another department commendation for that and for protecting my fellow officers who were in danger from Stevens."

"And what, if anything, did Stevens say to you after he was shot."

"Nothing. Two shots and dead."

"What did he say to you about Curtis Strong?"

Walsh grew red in his big Irish face. Inside the red was fire. He could pick this fat little man up and crush him. Who was he to question me about getting the scum of the earth off the streets of Stamford?

"Whose side are you on? What's going on here? Do I need representation?" Walsh said, breaking a bit.

"If you feel you do, by all means, that is up to you. But I've been told that there is an innocent man in Auburn Federal Prison. Can you help me out here?" Boriello said, trying to give Walsh an opportunity to tell the truth.

"Sorry, Lieutenant, but I have no idea what you are talking about."

"What if I told you that Curtis Strong is innocent? That the person who killed Augusto Santos is not Curtis Strong, but Billy Stevens. And what if I also told you that you are aware of this."

"You've got some rich imagination, Lieutenant."

"I've also got two witnesses that say you know this."

"And who might they be, members of the Strong family."

"No, members of our family."

"Cops. No way."

"You can do this the easy way or we can take it the next step."

"Are you threatening me?"

"I'm telling you what is going to happen next. Nothing is set in concrete yet. But when this conversation is over, I'll be thanking you for your assistance or reading you your rights."

Walsh was done in. The anger subsided, the rage calmed and strangely the fear was gone. "Yes, Lieutenant, Stevens did tell me that he killed Santos. I didn't believe him. I thought it was just a ploy to get his buddy out of jail."

"Why isn't that in your report on Stevens? There is nothing about a discussion, an admission of a crime by Stevens."

"Because I didn't believe the bastard. He was trying to do one good thing before he croaked."

"What else isn't in the report?"

"That's all."

"What about Parker Barnes."

The fear returned. He was so drunk that night two weeks ago he almost forgot. So it was the cops who were there with him who ratted him out. But Barnes, how did that get into the conversation. Stevens never said that. Did I say that? So drunk that I took what Al Paiva had me help him with seven years ago, the cover-up of Augusto Santos murder by Parker Barnes and the framing of Curtis Strong.

"Where'd you get that name," Walsh began a new stonewall.

"This is what was reported you told others. That Stevens first said he killed Santos and then he said Parker Barnes killed Santos."

"Well, Stevens never said that. He said he did it. I saw it as a friend trying to help a friend so I dismissed it."

"And Barnes?"

"No part at all in it."

"Why'd you bring the name up?"

"This came from the night at the Colony?"

"Part of it."

"Lieutenant, I was bombed. It was story time. We were laughing and having a good time, and I took it to another level of bullshit."

"So you will confirm that Stevens did tell you that Strong was innocent."

"What do you mean confirm."

"There's an innocent man in prison."

"He's not innocent; he's guilty as sin. Stevens was trying to save his ass."

"Sergeant Walsh, that's not up to you to determine. I need you to confirm in writing what Stevens told you, to make it an official part of your police report. Will you do this?"

"Why, so you can let a killer out?"

"How about we let the judge decide?"

"Do I have a choice?"

"No," Boriello said firmly.

With a limited written admission by Walsh of what he omitted in hand, one that Walsh gave up grudgingly, one that confirmed Stevens' dying confession of guilt and Strong's innocence, Boriello did two things. He went to the presiding judge of the Stamford Superior Court and got an order for a hearing for Curtis Strong. The second thing he did, and he wasn't sure how far to push this, is with Chief Brennan's agreement, he got Walsh placed on administrative duty until the issue was resolved. The administrative duty was on the graveyard shift from 11 p.m. to 7 a.m.; enough to keep Walsh unhinged.

"What the hell gives, Captain," Walsh said to Captain Al Paiva, to whom he reported, when the Captain told him of the decision to place him on administrative duty until after the hearing on Strong.

"Look, Boriello has dug in real deep on this," Paiva said.

"Yeah, and it's my ass he's hanging out to dry."

"Patience, Johnny," Paiva counseled.

"Patience my ass," Walsh replied. He hated it when someone, anyone, called him Johnny, as if he were twelve.

"Boriello retires in two weeks. They're setting up a hearing for Strong in the next week. No one cares about you—they just want to get Strong out. Bunch of freaking do-gooders."

"Well it looks like his freedom is coming at my expense," Walsh exhaled.

"Just take this, suck it up. You'll enjoy the peace and quiet of the 11-7. They get their hearing, the kid gets out, Vito retires, and I bring you back to your duties."

"And what about the Lieutenant's position when Boriello goes?" the ever ambitious Walsh pushed.

"One thing at a time, Johnny, one thing at a time," Pavia said, shaking his head as Walsh left his office. Then Pavia thought to himself, "the fucking gall. Bagged and looks for a promotion."

Walsh thought about telling Pavia that he screwed up by opening the murder door on Parker Barnes when he was drunk, but he decided to keep that to himself for the time being. He might need Paiva and an ace in the hole to get Paiva to help him out of this jam. After all he reasoned, it was Paiva in the background who helped him in the CJ Strong case by keeping pressure on the judge to not buy into a hung jury. It was Paiva who would continue to benefit from Barnes' senior's largess if they could keep Parker Barnes out of the picture for committing the murder of Augusto Santos. It was their dirty little secret that Paiva and Walsh knew CJ Strong never killed Santos.

63

Parker Barnes put together Tray Johnson's "going back to Paki-land" party at England, a Soho style dance club that resided in the quarters of a former hedge fund that went belly up. The building sat on the Connecticut/New York border in Greenwich.

It was the last time the friends could get together before Tray returned to Kabul and then special operations across the border in Pakistan. Winston Trout's wedding was later in the week and three of the friends would disperse the day following the wedding so they picked this night. The only problem was Tray could not come—he was insistent on staying with Silvana in Puerto Rico. Sebastian arranged for a hookup through his iPad to bring Tray in, who could also review the festivities on his own iPad. Since Sebastian would be in Arizona the next two days proposing solar farms to the State and its environmental commissioner, Hadley Lane, this was the one day besides the wedding day that they would all be together, except Tray, Parker arranged the party anyway. Parker, for his date, brought a plain but thoughtful and attractive looking young Asian woman.

Kish Moira had a tall, gracious Indian girl in a rich white dress on his arm that none of the friends had seen before and were frankly surprised; they did not know this beauty. Kish introduced her as Binky Patel.

Winston Trout came with the girl who would be his bride within the week, Emily Albright.

And but for the appearance of Sebastian Ball with Santa Alba and Edward Wheelwright with Valerie Samson, the stunning event of the night was Gideon Bridge with a very pretty woman whom he introduced as, "Bridgette Johnson, Tray's cousin."

Sebastian came with Santa as peace between the foursome was restored over dinner earlier in the evening at LaBretagne, a quiet French restaurant on the Post Road on the Stamford/Greenwich border. Edward and Valerie had arrived first at La Bretagne. Jean Daniel, the owner, greeted Edward, whose family were long time customers, and embraced Valerie as if they had known each other for longer than the moment. Mr. Daniel escorted Edward and Valerie to a circular table for four in the middle dining room. As they passed through the front dining room that was fully occupied, Valerie pinched Edward's arm. He grimaced.

"How come you never took me here?" she said with a smile as she looked around at the embroidered drapes, framing paned windows. The wallpapered room depicted scenes of a French countryside.

Other, older couples looked at the young pair and smiled as they passed by their tables. In their late twenties, the couple was easily half the age of the next youngest couple in the restaurant. Edward was clearly the only man in the room with color in his hair, or better yet, who even had hair.

At LaBretagne there was an air, a sound, a voice of people quietly enjoying each other's company. The sound had uniformity to it; no one distinct voice could be heard above the others. These people came here for the same reasons.

The middle dining room had ten tables, symmetrically positioned. There were four corner circular tables with six diners seated at each table, there were two tables on each side of the room that sat four, and but for one with two diners, the other three had four each. There was an empty table for two against the back wall that, on either side of it, had French doors entering the back dining room.

The round table square in the center of this middle dining room was where Mr. Daniel graciously deposited Edward and Valerie, pulling Valerie's chair out for her and doing the same for Edward.

As Mr. Daniel departed, Valerie said to Edward, "I love this place. When did you find it?"

"As you can tell, my dear, it's not mine, it's my father's. He loves coming here," Edward said.

"I can see why," Valerie said.

"Now, when Sebastian and Santa come, don't be nervous."

Valerie leaned forward and in her quiet restaurant voice said to only Edward, "I'm going to rip her fucking heart out."

Edward burst out laughing, turning the heads of the other dinners. He kept giggling and both kept laughing, but more quietly, just as Mr. Daniel reappeared from the front dining room with Sebastian and Santa.

Edward rose to greet them while Valerie remained seated.

Edward and Sebastian shook hands warmly, then, Edward turned slightly to greet Santa who was looking into Edward's eyes. Edward took her hand, brought himself to her and kissed her on the cheek, without ever looking into her eyes. Valerie kept her glance on Edward's eyes and smiled inside herself at the lack of recognition beyond politeness.

Mr. Daniel returned to the role seating new arrivals, and as the four sat down, Sebastian introduced Santa Alba to Valerie Samson.

"Nice to meet you," Santa said with a sincere smile, "I've heard so much about you."

"Thank you, And I you," Valerie said politely. And it was immediately noticeable. Valerie was the bright worldly woman, and Santa was the striving, although stunning, island girl. There was an enormous difference in composure, in who they were as young women; Valerie was tall, well postured, strong boned, and lovely while Santa was a pretty girl, attractively attired in a print dress more fit for the city. Valerie's features could be seen forward; she would still be beautiful when she became a grandmother. Santa, a carnal thrill, whose face, in time, would broaden and harden. But not yet.

The conversation through dinner settled on Tray's party later that evening and Winston's wedding until Valerie asked Santa, "I understand you and Tray's girlfriend are quite close?"

Edward had hoped the conversations would stay totally topical, not about each other. But he realized Valerie was a very competitive person and would have trouble with that. He would have to gently guide her through the mine fields she had no fear about entering.

When Valerie decided to prod the young woman from Puerto Rico, first Edward, then Sebastian guided conversations back to light, airy subjects like "Do you think Tray has killed any Taliban," or "When are the Winston Trouts going to be back from their honeymoon in Hawaii?" and finally, Sebastian let out, "Did Winny tell you I'm buying Trout Solar?" This shocked Edward since Winny did not. It also shocked Valerie who didn't care if she ever heard the word solar again. It pleased Santa to know that her "Sweetie" could buy anything.

And when the foursome entered the dance club England, the shock of seeing them all together brought, at first, smiles to the friends, knowing that their lifelong relationships were intact and could overcome even what Sebastian and Santa had put them through. But seeing Eddie and Val together brought pure joy.

"What a stroke," Gideon gasped across the table to Winston, "Eddie and Val. The empire strikes back." Winston smiled, in complete understanding at what Gideon meant. The omniscient Mr. Ball taking whatever he wanted and not looking back, and the striving Mr. Wheelwright realizing where real beauty lay. Those were the two thoughts that went through Winston Trout's mind. Gideon smiled with quiet satisfaction; his thought, "The world has righted itself as the real lovers we all knew are here with us."

The friends rose to greet Valerie, always the sweetheart among them, the longest lasting of any of their paramours, and here she was back in their midst.

At ten thirty Parker rose to the DJ's area where they had arranged the large screen, took a mike from the DJ, and introduced himself to the club. "Tonight is a special night—we have a celebrity among us—almost." And he nodded to Sebastian who brought Tray Johnson onto the large screen through the magic of an iPad and GoPro projector. "Ladies and gentlemen, please meet Navy Seal and Lieutenant Traynor Johnson who is on his way back to Afghanistan." The club crowd clapped. Parker went on to embarrass Tray, had him get Silvana in front of the remote camera. "And now you can also see why he won't leave Puerto Rico. We just hope he won't be going AWOL." Everyone laughed and joined Parker in a toast to his friend. Tray joined the toast and laughter, thanked them and saluted sharply.

The club was crowded at 11 p.m. Valerie knew her way around a club. She walked up to the DJ who was still setting up and gave him a note requesting two songs, Adele's "Rolling in the Deep" and Mark Ronson's "Bang, Bang, Bang." She requested the first to be played at eleven fifty nine and the second at twelve thirty. She handed him a twenty-dollar bill.

"Eleven fifty nine, exactly, yes?" she sought confirmation.

"Sure, honey. Thanks," the heavy set black man said.

When she came back to the table, not twenty feet from the DJ and on the edge of the dance floor, Gideon, who always had fun with Val, asked her which songs she requested. "Come on, Val, what do you want to hear?"

"You'll see, Gid," she said with a smile.

"A hint?" he begged.

. "You are so funny, Gideon," Val chided. "OK, here's your hint—New Year's eve, 11:59 p.m."

The friends sat in a large circle of chairs around two square tables, crowded with drinks in glasses of varying heights and colors, in the center. Until the DJ started playing tunes at eleven thirty, they were able to talk comfortably. The wedding, the Galleon insider trading scheme, Tray returning to duty, the Tsunami in Japan, Tray and Silvana in Puerto Rico, and where Gideon met Tray's cousin.

Val kept her eye on her watch, and at eleven fifty nine she looked up at the DJ who nodded to her. She rose, went to Edward and said, "Let's dance."

"Wait, you don't know what he's going to play," Edward said.

"I do," Val said, and she gave him a tug up.

"Oooh," Gideon chirped, "This might be fun."

A guitar started strumming and the voice of Adele began singing, "There's a fire starting in my heart..."

Eddie didn't know the words to "Rolling in the Deep." It was a new song for him, but he liked the sound of Adele's voice and the beat as Val led him on the dance floor.

They bumped and strode as others joined them on the floor. When the singer hit the key words, Val swooned, swung her hips left, grinding, arms pumping right, and the singer shouted the words:

"We could have had it all,
You had my heart and soul,
You could have had it all."

The song stomped forward, and Eddie realized the words in the middle of his grind. Val smiled; she was dancing with wild abandon. Her face was soaked with tears.

Eddie saw the power in the swaying beautiful woman taunting him and calling him back at the same time. He realized the anger in the song over a girl's lost love. He saw an exorcism taking place in Valerie.

Lost in the power of the music as the singer approached the refrain, "We could have had it all," Eddie moved closer to Val and inserted his own words singing, "We will have it all."

Val sang the new words as the refrain was repeated over and over.

They smiled, knowing, building a fire on an older flame, and with new fuel they realized what was almost lost forever.

Watching this, Gideon thought back to the dance he had witnessed one week prior with Santa Alba and thought, "Poor Eddie is in a quandary."

Gideon leaned over to Kish who was now seated next to him, "I could become mono-sexual if I had the choices of young Mr. Wheelwright."

Kish laughed at Gideon's words and said back, "Gideon, don't tell, don't ask."

Gideon looked at Kish and they laughed and looking at each other laughing, they laughed all the harder.

"What's funny, Kish," Emily, Winston's fiancée, asked with a smile.

"Gideon thinks he might like girls after all," he said, pointing to the dancing Val.

And Emily joined the laughter.

When Val and Edward returned to the table, Gideon whispered to him, "You certainly do attract rather intense women."

Eddie looked at him, questioning.

The very well-dressed Mr. Bridge leaned in again, "Santa's dance last week and what I just witnessed. You are fortunate beyond words."

"Thanks, Gideon, something to think about, huh?" Edward said as the club DJ put on another pounding beat.

Gideon rose, walked over to the other side of Valerie. He whispered in her ear: "The answer to your New Year's eve riddle: Out with the old, in with the new!"

Valerie looked up smiling, then laughing, "The smartest man in the world."

"I know," he said as he continued walking towards the men's room.

"What did Gideon say?" Edward asked.

"He said he liked the way I danced and that you're a lucky man," she answered.

"Funny, he told me the same thing," Edward said, with a crooked smile.

Santa Alba watched the dance. Sebastian sat next to her. Without looking at each other, he wondered what Santa was thinking, and she wondered if Eddie missed her.

Fifteen minutes later Gideon grabbed Winston's arm, "Oh, Oh. I smell trouble."

He was watching Santa Alba walk to the DJ with a note.

"Sweetie, would you please play, The Cure."

"Which, The Cure?" the fully stocked DJ asked.

"The sexy one with the horn that wails in the night."

"You mean Trombone Shorty?" he said with a smile.

"That's the one."

"You got it," he told her, surprised at the request for a New Orleans brass band. Didn't get too many requests for those tunes up here in Greenwich, he thought. In the city, in Harlem, all night long. Here, never had one request before. This should shake them up.

The rhythmic guitars started up, the drummer kicked in and the guitars foreshadowed the cry of the trombone. Then it came: a beautiful three-note wail, followed by a jazzy call, then a staccato bump joined in by the whole orchestra. But it was the trombone that woke up England. When you heard that sound, you knew why the leader of the band was called Trombone Shorty. It almost wasn't fair what he could do with music. The beat was infectious, and England was bouncing in place.

"Sebastian, Sweetie, dance with me," Santa Alba said reaching for Ball's hand.

Sebastian Ball had one left foot, but he thought the song had a lot of rhythm so he would try it.

It did not matter. On the dance floor, it soon became all about Santa Alba. She went out shaking her hips, hands above her head waving, first one on the floor, ahead of Sebastian. It was immediate. Everyone noticed right away, and it was clearly "Show time!"

What Santa Alba gave away in grace at LaBretagne earlier, she made up for here. Now the hair was undone, flowing across her shoulders as she wiggled toward a red faced Sebastian Ball, calling him forward with her fingers as the trombone wailed and as she shook her body to the left and then slowly moved it across its center and rolled right. Her head flung itself back.

"I love that move!" Gideon laughed to Winston. The two tables of friends were laughing at the boldness of the dance. Valerie had thrown down the gauntlet they theorized, and here was Santa picking it up.

As had happened in San Juan, the dance was so hot, what with pulling the pretty print dress to the high side of the thigh as she did a limbo shimmy toward Sebastian, that the floor was ringed with spectators encouraging Santa on. Sebastian was now way out of his comfort zone and meekly pulled back to the edge of the floor with the others.

The DJ knew a good thing when he saw it, and as the song was winding down, he easily restarted it without missing a beat. Santa was in her element.

It struck Winston that Santa must be lonely inside. How could a girl constantly seek that much attention? This was the second time in two weeks he was seeing the dance of the century performed for two different men, or was it. Maybe it was just for Santa. Maybe it was just for one man, Eddie.

The music hit a climax, and it paused as if it were a plane about to go into a dive. Then, Bang! The trombone gave a long wail in the night, next the whole band joined in and above it all the trombone with a strong hot melody carried Santa across the floor—legs flashing, arms swinging and always the hips punctuating.

Winston's fiancée, a modest, young lady, face flushed, asked Winston, "Does she do this all the time? Is this what you said happened in San Juan?"

"It's exactly what happened in San Juan. When the girl needs attention, she takes to the dance floor."

"Honey, not to be immodest, but I'd love to be able to dance like that."

"I'd love that too but only in our bedroom." They laughed. The two tables were having fun, even Valerie and Ed were laughing, enjoying the dance.

"Did she ever do that dance for you," Valerie poked Edward.

"No," he said smiling.

"Would you like me to do that for you?" she said grabbing him on the inner thigh.

Pulling back from the under the table grope, he laughed and said, "No, I love your dances and only your dances."

PART

5

64

Jim Conroy joined the New York City police department right out of the Army where he had achieved the rank of Sergeant First Class. He enrolled in John Jay College nights and studied criminal justice on the GI Bill.

Conroy grew up in Queens. His father was a cop as was his older brother and uncle.

At John Jay his minor was information technology. His studies continued an expertise he developed in the service, while stationed in Iraq, in using technology to follow money trails of Arab terrorists. He was part of an elite team working out of Baghdad Airport as part of Central Command's Terrorist Surveillance Unit.

These experiences and interest were noticed early on in the police department. Conroy had a beat in Times Square for all of six months when he began offering his opinions to the department on how to track financial cyber criminals operating in New York. Lieutenant Jack Kent, who had formed the Cyber Crimes Unit (CCU), noticed the stream of tips that flowed into the unit with a buck slip "from Officer James Conroy" attached to the information he offered along with his badge and unit numbers. These tips were usually followed up on by a call from Conroy inquiring how the unit was proceeding on his suggestions.

CCU was put together at the request of the Police Commissioner, who in turn was responding to a request from the Securities and Exchange Commission. The SEC had been taking extreme heat for a lack of oversight on securities crimes, particularly Ponzi schemes, wire fraud, and insider trading. The members of the unit were more seasoned detectives, so Kent thought some fresh blood would be good for the unit. He reached out and plucked Conroy off of the beat and made him a detective in the unit.

The unit stumbled onto a number of what looked like insider trading schemes coming out of Blackthorn Investments, the hedge fund. The hot line had received a call stating that one Sidney Rogers, a managing director at Blackthorn Investments, was buying large chunks of Rocket Solar before the company was set to announce a series of large contracts with Chinese companies. The female caller said that news of the contracts, which were to be made public within the week and which were worth seven hundred million dollars, would cause the price of the stock to rise dramatically from its ten dollar a share value.

This was the second such call in the past week on insider trading in Rocket Solar. Another individual named Leonard Crane, a trader with the Brunswick Fund, was identified as having made insider transactions on the same information that Sidney Rogers was trading on. This tip was also made by a woman. The police unit put surveillance in place on Rogers' and Crane's phones and computers. For Rogers they had access to his trading accounts at both Blackthorn and a smaller brokerage firm he was using for personal trades. His bank records were in the police unit's hands, and they were able to trace the funds movements from two different banks through the brokerage account at the smaller firm.

The pony in the surveillance was the linkage Rogers was able to provide through his phone contacts, and where, once identified as fellow conspirators in the insider trading scheme, the CCU was able to link in other individuals through their phone, computer, bank, and trading accounts. In the office of the CCU were "war walls" with "family trees" for different investigations underway. The individual at the top of the "Rocket Solar" tree was Sid Rogers. They had a picture of him, along with a sheet of key details, such as origination of the tip, date of the first trade, trading history, and profits and losses. Then beneath Rogers were other players in the scheme, their pictures if the unit could get them or a description of the individual if they did not. The Rocket Solar tree had four squares beneath Rogers, and they in turn had other blocks beneath them. There were two additional squares under Rogers that had names penciled in showing it was a work in progress. The first branch of the tree listed Rocket Solar in the square and beneath it were two pictures, Tom Barrett and his brother Rob Barrett; they were identified as CEO and VP of World Wide Sales, respectively, at Rocket Solar. The next branch was Blackthorn, and the name Valerie Samson with information about her and beneath her the name Alice Kraft was listed with information about her. The third branch was Barnes Construction with a picture of Parker Barnes. The fourth branch identified the Brunswick Fund and had a picture of Edward Wheelwright; beneath Wheelwright's picture were two names, Kishenlal Moira and Leonard Crane. A fifth branch was outlined in pencil with the name Trout Solar, and the name Winston Trout written in. A sixth branch was also outlined in pencil with the name Clayton Reed. It listed him as Sid Rogers's brother-in-law.

There were connecting lines showing linkage of who talked to whom. Lines were drawn from the Barrett brothers to Rogers, from Kraft to Crane and Wheelwright, from Samson to Wheelwright, from Wheelwright to Trout. However, beside Leonard Crane's name were lines connecting other family trees. From him, in only one week, they had found what they suspected were major securities fraud—all out in the open, very easily tracked. Besides Rocket Solar, going back in time every trade he made while at Brunswick or in his own accounts seemed to be based on inside information. From his phone records, they could see he would make a call to another securities firm, follow it up with several other calls to the same firm and phone numbers, and then he would make a trade. The Cyber Crimes Unit was able to trace the company whose stock Crane traded, and sure enough, their investment banker was the original firm Crane called. Then they started listening in to the calls, and their assumptions were confirmed—every time.

Joe Whelan, one of the senior officers on the Cyber Crimes team was providing a briefing for the SEC Deputy Director, Gail Donaldson, and took time to describe a couple of Crane's transactions and the path he took: "He'd call the investment banking firm, make a trade after the call; the police unit traces the investment traded right back to the investment bank he called. We're in the process now of identifying these individuals Crane's been talking to."

She interrupted, "And for this Rocket Solar stock, you said the numbers beside 'traded shares' for each person represented what each person has bought since Sidney Rogers made his first purchase six weeks ago."

"Yes, "said Whelan.

"But you said the two owners there," and she pointed to the Barrett brothers, "are not buying but selling. Is that right?"

"Yes, maam."

"Well, why would they be selling with news like this and everyone else who seems to know the news is buying."

"Good question. It's at the top of our list to ask the brothers when we bring them in once the news of the orders goes public. Right now it makes no sense."

Jack Kent volunteered, "Unless the brothers are pulling the wool over everyone's eyes and the orders are no good. So as the stock begins to rise, as it has, you sell into that buying."

"I see this tree you're talking about has links into the other three trees on the wall, but they all seem to be linked together to this Mr. Crane in Brunswick," the SEC Deputy Director went on.

"Exactly, maam," Whelan said, and unable to hide his glee, added, "He's a goddamn gold mine, maam! A lot of the information we're learning about Rocket Solar is new in the last few days. But these other links from Crane, he has tentacles everywhere."

The briefing concluded once Whelan covered the other three large family trees on the wall that were similar to Rocket Solar and tied umbilically to Leonard Crane.

65

Despair needs its own haven. Leonard Crane chose Bryant Park. The chess players were at work. A Pakistani and an Orthodox Jew were waiting for their turn at the table. Further back the street person with a gold front tooth waited at the other chess table to challenge the winner of a grueling match taking place.

Crane walked past them; there were three Chinese girls from the office building at the corner of Sixth Ave and Forty Second Street having lunch at one of the round iron tables. As he looked back at one who was particularly cute, he noticed that the chess players had all risen and were looking in his direction.

Crane looked ahead to see if he could notice what they were looking at. He saw the portable book mobile with rows of books for lunch time reading. He saw the two ping pong tables in use with two games underway, one with two Filipino men, the other with a man in a white shirt and tie playing a bearded college student.

He looked back again, and the chess players' faces seemed angry. The three Chinese girls were now looking at him, saying something he could not understand. The cute one was wagging her finger at him. Play at the ping pong tables stopped, and the four players were now walking towards him.

He quickened his pace. A black woman picked up a book from the mobile shelves and threw it at him, barely missing his head. He turned to look back at the chess players, and they were now running towards him. The three Chinese girls merged with the chess players.

397

The path was now four deep across and at least five people deep as the ping pong players joined in.

Crane was running along the flagstone walk heading toward Sixth Ave. The man playing bocce ball came up to the walk and cut him off. He ran towards Forty Second Street and jumped over the fence.

He was out of the park. All of his pursuers were lined up along the wrought iron fence, maybe twenty-five now, waving their hands and yelling at him, but he couldn't hear them.

Leonard Crane woke. He sat up in bed. A nightmare. There was no longer a place to hide. He was cornered. In two hours he would have to meet with Jim Conroy of the NYPD Cyber Crimes Unit. Conroy would be asking him about what he knew about insider trading in Rocket Solar; why else would Conroy want to see him.

Detective Conroy began the interview with Crane by telling him they knew he was engaged in insider trading and had frozen all of his assets and his trading accounts, including the three that he had used to trade Rocket Solar shares.

"We see you have two accounts with Merrill Lynch and one with Blackthorn Securities. All of the shares you have traded, roughly three hundred thousand, were bought on margin and are in Rocket Solar shares. Plus, in one of your Merrill accounts you have several hundred call options on Rocket Solar," Conroy said, adding, "Please tell us how you came to buy these shares at this time."

Crane, still alarmed at the call he received from Detective James Conroy to come in to talk with the NYPD as part of an investigation into insider trading, thought for a moment and agreed with his conclusion on the taxi ride to this police location that he would stonewall any questioning.

"Well, Detective, I do know the stock market and invest in it daily."

"I'm not asking you that," Conroy shot back, "I want to know what caused you to buy three hundred thousand shares of Rocket Solar on margin over four days when you do not have a job."

Crane's brain raced. They knew more. If they knew he was not working, then they had to have been watching him for some time.

"What are you saying, Detective, that it's against the law to own shares of stock if you don't have a job," Crane said, somewhat pleased with his response.

"No, Mr. Crane. I'm suggesting you have no way to pay for the shares if they don't rise. So obviously you felt very confident the stock was going to rise very soon," Conroy said, now moving a bit closer across the table that was not more than four feet wide, causing Crane some discomfort with movement into his personal space and causing him to pull back. "I want to know why you felt this stock would rise soon, as it did to $14.50, two days after you purchased the last of the shares, and one day before you sold all of them for a profit of almost 150 thousand dollars."

He needed to think fast. This cop was ahead of him, and he didn't know how far.

"I have resources of my own, Detective Conroy, and it is not unusual to be out of work for a few weeks as you switch between firms in New York," again he was pleased with his quick thinking, but he was running low on answers.

"Mr. Crane, the total cash in all of your accounts other than those containing profits from Rocket Solar is eighty thousand dollars. Hardly the wherewithal needed to cover if your bets on Rocket Solar went bad," Conroy said, and once again leaning into Lenny the Liar's space, "So, Mr. Crane, we don't have to approach our concerns with you this way."

"What's that supposed to mean," an upset Crane replied, not sure what would happen next.

"It means I said I have information that you engaged in insider trading. I shared some of the obvious information that caused us to look into you and your actions. We are hoping that you will cooperate with us on this investigation," Conroy said, thinking that this would be like pulling teeth to get Crane to open up. He would have to offer up the next morsel of evidence and see if Crane would start to crack.

At this point, Angella Sgorous, the SEC investigator in the room who had sat silently observing Crane, spoke, as Conroy and she had agreed beforehand.

"Mr. Crane, may I call you Leonard?" Angella Sgorous said.

"Yes, please," Crane replied with half a smile.

"Thank you, Leonard. As Detective Conroy has shared with you, we have been investigating trading in Rocket Solar for some time. Right now we cannot share all of the information we have with you, but we can say that your phone records in the week before your trades did show us you were talking to some of the same people we had been investigating. In fact it was those phone records that led us to get a judge to allow us to tap your phones. In the days prior to your trades and after, we have recorded conversations of you talking with others that confirm you were trading on inside information. This is a felony crime, punishable by up to twenty-five years in prison," Ms. Sgorous said, pausing to pour a glass of water. "Would you like one, Leonard?"

"Yes, please," Crane said dryly, so dryly it was only then he realized his mouth was totally without moisture and that he was sweating profusely. He reached in his pocket and with a handkerchief wiped his brow.

"As I was saying, these are serious crimes you are involved in," and she paused, taking a slow drink of water.

Crane was boiling inside, sweat poured from his pores, he could feel the back of his shirt soaked, sticking to the chair. He needed to get out of this situation.

"I want my attorney here," Crane said, exhausted.

"We can call your attorney, but once we do, the phase of cooperating witness is over. You will be arrested and charged with felony insider trading," Sgorous said.

"Or," Detective Conroy said, jumping back in, "you can use your head and tell us what you know about this whole scheme."

"What will happen if I am able to recall some other details?" Crane said.

"Well, depending on how helpful you are, we can recommend to the judge a lighter sentence," Conroy said.

400

"A lighter sentence! If I help you in this, there should be no sentence," a red-faced Crane said, now upset that he was being played.

"Mr. Crane, we have more than enough evidence to convict you and a number of others for insider trading in Rocket Solar. These crimes are being committed by you and others, and we have it recorded in your own words. We have other individuals we expect will cooperate. The first ones to cooperate get the softer deal. It just makes our job a little easier if we can have someone telling the story from your point of view, and for that we are willing to recommend leniency," and again leaning across the table, Conroy's and Crane's noses were not more than a foot apart. Crane wanted to rip his head off. The bulldog instinct in him wanted to rear up and crush this intruder, this accuser. "So, Leonard," Conroy said, sarcastically, staring him down, "What'll it be, your lawyer or a little help for us to put the big fish away."

That part appealed to Leonard. It wasn't him; it was the others. If the two brothers hadn't been so greedy and put this plan in place, he wouldn't be here. If Alice hadn't called him and told him about what their old boss Sid Rogers was up to, he wouldn't be here. If Parker Barnes and Kish Moira hadn't agreed to his plan to the insider trading, he wouldn't be here. In fact if Eddie hadn't got so high and mighty, he'd still be working at Brunswick and wouldn't have gotten fired.

"Yes," Crane said, "It does make sense to help you, but," he decided to try again, "if I give you everything, no jail time."

"Mr. Crane, we already have everything," Angella Sgorous said, emphasizing "everything." "Now can we get on with it? Please tell us how your involvement in Rocket Solar began, what was said and what you told others."

Leonard Crane slumped. He found himself trapped. He had to do the best he could for himself.

"Alice called me," Crane said.

"That would be Alice…?" Ms. Sgorous asked.

"Alice Kraft," Crane said, wondering one last time, did they really know it was her.

"What specifically did she tell you?" Conroy asked. Suddenly Crane remembered, she did not tell him Rocket Solar when they met. It was his own work that figured it out.

"Wait, she never told me it was Rocket Solar, just that there was a solar company that had received large orders from Chinese solar companies and that would cause the stock to rise."

"Mr. Crane, you said you would cooperate. If she didn't tell you it was Rocket Solar, who did?" Conroy persisted.

"No one," Crane said, pleased with his recollection, "I came back to the office and talked it over with Edward Wheelwright. He told me to do the research and see who it might be. I worked for an afternoon and figured out that it had to be Rocket Solar. Wheelwright...," and here Crane paused—high and mighty Ed Wheelwright wouldn't soil his clean hands, and Lenny the Liar crafted a piece of revenge for Mr. Wheelwright— "Wheelwright, I told him it was Rocket Solar, and he said he needed to think about it. He said if we were to do a large buy here, he should do it with me outside of Brunswick, sort of one off, one degree of separation. That was the way Eddie saw the mosaic of information; it had to be a one or two off. The further removed the better. He had me call Alice back and say we were not interested."

"Good, that's very helpful. Now, we need to know more about this Alice Kraft and the other people inside Blackthorn that she discussed," Sgorous said, adding, "Then we want to come back and talk about Brunswick and what you can share about a Parker Barnes."

"Fine," Crane said, but saddened they had Parker's name; he had to protect him. But he did see a real opportunity to settle more than one score in this discussion.

"Good, so let's go to Blackthorn. How did Alice Kraft describe what she knew; where did she get the information."

"We met and she described an opportunity to make a significant fortune, but we had to act quickly. She said her boss, Sid Rogers, was also trading on the information. Alice said the solar company had received three large orders from Chinese solar

402

companies that would send the stock soaring, doubling," Crane concluded.

"Thank you, Leonard," Sgorous said, and continuing, "now we have information that I need to ask you about at Blackthorn. What did Alice Kraft tell you about the involvement of the two brothers who run the company and own much of it?"

"Nothing," Crane said with a puzzled look.

"She did not tell you that they were selling in large quantities," Detective Conroy asked.

"No," Crane said, confused now, "Why would they sell? Everyone was buying. We made a bundle. That makes no sense," then Crane paused, thought for a moment, adding, "If that's the case, it would suggest that the brothers are cashing out while the stock is high or that the orders are no good?"

"So, you made buys for yourself. Do the figures we have sound right, about one 150 thousand in profit?"

"Roughly, but close enough," Crane replied to Conroy.

"Who else did you share this inside information with?" Conroy asked.

"You are still referring to the fact that I figured out which company Alice was talking about as inside information. I told you that she did not tell me the name of the company," Lenny the Liar rose up to protect his reputation.

"Mr. Crane, are you forgetting that we have phone recordings of your discussions?" Sgorous said.

"I met with Alice Kraft," Crane said.

"We also have a phone conversation between you and a rather upset Ms. Kraft with her telling you the name of the company was Rocket Solar," Sgorous said.

Crane's face reddened, bright red. Anger. Had he forgot she told him the name of the company? Wait, that was after he figured it out. It was not insider information.

"That was not insider information. I figured out the company myself before she told me that," the Liar persisted.

"Mr. Crane, are we back to that again?" Conroy said angrily, "The information you had is inside information; you traded on it and made illegal profits. We've told you those actions are punishable by up to twenty-five years in prison," the detective concluded firmly, adding, "Are we clear."

The "are we clear" was said forcefully enough that the Liar crawled back inside his shell, and Crane answered, "Yes, sir."

At this point Conroy stood up and walked to a dry erase board on the wall at the front of the room. "So, Leonard buys three hundred thousand shares, correct?" he said as he wrote, "Leonard— 300k shares."

"Yes, that's right," Crane replied.

"Now, Alice Kraft, how many shares did she buy?" Crane said. Sgorous looked at Conroy; both hoping Crane could shed light on her inside buying since they had not been able nail down her trading accounts. They figured this may have been done through relatives or friends, which is often the case.

"Alice wanted me to buy the shares. I don't know if she had access to enough money, quick enough to act," Crane said, continuing, "She knew through my trading desk at Brunswick Fund I would be able to buy plenty."

"And did you?" Sgorous asked.

"No, not there, not at that time. But once I saw the scale of buying that Brunswick was going to do on Rocket, I left," Crane said.

"You mean in the predetermined way that you had agreed to with your boss, what was his name?" Conroy said.

"Wheelwright, Edward Wheelwright," Crane said, adding, "Not quite. Once I saw the scale of buying they were going to do, I left. I wanted nothing more to do with it."

Sgorous and Conroy exchanged knowing glances again, that Crane had changed his story. Conroy let it pass, for the time being.

"So, let me get this straight, after you left, you bought three hundred thousand shares."

Crane, a little unsure of why Conroy repeated that said, "Nothing. Those buys are small change. Wheelwright heads up Brunswick fund. They bought millions of shares."

404

"And how were these shares purchased," Conroy asked, as they did not show a number anywhere that large flowing through Brunswick Fund.

"Through Brunswick Fund."

"And you know this how? Who told you they bought millions of shares?" Conroy asked.

Why are they asking that question, surely they know of the trades. He paused, something was not right.

Conroy asked again, rephrasing the question. "You said you had left Brunswick Fund; you said you knew they bought millions of shares. But my question is, how do you know they bought those shares?"

Lenny the Liar was confounded. Was he trapping himself somehow in this? Would this affect Kish? Could he end up getting Parker in trouble? He had to protect Parker at all costs. Eddie told him. "Eddie Wheelwright told me," Conroy blurted out.

"When did he tell you this," Conroy asked, knowing they had no taped phone conversations between the two men discussing the purchase of Rocket Solar stock.

"Probably the day after I left. No, more like two days later, and that's when I bought my shares."

"And you're sure it was Wheelwright you talked to?" Sgorous asked.

"Yes, it was Wheelwright," Crane said, feeling comfortable at ensuring Mr. Highandmighty was duly implicated.

Sgorous looked at Conroy. These trades were not showing up. The SEC had nothing on trades by Brunswick Fund although they did have phone calls between a number of people at Brunswick Fund and Blackthorn Investments in the timeframe they were discussing. The only trade of any consequence out of Brunswick Fund in this time frame was an account of one Parker Barnes.

"Tell us about Parker Barnes. He has an account at Brunswick Fund. And he traded in Rocket Solar in that time frame?" Sgorous asked.

Crane thought, protect Parker. "I don't know."

"You don't know what, Leonard," Sgorous said, puzzled by Crane's response.

"I don't know if a Parker Barnes bought shares in Rocket Solar," Crane replied.

"Mr. Crane!" Conroy shouted.

Crane jumped back in his chair, he was so startled by Conroy's shout.

"Mr. Crane," Conroy shouted again. "We know you made a phone call to Parker Barnes one day before he bought over one million shares."

"I don't know," Crane said stiffening. Sgorous noticed this, saw Crane's jaw tighten and waited with Conroy for Crane to speak. The silence grew.

"Leonard," Sgorous began, "We're trying to give you room to help us. Now tell us about Parker Barnes. Who is he, and how did he become involved in Rocket Solar?"

"I really don't know," Cranc said dumbfounded. He did not know how to get out of this.

Conroy rose, "That's it. The deal is off, Lenny."

"Why? Wait, why?" Crane pleaded.

"We know you contacted him. Shortly after this contact he buys a million shares. Last chance, Crane. If we don't hear right now what you were up to with him, we're arresting you and walking out of this room," Conroy concluded, with his palms on the table, leaning across it into Crane's space once again.

Crane's body language was beautiful, Conroy thought, as Crane slumped, now defeated.

"Parker Barnes was my college roommate," Crane began softly.

"Speak up, Lenny," Conroy said loudly.

"We were roommates at college," Crane said in a raised voice. "I called Parker, and then met with Wheelwright's partner and Parker."

"Who is Wheelwright's partner?" Sgorous said, wanting confirmation.

"Kish Moira. We all went to school together as kids. I met with Kish and Parker in Kish's office. I told them about Rocket Solar. Earlier, as I mentioned I told Wheelwright about Rocket. I know

Parker bought a lot in his account. And I'm certain Wheelwright and Moira bought millions for Brunswick Fund."

"Now what else can you tell us about other trades with Rocket Solar?" Sgorous said.

"That is it, that's everything," Crane said realizing now he had betrayed Barnes.

"Lenny, we're going to verify everything you have said here. If there's anything that's not true, any leniency we would recommend would come off the table," Conroy said, looking for one last tidbit Crane might be holding back on.

"No, that's everything," a dejected Crane told Conroy.

"Alright, you're free to go," Angela Sgorous told Leonard Crane. "We'll be in touch in a couple of days. Please do not leave the city without contacting either Detective Conroy or me."

66

For a late spring morning, it was unusually cool, but refreshing, he thought as he began his run at Tod's point. He had parked by the main concession stand and stretched his legs on the back of a bench. He looked out at the waters of the Sound; they were bright, shimmering from the early morning sun.

Out behind the concession stand, the woods began, first up through a glade of small hills with picnic tables. The sun came through waves of shade from the tall thin trees. He struggled with the hills at the very start of his run. A hawk flew in front of him and landed on a tree, head high and to his left. It surprised him that the bird came so close to him. As he passed not more than five feet from it, he turned twice to make sure he was not in the bird's brain as a breakfast bite. He laughed at the thought and continued up the hill.

A giant boulder sat at the top of the hill, which was a confluence of two paths coming up from the glade and two paths descending, one into woods towards the holly grove and one rolling down through a broad green meadow to the sea that was framed by woods on either side. He took the meadow path, easing his jog down through the thick green grass. Three quarters of the way down he turned right into an opening and a path to the woods. The path wound its way towards the reeds by the sea then turned up to a small clearing. A lone picnic table sat in the middle of this serene setting framed by brush, pines and hollies. There were six paths leading out, and he continued on a route he had known well but travelled less frequently, into woods, out into another clearing with more tables. The waters of the Sound were forty feet away before a new path appeared, broader, more worn into deeper, darker woods.

Chipmunks dodged him as he picked up his pace, and his lungs filled with the crisp morning air. The path wound its way through the wood for about a quarter mile before opening to the clam bake area. It was like opening a theater door into the bright sun—a two-acre field lay before him glistening in the bright sun. He crossed the field diagonally running past a small house for bathrooms and past the long cupola covering picnic tables. Across this field, along this run is where he took his four-year-old son on his first run. Once across the field, he entered a path of head-high reed grasses on his left and woods to his right. It was training day, and just ahead of him a baby dove was practicing. As he approached the parents took off, leaving junior to figure a way off the path. Junior flapped and flapped, moving down the path ahead of him and finally was overtaken but left only panting from this first encounter as the man passed by to the left of the bird.

Another memory rushed forward—the time he and his son took their first weekend away together, just the two of them. The son was twelve, and he took him to Cooperstown to the Baseball Hall of Fame. The Hall was a wonder for the boy who was into baseball, but what flooded his memory was the intimacy of their time together. They stayed at the venerable Otesaga Hotel on the lake of the same name. In those three days, he let the boy pick from a list of activities—the twelve-year-old played his first round of golf, they fished for the first time in two years, they took their first canoe ride, they ate dinner quietly on the patio of the Otesaga, and they had breakfast on the veranda. On the second day, they found Cooperstown Fun Park and played miniature golf, hit baseballs from a batting cage and drove balls on a range. That night they drove to Unadilla to a drive-in movie, another first for the boy.

At the end of the reed trail, he came to a divergent path: onto a road or back through a small jog to the outer trail that went by the waters of the sound. He chose the latter, not thinking of Robert

410

Frost as much as the echo of what lay ahead. Turning left he glimpsed the city to his right. Thirty-five miles away Manhattan Island stretched out from north on the right to the left and south, missing its two tall towers at the end. He remembered that day. He was off and at home. He got a call to turn on the TV. And for an agonizing half hour, he watched the horror. When he could stand it no longer, he came to the point and ran, fast and furious to get away from it. But when he got to this very point, there it was. A stream of black smoke rising up from where they stood. And then nothing, the smoke changed to white. He did not know why the color of the smoke changed until he returned home and saw they were gone. Just up ahead along the path a bench looked out toward the city. It had the name of a son lost that day. And he thought about his own son, who called him crying. Sobbing about what had happened in the city he would live in after college, about all the people lost in the storm of fire and collapse. He told his son to pray for the souls lost that day; he told him to thank God for his life.

He came off the shore trail, down through a short winding path to a broader road under a canopy of tall elms, back across an earlier glade, across the meadow to the sea and into another short path back to the shore road.

It was 7 a.m. As he reached the concession stand, his t-shirt was soaked. He had run faster than he expected. He was exhausted, and even though he hadn't run lately, he knew he would be alright. Optimism was pulsing inside of him. Mark Wheelwright was looking forward to seeing his grandson, again, this day. He was looking forward to spending time with the little boy. More memories of his own son Edward kept rushing forward. He wanted time, time to repeat some of these memories with his grandson.

67

Against the split horizon of a charcoal sky and unseen water, the running lights of the "Construction" appeared. The boat snaked its way into the channel from Long Island Sound, narrowly past a few wrecks lying dead, half sunk; past a decrepit house boat that had a dim light from inside; past three barges that lay in a row partly filled with scrap metal from an adjoining junk yard; and past a speed boat tied up on the front end of the pier that was one of three making up the "marina." If this canal were an alleyway, you wouldn't walk down it at night.

Chunk DeLuna and three of his men pulled the white van out of the black shadows as Parker Barnes docked his yacht at the End of the World Marina in Norwalk. It was dark, dirty, and isolated. Barnes picked the spot because it got little use; only a couple of large sail boats docked here. The landing area was in an industrial setting with little nighttime traffic. Visiting boats such as his were left to themselves.

Barnes drove DeLuna to this site three weeks earlier to familiarize DeLuna with the location and to talk through how they would unload, which they now began as soon Barnes had secured the boat with the mooring ropes. DeLuna spoke only once to his men, in Portuguese, and then his men worked in silence. Quickly they had the panels off the inside of the cabin. In little over forty-five minutes, all packages of drugs were off the boat, and the panels were back in place.

Barnes took a deep breath as he stood ready to unhook the ropes and sail out. DeLuna gave him a hearty hug, and in less than one hour, DeLuna and his men were in the van heading for his drug distribution center in Stamford. In two days the drugs would be cut, diluted and repackaged creating a street value of some thirty million dollars.

Now in the seam, between the clouds of the night and the fog of morning, Parker Barnes guided his boat down Long Island Sound to Stamford.

It was 5 a.m. when he docked and tied the boat up at the Stamford Yacht Club.

Barnes and DeLuna had executed the plan they drew up weeks earlier when Parker realized how overextended he was, and while talking to DeLuna about his plight, the little cement maker told him more about his other lines of work. Barnes would be paid three million for the transaction, which involved meeting one of DeLuna's cement freighters ten miles south of Montauk Point, off-loading the drugs into his yacht's panels and meeting DeLuna at the marina in Norwalk.

Barnes took a deep breath of the early morning air; he was exhausted. The world was asleep, and he returned below to the cabin. He laid down on the bed and slept.

68

Parker Barnes woke up at four in the afternoon on his boat
docked at the Stamford Yacht Club. Somewhat dazed from the
long night and an uncomfortable sleep aboard the boat, he washed
up, shaved, and changed his clothes.

He got off the boat, walked along the ramp to the parking lot
without seeing any of the clubs members, and drove off in his
Mercedes SL. Two minutes later he was home.

At 6 p.m. he joined his mother and father for dinner.

"I tried to reach you today, twice," Jonathan Barnes began in a
tone that sounded accusatory, as usual. "Your assistant said you were
out—both times I called."

"Yes, I was with Mr. DeLuna all day discussing the cement
requirements and the framing that his company is going to need to
do for us," Parker said.

His father smiled, "Good. I like the little guy, and I like his
prices."

The three made small talk over dinner: the responses from
friends to Jonathan's run for the senate, the times of Winston's
wedding and reception and who was Parker bringing, and that Mrs.
Strong's son may be innocent and about to receive a new hearing.

"CJ got screwed on that," Parker sneered, almost like he forgot
why.

"Parker, shut up," his father said, mindful that Mrs. Strong,
their housekeeper was still in the house. The three exchanged the

415

uncomfortable glances that come from seven years of covering up a crime in which they knew who did it and who did not do it.

After dinner Parker left the dining room and went out toward the carriage house where he had personal quarters, separate from the main house. It was his refuge while under the roof of his father. He would go to watch TV or use his computer, read, or simply spend the night there.

This night he would start to plan how to use his new riches.

As he exited the main house through the side door, Mrs. Strong was coming back inside.

"Parker," she exclaimed, "have you heard? Curtis is about to be freed."

Barnes looked at her; this was different than what his mother said, "Yes, Mom mentioned he was going to get a new hearing."

"They say they know my boy didn't kill that drug dealer. Now after all these years, he's almost free."

"That's wonderful, Mrs. Strong. I'm sure you are very happy," he said with mild enthusiasm.

"Yes, you don't know how happy."

Barnes put his arm around the woman then continued on his way.

As Barnes entered the door to the carriage house he said out loud, "Well, if CJ didn't kill him, I wonder who did." He laughed, out loud, and kept smiling as he felt his cell phone vibrating. He pulled the phone from his pocket as he closed the door.

"Hello," he said not recognizing the phone number.

"Barnes, we got trouble." It was Chunk DeLuna. He recognized the pitch of the voice with the Latin accent.

"What's up," Parker replied casually for he was not prepared for what came next.

"You're my one call," DeLuna said. "They caught me with the truck. The cops got the whole thing. I need you to get me out of this."

Barnes did not quite believe what he was hearing. "Where are you, Chunk?"

"I'm in jail in Stamford," came the reply

Barnes felt a rush, but it wasn't the good kind of rush from cocaine. It was fear and anxiety combined. Fear they'd been caught, anxiety over not knowing what to do.

"What do you want me to do?" the question Barnes asked was not intended to help. It should have been phrased, "What do you expect me to do," since Barnes intended to do nothing.

"Don't play games with me, Barnes. Get me out of this."

"How do you expect me to do that? Be serious, DeLuna. I can't involve myself in this," Barnes said

"You are involved," came the reply from DeLuna and in rapid fire he added, "And if you don't want to be sitting in the cell with me and my cellmate, you'd better get your ass down here with a lawyer and bail."

"Have you called a lawyer?" Barnes asked feebly.

"Listen. They tell me I got one call. You're it. I was at your old man's party and so was everyone else who can fix this thing."

"DeLuna, my father is running for Senate. We can't do anything. Damn."

"Let me put it this way," DeLuna said raising his voice, "if I'm still here this time tomorrow, you will be also. OK, cop's telling me my time's up. Do it." And DeLuna hung up.

Parker Barnes sat in a large lounge chair. He was in full panic. Surely he was going to jail, even worse was the thought that his father would cut him out of the family and out of his rightful fortune. He could hear Jonathan. The harang would go on for hours, for days. There was enough ammunition here for his father to crucify him—drugs, theft from the company, our reputation. "The Senate—you've destroyed my chance to help lead the country," those would be his father's words. It wouldn't be the money or even the drugs that would push Jonathan Barnes over the edge. It would be the blow to his ego.

For the first time in two months, Parker felt the weakness returning. It left him powerless to act and think in the right way. He was starting to feel a craving. But first he needed to act. He needed help and he could not ignore this problem.

69

Parker Barnes was a singularity. He was alone on a planet of seven billion people. Walt Whitman wrote, "We are large, we contain multitudes." Parker Barnes, to all who knew him, seemed that way, large, containing multitudes. There were many ways to view him—as an athlete and sailor, friend and companion, student and professional, and son. But for all his roles in life, for all his seeming multitudes, Parker Barnes was alone, in himself.

Einstein wrote, "The significant problems we face cannot be solved at the same level of thinking we were at when we created them." And therein lay Parker Barnes' problem. At each level of treachery to himself, he created an infinitely more complex problem, and he utterly lacked the ability to find a path out. For as he got older, each problem got more severe. When he was sixteen, he began using drugs, and while he would control their use, by the second year of using he became reckless. He no longer could find his way back after that first year. When he was seventeen, he stabbed Augusto Santos to death and allowed Curtis Strong to go to prison for that crime these past seven years. The guilt that built from that initial "accident" grew daily, and all he had to do to be reminded of it was to look at the saddened face of his family's housekeeper, CJ Strong's mother. By the time Barnes was twenty-five, he was not the joyful young boy from the Brunswick School. Drugs and guilt now wracked him. Greed loomed and he seized upon it, misappropriating two million dollars from his father's firm to invest in the Brunswick

Fund, to keep up, to be one of the boys. Then he compounded that crime by taking several million more to invest in Rocket Solar in an insider trading scheme to pay back the first theft. But Barnes thought maybe his luck was turning as news of the Chinese orders was out and Rocket Solar was up sharply.

Parker Barnes was smart in the sense a master criminal is smart and develops contingency plans. Barnes did develop a contingency plan in case the tip from Lenny Crane did not work out, and he would need to replace the larger sum on the Rocket Solar investment. With Chunk DeLuna as an ally, partner and drug supplier, they came up with a plan to smuggle drugs into the US on Barnes' yacht. He would do this just once, he promised himself. One time, a shipment large enough to repay all "loans" to the family firm would allow him to finally relieve the steady pressure he found himself under. It was a plan; if it failed, that would seal his fate, a plan so warped, so removed from the reality of the life he lived there would be no escaping the consequences. It was a plan only the singularity that was Parker Barnes could have developed.

Daniel Defoe wrote about Robinson Crusoe and his survival and his search for a way off the island. It had been three years since Crusoe had been marooned that he found himself with the idea of building a canoe to row to the land he saw in the distance. With his crude tools, he felled a cedar tree that was fully "five feet and ten inches in diameter at the stump" and for weeks he trimmed it, hollowed it out and shaped it. Only in the end did he realize he was one hundred yards from water and the land rose up between the canoe and the water.

It is a forlorn Crusoe who laments, "And now I saw, though too late, the folly of beginning a work before we count the cost, and before we judge rightly our own strength to go through with it."

The folly of Parker Barnes was his inability to think through the consequences of his actions. The fog of drugs, the weight of guilt, the anxiety of theft, the urgency of greed, the disappointment of a father, and the disappointment in a father were a cancer on his conscience. The promise that Whitman saw in the human condition no longer existed in Barnes. The layers of life ill lived buried the promise of youth. Problems became so significant they could not be solved; holes closed behind impulses acted upon. Ultimately the individual was alone in his stew. This singularity, alone.

And now the captured Chunk DeLuna was making his one call from jail and it was to Parker Barnes. Barnes needed to talk with someone, to think this through. Lenny. If Barnes trusted one person in this world to help him, it would be Leonard Crane. The same Lenny Crane who two days earlier had entered into a plea bargain with Cyber-crimes investigator Jim Conroy and the SEC.

Barnes dialed Crane.

Leonard Crane's cell phone rang at the apartment of the girl he was dating. They were sitting on a couch watching TV. The caller ID showed it to be Parker Barnes. The phone continued with the crazy, noisy ring tone of the song "Cotton Eyed Joe."

Mr. Crane's lady friend asked, "Lenny, aren't you gonna answer that fuckin thing?"

"No, it can wait," he replied and shut the phone down.

Crane had never not taken a call from Parker Barnes before. But he had also never sold him out before. As part of the plea bargain with Conroy, he had to state exactly what each person did that he came into contact with during the purchase of Rocket Solar shares. Lenny the Liar told the whole truth. He fully implicated Parker Barnes on insider trading charges. While Lenny the Liar told the whole truth, it wasn't nothing but the truth. He also implicated Edward Wheelwright.

"Damn, Lenny, pick up," Parker screamed at his cell phone. He snapped it shut. The craving was growing. He had to act now. He opened the phone again and hit two buttons—the number for Gideon Bridge.

"Gideon, I'm in trouble, and I need your help," Parker said into the phone and the recorded message from Bridge.

It was 10 p.m. The craving was now overwhelming. He picked up his car keys and wallet and went out into the night.

70

J ames Ford was allowed to accompany the transfer jailer who was charged with delivering Curtis Strong to Stamford Police HQ for a hearing on the following Monday. Ford and Lt Vito Boriello of the Stamford Police had succeeded in finding multiple pieces of evidence that they believed proved Strong had been wrongly convicted, the lead piece being John Walsh's written statement that Billy Stevens confessed to him that it was he and not Curtis Strong who had killed Augusto Santos. They had arranged for a hearing that in all probability would result in the conviction being set aside, and then it would be up to the District Attorney to decide if the case against Mr. Strong was worth pursuing. Boriello had been persuasive enough that the DA had agreed that if a judge set the verdict aside, then he, the DA would not pursue a new trial. The DA agreed to be present Monday also.

They brought Strong in late Friday afternoon. He would remain in jail over the weekend until the hearing and until a determination was made by the judge. In the meantime, Ford and Boriello had arranged a series of meetings on Saturday, first with Mrs. Strong at 9 a.m.; then at 10 a.m. the public defender who would represent Strong would meet with his client. At 11 a.m. Strong and the public defender would be joined by Ford and Boriello to stitch together the order they would present evidence: evidence of a sham trial with incompetent representation of the defendant and evidence of a highly partial and conflicted judge and prosecutor. Evidence of a badgered jury would be presented with sworn statements from two jurors. Evidence would be presented in the sworn testimony of the defendant that he merely went to the aid of an injured man who was calling out for help.

Strong was taken to the same jail area he had originally been in seven long years ago. Ford and Boriello accompanied him after Boriello had accepted receipt of the prisoner from the Auburn Prison transfer jailer.

"You'll get a good meal. Have a good night's sleep, and we'll see you in the morning," Ford said.

"Thank you for all you have done for me, Mr. Ford. And you too, Lieutenant Boriello."

"You're welcome, and I am finally glad to meet you. I called your mother, and she will be here to see you at 9 a.m. We have a busy day, so sleep well. We'll get you out of this mess soon," Boriello said with a smile.

They shook hands, and the Stamford officer on jail duty opened the cell door and let Strong enter. He closed it after him and locked it.

"Richie, take good care of him tonight. He's been through a lot," Boriello said to Officer Richard Long.

"Sure thing, Lieutenant," Long said, accompanying Ford and Boriello out of the small cell block.

Strong had a calm evening. He was brought dinner. He read from a novel he brought with him. At 9 p.m. he was asleep.

At 10 p.m. he was awakened. The jailer brought another prisoner in to this cell. The cell was large enough; on either side of the small room, there were bunk beds. Strong hoped that they would not be filling all four beds. He'd had a long eventful day and was looking forward to seeing his mother and his attorney.

This new prisoner was snarling; he had a wild look in his eyes.

When Officer Long took the cuffs off the new prisoner, he said to him, "Now behave yourself, Poncho. When your attorney gets here, I'll come and get you."

Strong did not get up from his bunk. He ignored the new man and rolled back over in the lower bunk on the left hand side of the room. The new prisoner sat on the lower bunk on the right hand side of the room. He was restless.

"What did they get you for," he said in a clipped foreign accent that Strong believed was Spanish.

Strong did not answer and stayed facing the wall.

"Fuckers. Got me. Got my whole shipment."

Obviously this was not going to work. Strong turned over and looked at the man. He looked like that little guy from the old TV show that shouted, "The plane, the plane."

71

The offices of the insider trading task force, made up of the NYPD Cyber Crimes Unit and the Enforcement Branch of the Securities and Exchange Commission, were spread over three floors in the building they were using. The building itself was mostly empty, seized by the government after the collapse of Lehman Brothers. It was a building Lehman had been renting for its back office operations. Lehman had been running behind on its rent for over a year; it was early in 2008, and the writing was on the wall for Lehman. It would die a death like Caesar, with all who surrounded him stabbing him and no one stepping in to stop it.

Five days after Lehman vacated the space, the city seized the building, and it sat vacant once again until the task force moved in. It was a narrow cement structure built around 1930. The building was designed for small professional offices; lawyers, accountants, and advertising firms—the size of many businesses in the 1930s before the growth of mega corporations that today not only took whole floors in skyscrapers but who took whole skyscrapers. The narrowness of the building meant you could not house large operations on any one floor. At this particular time, for this particular use, these size constraints would work well for Jim Conroy. The plan was simple—simultaneous arrests, simultaneous interviews—on separate floors where there was little chance of one crook seeing another crook. Warrants were issued on Thursday, and arrests were targeted for 10 a.m. Friday.

Precisely at 10 a.m. brothers Tom Barrett, the president and CEO, and his brother Rob Barrett, the VP of World Wide Sales, were apprehended and brought in for questioning from their offices at Rocket Solar. Sid Rogers and Alice Kraft were similarly were picked up at their offices at Blackthorn Investments. It was only hours later after questioning that formal arrests were made.

Not "apprehended" but invited in for interviews by members of the task force at precisely the same time were a number of others tangentially involved in the case where no direct evidence yet tied them to profits from insider trading. These included Valerie Samson from Blackthorn who through Blackthorn initiated a "Buy" recommendation on Rocket Solar three days earlier and had calls back and forth to Edward Wheelwright at Brunswick Fund; Edward Wheelwright and Kishenlal Moira from the Brunswick Fund; and Parker Barnes, a private investor, each of whom had been identified by Leonard Crane as trading on insider information on Rocket Solar, but where the task force had yet to find trades in the stock at Brunswick or in the men's accounts, and Winston Trout, who as head of a competitor solar company, Trout Solar, had numerous contacts with Edward Wheelwright, on the same dates that Wheelwright had talked with Val Samson and Alice Kraft from Blackthorn Investments. All the interviews took place in New York, except for Wheelwright and Samson, who were interviewed in Greenwich and for Parker Barnes who could not be located at his office or home.

While the task force had more than enough evidence for convictions against the Barrett's and Rogers for profiting from insider trading and sufficient evidence against Alice Kraft for conspiracy to commit insider trading, they interviewed the others to see what else fell from the tree. They were searching for evidence against those being interviewed; failing that, they felt the interviewees may be able to shed more light on the investigation.

This unusual approach was taken to limit the damage that was about to happen to stockholders in Rocket Solar. The SEC had insisted that they needed to move at this time since the stock of Rocket Solar, partly due to the Valerie Samson recommendation and

"Buy" rating, was rising and more investors were buying into it. The apprehensions were not made public, and the interviewees brought in for questioning were kept out of the limelight. During the day on Friday, Rocket Solar rose another $3 per share to $17. Friday, and over the weekend the task force had to move quickly, formally arrest those where the evidence was irrefutable, gain additional evidence against those who may have been participating in these schemes, and then announce the scheme publically. Some stories were bound to appear over the weekend as the apprehensions and interviews of those involved were drawing attention. Many innocent investors were about to lose thousands, even hundreds of thousands of dollars.

The surprise of the day was not to any new dimensions the investigation took but to the individuals themselves involved or not involved. For example, Valerie Samson and Edward Wheelwright had been on vacation time during the week, getting reacquainted with each other and their son. So it was no small surprise to Valerie that she had issued a "Buy" recommendation on Rocket Solar, something that she was easily able to refute while the investigators were at the Greenwich Police station with her, where they arranged space for the interview, simply by pulling up on line her final of the recommendation that said, "Sell." This was further confirmed on the spot by a call to her boss who told of the pressure Sid Rogers was putting on Valerie for a "Buy" rating, which she refused to issue.

Edward Wheelwright was astounded that calls to him from Alice Kraft and Valerie Samson and his calls to Winston Trout were being construed as evidence of insider trading where nothing could be further from the truth. To back his version up, he cited proof that he fired Leonard Crane for cause, the cause being unethical behavior. Additionally, Alice Kraft confirmed that Wheelwright had called Samson, who got Kraft to stop any further attempts at insider trading. Kraft also told the officers that it was Wheelwright who had been very good in helping her understand her errors. Finally, the confirmation of no trades at all in Rocket Solar vindicated Wheelwright.

Kish Moira admitted that Crane and Barnes had come to see him and wanted to buy hundreds of thousands of shares of Rocket Solar, and after Crane and Barnes had left, he decided to talk with

Wheelwright. It was then that he learned why Crane had been let go. He explained to the investigators that, while he and Wheelwright were partners, Wheelwright handled the people end of things and he handled the technical. On investments he told them they made joint decisions, particularly the brothers' investments. The reason he had gone to Wheelwright in this case is that from what Crane had been saying to Barnes in front of him it sounded like a bad deal, like Crane had some type of insider information. Wheelwright explained what had been going on and together they invested Barnes' money in Trout Solar, a trust the brothers had given Edward and Kish, to make the right investments, no matter what.

Sidney Rogers initially denied all charges. Throughout the day his story changed several times, and new information was called in. When confronted by the wire taps, his own e-mail between the Barrett brothers, double confirmation by Samson and her boss that it was Rogers who initiated the "Buy" recommendation on Rocket Solar, and records of hundreds of thousands of shares of Rocket Solar bought and partly sold by him, Rogers was ready to confess to his part of the entire scheme for some leniency.

"And in return, what help can you provide so we understand how this all began?" Jack Kent asked.

"I can tell you exactly what and how the Barretts were doing what they were doing."

"Explain."

"And for this I will get?"

"Consideration as a cooperating defendant."

"Meaning no jail time?"

"Far from it. You will be going to jail for a very long time. Just not as long as you might otherwise."

"Forget it."

Jack Kent said, "Well you might have saved yourself ten years, since we know exactly what the Barretts were up to. Now you'll have to do the complete twenty-five years. Valerie Samson was able to give us a complete rundown on the orders from the Chinese solar manufacturers, their out of date technology, how Rocket would announce the orders after you did all your buying, and how you and the Barretts would be out of the stock in six months when the orders were confirmed as no good."

"That's all bullshit," Rogers screamed.

"You must have really pissed Samson off by changing her recommendation. She actually gave us tapes of your last couple of conversations. Threatening a lady is not a good idea."

"Yeah, well she also was willing to deal on that 92nd Y. She would give the recommendation if my wife got her kid in."

"Yes, we have that on tape as well. It looks to us like she didn't act on the position you were able to secure. Looks like your wife may have to resign from the board there. That place sure gets a lot of attention from you financial types trying to get your kids in there," Kent concluded, unable to resist the jab.

By 9 p.m. Friday night, Tom and Rob Barrett had been read their rights and arrested for securities fraud. Similarly, Sid Rogers was arrested for securities fraud and profiting illegally from insider trading. Leonard Crane was formally arrested for attempting to aid insider trading. He was not charged with insider trading and would not profit from any trades he made since the markets were closed, and his various accounts held several hundred thousand shares that would be under water come Monday. Alice Kraft was not charged and was listed as a cooperating witness.

Wheelwright, Moira, and Samson, after a full day of questioning that went well into the night, were thanked for their cooperation and asked to give signed statements as cooperating witnesses, which they did.

In the car, on the way back to their home, Valerie said to Eddie, "A couple of Saturdays ago I had an opportunity I wanted to talk with you about. Do you remember?"

"When we met over at Tod's Point? I thought that was just a ruse."

"A ruse? For what?"

"You know, to get back together," he said and then winced as she whacked him in the gut as he drove.

"You conceited bastard. Did you think I couldn't live without you?" she laughed.

"Yes, because I could not live without you. It seemed a perfect way to get us together."

"Well I'm glad it worked out, but that wasn't the reason."

"So what was the opportunity that was so important?"

"Never mind."

"Seriously, what was it?"

"I forgot."

"Val?"

"I was going to suggest me joining Brunswick Fund to do research."

"Really?"

"Was."

"It's a great idea. The thought of the powerful McGuire brain and the beautiful McGuire girl beside me all day. We'd need a private office."

"Where does your mind go? Anyway, that was the idea. After today I think I will be very content being Mrs. Wheelwright, the mother of our son."

"An even better idea."

Wheelwright called Kish Moira from his cell phone as they pulled into their driveway. "How'd it go, Kish?"

"Fine, they thanked me, had me sign a statement on what I told them. How about you?"

"Yes, same thing."

"Eddie, thanks. That was a brilliant move not to follow Lenny and Parker into Rocket Solar."

"We want to get ahead, Kish, but not that way. Your instincts were right in bringing the transaction to me so we could discuss it. That's why we're a great team."

"Brothers till the end."

"I'll see you at the church tomorrow; I'll get a car to bring you out."

"Big day for Winny. I'll bet he doesn't sleep all night."

"After today, neither will we. Good night, Kish."

"Night, Eddie."

"You guys make me sick with this brother shit." Valerie said sticking a finger down her throat.

72

At 2 a.m. on the day Winston Trout was to wed, he and his six
Brunswick friends were abed. But only one slept in his own bed.

In the mansion, Ball Hall, the fluffy white Snowman of his
childhood sat on the dresser next to Sebastian Ball's empty bed. This
night Sebastian was in bed with Jane Lane, wife of the Arizona
environmental commissioner, who Ball had been calling on to get a
large solar farm approved for the Arizona desert.

And young Mr. Wheelwright was not in his usual bed with
Santa Alba but back home, in the guesthouse. Lying silently,
contentedly naked next to him was the former future, now future
again, Mrs. Wheelwright, Valerie Samson.

Kish Moira lay uncomfortably, not in his home in Murray Hill,
not in his bed, but on a couch in his office. Sugar plum fairies were
not in his dreams; what jumped over the fences in the meadow were
not sheep. Millions of Rocket Solar panels were lined up, row after
row, for miles in the Arizona desert, attached to the Western Grid.
The lines ran alongside the path of the Colorado River, and as the
river filled the pipes of homes in Los Angeles, the lines in the grid
brought in the power for the homes. When the power went into the
homes, they all burst into flames. Hundreds of thousands of homes
in Southern California all on fire, a great conflagration sent walls of
flames into the hot, dry valleys. Kish was jolted awake. He lay fully
clothed, sweating in the dark on the couch. Four days earlier he had
worked all evening reviewing the executions of the day's trades in

Trout Solar. Earlier, he knew Edward would be upset for the risks he proposed taking in Rocket Solar, but after talking with Parker Barnes and Lenny Crane two days before, he agreed to buy all the shares Parker wanted. Parker gave him checks for four million dollars in eight transactions from Barnes Construction to his personal account in the Brunswick Fund. Kish didn't understand the reason for separate checks of five hundred thousand dollars each, but Parker was always doing things a little differently anyway. Kish, after listening to Barnes and Crane made a determination that the information they possessed about Rocket Solar was not insider information since it was twice removed from the source, decided to match their five million with five million from the fund. Throughout the day he held back from purchasing one million shares in the solar company. The stock's volume was rising to three times its daily average, and the stock price had moved up three dollars. They could still be in early, Kish thought, and would make a killing. Something though told him to review all of this with Edward Wheelwright before pulling the triggers. Wheelwright realized his own mistake in not keeping Kish up to speed on why he fired Crane and what he knew about Rocket Solar. After a brief discussion, Kish got it, and both agreed to do the transactions, but not in Rocket Solar, in Trout Solar. Kish fell back to sleep, exhausted from the questioning by the SEC over potential insider trades of Rocket Solar, not one of which Brunswick Fund made. He promised to say a prayer of thanks at Winston's wedding to whichever God had watched out for him and Eddie.

Chunk's sister, the beauteous washer woman of San Blas, slept a sleep of joy, the strong arms of the warrior Tray Johnson around her, in her modest home in Coamo.

The groom to be, one Winston Trout, was focused on every detail of the wedding and went so late he took the guest apartment above the Stamford Yacht Club where the reception would occur the following day. And in the guest room next to him was not his bride to be but her father. He worked side by side with his son-in-law-to-be. They had become fast friends, and James Albright treasured the man who would be his daughter's husband.

This night NY City Police investigator Jim Conroy slept well in his own bed, having worked with prosecutors and the grand jury to return indictments against six individuals for insider trading in Rocket Solar.

This night Curtis Strong thought of liberation, knowing in three days he would appear in Stamford Superior Court for a hearing that would possibly free him after seven years, two hundred fifty-five days, and looking at the illuminated hands of his watch, five hours in prison. Next to him in his cell and waking him was the noisy Latino pacing back and forth saying he had a get-out-of-jail-free card.

This night Stamford Police sergeant John Walsh would be sleeping with the fishes.

This night Parker Barnes would not be sleeping at home.

Gideon Bridge was asleep in his bed; soon to be awakened, not once but twice.

73

When the warrant for the arrest of Parker Barnes came into the Stamford Police, the notice was given to Captain Al Paiva. The receiving sergeant recognized the name and got it to Paiva, who normally ran interference with the big names; in Stamford no name was bigger than Barnes. The company had practically built Stamford; it had built this police headquarters building.

Pavia looked at the Federal warrant, noted that the complaint had come out of the NYC police department, cosigned by the SEC requesting their cooperation in arresting Barnes and notifying them, so they could pick him up once he was in custody.

"Look Sergeant Conroy, we'll pick him up for you, but you're not taking him out of this town. His father owns Stamford. You can come here and talk with him," Pavia said firmly into the phone.

Conroy apparently did not like that approach because in the next second, Pavia exploded at him, yelling into the phone and standing up as he did it. "I don't give a good goddamn what the NYPD wants. This is our city. You want our cooperation, you come here. We have to live with these fucking people after you leave."

There was acquiescence. "Fine then, I'll call you when we have him here. You can come in in the morning and interview him. By the time you finish the interview, his attorney will most likely be with him and he will have been bailed out."

Paiva debated calling Jonathan Barnes. If it were a local warrant, he could work around it, even get it pulled and let the cops talk through the issue without arresting the young Barnes. This was different. With a federal warrant, he had little leeway, in fact none, other than what he was able to negotiate with Conroy.

Paiva decided to let the warrant go through. When he got the call from Jonathan Barnes, he would simply plead ignorance. But in letting the warrant go through for Barnes' arrest, Paiva talked to the evening watch commander and told him to wait for Barnes to leave the house. Do not do it on the Barnes' grounds.

"What if he doesn't go out for the night?" was the question back from the watch commander.

"Then we just sit there until he does."

That would be unnecessary. At around 10 p.m. Parker's Mercedes XL shot up Rogers Rd. The unmarked car followed him onto Occan Drive West, and when Barnes peeled out onto Shippan Avenue, the undercover car with two detectives and one warrant pulled Barnes over.

The officers in plain clothes approached Barnes from both sides. He saw them out of each mirror. For a second his mind said, "take off—it's a trap." He thought of his argument with Chuck DeLuna just a few minutes before. Were these his men? But when the officer on his side said calmly, "Sir, may I see your driver's license," Barnes relaxed. He must have been going too fast up Shippan Ave and didn't see them hiding in a speed trap.

"Yes, sir," Barnes said, pulling out his wallet and showing his driver's license.

"It says here you are Parker Barnes. Is that correct, sir?" the officer asked.

"Yes, officer. Was I speeding? Sorry." Barnes said, before confirmation that he was stopped for speeding.

"Mr. Barnes, would you please step out of the car?"

This was strange he thought but followed the officer's request.

Once out of the car the officer said, "Mr. Barnes, please turn and face your car with your hands on the roof."

"Officer, what is this about," Barnes asked, while complying.

The second officer came around from the back of the car and patted Barnes down.

"He's clean."

"Mr. Barnes, I have a warrant for your arrest. We are going to take you to the Stamford Police station."

"This must be some mistake, I don't have any outstanding tickets; nothing else is wrong," Barnes said, now in a plea.

"Mr. Barnes, the charges in the warrant are for insider trading in stocks," the first officer said to Barnes.

"That's impossible."

"This is a federal warrant. Once you are in custody, an agent from the SEC will be arriving to go over the charges with you in more detail. Our job right now is to bring you in," the officer continued. "We'll lock your car up and take the keys."

The second officer put handcuffs on Barnes and placed him in the rear of the Ford sedan. The second officer locked Barnes' car.

They were at the police station in ten minutes. Barnes was read his rights along the way. He remained silent, wondering how this involved him. The tips that Lenny gave him and that he had Kish execute were for Rocket Solar. Everything was fine there; the stock was a rocket, up 30 percent in the past three days. Could they have somehow found out about Lenny's information to him? Could Kish have... "Oh my god," he said audibly.

"What's that, Mr. Barnes," the booking officer asked as he fingerprinted him.

"Nothing," and what had startled him was that Chunk DeLuna was most likely in this very jail. "Oh, my god," he said again, but this time to himself.

"As the arresting officer has stated to you, we are helping execute a federal warrant. The filers, the New York City Police Department and the SEC will be sending representatives here in the morning to formally charge you. You will have a special arraignment, and then you will be eligible for bail."

"I want to call an attorney this moment; there is no reason for me to be held overnight here," he said, determined to not share the same space as DeLuna.

"Once we're through here, I'll get you a phone, and you can call your attorney."

When they completed their work, Barnes was allowed to make a call from a cubicle that gave him some privacy. He dialed Gideon Bridge. This time for himself. Once again he received Bridge's answering machine. He thought of hanging up and calling his father, but that would be worse.

"Gideon, it's me Parker. I'm in the Stamford Police Station's jail on some charge of insider trading. I need you to come here tonight and get me out of this. Please hurry. Thanks."

"All set?" the processing officer asked, approaching Barnes.

"No, not really," Barnes said in a panic.

"Well, I'll take you to a cell. You can wait there until your attorney gets here."

"I'd rather not," Barnes said defiantly. "I would like to wait right here until he comes."

"Here?" the officer said, "You can't wait here; we have things to do. You've been arrested. When that happens you wait in a cell until the next event takes place." The officer said back firmly, expecting trouble, and letting Barnes know if there was trouble, the officer was ready for it.

"Please?" Barnes begged.

"Mr. Barnes, this happens all the time; there is nothing to worry about."

Barnes thought of telling him that if DeLuna was there his life could be in danger. But that may make matters worse. Maybe DeLuna, seeing him also jailed, would keep his mouth shut.

"Come along now," the officer said as he walked towards a door.

The door led down a flight metal and cement stairs. Very firm Barnes thought, the whole building has the feeling of a fortress. Every stair he descended seemed to be taking him further from the privileged life he led. When they reached the bottom, they went through another door. An officer sat behind a desk; beyond the desk were metal bars and gates. For all the trouble Barnes had been in his life over drug use and driving while intoxicated, he had never been jailed. The thought of losing his freedom, of being unable to do whatever he wanted, whenever he wanted, was paralyzing him.

"This is Mr. Parker Barnes, Jerry," the processing officer said to Officer Jerry Lott, a very large, barrel chested man who was probably serving out his time here until his pension.

"Let's see. Would you like a single or a double, perhaps a water view?" Lott said sarcastically. "Ah, here we are, I have a lovely single. It's in a noisy neighborhood, but things usually calm down by 11 p.m."

He opened the sliding gate with his keys, and he and Barnes walked down an aisle of about twelve cells, six to a side. Every cell had one or two men in them.

"Here we are, your room with a view," he said, sliding the barred gate to the cell to the left as Barnes entered.

"I trust you'll sleep well; see you in the morning," and he slid the metal gate shut.

"When my attorney comes," Barnes began quietly as he could see there were men in the cell directly across from him on their beds, "would you please come and get me."

"Yes sir, if your attorney comes tonight, we will get you. I'd get a good night sleep. Usually the lawyers don't show up till morning," and the officer walked back up the aisle.

"Your attorney?" it was the voice of DeLuna, "Don't you mean our attorney, Mr. Barnes, sir," and he slurred the "sir" in the same sarcastic manner as Officer Lott.

No nightmare could be worse than this. Parker Barnes was in jail, and Chunk DeLuna was in the cell across from him.

The other occupant of the DeLuna cell was startled by the name Barnes. He listened as his cellmate DeLuna spoke across the bars. It was only an hour before that DeLuna had started confiding in the black man about the deal that had gone bad.

"We had it complete. All the drugs came off the boat. Hell, I even gave the kid who brought the drugs in his boat half his money up front. If I can't get out of this, I'm screwed. I'll be out a million and a half and have nothing to show for it."

As DeLuna told his tale, nothing about it seemed familiar. CJ Strong thought now, how could he have missed it—rich kid, own boat, father's a big shot builder, running for Senate. Hadn't CJ's mother told him that her employer Jonathan Barnes was running for Senate? Yes. But Strong had been so focused on tomorrow, Saturday, the meetings, then Monday the hearing with the judge, he did not pick up on it.

"Barnes," DeLuna feigned a whisper, loud enough for the entire cell block to hear. "When we getting out."

"DeLuna, shut the fuck up," Barnes screamed in a low stifled rage. "Are you nuts? Be quiet. This has nothing to do with you."

"What, you got yourself arrested on something else?" DeLuna said, and then added. "God's punishing you. You were going to leave me in here, and He didn't think that was right. When your lawyer comes, we walk out together."

"Damn it, DeLuna, be quiet," Barnes said, knowing that the runt across the way was a caged animal. Barnes could sense his relentlessness.

"Barnes. What did they get you for? Is it something with us?

"I already told you, it has nothing to do with you."

"Then what. Tell me. I have to know," DeLuna persisted.

"Insider trading. Buying stocks with information only company people should have," he blurted out to shut him up.

"I know what that is. Did you do it?" DeLuna asked.

"No. Now be quiet," Barnes said

Turning to Curtis Strong on the bed, still facing the wall, DeLuna said, "This is my boy across the way. He's the one I've been telling you about. Big shot. He and his old man. It was his boat we used to bring the stuff in. That's why he's going to get me out of this," DeLuna concluded, having said this loud enough for Parker Barnes to hear.

Barnes was trembling. "Mother of God," he said to himself. "This imbecile is going to take me down with him." "DeLuna, be quiet. We'll never get out of this if you don't shut up."

"Then tell me how this is going to work. How do we get me out of here?"

"I've got calls in to my lawyer. He'll be here. He'll get me out. I'll get you out. Now stop."

DeLuna sat back down on his bed. He whispered across to Strong, who had not responded to anything DeLuna had said since he came in the cell, and now figured DeLuna was talking to him as you would to yourself, only Strong could hear everything. "This kid is gonna fuck me. I know it. He says he'll get me out of here. I don't think so. Well I've got a surprise for him," DeLuna continued in his monologue, loud enough for Strong to hear but muffled to Barnes in his cell. "The surprise he's gonna get is that I'm tougher than anyone alive. I can take anything. If I go to jail for this, he's coming with me. If they give me twenty-five years for bringing millions of dollars of drugs in, they're gonna give Parker Barnes twenty-five years for bringing millions of dollars of drugs in."

Around midnight DeLuna created a scene, screaming for the jailer. He made a case that his one call was to someone who couldn't help him. He needed to call his girlfriend and he would be quiet. The jailer had another officer come downstairs; they cuffed DeLuna from the front and took him to a small office by the front of the jail by the stairwell. The officer handed him his cell phone. "Make it quick and be quiet."

"Lupe, Estou na cadeia em Stamford Estação de Polícia," DeLuna said in Portuguese and continued, "you need to get Carlos. This has to be done quickly. Tell him it's the Olinda operation again. (Olinda had become the gang's code for putting an operation together to attack an enemy location.) He'll need all of the boys to get me out of here. He needs to do it before tomorrow morning."

The jailer returned, "OK, Poncho, time's up. Hand over the phone."

"I love you, Lupe. Help me, quickly or I'm done," and he closed the phone and handed it back to the officer.

In the meantime, while DeLuna was out of the cell, Curtis Strong called across the aisle to Parker Barnes, who was lying in a funk on his mattress.

"Parker, it's me, Curtis Strong."

Barnes thought he heard his name. He got up off the bed and moved to the bars where a black man in DeLuna's cell was looking at him, speaking to him.

"Parker, it's me, Curtis Strong," he repeated.

"Curtis," he stammered in disbelief, "how the hell," Barnes said, beginning to comprehend what Strong's mother said about him going to be freed. "Curtis, Hi."

"Parker, listen, this guy in here with me has been saying he's going to take you down with him."

"No way. Nothing to that." Barnes said. "He's a vendor of my father's, importing cement."

"Says he brought the drugs they caught him with in your boat. Says he left a bag behind, hidden, for proof, for his insurance."

"Shit," Barnes said.

"It's true?"

"He's a sly little bastard."

"Parker, is it true?" Strong said as they heard the jailer open a gate at the end of the block.

"Yes, but damn it, Curtis, please don't say anything," Barnes pleaded.

"I won't say anything," Strong replied as the jailer returned DeLuna to his cell.

DeLuna noticing both men at the cell bars, asked Strong, "Are you and my boy Barnes there becoming friends?"

Strong went back to his cot without answering.

DeLuna said to Barnes, "Bet you, I get out of here before you."

The jailer returned to DeLuna's cell. "It's getting late; you said you'd be quiet if I let you make the call. No more talking."

DeLuna nodded and laid back on his bed. Soon he was asleep, snoring loudly. "Finally," Strong said to himself.

Now it was Strong who was astir. But what of Barnes. How could Strong help him. He smiled to himself, "You are the one who's nuts. Why help him. You did ten years in prison for what the guy in the other cell did. And you want to help him? Yes, came his answer. It was the Barnes family who looked after Mrs. Strong. They even tried to help him, by hiring an attorney when he was charged. And then it hit him. Did old man Barnes know what Parker did? Is that why he hired the attorney? Is that why he took care of my mother? Is that why Parker got away with it? No, that can't be. Billy Stevens said it was just the two of them. They got away, no one else ever knew. As sleep started to take him, his last thought was, no, I must help.

At three in the morning, Officer Clark Watson came to Barnes' cell, opened the door and gently shook Barnes awake.

"Your attorney is here."

Barnes got up quickly and quietly, and followed the officer down the aisle, careful not to breathe for fear of waking DeLuna.

They went upstairs and to a glassed-in office. "In here, Mr. Barnes." Officer Watson said, and as he walked around the officer, there was Gideon Bridge.

"Got your message when I woke up to take a leak. What the hell's going on, Parker?" Bridge said.

Bridge shook his head as he listened to Barnes tale. He said he believed Barnes, that he did not buy any of the stock in Rocket Solar based on inside information. He said Barnes should just spend the night, and he would be back first thing in the morning when the NY police and the SEC were here. They would all meet, and he would get this straightened out.

At 3:30 a.m. Barnes went back to his cell and exhausted, quickly fell into a deep sleep.

74

After Lupe heard from Chunk, Lupe, from DeLuna's apartment on 28th St in Chelsea, called Carlos at his condo in Port Chester. There was no answer. She called him on his cell phone and got him. "Carlos, Chunk has been arrested. He's in jail in Stamford."

"That's what happened," he said.

"What do you mean?"

"After we got the shipment," then he paused. DeLuna was very strong on compartmentalizing gang knowledge. Carlos was not sure that Lupe was aware of what they were up to.

"They got him, and the shipment," Lupe said. So much for compartmentalizing. "He said you need to get him out or he's done for."

"I see," he said, his mind moving toward thought, rather than the girl he lay on top of. He rose up, "What else did he say?"

"Not much, it was short. He did say it's the Olinda operation."

"Shit, this is going to be hard. Where are you going to be, Lupe?"

"I'll come there if you want?" she asked.

"No, you stay there, in case we need you. I'll call that lawyer, the one Chunk set up. We'll use him."

"Carlos, are you stupid. Chunk said it's the Olinda operation. I know what happened in Olinda. You guys didn't use any lawyers," Lupe said. Chunk's gang had come to respect Lupe, and she could be as hard as Chunk to deal with. "Now listen to me Carlos. Chunk said you need to do this before tomorrow morning."

"That's impossible!" Carlos said loudly.

"Carlos, he needs you and the boys to get him out or it's all over for him and us."

"I'll get back to you," Carlos said and closed his cell phone. He unplugged himself from the girl, said something to her and she left the room. His head began to hurt—the pressure to act was enormous. He only had hours. He opened the cell phone again and began pushing buttons. His direction was the same to each of them: "Come to my place in one hour, ready for war and bring your vests."

His last call was to two brothers in Stamford. "I need you both at my place in one hour."

The two brothers Henri and Francois Piermont, Haitians who were part of his dealer network in Stamford, had been arrested recently and had been held in the same location as Chunk and would be valuable in locating Chunk quickly. These Haitians had been very helpful to Deluna in establishing the US drug operations in Stamford and New York City when Chunk and Carlos and their original gang members moved to the US as Chunk began securing cement contracts with Barnes Construction. Deluna's childhood friend, Angel Pagan, took over all operations for Chunk with his own crew in Brazil. The Haitians were loyal and dependable. They were also known for their ruthlessness and their imposing size would be an asset in what Carlos was planning.

At 5 a.m., two cars and six men, three in each car, pulled up to Stamford Police Headquarters. The June morning air was cool but comfortable. They parked the cars in the street and took two duffel bags from each car. It was just becoming light, the street was deserted and no one was stirring around the station.

When they got to the front of the building, the six men gathered round the four duffel bags. They were dressed in jeans and t-shirts and Kevlar bullet proof vests. They reached in, each taking Uzi sub-machine guns and extra clips, which they were jamming into their pockets.

448

Carlos reminded them, once more, "We follow the brothers. I do the talking. We only shoot when confronted."

Inside Police Headquarters there were five officers on duty. One at the front desk, a duty sergeant in back of him, two dispatchers, one officer downstairs in the jail. Also, a patrol officer, Rita Vercillo, arrived early to work out in the small gym at the rear of the building. It was her way of getting some privacy from the testosterone bunch that came in at 6 a.m.

As soon as they walked in the front door, the front desk officer instinctively punched the alarm button. He was alert, looking forward to the shift ending in two hours. He had been keeping himself busy with the crossword puzzle from the Stamford Advocate. At 5 a.m. six Latino guys walking in the front door of police headquarters gets your attention. It's not a big jump from that to the Kevlar vests and Uzis for you to realize you have fifteen seconds to live.

The alarm button rang, Klaxon like, loud and long. It stunned Carlos how fast they needed to spring into action. He opened fire on the front desk, the heavy glass shattered. The Piermont brothers blasted away at the metal door, shooting the lock away. They pulled the door open as the desk officer fell over dead. The duty officer in charge, Sergeant John Walsh, drew his service pistol but never got a shot off as he was hit by a hail of bullets from Pedro. Carlos positioned Pedro in the office area that gave a view to the front door, the office area and the stairwell leading down to the jail. The other three followed the two Piermont brothers downstairs quickly.

The alarm gave the officer in charge of the jail time to draw his weapon. He stood to the right of his desk, behind a wall that enables him to see anyone coming thru the staircase door.

Henri Piermont was the first through the door. The jailer saw the machine gun, saw Piermont raise it and shot the bigger of the two brothers dead.

Francois held the others up. "Damn, he shot Henri."

Carlos pulled Francois aside, "We have to go in there. Now."

"There's another way. A back door that comes in through the jail."

"Isn't it locked?"

"I never heard them unlock it. But I don't know how to get in there."

"OK, you stay here. Come on boys, we need to hurry."

The three ran back up the stairs, across the office area toward a back door in the rear.

Rita Vercillo, the officer who arrived early came up out of the gym with her gun drawn. She was pulled aside by the two officers in dispatch.

"There's shooting out front, and it sounds like downstairs," the older of the two dispatchers said, "Go out the back door, and come around the side of the building, flat up against the front door. Stop them there if they are coming out."

"Got it," and Vercillo was off and out the back door.

Three seconds later Carlos along with two other gang members burst through the door at the rear of the office area. Five guns fired in the next second. Two officers and one gang member fell dead. Carlos had a bullet pass through his right leg, along the surface.

Carlos saw the rear staircase door. It was ajar; left open by the officer coming up from the gym.

Francois meanwhile attempted to enter the jail area and was met by a volley of shots from the jailer's service pistol.

Carlos and Paco, Pedro's brother, descended the stairs. It brought them past the gym, a kitchen area and to the cell block entrance. There was no door. They looked in and saw all of the prisoners at their locked cell gates yelling. They saw the jailer at the other end of the cell block, hiding behind a wall and saw an exchange of gunfire with Francois.

The jailer began reloading his weapon when Carlos charged down the aisle.

"Francois, now," Carlos yelled.

The officer froze; he saw a figure running at him from inside the cell block. He fumbled with his gun as Carlos approached the bars and fired at him, killing him.

"Francois," Carlos called out. "Come in, we got him."

450

The large black head poked through and saw Carlos. He opened the door fully and bent down to his brother.

"Francois, get the keys."

Francois made the sign of the cross on Henri's forehead, rose and took the keys from the dead officer's belt. After a couple of tries with keys, he found the one that opened the main gate.

Chunk DeLuna was screaming with joy from his cell. Carlos rushed over with the keys. In a moment he had the gate opened.

"Blackie, come on," DeLuna said to Curtis Strong.

Strong said nothing and remained standing by his bed.

"Suit yourself." Deluna said, then turning to Parker Barnes, "Hey Barnes, want out?

He didn't wait for an answer but instructed Carlos to open Barnes cell. Carlos handed DeLuna a pistol that was tucked in his belt.

Once Barnes cell was ajar, DeLuna walked in, "Come on. You're coming with us."

"DeLuna, no. Leave me here," Barnes said pulling back.

"Bullshit, I'm safer with you with me," and DeLuna grabbed the much taller Barnes by the arm, and looking at the gun Carlos had pointed at him, Barnes went with DeLuna.

Paco, Francois, and Carlos proceeded to the front staircase with Barnes and DeLuna behind them.

Curtis Strong reacted to DeLuna pulling Barnes with him. He saw the downed officer's gun, the officer whose last action in life had been to reload a clip in his gun without firing a shot. Strong followed behind the men who had now entered the stairwell. He picked up the dead officer's gun. He saw Henri Piermont's Uzi and picked it up as well. There was not time to wonder why he would now risk his life for the man who had caused him to be imprisoned for almost seven years. It was not a thoughtful reaction but an instinctive one, one borne of loyalty. It was a misplaced loyalty to a family that he believed protected his mother and had tried to protect him. It was a misplaced loyalty he had only recently come to realize—that in providing the lawyer to defend him, it kept all of the Barnes family's options open to protect Parker. If the evidence seized was weak in the prosecution of Strong, the defense could be made weaker. It was a loyalty infused in him to protect what he cared about. It was why he would not give up Billy Stevens, who for all those long years he believed had killed Augusto Santos by himself. It was the way he was programmed, the way his mother and father raised him. It was why in this split second he was moving to protect Parker Barnes.

Officer Vercillo, now positioned in front of the building, peeked in the front door and saw the shattered glass, saw the broken door, and saw Pedro facing the rear of the office area. As she came around the building, she heard a furious amount of shooting that ended quickly. She reasoned the officers in dispatch had shot some of the intruders. She felt she could take out this one before her. She reached the front door, pulled it quietly open and slipped in. Pedro thought he heard something behind him. Before he could turn he took three shots to the body and fell dead.

Officer Vercillo now saw the desk officer and the duty sergeant, John Walsh, who she had spoken to not thirty minutes before. She went to each, felt for a pulse. They were both dead.

Just then, shots rang out from the jail downstairs. Vercillo ran back to the dispatch area. Both officers were dead, with one of the intruders dead beside them.

She heard yelling from the jail downstairs. She knew whatever was happening was going to come up through front stairwell from the jail in less than a minute. She picked up one of the dead officers pistols, the same issue as hers.

Officer Vercillo then positioned herself strategically between the front door and the stairwell, behind the duty officer's desk. The sound of the alarm was now audible—it hadn't stopped but Vercillo only heard it in the first minute of confusion and now from where she watched, and waited.

Carlos and Paco burst forth into the station's open area from the stairwell. Vercillo killed Paco first, then hit Carlos in the arm. He pulled backward into the stairwell.

Entering the bottom of the stairwell Curtis Strong called to Parker, "Barnes, look out," and he raised the jailer's pistol and shot

Chunk DeLuna in the back. As Francois Piermont turn and fired on him, Strong shot him twice in the stomach. He fell forward and then tumbled down the stairs. Strong pulled himself to the wall as Francois passed by, and then he raced up the stairs just as Carlos retreated back. Barnes picked up the other Piermont's Uzi, spun and fired into Carlos. The blast into Carlos' chest sent him reeling back into the squad room where he fell dead.

"You got him," yelled Vercillo, who in the moment before had begun fearing for her life.

Barnes and Strong came through the stairwell door cautiously.

"Freeze," the on-edge Vercillo screamed at the two men who emerged in the orange jump suits of jailed prisoners. "Drop those guns or I'll blow your head off."

Strong dropped both guns. Barnes dropped his and said, "Don't shoot."

"On the floor both of you with your hands above your head," and as they dropped down, Vercillo moved in and kicked the guns away from their reach.

Vito Boriello's alarm sounded at five past five. It wasn't his alarm clock; it was the alarm that was put in his house ten years before.

Rose Boriello woke up beside him, "Vito, what is that noise?"

"It's the alarm from the station, trouble," Boriello said, bounding his round body out of bed and heading to his closet. "Someone's in trouble at the station."

"Be careful," his wife said as he left the room.

He was dressed and out in ninety seconds. He pulled his car right to Police HQ's front door two minutes later. At that same moment, Sergeant Chris Redwine pulled up next to him. It was 5:12 a.m. They both broke from their cars on the run.

"What the hell is it, Vito," Redwine asked with pistol drawn.

"I don't know, Chris, but it's not good," the fat lieutenant said as they reached the front door.

They entered, each from a side and quickly saw the bodies of two fellow officers. Then Officer Vercillo standing over Barnes and Strong swung toward them as they entered with her pistol aimed at them.

"Hold up, Rita," Redwine said.

A broad relief came over Vercillo as she saw other living officers, "Thank God."

Boriello said to Redwine, "You cuff those two." And as Redwine bent to his duty, Boriello asked Vercillo, "What went on here?"

"I'm not really sure, Lieutenant. I was in early, working out. I think we had an attempted jail break with lots of help from the outside. Two dispatchers are dead, also the desk officer and Sergeant Walsh. I don't know about downstairs."

"Come with me, cover me," Boriello said as he stepped into the stairwell. They found DeLuna dead at the top of the stairs and Francois Piermont dead at the bottom of the stairs. Through the door to the jail, they found Henri Piermont and partially, out of sight behind a wall, the officer on jail duty.

The nine prisoners still behind bars were agitated and yelling. Boriello walked to the aisle in the middle of the cells and said, "You boys alright?"

"You fat fuck, those assholes could have killed us all," yelled a tall thin man, drug abused, whose better days were behind him.

"Calm down, there's a lady present," Boriello shouted. "We'll be getting some help in here soon."

Boriello shook his head, and he and Vercillo went back up to the main squad room. More officers were arriving, some from patrol as the alarm also went into their cars. Boriello took charge, gave orders to get ambulances in; he called the Chief, whose wife said he was on the way in. Captain Paiva arrived.

By 5:34 a.m. ambulances had arrived; officers were treating the whole station house as a crime scene. At 6 a.m. interviews were begun with Vercillo, the only surviving officer in the station at the time, and Barnes and Strong who had witnessed the mayhem and took down three of the killers.

By 7 a.m. the first reporters were at the scene, now cordoned off by more than one hundred feet. Detectives were pouring over the two cars used by the assailants. The four duffel bags, some still holding Uzi clips, were taken inside the station as more evidence. The first bodies began being removed by 8 a.m.

At 9 a.m. the chief of police, John Brennan, Captain Paiva, and Lieutenant Boriello were meeting to piece the siege together. It appeared that six gunmen tried to break the prisoner DeLuna out of jail; in the process they killed five Stamford officers, including duty officer Sergeant John Walsh. It also became clear to the three police leaders that Officer Vercillo killed two of the intruders, the officer on jail duty killed one, and a dispatch officer killed one. And the two prisoners, Barnes and Strong, killed two others and the prisoner DeLuna.

"Not only do we have as a prisoner Curtis Strong, who we know is innocent of that murder seven years ago," Boriello was fuming, "now we have Parker Barnes, who we just got a call from Manhattan that his arrest warrant that we executed for them is in error. He should not have been arrested. They were preparing to interview him."

"What are you telling me," the chief said, "I've got five dead cops and two heroes as prisoners who are both innocent?"

Captain Pavia piped in, "Well, we do have seven dead bad guys," and he said it with a smirk.

"What in the fuck do you find funny in this whole goddamn thing," Chief Brennan said, slamming his fist on his desk.

""Nothing, sir," Paiva snapped. He hadn't called the chief sir in the five years he'd been chief, but now seemed an appropriate time.

"Paiva, who's your friend at the *Advocate*?"

"Mike Slade, the editor?"

"Get him in here; we've got to control this story or we all look like horses' asses. Give him the exclusive and have him feed every detail to the NY Times. I don't want to win the local battle and lose the war with the city."

"Yes, sir. In fact he's in the building. We've given the press a temporary office on the second floor."

"Good and I want a very good write-up on how fortunate we are to have had NYPD screwup and have us bring Parker Barnes in and what a hero he is in killing one of these vermin dealers. And what's the black kids name again."

"Curtis Strong," Boriello said.

"Well make sure they say something nice about him too."

"Sir, if I may," Boriello interrupted, "even Barnes acknowledges that Strong is the hero."

"Strong gets us nothing. Barnes is the key. It's him the media will focus on. They'll try to paint it as our screwup."

"Chief," Boriello began, "think about this. We're the ones who have gotten Strong sprung. We're the ones who found out he was innocent. We paint the picture of the dual heroes; the community could use a black hero."

"Fuck black heroes," the chief said. "Vito, are you forgetting who put him away in the first place? Us, the Stamford Police department. And are you not aware that the diligent officer sitting beside you is the one who made sure that young Mr. Barnes was never charged in that murder?"

"Chief," Captain Paiva protested.

"Shut up, Paiva," the chief intoned.

"You mean it is true?" Boriello asked.

"Yes, sadly it is true. Paiva here was always the one to handle the dirty work for the big boys. We've kept it as our dirty little secret all these years. And now, here it is out in the open."

"But you knew I was working with Jim Ford on this."

"That's why I gave you to him when he called me. I knew you'd get to the bottom of it. I knew you'd get the kid out finally. Damn, that's the one thing that bothered me in my whole career. After a day like today, it doesn't seem to matter as much," and the chief paused, a long tired sign came out. He looked at his two officers. "Most everything we do is good, very good. And every once and awhile we screwup, not intending to cause harm, but when we do what we did to Curtis Strong we cause harm, irreparable harm."

"Here's our chance to fix it then," Boriello said, and to himself he thought, "I have been on this planet too long."

"Well then fix it, but do no harm, Vito. I don't want this department looking like fools over this."

"I'll fix it," Boriello said.

"I'll help," chimed in Paiva.

"You stay the fuck out of the way," the chief said. Then he summoned the guts he had lacked for years in competing with Al Paiva. "Al, I want your resignation on my desk by tonight."

"What," Paiva seemed to scream, but it was a silent scream, more a squeak.

"You heard me; now both of you, get out."

75

I t was the wedding day of Winston Trout. The bride to be and the groom to be were separately busy with their individual preparations although Winston was somewhat worried about his brothers. He was surprised about how very quiet his cell phone had been from the prior evening. It was 7 a.m. on Saturday morning.

And he would have been surprised if he knew that Tray Johnson was in San Juan at this hour. And he would have been surprised to learn that contrary to his plans, Sebastian Ball did not return on a flight on Friday after his meeting with Jane Lane's husband and an overnight tryst with Mrs. Lane. What would also have surprised him was that the cell phone of Parker Barnes sat in the property room of a partly destroyed Stamford police station.

But he would really be shocked if he knew that the two-year-old ring bearer stayed at home with his grandfather as Edward Wheelwright Jr. accompanied Valerie Samson to interviews with the SEC and NYPD in the Greenwich Police station, and that while they were being questioned in separate rooms, Kish Moria was being questioned at the NY Office of the insider trading task force.

His final surprise would have been that Gideon Bridge, was bringing a female date to the wedding.

This morning what had Jim Conroy upset was the screwup by his team that turned a request for an interview into an arrest warrant for Parker Barnes. And it didn't happen that Mr. Barnes was any inside trader, having purchased not Rocket Solar but Trout Solar. He happened to be the son of one of the wealthiest contractors in the northeast and a candidate for the US Senate from Connecticut. Compounding it all was the fact that somehow Barnes is now a hero in a crazy jail break attempt where he was being held. Seems that Barnes shot and killed at least one of a gang of drug dealers who were trying to break one of their own out of the Stamford Police station. "So much for coordination," Conroy said to himself.

****

At the altar of St. Mary's Church, an old gothic reminder of the strength of Catholicism in the late nineteenth century, his second best man appeared. The wedding neared.

It was 4:45 p.m. as Kish came in a limo. As he walked in from the side altar, he stood beside Winston and Gideon, another of Winston's best men who had arrived earlier. Winston asked, "Where are the rest of our brothers?"

"Don't worry, they'll be here. It's early yet," Kish said.

"In fifteen minutes the ceremony starts. Kish, do I smell curry?" Winston asked.

"It's a long story, I'll tell you later."

"Good luck getting anyone to dance with you," Winston said.

Other friends of the brothers were ushers, accompanying guests into the cavernous church. Tom Brandon, IT director of Brunswick Fund and former classmate of Wheelwright at Harvard, ushered in Santa Alba, who wore a rose dress she designed herself, with matching wide brim hat. With her olive skin as a perfect complement, she was radiant. She smiled warmly at the men on the altar in their tuxedos. Before being seated, she walked to the altar, put her hand on the arm of Gideon Bridge and kissed him.

Winston and Kish looked at Gideon; all three smiled broadly before Winston asked. "Want to talk about it, Gideon."

"Actions speak louder than words," was his reply.

The Saturday *New York Times* had the following story on the front page:

460

"Six arrested in insider trading scheme in Rocket Solar stock," read the headline.

"In a joint investigation coordinated by the NYPD Cyber Crimes Unit and the SEC, police arrested six individuals on insider trading charges in the company, Rocket Solar. Arrested were the two founding brothers in the solar equipment manufacturing company, Thomas Barrett, the CEO, and Robert Barrett, the VP of Sales. Also arrested was a financial executive at Blackthorn Investments, Sidney Rogers, Managing Director of Equities Trading and a former Blackthorn Investments trader, Leonard Crane. Additionally, two associates of Mr. Crane, brothers Joshua and Saul Kaplan were being held on warrants for insider trading and wire fraud.

"NYPD Detective James Conroy, speaking for the task force assembled to curb insider trading, stated, 'Today we have broken an insidious insider trading scheme conducted by the two brothers who started Rocket Solar. They sought to drive the price of Rocket Solar stock up with false orders from three Chinese companies that they knew would eventually be cancelled and cause the stock of the company to plunge. Sidney Rogers manipulated Blackthorn research reports to put out an incorrect "Buy" rating on the stock, which was rated a "Sell", by Blackthorn analysts. He did this after having purchased several hundred thousand shares in his own account. Additional work is being done to identify other individuals inside Blackthorn who are suspected of insider trading. These arrests and this scheme are being announced at this time to prevent further losses for investors in Rocket Solar. The two associates of Mr. Crane profited by buying shares of the stock with insider information from Mr. Crane, which he and they used for personal gain.'"

At four fifty, in his full Naval dress uniform, into the church walked a ramrod straight Traynor Johnson. Taking his right arm was Silvana DeLuna and holding Silvana's right hand was her daughter, Mare. Silvana spotted Santa Alba in the second row, on the left hand side of the aisle, and she nudged Tray. He got the hint and ushered Slivana and Mare in beside her friend. Santa picked up the child and kissed her and hugged Silvana. Tray proceeded to the altar where he was greeted by the groom and his fellow best men.

"Three down, three to go," remarked Gideon.

Admiral Johnson, after getting the call from Tray while he was in the air in Sebastian's plane, laid out dress uniforms for both of them. He proceeded to Westchester Airport and the Executive Jet's hangar and picked up his son, Silvana and Mare. They returned to the Johnson house, changed, and now exactly one hour and ten minutes after the pickup, Admiral Johnson in his full dress uniform walked up the aisle after parking his car. He went into the second row with Silvana and Mare. Silvana introduced Admiral Johnson to Santa Alba who hugged the admiral.

"I love a man in uniform," she said. The Admiral laughed; Tray had told him of her ability to express her warmth.

Sebastian Ball arrived, and one of the ushers pointed him to where Santa Alba was. He smiled his big smile and strode down the aisle. At the pew where she was seated, he greeted the Admiral, warmly welcomed Silvana who thanked him for providing his plane. He stepped over to Santa and was about to hug her when she pulled back.

"Keep going. I'm with Gideon," she said icily.

"What," he whispered, though loudly enough to turn heads. He was stung.

"You heard me."

"What's wrong, Santa?"

"What's wrong? Try Mrs. Jane Lane."

"What are you talking about?"

Santa stepped out of the pew to the far side of the church in an apse, and Sebastian followed. "I tried to reach you. You were coming home yesterday."

"Yes, but I got detained."

"With Mrs. Lane."

"No. On business."

"She was your business."

"I had other business on the trip."

"She called this morning."

"Huh," he said. The audible whispers and body language of the two were attracting attention.

"What do you mean she called?"

"As in, on the phone."

"And?"

"And she left a message. A quite loving message."

Ball looked at Santa said nothing further. She walked back to her seat. He proceeded to the altar with his brothers.

"Four down, two to go," Gideon said.

When Santa called Gideon at 4:45 a.m., she was in tears. He was getting no sleep at all after his earlier visit to the jail to see Parker. Santa told Gideon about the phone call from Jane Lane and asked if he could come over.

Gideon kept a small mansion on the water by the Riverside Yacht club in Greenwich. It was a five-minute drive from his home to Ball Hall. Since Santa intended to take as much of her clothing and personal affects as possible, in this her second move in two weeks, Gideon drove the Escalade. When he was let through the main gates at Ball Hall, he proceeded to Sebastian's living quarters, which were in a separate Mediterranean style villa on the property.

Santa was waiting and together by 6:30 a.m. they had the SUV packed with her things. She hugged him and thanked him. When they finished moving everything into one of his guest bedrooms, she took Gideon's hand.

"But this is not where I intend to sleep. Show me your bedroom."

"Santa, while that would be quite lovely for almost any man on the planet, you do know I'm gay?" he asked with a half-smile.

"So what. You're wonderful."

"Now that we both are aware of that, let me introduce you to Adam," who emerged as if on cue from Gideon's bedroom in light blue silk pajamas.

Santa paused, smiled broadly, and said, "Will you at least take me to Winston's wedding?"

"Adam?" Gideon asked.

"Sure, I didn't know any of them anyway," and Adam said to Gideon, "but you owe me."

Gideon put his hand around the back of Adam's neck and pulled him to him, kissing him on the lips.

Santa cringed.

At four fifty-five the limo with Winston Trout's bride-to-be pulled up. Emily Albright sat in the limo with her father for a moment. Just then Valerie McGuire Samson arrived with Edward Wheelwright, who was trailed by Mark Wheelwright carrying his grandson.

Valerie went to the darkened limo windows and knocked. She waited as one of the rear tinted window was lowered.

"Am I allowed to peek in?" Valerie said peering in, and there in the rear seat was a most gorgeous Miss Emily Albright.

"You are, but he isn't," Emily laughed.

"Turn away, you beast," Valerie said laughing and gave Eddie a gentle shove. Turning back to Emily she said, "You are going to take his breath away; you are so beautiful." She reached in and touched the side of Emily's cheek. "See you inside."

As they entered, the Wheelwrights were ushered to the front, to the third row, just behind Santa and Silvana. The ladies all smooched, and Edward walked to the altar. All of the best men were dressed identically but for Tray and except Parker Barnes, who hadn't arrived yet and it was four fifty-nine.

"Five down and one to go," Gideon said.

After Gideon had seen Parker at 3 a.m., he made several calls and was assured he would be able to get Parker out by 9 a.m. no matter what. At eight forty-five as he prepared to go back to Stamford Police, he got a call from Lieutenant Vito Boriello stating that Mr. Barnes was being released. He was arrested in error and that Stamford Police Chief John Brennan would like to speak with him. They set a time of 10:30 a.m. for Chief Brennan to call. And at 10:30 a.m. Chief Brennan proceeded to tell Gideon it was all a terrible mistake by the NYPD. Parker was to have been merely interviewed. "However," the chief said, "thank God Parker was here.

He saved lives by helping take down the criminals who murdered innocent Stamford police officers."

That statement would appear in a special afternoon addition of the *Stamford Advocate*, under the byline of Mike Slade. It was the lead story on all Connecticut and New York radio and TV stations throughout the day Saturday.

The News at Noon segment of one of the New York stations had in full color, now in civilian clothes, Parker Barnes and CJ Strong at a Stamford Police Headquarters news conference, with captions beneath them that read, "Local heroes save police lives, stop murderous criminals." The story later spread to multiple channels throughout the day, on all the major networks as well as local cable stations. Pictures of DeLuna and scenes of carnage kept playing as the two heroes talked.

At 5 p.m. Parker Barnes arrived at the church in a long stretch limo accompanied by the same attractive Oriental woman who had been at Tray's going away party. Exiting the limo after Parker was a beaming Jonathan and Mrs. Barnes. Following the Barnes out of the limo were Curtis Strong and his mother, Louise. Strong had quickly been released under his mother's supervision until the following Monday when he would be exonerated.

At that same moment, Emily Albright was exiting her limo on her father's arm.

Parker held up going into the church until Mr. Albright gave him an indication that he should go first.

As the six members of the Barnes and Strong families started down the aisle, a clamor began. The six were smiling broadly, looking at each other. Slowly, from the back of the church people began standing and clapping. The bride was not yet in the church.

As the party of six reached the middle pews, more people rose joining those in the rear, clapping; even some cheering accompanied the clamor. News had spread fast. By midday, the whole city of Stamford, surrounding Greenwich, Fairfield county and all of the metropolitan New York area had been made aware of the daring attempt at a jail break in Stamford, of the heavy loss of life of the officers and the two men who were now in their midst. Parker Barnes and Curtis Strong Jr., who between them killed three of the seven murderous drug dealers and most likely saved countless other officers lives, were heroes.

The Barnes and Strongs entered the pew with Val Samson's family. Mark Wheelwright and Jonathan Barnes shook hands.

"Congratulations," Wheelwright offered.

"Congratulations, yourself, Grandpa," Jonathan Barnes said with a broad smile.

Parker started his walk to the altar, turned and went back to the pew. He had lent Curtis a suit, since they were similar in size, although Curtis' muscles were straining the seams of the suit coat.

"I want you to come up on the altar with us," Parker said to Curtis.

Strong pulled back. "No, you go ahead with your friends."

"I'm not going up there with my brothers if you don't come," Parker said while standing in the aisle. "Curtis, in my life no one has been more of a brother to me than you. I just never knew it until today." Then Parker leaned forward, hugged CJ, and gave him a tug out into the aisle.

As the two brothers walked to greet their other siblings, the congregation stayed on their feet.

The six brothers at the altar stepped forward to greet Parker. And by bringing Curtis forward, they understood they had been joined by a new brother, whom they also greeted warmly. They knew a partial reason for his inclusion in their family, but they would never understand fully what Curtis Strong had done for Parker Barnes.

At one minute past five, Emily Albright entered the rear of St. Mary's church with every pew full and every person standing and clapping.

Emily was quite delighted with this reception and glowed as she arrived at the altar to meet her groom, Winston. With Winston's now seven brothers for best men and Emily's four maids of honor, her sisters, her real sisters, they were married.

Postscript:

O nce the wedding was over, Stamford Police were waiting with a warrant for Parker Barnes arrest since police got a tip from a woman with a Latin accent that he had smuggled drugs into the US on his yacht. Police checked and found a package of cocaine exactly where the woman said it was. They also found traces of cocaine under other panels on the boat. The one package matched the packaging and quality of that previously seized from Chunk DeLuna.

The following Monday, Jonathan Barnes dropped out of the race for the Democratic nomination for US Senate.

Kish Moira is engaged to Binky Patel, the tall Indian girl in the white dress seen at Tray Johnson's going away party and accompanying him to Winston's wedding. She is Kish's cousin. Gideon Bridge calls her the Kishing cousin.

Five months later Edward Wheelwright and Valerie McGuire Samson were married, which followed by one month Valerie's divorce from David Samson.

Seven months later Gideon Bridge was elected as President of the Knights of Columbus, a Roman Catholic order of lay people engaged in doing good works. Three months after that, Gideon was married to Adam Llyenthal. Santa Alba was the bride's maid. Five of Gideon's six brothers were his best men.

Sadly, Tray Johnson did not return from Afghanistan. Admiral Johnson mounted several search and rescue attempts both through the Navy and privately with men in his former command. Captain Tray Johnson's unit's attempt to extract a friendly Afghan tribal leader being held by Taliban led to the unit's destruction. Several bodies from the unit were recovered. Captain Johnson is listed as missing in action. Admiral Johnson travelled to Coamo one month after Tray went missing to tell Silvana DeLuna. The night the Admiral left, Silvana wept quietly on the stoop of her home, holding her daughter Mare between her legs. Silvana held a piece of paper and reread the last letter she had received from Tray.

Ten months later Trout Solar was on its way to becoming a world leader in producing solar panels from their large complex that was being built in the Arizona. The state of Arizona and its Public Service Commission approved all plans presented by Winston Trout and Sebastian Ball to build their plants and solar farms in the Sonoran dessert. The solar farm they are to build next to the manufacturing facility will produce 20 percent of Arizona's electric energy within five years. Two additional large scale solar farms are planned for Nevada and California. Based on the scale of the Trout's solar farm and planned farms, the US Government has committed that if Trout is successful in generating large scale energy it will begin looking at dismantling three dams upstream on the Colorado River.

Five months into the Arizona dessert venture, faced with insurrection at the hands of Arthur and Winston Trout, Sebastian Ball Jr. spun Trout Solar off from Ball Enterprises in an IPO that netted him close to four hundred million dollars. The Trout's wealth grew by eight hundred million dollars from the transaction.

Leonard Crane was sentenced to three years in prison for his part in the insider trading scheme in Rocket Solar. It was the lightest sentence of the six originally arrested. Rocket Solar now trades on the Pink Sheets at twenty-seven cents.

Mark Wheelwright is clean and sober and providing child care for his grandson Edward since Valerie and Eddie work together at the Brunswick Fund.

Epilogue:
The Warrior

———————————

The two judges split, therefore in the case of a tie, the referee became the third and deciding judge. He said "red" and Tray had lost. It was his first match in his first tournament. He didn't know what to think, but he was only eight, so what should he think. He had been sparring in Kempo Karate for seven months and made his way up through several belts. But he did have an expectation of winning. It had been bred into him for some time, not by anyone, rather, by competition. Four years of soccer, two years of flag football, playing both ways as linebacker and running back, two years of basketball as a point guard, and beginning his second year of baseball as a second baseman had conditioned the boy for competition. And he was eight years old.

The tournament with four participating towns was double elimination so there would be a second chance. Tray won his second match quickly on three straight points. First to three wins. His third and fourth matches got tougher and so did Tray. Kempo Karate being a mixture of Japanese and Chinese karate, boxing and kicking, in the third match Tray scored a decisive kick to the mid-section of the larger opponent. The fourth match was a nail biter; tied two to two Tray scored his third point with a punch to the head of his opponent.

With the equipment the boys wore—helmet, gloves, shin guards, cups, and mouth pieces—the Kempo Karate students are pretty well protected. In Tray's fifth and sixth matches, all that equipment still did not provide enough protection.

In the fifth after both boys bowed to each other and their teachers, they clashed with no points awarded. This happened two more times, and Tray was being tested. Both boys earned two points each. Tray's opponent then poked a thumb in his eye. The referee stepped in—Tray was alright, no points. Tray launched a quick kick once action resumed and scored the winning point. In the sixth match, Tray was down a point, and his opponent caught him in the face with a punch so hard it knocked his mouthpiece out. The mouthpiece was reinserted and action began again. His opponent attacked; Tray spun away then quickly attacked leaping into the air like a Ninja. A quick punch to the opponent's head made it two to one, Tray still trailing. Tray attacked with a kick next. Two to two. Tied and confident Tray again took to the air, leaping over his opponents kick and knocking him in the head for a victory.

Tray now had five wins and one loss. He was in the semifinals. With only two opponents left, Tray was facing his third straight match without a break. He was literally taking on all the surviving combatants.

Battle toughened from the five straight wins, a growing black eye, a cut lip, and tactical strategies forming, Tray got his sixth win in relatively easy fashion with three quick scoring jabs to the head.

Now, as the judge explained to the other eighteen competitors and their parents, third and fourth place trophies had been decided. What outcomes remained were for first and second place. Tray's opponent, who beat him in his first match, only needed to beat Tray and he would be champion. Tray, however, to win first place would need to beat his opponent, who was undefeated at seven and zero, twice since it was double elimination.

Tray after his first loss, sat on the sidelines watching the other boys spar, particularly the style of the combatants. Who favored thrusts with kicks; who preferred punches. Tray's parents were happy for him, but this was Tray's sixth straight match without a break.

Tray came out cautiously, and when his opponent attacked kicking, Tray leaped over his leg and landed a hard blow to the head. Point Tray. They battled to a draw on two more charges, then the opponent landed a kick. One to one. After several clashes it was tied two to two. On the fifth point as they clashed, Tray was knocked down—no point awarded. As Tray got up, his opponent charged him. Tray spun away, and as they faced each other, Tray looked fresh, fresher than his opponent, fresher than an eight-year-old had a right to be after eight matches in less than two hours.

Tray struck, leaping to right of his surprised opponent and hit a glancing blow to the front of the head. Third point and win for Tray. The other boy had reeled backward from the blow and fell to the mat. Tray advanced and helped him back to his feet.

Championship match. Both combatants now seven and one. Winner gets a large three-foot-tall trophy proclaiming them Kempo Karate champion of the Fairfield County.

The picture of Tray holding that large trophy attested to the quick finish to his ninth match, which Tray won, three points to one. The pictures show the fifty-three inch, fifty-five pound warrior with a cut lip, swelling and bruised eye holding the thirty-six inch, twenty-pound trophy with his black gloves and black head gear still on. He is a barefoot Ninja in black pants and shirt. He doesn't smile, not yet, as opponents and other members of his dojo congratulate him. He is in a battle state. Those six straight matches without a break keep him at a heightened state of readiness. Slowly though, the boy lets go, the gear comes off, the warrior smiles.

****

The Blackhawk went down. The warrior was down. The mission was to extricate a local tribal leader from a Taliban camp he was being held in along the Pakistan border. Tray Johnson was leading a team of four Navy Seals, six Marines, and four Afghan Army non-coms. The mission came together quickly after the local leader, who had been a friend to US Forces, was taken prisoner by Taliban insurgents. Mohammed Monsour had aided a downed

American flier in the past, hiding him from Taliban searching his village.

As the chopper approached the coordinates of the location Monsour was said to be held, the Blackhawk was hit by a rocket-propelled grenade. The grenade didn't do much damage as it exploded after bouncing off the reinforced under carriage. What happened next though proved fatal to the mission. The copter pilot, a Navy Chief Warrant Officer, pulled the chopper up, like he had the reins of a horse. That maneuver, meant to begin a sharp left turn away from the source of ground fire, pulled it directly into the path of a shoulder fired missile.

The missile exploded to the rear of the side door killing half the soldiers on contact. The chopper began a dizzying death spiral and crashed nose first about four miles away from the enemy.

Tray Johnson was wounded in his left forearm, a gaping gash that let blood flow freely. Johnson quickly applied a tourniquet with his belt while trying to find his way out of the black smoke of the coffin that held his men. The chopper lay at a forty-five-degree angle with the nose buried in the gravel of the flat plain just beneath a six-thousand-foot mountain. The tail of the craft stuck up at that sick angle with its vertical rotor still spinning wildly. As Tray moved toward where he believed there was an exit, he groped from soldier to soldier in the dark, searching for a sign of life in his men who were still strapped in, in death. There were no pulses, no noises. As the black hawk burned he yelled, "Guys, can you hear me. Anyone." The only noise was from the inferno that was engulfing the helicopter. With his right shoulder Johnson slid the right side door open. Flames were moving quickly up the length of the whirlybird.

Johnson jumped down the eight feet and rolled on the ground, got to his feet and ran to the front of the helicopter. There he found the body of the pilot, somehow blown out of the middle of the chopper. The black hawk apparently hit at an angle as it crashed and blew out the left front side of the aircraft, splitting it in the front, ejecting the Warrant officer pilot through the window.

Johnson checked for a pulse and did not get one. Alone, he could hear the roar of the fire. Off in the distance he heard another roar. It was the sound of gunfire from Taliban combatants in Toyota pickups racing to see what they had plucked from the night sky.

The flames lit the area up, and Johnson moved to put the fire between the Taliban and him. He could move toward the small hills, off a quarter mile away, as long as the fire would keep the approaching trucks from seeing him.

"Lieutenant, help me," a voice hollered from the Blackhawk. The fire burned so bright Johnson could not see who it was. He moved back beside the chopper and looked for a way in.

"Here, down here, LT," the voice came from underneath the copter.

It was one of the Marine sergeants who was somehow outside the helicopter, wedged beneath the mangled left side.

Johnson needed to work quickly; there was no time. The fire inside and to the front of the chopper raged. He could hear the Toyotas as the men fired their weapons into the air.

"Damn," Johnson said trying to budge the chopper, back pressed against it, feet, legs pushing downward; a man weighing less than two hundred pounds trying to move a machine weighing seven tons off a fallen comrade.

"Don't leave me, Sir," the Marine pleaded.

"I'm with you," Johnson said, "But you better start praying for us. We're in deep shit."

Don Reynolds, the Marine, could feel himself losing consciousness and after watching Johnson trying several positions, looking for leverage, he asked Johnson, "It's not working, is it?"

"Not so far."

"Sir, you better save your own ass."

"Yeah, you're right. I should." And as he said the word "Should" an explosion rocked the chopper, lifting it up from the diagonal and it rolled to its right and off of Sergeant Reynolds.

Johnson was knocked to the ground. Shocked but aware. And there in front of him Don Reynolds lay. Uncovered, freed from beneath the dead black bird.

With two broken legs and in agony he pulled himself along the ground away from the inferno and toward Johnson.

"You must pray pretty freaking hard," Johnson said bringing a momentary smile to each of their burnt and blackened faces. Johnson noticed the condition of Reynolds mangled legs.

Above the roar of the flames both soldiers heard the trucks coming near, more shots fired into the night sky celebrating their kill.

"Lieutenant, go, you can't help me," Reynolds pleaded.

As Johnson hoisted Reynolds over his right shoulder he said, "I might need a bargaining chip with those assholes. You're coming with me." Reynolds laughed through the pain as Johnson wrapped an arm around his broken bones.

Through the pain, with strength, training, mission focus, and fear, Johnson stepped off into the Afghan night. In the dark, two hundred yards away, Johnson injected Reynolds with morphine as the two soldiers watched the Taliban, by the light of the burning Blackhawk, desecrate the body of the pilot who had been ejected.

****

Epilogue II:

Two years had passed since Tray Johnson went missing in action in the Afghan night. Silvana DeLuna kept her laundry business. Mare had started school. It still rained slowly in the mountains of San Blas de Cuomo.

And when the rain stopped, the sun came back out. Silvana heard footsteps coming up the short flagstone walk. A customer. But which one. She played a game with herself, trying to identify the walk, the shuffle of a shoe, the spike of a woman's heel. This was a new sound. A shuffle, shuffle, click. The third sound did not make sense.

Silvana looked up into the late day sun shining through the door. She remembered another time when the shadow of Tray blocked that door.

"Yes, can I help you," Silvana said looking into that same sun, blocked by that same outline she had seen two years before.

"Are you packed yet?"

And peace came to her heart.

Where to find Tom Connolly online:

Twitter: http:www.twitter.com/tomcontcg

Facebook: http:www.facebook.com/tom.connolly775

Linkedin:
https://www.linkedin.com/profile/view?121210778%2FTomConnolly

Smashwords: http://www.smashwords.com/interview/tomcon

COMING THIS FALL, look for the Beast of Brazil, a pre-Olympic shocker: A murderous Brazilian drug kingpin from Recife owns a cement company as a front for his criminal operations. He has won bids for three upcoming Olympic venues. His criminal empire is stretched beyond his ability to manage it, the cement company's capabilities are overpromised, his lover, Lupe Montserrat, is questioning her values for staying with Chunk DeLuna and as the Olympics near, an underground river in Amazonia is undermining one of the Olympic sites DeLuna is building. The Beast of Brazil is a man at wit's end.